THE AVON ROMANCE

Four years old and better than ever!

We're celebrating our fourth anniversary...and thanks to you, our loyal readers, "The Avon Romance" is stronger and more exciting than ever! You've been telling us what you're looking for in top-quality historical romance—and we've been delivering it, month after wonderful month.

Since 1982, Avon has been launching new writers of exceptional promise—writers to follow in the matchless tradition of such Avon superstars as Kathleen E. Woodiwiss, Johanna Lindsey, Shirlee Busbee and Laurie McBain. Distinguished by a ribbon motif on the front cover, these books were quickly discovered by romance readers everywhere and dubbed "the ribbon books."

Every month "The Avon Romance" has continued to deliver the best in historical romance. Sensual, fast-paced stories by new writers (and some favorite repeats like Linda Ladd!) guarantee reading *without* the predictable characters and plots of formula romances.

"The Avon Romance"—our promise of superior, unforgettable historical romance. Thanks for making us such a dazzling success!

PROUD SURRENDER

KAREN JOHNS

▲ AVON
PUBLISHERS OF BARD, CAMELOT, DISCUS AND FLARE BOOKS

For

My husband, Terry,
who has shared and enriched my life
throughout the years

AVON BOOKS
A division of
The Hearst Corporation
105 Madison Avenue
New York, New York 10016

Copyright © 1987 by Karen Kimpel Johns
Published by arrangement with the author
Library of Congress Catalog Card Number: 87-91152
ISBN: 0-380-75379-0

First Avon Printing: August 1987

Preface

This novel is a combination of fiction and fact. The plot is strictly an invention of my imagination, as are the main and supporting characters. If any fictitious character in this book possesses a name identical to that of any person, it is merely coincidental; the one exception is the imaginary character, Mary Belle Moore Waddell, whom I named after my maternal grandmother.

Many of the homes and buildings in Vicksburg mentioned in the text still exist, and some are open to the public. Local churches and civic organizations have also been used. Streets, rivers, fortifications, and other geographical locations, such as Fort Hill, Gravel Branch Ford, Milliken's Bend, and so on, were real. The Devans' plantation, Belle Glen, and neighboring plantations belonging to the Moores and Waddells are purely imaginary, though there were plantations in that proximity at the time of the war.

Historical events pertaining to the Civil War and particularly the siege at Vicksburg have been carefully woven into the story and, to the best of my knowledge and understanding, are factual. If any of these facts have been presented erroneously, or are in any way distorted, it was done unintentionally, for I have endeavored to the best of my ability to present them as accurately as possible. Names of well-known historical, political, and military figures have been used, authentically in relation to actual historical events, but inauthentically in relation to fictitious characters.

I am indebted to many who have provided me with various

research material. I would like to take this opportunity to express my appreciation to the librarians at the Memphis/Shelby County Library, who helped me to obtain numerous resource books that were needed. I am also extremely grateful to several people in Vicksburg who have provided me with invaluable information, including copies of old newspaper clippings, letters and papers written by the besieged, and other bits of pertinent information pertaining to the siege. A special acknowledgment goes to the following: Gordon Cotton, Director of the Old Court House Museum; C. Bowie Lanford, Chief Park Interpreter of the Vicksburg National Military Park; the late Ray Terry, who kindly gave my husband and me an extensive tour of the entire battleground; his wife, Blanche Terry, Assistant Director of the Old Courthouse Museum, whose ancestor Henry Schuler is briefly mentioned in the book; and Elizabeth C. Taylor, Assistant Director of the Information Center of the Warren County Tourist Commission, another descendant of one of the besieged citizens.

I also want to thank my sons, Steve and Mark, for their encouragement—and *especially* Scott for his constant support and thoughtful consideration. Above all, I want to give special credit to my husband, Terry, who was the first to edit the entire manuscript. His insight and assistance have been invaluable, and he deserves much credit for this book's completion.

Last but not least, I wish to express my sincere gratitude to my agent, Robin Rue, for her enthusiasm and professional guidance; to my editor, Ellen Edwards, for her support and interest and particularly for the excellent revisions she suggested; and to those on the staff at Avon Books who have worked diligently on the publication of *Proud Surrender*.

Karen Kimpel Johns

Part I

Chapter 1

July 4, 1860
Vicksburg, Mississippi

Tad Devan sighed with exasperation and realized he would soon be capitulating to his younger sister's wishes, as usual. When petite Kitty Devan chose to use her feminine charm as a weapon, she was positively devastating, even to him. Charged with vitality, she exuberated a vibrant personality that was unique, electrifying, and totally captivating. Her moods, however, were unpredictable. Though blessed with a sunny disposition, she also possessed a stubborn streak and, when crossed, a volatile temper. In all of her seventeen years, she had never been easily swayed from a course of action once her mind was made up, and it was apparently made up now.

Kitty's enchanting smile suddenly faded, and her dainty lips drooped as she raised her delicate chin and shot her brother a petulant look. Her growing impatience for his answer was evidenced by a sudden narrowing of stormy eyes as her hands came to rest on her tiny waist.

"Well, Tad, will you or won't you place the bet for me?" she asked irritably, flicking an unruly tendril of raven hair from her heart-shaped face. Her defiance did not stem from the fact that Tad was only her half brother—her mother's son by a former marriage whom her father had long ago adopted. She simply did not like to be thwarted.

Realizing this, Tad shook his head in despair and made one last attempt to reason with her. "I can't, Kitty. Pa'd have a fit if he ever

3

found out," he asserted weakly. "You know how set he is against ladies gambling."

"What Pa doesn't know isn't going to hurt him. We're not going to tell him, so how'll he find out? Besides, I've had my heart set on placing a bet on Golden Boy for weeks now. After all, he is our horse, and we both know he's going to win."

Knowing he was weakening, she flashed a deceptively sweet smile and played her trump card. "Please, Tad, I'd be ever so grateful. In fact, if you'll place the bet for me, I promise to be particularly nice to Dede this afternoon."

"I should think you'd be nice to Miss Jackson in any case, considering she's visiting our closest neighbors, the Waddells," he replied stiffly.

"Much to my regret. Thank goodness she'll be returning to her aunt in Natchez pretty soon. She hasn't the sense God gave a goose, and her constant chattering is enough to bore anyone to tears. I swear I don't see why you're so smitten with her, but if you'll do this for me, I'll bend over backward to be friendly to her."

Tad was tempted, but not totally persuaded. "And if I don't place the bet for you, what then?"

"Not only will I ignore Dede, I'll simply have one of my friends place the bet for me. Let's see, there's David Shelton, Dennis Sasser, Wade Waddell, or—hmmm, maybe I'll just ask one of the Moore boys," came the pert reply as she ticked off the names of her beaux.

"You wouldn't!" Tad sputtered with a worried frown.

"Oh, but I will—unless, of course, you do as I ask."

"All right, you win," Tad muttered, unhappily pocketing the five gold coins she handed him. "But this is the first and last time I'm placing any bets for you, so don't ask me again."

"Why, I wouldn't dream of it," came the tongue-in-cheek reply as, standing on tiptoe, she planted a light kiss on his cheek. "Now, there's no need for you to escort me back to my seat. Just place the bet, then you can get back to Dede."

Without giving him a chance to reply, Kitty turned and nimbly picked her way through the milling crowd.

What a glorious day, she thought happily. But wasn't every Fourth of July? Except when it rained, perhaps, but even that never prevented the most celebrated festivity of the year from proceeding. Rain or shine, on the Fourth everybody in Warren County congregated at the fairgrounds for the annual fish fry and horse races. As was customary, the last and most important race would commence right after the noonday meal, which was already well under way.

Pausing to catch her breath, Kitty glanced toward the back of the racing stands, where several Negroes were tossing hunks of catfish into cauldrons of hot, bubbling grease. The tantalizing aroma of the golden-fried morsels permeated the air, reminding her that she had not yet eaten a bite. Her stomach suddenly rumbled in protest.

She was on the verge of moving on when she spotted their house servants from Belle Glen, the Devans' plantation, and her lips curved into a pleased smile. Like other house servants, they were frying fish and busily tending to the meal's preparation, but even from a distance she could tell that they, too, were enjoying the outing. She was glad they were permitted to accompany the family on the Fourth, for it was unthinkable that they should miss such an important celebration. They were, after all, a part of the family.

Uncle Thad, now old and wizened, and the rotund Mammy Lou had resided at Belle Glen longer than anybody else, ever since Kitty's grandfather had built the place. Mammy Lou never let anybody forget that fact, ruling the entire household with a firm hand. She was bossy, a veritable old matriarch; yet everyone loved her, including her father, Dave Devan. He ran the plantation, but Mammy Lou ran the Devans.

Working beside Mammy Lou were the Devans' other house servants, Doshe and her robust husband Lemme, along with their four grown children: Zeke, Gus, Shasta, and Daisy—the latter resembling her mother with her light coloring and skinny frame. Theirs was a happy family, and if Mammy Lou bossed them unmercifully, none of them questioned her authority or resented her gruffness. Even from where Kitty stood, it was obvious that the lovable tyrant was running true to form today, issuing orders to first one, then another, as she ladled slabs of fried fish from the sizzling cauldron onto a platter.

Handing the heavy dish to Daisy, she waddled toward the long tables that were situated beneath a group of shade trees a short distance away. With a shake of her turbaned head, she began rearranging the tantalizing display of food that covered the entire length of one table.

Every family had contributed something. Heaping platters of catfish and fried chicken were accompanied by long ears of roasted corn, bowls of potato salad, baked beans, and slaw. One table was filled with wicker baskets of corn pones, buttermilk biscuits, and golden mounds of fresh, delicately molded butter. Another was ladened with delectable pies, cakes, and a varied assortment of canned fruits, jams, preserves, and jellies.

Turning away from the appetizing display, Kitty hurried toward the shade tree where she had left her best friend, Sally Collins, seated with the Moore brothers, Ben and Buck. As she drew near, she saw that Lorna Lou Waddell and her brother, Wade, had also joined the group. All were eating, and spying an extra plate filled to capacity on the bench beside Wade, Kitty could only hope he had thoughtfully brought it for her.

"Where on earth have you been, Kitty?" Sally asked, scooting over to make room for her on the narrow bench.

"I've been talking with Tad," she answered, handing her parasol to Ben.

"You should have let us know where you were going," Sally remarked. "David Shelton and Dennis Sasser have been looking all over for you."

"If Miles were here today, I bet you'd stay put," Lorna Lou teased, knowing that Miles Blake was Kitty's favorite beau. "By the way, where is he?"

"In Jackson. Judge Crane needed a document from the court-house, and since Miles is his assistant, the judge sent him rather than go himself. He'll be back in time for the ball at Mayfair tonight, though."

"And as usual, he'll monopolize you. The rest of us probably won't even get a chance to dance with you," Buck remarked sourly.

"I'll bet that won't stop you from trying," Sally quipped.

Everyone chuckled, for it was no secret that Kitty was one of the most sought-after girls in the county. Not only was she strikingly beautiful, she was also unpretentious, intelligent, and an extremely good conversationalist. She had a unique talent for drawing others to her, regardless of their age or sex. Only those who envied her were the exceptions to the rule. Unfortunately, Sally's older sister, Celia, fell into this category.

Seating herself beside Sally, Kitty carefully arranged her white-and-blue-sprigged organdy skirt to cover the tips of her tiny, blue-slippered feet, then accepted the plate of appetizing food Wade offered her. Thanking him, she bit daintily into a crisp piece of chicken, savoring the delicious taste while the others continued their discussion about the day's festivities. She remained silent while eating, then, replete at last, she handed her empty plate to Buck.

"I'm sorry Mary Belle couldn't come today. Is her sprained ankle any better?" she inquired about his sister.

"Better than her temper." Buck grinned. "She was fit to be tied when Pa told her she couldn't come with us today."

"Will she be at the ball tonight?" Kitty asked, thinking it would be a shame if the fiery little redhead had to miss the dance that her parents, the Moores, were hosting at their home, Mayfair.

"Wade's coming, so she'll be there all right, even if she has to crawl downstairs on her hands and knees," came the laughing reply.

It was a known fact that Wade had been seeing a lot of Mary Belle lately, but he nevertheless flushed with obvious embarrassment. Seeing his discomfort, Kitty stood up and placed her hand on his arm.

"Wade, would you mind walking me over to the stables? I'd like to check on Pa before the race begins."

Wade happily agreed, and after promising to rejoin the group in the stands before the last race commenced, the two of them slowly made their way through the crowd.

It was exceedingly hot and noisy, but everyone seemed to be enjoying themselves. Grown-ups gathered together beneath the shade trees and visited while their children played in the broiling sun, girls participating in games of drop the handkerchief or ring around the mulberry bush and boys clustering in tight circles to shoot marbles or demonstrate their expertise with penknives in games of mumblety-peg. Behind the racing stands, one of the Devans' servants, Gus, strummed on a banjo carved from a long-stemmed gourd and sang "Li'l Liza Jane" while a handful of Negro women laughingly clapped to the rhythm, unmindful that some of their menfolk kneeling a few yards away were shooting craps.

Caught up in the mood of the day, Kitty was even agreeable to listening to Wade's rattling on about the presidential election that was to take place in the fall, though she staunchly disagreed with him that, should the wrong candidate win, the South would secede from the Union.

"Mississippi secede? Never!" she scoffed. "Why, if we did that, we couldn't celebrate the Fourth."

They were still debating the point as they neared the stables, but Kitty's voice trailed off when she suddenly spied a familiar face in the crowd, a handsomely dressed man who was leaning indolently against a nearby hitching post. Bret O'Rourke!

She had not seen him since his last visit to Belle Glen two years ago, but he was as arrogantly handsome as ever. Tall, broad-shouldered, yet narrow in the hips, his entire appearance exuded a sensual virility that was impossible to ignore. As his emerald-green eyes boldly met hers, a slight grin quirked the corners of his mouth, lending a diabolical look to his tanned, clean-shaven face and leaving no doubt in Kitty's mind that he, too, recalled their last encounter.

It had been New Year's Eve—in fact, only a month before her mother, Jody, had unexpectedly died of pneumonia. The Devans had given a ball at Belle Glen, the first Kitty had ever attended. Only fifteen at the time, she had looked forward to the festive occasion for weeks, secretly visualizing being admired and courted by every eligible male present. Her dreams had materialized in all respects save one—Bret. Though he was a guest in their home for the holidays, he had not once asked her to dance. Finally she had boldly asked him, but he had merely laughed and, tweaking one of her long curls, told her he would consider her offer in a couple of years—*after she had grown up!* The next morning he had cut short his visit and returned to Memphis, and she had not seen him since.

Still, the memory of his smug, condescending tone and his rejection rankled even now. Fortunately, Wade failed to see Bret and led Kitty right past him, sparing her the necessity of having to speak to him. Her mind was jerked back to the present when Wade spotted her father and quickly escorted her to his side.

Giving Dave an affectionate hug, she felt her dark mood lift. She adored her father, believing him to be the most wonderful person in the world. When her mother had died, they had experienced a mutual loss that had bound them even closer. Sorrow, however, had left its mark on Dave, aging him before his time, and this realization saddened her. His carriage was still proudly erect, but his face was more deeply lined, and his hair, formerly touched with gray, was now almost totally white. Not wishing to dwell on the startling change in him, Kitty turned her attention to the discussion at hand.

Dave was informing Wade that there would be seven other horses running against Golden Boy in the last race, one of them a newcomer.

"Don't tell me that's the newcomer," Wade said with a chuckle, pointing to a pathetically thin-looking gelding that was being led out of a nearby stall by a colored boy, apparently the jockey. As horse and rider drew abreast of them, he jokingly asked: "You gonna ride that bag of bones or carry him?"

"Naw, suh, Ah ain' gwine tuh haf tuh carry dis hoss." The youngster grinned. "Dis heah's Lightning, an' he's gwine tuh win de race!"

Kitty's eyes widened with astonishment, and even Dave laughed at the boy's bold assumption, for the horse looked to be anything but a winner. About fourteen hands high, with a white star on his forehead and white-stockinged hind legs, the mild-mannered creature was unusually stringy and lean even for a gelding. In fact, the animal appeared to have little of the necessary strength or stamina, much less the temperament, to compete in such a long and demanding race.

Undaunted by their amused disbelief, the boy beamed at them. "Reckon Ah best git along. Mist' Bret dun tole me tuh walk Lightning 'round sum befo' de race."

Dave sobered immediately. "Did you say 'Mister Bret'?"

"That's right, Dave, he did," came a deep voice from behind them.

Kitty's heart lurched, then sank, her eyes clouding with dismay as she turned to find her father shaking hands with the very person who had rekindled her resentment only minutes before. Despicable as ever!

"Bret, you son-of-a-gun, when did you get back in town?" her father asked with obvious surprise and pleasure.

"A few days ago. Been meaning to pay you a visit, but I've been tied up with business ever since I arrived. I figured I'd be seeing you today, though," Bret replied, his gaze moving away from the older man to rest on Kitty.

"Kitty," he acknowledged with a slight nod of his head, an appreciative gleam flickering in his eyes. "Pretty as ever and . . . just as I've remembered."

Kitty stiffened, knowing his last words were merely a backhanded compliment that indicated he still looked upon her as a child.

Determined not to let him get the best of her, she forced a smile to her lips.

"And you, Mr. O'Rourke, are just as *I've* remembered," she replied.

"Mr. O'Rourke!" Dave exclaimed with astonishment. "Why all the formality, honey? Bret's known you ever since you were born, or have you forgotten how you used to tag around after him all the time when you were younger?"

"Oh, I hardly think she's forgotten, Dave," Bret intervened with an amused grin, adding, "Especially not all the scrapes I used to get her out of. For such a little tyke, she could get into more mischief than a barrel of monkeys."

Kitty flushed irritably. Other men might consider her to be a fully grown and beautiful woman, but obviously not Bret. He still remembered her as the mischievous little hoyden whom he'd been forced to tolerate in his youth, when his father had been employed as the Devans' overseer at Belle Glen. Unable to think of a scathing reply, she was relieved when her father changed the subject.

"How long are you going to be in town, Bret?"

"Oh, I'll be spending quite a bit of time down here, now that I'm opening up another cotton brokerage in Vicksburg," he answered.

"Why, that's wonderful!" Dave exclaimed. "See, honey, I told you all along that Bret would make something of himself," he added proudly.

Indeed he had! After Bret's father had died, Dave had insisted the seventeen-year-old boy move in with them, an arrangement that had been totally disagreeable to Kitty and had lasted for a year. She'd been only seven at the time, and her attitude toward Bret had vacillated between childish resentment and reluctant admiration. She had not been sorry when Bret turned eighteen and, soon after, obtained a job in Memphis scouting cotton for one of the brokerages.

Unfortunately, Bret had kept in close touch with them throughout the intervening years, always visiting Belle Glen whenever he was in the vicinity on business and frequently spending holidays with them. Then, after her disagreeable encounter with him at the New Year's Eve ball, his visits had suddenly and inexplicably ceased, much to her relief. Still, he had continued to correspond, and Dave had continued to sing his praises.

No, she hardly needed to be reminded that Bret had made the

most of his opportunities during the past ten years. He owned a thriving cotton brokerage in Memphis and was obviously prosperous, but this did not alter her opinion of him. As far as she was concerned, he was as arrogant and unpleasant as ever, and all the money in the world was not going to make him acceptable to her. She was, therefore, dismayed when she heard her father invite him to spend a few days at Belle Glen, and despondent when the invitation was accepted.

"By the way, where are you staying in town?" Dave asked.

"At the Prentiss House for the present, but I'll probably rent a room elsewhere if I have to stay long."

"Are you going to hire a manager for this brokerage?" Wade asked.

"If I can find the right man. If not, I'll take up residence here and run this one myself. I've a good man working for me in Memphis, one who's quite capable of running my affairs there if I have to stay in Vicksburg."

"Well, let's hope you do." Dave smiled. "But back to the present, that old nag doesn't really belong to you, does it, Bret?"

"Yep." The younger man grinned.

Dave stroked his chin thoughtfully. "Hmmm—maybe there's more to that animal than meets the eye."

"You can't be serious, Pa! Why, it's downright mean of Bret to make that poor old bag of bones run in any race, much less the two-mile," Kitty asserted indignantly.

Bret and Wade chuckled, but Dave merely shook his head. Bret was shrewd, and Dave knew it.

"Bret doesn't usually back losers, nor underestimate winners," he said.

"Well, not even Bret can be right all the time," she retorted.

"I guess we'll just have to see, won't we. Would you care to make a friendly wager on the race?" Bret asked smoothly.

Kitty stiffened, wondering if he had somehow learned of the bet she'd forced Tad to place for her on Golden Boy. "A lady doesn't bet," she snapped.

"True, but I rather thought *you* might—unless, of course, you're afraid you might lose."

"Very well, what would you like to wager?" she asked crisply.

"Let's keep it simple. If I lose, I'll buy you the prettiest bonnet in town."

"And if you win?" she asked, masking her uneasiness.

"Then tonight, my dear, you'll forfeit the last dance to me."

Kitty frowned. "You'll be at the ball tonight?"

"That's right. Buck invited me earlier this morning."

"Very well. I must say it's going to be a pleasure seeing you lose for a change," she responded pertly. Lightning couldn't possibly win!

The black boy who was to ride Golden Boy led the handsome chestnut out of the stall and headed toward the starting post, reminding them that the race was about to begin. It was Wade who suggested to Kitty that they resume their seats in the stands, then asked Bret to join them. For a moment, Kitty feared he might accept, but fortunately Dave invited Bret to accompany him to the starting post and watch the race from there. With a relieved sigh, she opened her lacy parasol and held Wade's arm as he escorted her to the stands.

A grimace appeared on her face when she saw that Lorna Lou and Sally were saving them seats right in front of Tad and Dede. She seriously doubted Dede knew the first thing about racing, and she could only hope the girl would not twitter in her ear throughout the race.

Remembering her promise to Tad, she managed to smile and greet the couple with far more enthusiasm than she was feeling. "My goodness, Tad, you've kept Dede to yourself all day. Why, I haven't even had a chance to talk to her," she remarked lightly.

Dede beamed with pleasure. She was awed by Tad's pretty and vivacious sister, and being more than a little fond of Tad, she was anxious to know Kitty better.

"I told Tad to try and seat us near you so we could visit," she replied in a childlike voice.

"Bret's here, Sis," Tad intervened. "Have you seen him?"

"Yes, unfortunately," she answered a trifle shortly. "He's over at the starting post with Pa."

"Who's Bret?" Dede asked.

Kitty sighed. "Nobody important. His pa was our overseer."

Tad grinned, fully realizing Kitty's resentment as well as the reason behind it. "True, but he happens to be a very prosperous businessman, now." He turned toward Dede. "You remember, Dede, I introduced you to him this morning."

"Oh—you mean that handsome gentleman who has such nice manners," she remarked.

"I'd hardly call him a gentleman, Dede," Kitty stated. "Money can't buy good breeding, and that's something Bret O'Rourke will never have."

Wade whistled softly at the rebuke. "You sure don't have much use for him, do you, honey?"

"None at all," she replied, feeling suddenly embarrassed. "And please don't call me 'honey,' I'm sure Mary Belle wouldn't appreciate it. After today, I doubt she'll ever speak to me again."

Not wishing to bicker further, Kitty glanced toward the starting gate, her gaze resting on Dave and Bret, who were watching Sally's father, Henry Collins, draw the starting line in the dirt with his riding crop. With aplomb, the heavy-set man mounted a low platform box, extracted a red flag from his inner coat pocket, and inserted a cartridge into a small revolver. The jockeys had settled their nervous horses well in back of the line but now walked them toward the start. Two horses, Apollo and Fury, suddenly whirled, their sleek coats flashing in the sun as the riders struggled to bring them under control. This commotion, though brief, set Golden Boy to rearing and plunging.

Dave swore and shouted, "Hold him, Zeke, blast your hide! Get him back to the starting line."

A drum began to roll, and a hushed stillness swept over the spectators. A moment passed, then a loud shot suddenly dispelled the silence; the spectators jumped to their feet and shouted wildly as the mighty hooves tore down the dusty track. Apollo and Golden Boy got off in front, with Fury coming in third and Lightning, surprisingly, fourth. This changed in the next few minutes, as Golden Boy got to the fore just before rounding the second turn. Lightning sprinted past Fury, then Apollo, and finally took the second lead. Spectators shouted frantically as the magnificent beasts, soon neck and neck, thundered down the track.

Nearing the third turn, Apollo dropped behind Fury, and Lightning pushed ahead of Golden Boy by a length, which was soon shortened as the latter began to close up the distance. The other horses now outpaced, it was just Lightning and Golden Boy as they neared the head of the stretch. Lightning, with one last burst of speed, shot ahead and miraculously held his own down the final stretch, despite the determined efforts of Golden Boy and Fury, who were racing nose and nose a full two lengths behind the gallant gelding.

As Lightning streaked across the finish line, deafening cheers of excitement, mingled with moans of disbelief, filled the dusty air. Kitty glanced toward the winner's circle, where Bret, accompanied by Dave, was confidently striding forward to claim the prize money.

Kitty's eyes narrowed and anger threatened to consume her as she realized her folly in agreeing to Bret's wager. Now she would not only have to admit defeat to that hateful man, she would also have to allow him to dance with her, a thought that was completely unnerving in itself. Damn the man—why must he *always* win!

Chapter 2

Miles Blake glanced down at Kitty and smiled, his arm tightening around her waist as he noted the faraway look in her eyes. Though an egotist, he was not a fool, nor did he misinterpret the reason for Kitty's silence now. Bret O'Rourke. The fact that she professed to dislike the man did nothing to alter his opinion that she was, in fact, strongly attracted to him. The realization rankled, and his steps quickened as he waltzed her around the crowded ballroom at Mayfair.

A frown marred his handsome features, and he inwardly cursed Bret's return to Vicksburg. Kitty belonged to him and always had, ever since they had played together as children. But even then his every attempt to impress Kitty had seemingly been thwarted by Bret, whose three years' seniority had given him an edge in competition as well as authority. Damn him, Miles thought sourly, remembering how Bret had always excelled in everything he had tackled so that, even as a child, Kitty had been completely besotted with him.

Still, his childhood memories were not totally bleak. At one time, his family had owned the Moores' plantation, which was situated near Belle Glen. During those years, he had played almost daily with Kitty and, of course, Tad. Then the cholera epidemic had claimed his parents, and soon afterward, his grandmother had died of a heart attack. The plantation had been sold, and the money from the sale had been put into a trust fund for him and his younger sister. The two of them had moved into town to live with a distant cousin, the elderly Widow Benton, whom they called Aunt Phoebe. Yet even after they had moved into town, he and his sister had been frequent visitors at Belle Glen. When Bret moved to Memphis a year later, Miles had been delighted.

For years, Miles had been determined that Kitty would someday marry him. It never occurred to him that she might refuse, despite the fact that she was constantly courted by every eligible young male in the vicinity. When Judge Crane made him a full-fledged partner in his law firm, he would ask Kitty to marry him, and he felt confident she would accept. Still, Bret's reappearance on the scene was somewhat unsettling. Kitty's voice suddenly interrupted his thoughts.

"Have you heard from Beth lately?" she asked, referring to his sister, who had recently married and moved to Memphis.

"Yes, I received a letter from her last week. She and John have settled into their new house and are doing fine."

She would have questioned him further, but at that moment her eyes fastened on Bret, who was dancing with Celia Collins. A feeling of unreasonable frustration swept over her when she noticed the way he smiled down at the flirtatious girl.

"Isn't it strange that Bret didn't mention Beth at the races today," she remarked a little too sharply. "Surely he must have visited them while he was in Memphis."

"Not necessarily. A man with Bret's reputation is not always welcome in the more respectable homes."

"Beth would never snub Bret. You know she's always liked him."

"True, but if John is aware of Bret's reputation with women, as I'm sure he must be, he probably discouraged Beth from associating with him."

"Fiddlesticks! Bret's reputation isn't half as bad as you make it sound."

"Oh, but it is. Surely you heard about Bret and Mrs. Baxter's . . . er, questionable friendship when he was in Vicksburg a couple of years ago," Miles returned with a derisive smile.

"Colonel Baxter's wife, Selina?" Kitty gasped. "You can't be serious! Why, the colonel was alive then."

"Yes, and the town gossips were having a field day. Of course, your father and Tad have always shielded you from unpleasantness, so it's not surprising you didn't hear about it at the time."

The music stopped, and as Miles ushered her to a vacant seat, her mind was in turmoil. Not for anything in this world would she dance with Bret now, bet or no bet. But how was she going to get out of it?

Pleading a headache, she excused herself and frantically looked around the room for Dave or Tad. Surely one of them could be persuaded to take her home early, but neither was in sight. The next-to-last dance was under way, so there was little time to lose. It seemed her only means of escape was to be the isolated veranda, and with a determined step she edged her way around the room and slipped through the open French doors.

Safe at last, Kitty gave a relieved sigh and walked over to the dark corner of the veranda. It was doubtful that Bret would think of looking for her out here. The pleasure of her duplicity was cut short when a slight noise caused her to turn and see a tall man saunter out to the veranda, extract a cheroot from his coat pocket, and light it. Kitty's hand flew to her mouth to stifle the gasp that would have exposed her.

Bret! Had he seen her leave the crowded room, or was he merely out here to smoke? It hardly mattered. Realizing it was only a matter of seconds before he discovered her, Kitty spurred herself into action. Hitching up her white eyelet gown, she swung one leg over the porch railing, then the other. It was a good four feet to the ground, but in the dark, the drop seemed far more menacing. For a moment she hesitated; then, recalling that Bret was only a few feet away, she closed her eyes and dropped to the ground.

As luck would have it, the back of her hoopskirt caught on a nail. Unable to turn around in order to free the material, Kitty struggled silently for a few seconds, then thrust herself forward, giving the back of her hoop a vicious yank. But to no avail. Aside from tearing the material even more, not to mention popping the button off the waistband of the hoopskirt, she had gained nothing. She was totally helpless, and a muttered oath escaped her lips.

"Tsch, tsch, tsch—such language!" a deep voice chided teasingly.

Kitty gritted her teeth and counted to ten before turning slowly to face Bret, who was standing directly behind her on the veranda and grinning with unconcealed amusement.

"May I be so bold as to ask what in God's name you're doing down there?" he asked.

Kitty shot him a venomous look. "What does it look like I'm doing—playing hide-and-seek in the bushes?" she hissed, giving her hoop still another yank.

Bret chuckled and, resting his forearms on the railing, gave her a devilish look. "If you are, Kitten, I could suggest a more, shall we say, entertaining pastime."

"Nothing you suggest could ever be entertaining to me."

Bret straightened and, with a diabolical grin, gave her a polite bow. "In that case, I'll relieve you of my unwelcome company."

"Don't you dare, Bret O'Rourke!" Kitty cried, her blue eyes widening with alarm. It would just be like him to leave her to her own predicament. Realizing this, she nibbled nervously at her lower lip, then added, "I mean, please don't go."

"Ah, you do welcome my attention. And to think I misjudged you—that I even thought for a brief moment you might possibly be trying to welsh on our bet by avoiding me. No, don't say anything," he continued, seeing she was about to deny the accusation. "After such unworthy thoughts, I can only beg your forgiveness and take my leave of you."

"Oh!" Kitty sputtered, stomping her foot. "You low-down varmint, don't you dare leave me out here like this! I'll tell Pa if you do."

"And what will you tell him, Kitty?" he asked, amused. "That you got caught in the bushes while trying to renege on our bet? I trust that was your intent."

"It wasn't!" she cried, then, seeing his disbelief, she sighed. "Oh, all right, maybe I was hoping to avoid you. Now will you please come down here and help me?"

Bret chuckled and vaulted lithely over the railing. Coming to stand before her, he lifted her quivering chin with one large forefinger, placing his other hand on her tiny waist.

"You know, it never ceases to amaze me how you can get yourself into such god-awful predicaments," he commented wryly.

Kitty jerked her chin away, anger threatening to consume her. "You're despicable! Now will you please stop talking and get me out of this mess."

"And what will you give me if I do?"

"I'll honor our bet."

"Not enough. That you were going to do anyway."

The music had stopped, and a few couples were beginning to stroll out to the veranda for a breath of air before the last waltz. Kitty suddenly panicked, fearing they would be seen and that she would become the object of ridicule for weeks to come.

"All right! I'll do anything you want me to do. Just get me loose before everybody sees," she whispered angrily.

Bret chuckled and stepped behind her. Pausing to observe the source of her problem, he then deftly freed the material from a rusty nail.

Kitty flushed with embarrassment, for despite the fact that Bret had seen her in pantalets when she was younger, she was hardly a child now, and such an intimate view was not ladylike. Mammy Lou would have a fit, she thought, but before she could dwell on this, she was faced with another problem. The waistband of her hoop-skirt, now unfastened, was sliding to her hips. Panic seized her as she tried frantically to think of a solution.

Unaware of her latest problem, Bret gave her a mocking bow and extended his arm to her. "Now, shall we join the others in the ballroom?"

"I can't," Kitty murmured.

"Welshing again?" he queried derisively.

"I swear I'm not, Bret, but I can't go inside. You see, I—I'm feeling a little faint."

"You? You've never fainted in your life! Now what's the real reason?"

Anger bolstered her spirit. "If you must know, I've popped the button off the waistband of my hoopskirt. Just what do you suggest I do?"

"Well, one thing's certain"—he grinned wickedly—"we can't just stand here until we're discovered. I, for one, have no intention of entering marital bliss by way of a shotgun wedding!"

"Will you be serious!"

Genuine anguish was mirrored in Kitty's lovely eyes, and realizing the extent of her concern, Bret sobered. Looking around, he spied the outline of a rose arbor just to the left of them. Nodding in that direction, he asked if she could make it as far as that, where the damage could most likely be repaired. Kitty only shook her head.

"Well, as I see it, you can't fix that blasted hoop here, nor can I carry you over there without anyone noticing, much less speculating on my intentions. You're going to have to make it over there on your own two feet, I'm afraid. If you can hitch the hoop up in front, I'll just ease my arm around your waist and get a hold on it from the back," he suggested, carrying out his plan despite Kitty's attempt to pull away from him. Before she could protest, he eased her out of the shrubbery and propelled her toward the arbor.

Once their destination was reached, Kitty sighed with relief, then frowned. "Now that we're here, just what do you propose I do? I felt the button pop off, so how am I going to fix that?"

"For one with so much imagination, your lack of ingenuity disappoints me, my sweet," Bret remarked dryly, removing the diamond stickpin from his cravat. "Here, see if you can manage with this." He put the pin in her hand, then turned to step outside.

Uttering an oath, Kitty snatched up her voluminous skirts and, after making sure that Bret's back was turned, tried to secure the waistband with the pin, which refused to stay in place. After sticking her finger for the third time, she gave a despairing moan.

"This isn't going to work. The pin won't hold."

Bret reentered the arbor and, folding his arms, regarded her thoughtfully. "All right, turn around and lift up your skirts," he said matter-of-factly.

"I'll do no such thing!"

"Look, Kitty, you haven't any choice unless, of course, you intend to remain out here by yourself."

Kitty looked up at him in horror, completely forgetting that the ball was almost ended anyway. She disliked dark places, particularly such places as this, which, in her mind, undoubtedly housed various kinds of pesky insects.

Seeing her indecision, Bret smiled and stepped closer. "That's better. Now, if you'll just give me the stickpin and turn around, I'll be as quick as possible."

Reluctantly, Kitty did as she was told, lifting the back of her three-tiered skirt with a mortified jerk.

"Can't you hurry?" she grumbled, wiggling with impatience. It seemed as though he was taking an unusual amount of time.

"Ouch! Keep still, you little minx!" Bret exclaimed, stopping briefly to suck the finger he had just jabbed. Once again he bent to his task, and in a few moments he managed to secure the troublesome waistband with the pin.

Straightening her wide, red-satin sash, she turned around. "Oh, your finger is bleeding. I hope you didn't get any stains on my gown. Give me your handkerchief," she ordered. Without waiting for him to comply, she deftly extracted a handkerchief from his inner coat pocket and began dabbing at the small spot of blood on his forefinger until the bleeding subsided.

As she returned his handkerchief, strains of the last waltz floated out to them. Gently taking her arm and leading her out of the arbor, Bret paused and looked down at the slight figure beside him.

"I believe this dance is mine," he said softly, and encircled her waist with his arm. His seductive eyes locked with hers, silently compelling her to obey.

"It seems I have no choice," she murmured. She tried at least to maintain an appropriate distance from him, but even this bit of decorum was denied her. With a slight jerk, Bret drew her to him, and she became confusedly aware of the hard strength leashed in the tall, virile body now so close to her own.

Slowly, they moved to the tempo of the music, his eyes never leaving hers as they swirled under the shadowy trees that dotted the dark, deserted lawn. A whippoorwill called out and was seemingly answered by a chorus of locusts, but Kitty was aware of none of this. Nothing seemed real—nothing except the man who was holding her in his arms, caressing her with his eyes. Suddenly he stopped, drawing her closer until her breasts were crushed against his hard chest. She was only vaguely aware that the music had ended. As though mesmerized, she wound her arms around his broad neck when he slowly lowered his head.

"Bret," she whispered, wanting to feel the touch of his lips, which were now only tantalizing inches from her own.

In the next instant, he was unexpectedly removing her arms from his neck and gently putting her from him. Surprised by his rejection, anger washed over her, but before she could speak, the sound of approaching footsteps reached her ears. Apparently Bret had also heard the noise, which explained his sudden withdrawal.

Peering into the darkness, Kitty recognized the intruder as one of the Moores' servants. A closer look revealed he was quite distraught.

"Dere you is, Mist' Bret. Ah's been lookin' all ober fo' you," he exclaimed, mopping his moist brow with the back of his hand.

"Well now, Samuel, it must be something mighty important for the likes of you to be hurrying. What's the trouble?"

"Hit's yo' warehouse, Mist' Bret. Some of de white folks dun set off fireworks tuh cel'brate de Fo'th, an' dey's dun caught yo' warehouse on fire. Mist' Shelton rode out heah fas' as he could wid de news. He's up at de house waitin' fo' you."

A muttered oath escaped Bret's lips, and for a moment he was totally oblivious of Kitty's presence. Then he felt a slight pressure on his arm and realized she was trying to get his attention.

"Maybe it isn't as bad as it sounds, Bret," she suggested, surprised by an overwhelming desire to comfort him.

"Let's hope not," he answered somberly as, taking hold of her arm, he quickly ushered her back to the house.

Chapter 3

Bret gazed unseeingly from the bedroom window into the midnight darkness that enveloped the sleeping town below. Since the fire had taken its toll of his warehouse three weeks ago, he had spent every waking moment supervising the construction of a new and larger building on the same spot. With cotton pickin' time just around the corner, there had been no time to spare, and he had often worked side by side with the blacks borrowed from Belle Glen. Now he was tired, bone-tired, and completely oblivious of the provocative woman who watched his reflection in her dressing table mirror while thoughtfully brushing her long golden tresses.

Selina Baxter was no fool, nor at twenty-six was she a starry-eyed romantic, for whatever illusions she might have had about love had disintegrated during her seven years of marriage to the colonel. Not that she regretted the bargain even now. She had merely traded her youth and body for financial security, and true to his word, the colonel had turned a blind eye to whatever she did on the side, as long as she was discreet. The one thing she had not achieved was respectability, but even that no longer mattered. What did matter was the man who, tonight, would share the intimacy of her bed.

There had been other men, of course—many men, as a matter of fact. But none were as virile or as expert a lover as the man who stood across the room. In a ruggedly arrogant way, he was quite the most handsome man she had ever encountered; no one even came close—except, perhaps, Miles Blake. But then Miles's ardor was often tinged with masochism, a trait that had occasionally caused her more pain than pleasure. Bret had never resorted to such tactics, nor

23

did he need to; his strong, masculine body always fulfilled her every need.

He had not changed during his two years' absence, other than to become even more experienced in various methods of exciting her. He was as elusive as ever, never committing himself to her in any way, never pretending that what he felt for her was love. Love? She doubted seriously that he knew the meaning of the word, despite his lusty appetite for sex. Yet for a ruthless man he could be very gentle and considerate. She wondered briefly what it would be like to be loved by such a man. An unconscious sigh escaped her, causing Bret to turn from the window and look at her.

She was a very alluring woman and, considering the numerous late nights he had spent with her during the past weeks, a very generous one. Seeing her in the clinging, almost transparent wrapper that accentuated the voluptuousness of her mature figure, a familiar stirring rose in him. Setting aside his whiskey glass, he watched appreciatively as she strode over to him.

"Tired?" Selina asked, running her fingertips down his neck and pressing against his hard length.

"Not *too* tired," Bret murmured, clasping her buttocks with both hands, molding the curves of her body closer to his own. "Not too tired for you, that is," he added, tantalizing her neck and shoulders with his lips.

Selina nibbled at his earlobe, mounting excitement filling every fiber of her body. "You work too hard, you know. You never come to me until so late," she murmured.

Bret pulled away slightly and, arching one brow, gave her a knowing look.

"If it's too late, I can always leave," he remarked with a sardonic smile.

A low chuckle rumbled in her throat. "Damn you, Bret! You know I'm not going to let you leave now."

Selina was a tall, well-endowed woman, but Bret easily picked her up in his powerful arms and strode over to the ornate four-poster bed. The room was dimly lit, yet while his fingers deftly removed her wrapper, then quickly discarded his own clothing, his emerald eyes never left her face. It was a sultry night, and a light film of moisture glistened on his broad chest and back. His gaze darkened appreciatively, raking over her seductive figure, from the voluptuous breasts and curvaceous waist to the well-rounded hips, then lower.

His hungry look was returned as Selina eyed his tall, sinewy frame, her hand trembling slightly when she reached out to touch him. Slowly, her fingers trailed over his taut body, coming to rest on his hard thigh. He moved slightly, shifting his stance, and as her gaze fastened on his muscular torso, she was acutely aware that she had never seen a more magnificent man. Her eyes narrowed, mirroring her eagerness while slowly traveling the length of him, sliding from his darkly tanned chest down to the narrow hips and strong, well-shaped legs.

She reached for him, pulling him down beside her. Impatience mounted in her, though she knew she would have to wait. Bret never hurried when making love to her, often tantalizing her to the point where she was half-crazed with lust before he finally took her.

What she did not realize was that Bret's need was greater than her own tonight, for ever since he had seen Kitty buggy riding with Miles earlier that afternoon, visions of the beautiful girl had tormented him. Though he had made a point of avoiding Belle Glen since the night of the fire, he had been unsuccessful in banishing her from his thoughts, a fact that irritated him to no little extent. Even now, as his lips teased Selina's soft flesh and his hand stroked the smoothness of her shapely thighs, his mind was temporarily invaded by Kitty's image.

With an agonized moan, Selina arched, and, sensing her lusty eagerness now matched his need, Bret covered her writhing body with his own. Unlike other times, he took her savagely, enjoying her muffled cries of pleasure. Enjoyment was brief, however, for a vision of raven hair and violet-blue eyes clouded his mind. When at last Selina reached the peak of her fulfillment, it was Kitty rather than the woman moaning beneath him who released the dam of his passion—Kitty's lips he devoured until, with one last shudder, he stilled and slowly rolled away from her. A feeling of disgust and self-loathing swept over him.

Unaware of his inner turmoil, Selina stretched and sighed, languidly trailing one finger down his chest.

"Ummm, that was even better than usual," she murmured, snuggling contentedly against his side and laying her head on his chest.

Bret began absentmindedly stroking her hair. Moments later, her even breathing told him she had fallen asleep, but though he, too, was exhausted, he knew sleep would elude him tonight. Inwardly, he cursed himself for a fool as Kitty's image reappeared to haunt

him. Why in heaven's name could he not forget her? As a child, she
had been a thorn in his side—spoiled, impetuous, and in general a
menace. The intervening years had hardly improved her disposition;
she was as obstinate and unpredictable as ever, her resentment of
him no less than it had been when she was younger. Hell, he
thought, she's little more than a child now. But his mind quickly
refuted this.

She was a woman, a very desirable woman. He had made this
unexpected discovery almost two years ago, on the night of her first
ball. Then, he had been surprised, unnerved, by the arousal Kitty
had awakened in him. He had been sorely tempted to make love to
her that night, though he had treated her innocent flirtatiousness in a
falsely condescending manner; yet it was the startling revelation of
her enticing beauty, the desire she had ignited in him, that had
hastened his departure from Vicksburg. Realizing his vulnerability
where she was concerned, he had not been eager to return, but the
opportunity of acquiring another brokerage had been too great to
resist.

If he had thought that time would lessen his attraction to her, he
now realized his mistake. He wanted her far more than he had ever
wanted any other woman, and the knowledge of the intensity of his
desire filled him with disgust. A virile man, he had known many
women, experienced and otherwise, but none of them had been the
daughter of an old and respected friend. No, Dave Devan was more
than a friend—he'd been almost like a father ever since Bret could
remember. To have Kitty, he would have to marry her, and marriage
was out of the question at the present, even if he had been willing.
He was far from ready to settle down, and when he did reach that
point in life, he fully intended to choose a woman who would
respect him as an equal. He seriously doubted Kitty would ever feel
that way about him simply because his father had been the Devans'
overseer.

No, marrying her was out of the question; but if marriage to her
was impossible, an affair with her was inconceivable. There was no
solution in sight, and for the first time he questioned his wisdom in
returning to Vicksburg.

Kitty impatiently tapped her fingers on the arm of her chair and
watched while her brother continued to work at the desk. It was hot

in the study, and she was waiting for him to finish so she could question him about his visit to Bret yesterday.

She doubted, however, that he would enlighten her even if he could. At least, not about the matter that was utmost in her mind—whether or not Bret was having an affair with Selina Baxter. Miles had as good as said so only a few days before. Of course, Miles had never liked Bret, she reminded herself, reasoning that he could have been speaking from vindictiveness. But she had to know for certain. She refused to examine her interest too closely, reasoning that it was only natural to be curious.

"Will you please stop fidgeting, Kitty!" Tad snapped without looking up from his work.

Kitty's eyes widened with surprise at her brother's unusual abruptness, then narrowed angrily. "I'll stop fidgeting when you stop working so I can talk to you. My goodness, Tad, you've been as cross as a bear ever since that scatterbrained girl went back to Natchez," she remarked unkindly, referring to Dede Jackson.

Tad shut the ledger with a loud snap and looked irritably at the young woman who, until recently, had always come first with him. Now, however, it was Dede who came first, Dede whom he had decided to marry.

"Dede is not scatterbrained," he said with forced patience. "She's a lovely, sweet girl who has many commendable attributes. I'm surprised at you, Kitty. It's not like you to be unkind, and quite frankly, I'm getting tired of hearing you downgrade her."

"Good grief, Tad, to hear you talk I'd almost think you were planning to marry her!" Kitty exclaimed.

"If she will have me, I intend to do just that," came the startling reply.

Dumbfounded, Kitty stared at Tad with open amazement. But before she could argue the point, Tad continued.

"You're not being fair, you know. Dede is a very lovable person, and she thinks the world of you. She's always saying how pretty you are, and how she wishes she could be more like you. She wants to be your friend, and if you'd just give her a chance, I'm sure you'd like her.

Kitty seriously doubted it but was prevented from arguing further by a knock on the side door. Obviously relieved by the interruption, Tad walked over and opened it. It was the overseer, Charlie Jones, and his two gigantic sons, Alvin and Billy Mac.

"Hello, Charlie," Tad said, giving the man's name the typical southern pronunciation and dropping the "r."

"Howdy, Mist' Tad. Yer pa here 'bouts?" Charlie asked, mopping his brow with the back of his big, calloused hand.

"No, he went over to the Waddells' to see about buying another brood mare," Tad replied. "I don't know when he'll be back. Can I help?" Remembering how hot the midday sun was, he stepped aside to allow the older man to enter. "Come on in."

"Thanks. I reckon I can chew over my problem with you as well as yer pa." The big man grinned, then turned to the young men standing docilely behind him. "You boys git over to that shade tree an' set a spell—but don't go fertalizing friendships with any of them colored gals workin' 'round here," he added warningly. "And mind yer manners."

Another grin broke over his friendly face as, stepping inside, he spotted Kitty. "Why, howdy, Miss Kitty. My, ain't you a sight for sore eyes this morning—jes' pretty as a speckled pup!"

Kitty smiled prettily, for she was quite fond of the homely man, despite the fact that he was often boisterous and had a sense of humor that was sometimes crude. One could seldom believe half of what he said; it was a known fact that Charlie Jones was a spinner of tall tales and a real character.

"Mornin', Charlie. How are you?" she responded, rearranging the folds of her red, dotted-swiss dress to conceal the tips of her black slippers.

"Fair to middlin', I reckon, Miss Kitty," came the affable reply as Charlie extracted a red bandanna from his hip pocket and mopped the moisture from his craggy face.

"Looks like you've been workin' up a sweat this morning, Charlie," Tad observed. "Those darkies keeping you busy out in the fields?"

"Busy! Lawd, I've been so busy, I feel like a dog chasin' his tail!" Charlie exclaimed with a guffaw. " 'Course, most of our field hands tote their own load, but there's always a few of them who don't do nothing but stand around po'mouthin' all the time."

"What about?" Tad asked.

"First one thing an' then another. They're hungry, tired, hot—or jes' feeling por'ly in general. Por'ly, my foot!" Charlie snorted. "They's jes' plain lazy. Why, they ain't another slave owner in

Mississippi who treats his people any better than Mist' Dave duz—most of them not as good.''

"There are always a few misfits, Charlie. You know that. Just keep an eye on them and make sure they don't stir up any trouble. If they persist or become unmanageable, then we may have to sell a few of them," Tad remarked, "but let's hope it doesn't come to that.''

"Naw, sir, let's hope it don't, but I think you better let yer pa know about it jes' the same. One rotten apple kin spoil the whole dang barrel, an' a few troublemakers kin stir up a mess of trouble. We shore don't wanna be caught sleepin' at the switch, if'n you know what I mean," came the dead-earnest reply.

Tad did, though it was hard for him to believe that any of their slaves would actually try to escape, much less stir up a rebellion. Still, one could not overlook the fact that there was an increasing number of slaves escaping to the North each year—slaves who were aided by northern abolitionists via the Underground Railroad to the "promised land"—Canada.

Realizing this particular subject could go on forever, Kitty intervened. "Goodness, Tad, it's almost one o'clock. I 'spect Charlie's wife is waitin' dinner on him," she remarked, hoping to end their conversation so that she could have Tad to herself again.

"Naw'm, we've already had dinner. The missus sed it wuz too hot to git over a stove, so the boys an' me jes' had a mess of cold 'coon an' collards,'' Charlie replied, referring to the cold chicken and cornbread leftover from the night before that he and the boys had devoured at noon.

To Kitty's dismay, the conversation was not about to end, thanks to her brother.

"Speaking of 'coon, Charlie, you been hunting any lately?'' Tad asked. If there was one thing Charlie was good at, it was hunting.

"As a matter of fact, me an' the boys did go huntin' a spell back. Lawd, that wuz something, I'm tellin' you!'' With great enthusiasm, Charlie embarked on a tall tale that made Tad roar with laughter. Even Kitty giggled for a few seconds, despite the story's lack of believability. Then, realizing that in all probability a few more tales would be swapped, she sighed and arose.

"If y'all will excuse me, I think I'll step outside and see if I can find Lemme. He said he'd shake some peaches down from that tree in the back so Mammy Lou can make a cobbler for tonight.''

"Don't let me run you off, Miss Kitty. I wuzn't aimin' to stay," Charlie stated almost apologetically.

"That's all right, Charlie. I was fixin' to leave when you came," she lied sweetly, feeling somewhat vexed that her questions regarding Bret were still unanswered.

"Proud to have seen you, ma'am." Charlie smiled and opened the door for her to leave.

"Why, thank you, Charlie. And if there are enough peaches, I'll send your wife some before suppertime," Kitty replied over her shoulder, lifting her skirts and descending the porch steps.

An hour later the peaches had been gathered, but in spite of the heat, Kitty was reluctant to return to the house. A slight breeze stirred the hot air, and finding a good shade tree, she sat down and leaned against it, closing her eyes. Within minutes she was asleep, a sleep that was painfully terminated some time later, when a colony of red ants from a nearby anthill inched over toward her and crawled up her legs.

Still drowsy, Kitty stirred uncomfortably, then came fully awake, aware of the prickly, stinging sensation that extended from ankles to knees on both legs. Perplexed, she glanced at her feet and spied the source of discomfort. A pained cry escaped her. Jumping up and hoisting her pantalets, she began slapping at the tiny creatures, hopping first on one foot and then the other. Near hysteria, she was unmindful of the tall man approaching her until a deep chuckle caught her attention.

Still slapping at the pesky ants, she managed to glance toward the sound, her eyes darkening angrily when she discovered Bret leaning indolently against the nearby fence, amusement etched on his face.

"Don't just stand there. Do something!" she cried.

"Well, well! Can it actually be you're in trouble again?" he chided before sauntering over to her.

"Oh, you're a despicable varmint!" she exclaimed furiously, pausing long enough to cast him an angry look. "That's right, laugh at me. You've always enjoyed seeing me suffer." She resumed swatting the minute attackers, too distraught to care whether or not Bret caught a glimpse of her shapely legs.

"My dear Miss Devan, I assure you nothing is farther from the truth," he quipped, then added seriously, "And if you weren't so quick to fly off the handle, you'd know it. Now, stand still and lift up those pantalets," he instructed, bending over to assist her.

Disregarding propriety once again, Kitty did as she was told, squirming miserably while Bret proceeded to brush away the troublesome insects.

"Trust you to find an ant bed to fall asleep in! Good Lord, don't you ever watch where you're going?" he muttered, then reared back on his heels to look up into her distressed face. "I'm afraid there's no help for it. You're going to have to come out of those damned things," he stated, referring to the pantalets, which were now thoroughly infested.

"What!" Kitty cried, immediately indignant. Then, recognizing the necessity of complying with his suggestion, she scurried behind a clump of bushes and divested herself of the garment. A few minutes later, rid of her tormenters and back into the frilly pantalets, she reappeared, her stubborn chin lifted as she silently defied Bret to laugh at her again.

"Oh, how I'd like to whittle you down to size," she whispered vehemently.

"Feeling better?" Bret asked with a devilish grin.

"Quite, thank you."

"In that case, how about strolling down to the creek with me?"

Kitty knew that he was referring to the creek where they had fished throughout their youth. The idea seemed suddenly appealing. Picking up the wide-brimmed hat that had fallen off during her recent struggle, she hesitated only briefly before nodding and accepting his outstretched hand.

A quiver of anticipation ran down her spine as their fingers touched, and she glanced up at him shyly. Though his expression seemed genuinely friendly, she was reluctant to let down her guard, half expecting his now amicable mood to give way to mockery at any moment.

The creek was not far, and they walked in silence for the first few minutes, Kitty still smarting from her humiliating experience. Why must she always make a fool of herself in front of Bret? she wondered.

As though reading her mind, Bret smiled down at her. "You know, Kitten, rescuing you is becoming a habit. In fact, I don't know how you've managed without me these past few years!"

Seeing the furious look on her face, he mockingly threw up his hands before continuing. "Now don't get your feathers ruffled. I mean, you do have a way of going off half-cocked and landing yourself in rather unusual circumstances.''

"If you had any manners, you wouldn't keep bringing up the past. It's a pity you can't be a gentleman—like Miles, for instance.''

"Ah, yes—Miles,'' Bret murmured thoughtfully, a slight frown creasing his brow. Selina had told him of the rumors that Kitty and Miles had been seeing a lot of each other.

Seeing his frown and hoping to nettle him further, Kitty said: "He's doing quite well with Judge Crane, you know. It's just a matter of time before he becomes a full-fledged partner in the judge's law firm.''

"You seem to know a lot about Miles. Don't tell me you're getting serious about him at this late date.'' He grinned, remembering the many set-tos Kitty and Miles had had during their childhood.

"I might be at that. Miles is handsome and smart, and he knows how to treat a lady—which is more than I can say for you.''

"If I were you, Kitty, I don't think I'd take Miles too seriously.''

"Well, you're not me, and if you think you're going to give me brotherly advice, you're barking up the wrong tree.'' Remembering Selina, she added: "Besides, you're a fine one to talk. Why, half the town's whispering about you seeing so much of Selina, and the other half's at least wondering about it.''

Bret's eyes sparkled. "Tell me, Kitty—have you been whispering or just wondering?''

"Neither,'' she snapped. "I couldn't care less what you do nor whom you do it with. As far as I'm concerned, you and Selina are two peas in a pod. You're both immoral and . . . and unrefined.''

"That's enough.'' Anger sparkled in his green eyes as his grasp tightened on her arm. "Malign me all you like, but leave Selina out of it. She may not be a lady by your standards, but she's one of the few women I trust and respect.''

Kitty stopped in her tracks, completely flabbergasted. "Respect! *Enjoy*, don't you mean,'' she remarked sarcastically.

"That, too. She's a very enjoyable woman to be around, more so than most,'' he answered with complete honesty. "She happens to be a very big-hearted person and a very kind one. Oddly enough, I've never heard her say a cross word or an unkind thing about anybody, which is more than can be said for others I know,'' he added meaningfully.

A flush appeared on Kitty's face as she turned to look at him.

Resentment stirred oddly in her breast. "Oh, I'm sure she's *most* generous. Aren't all whores?" she retorted.

Grabbing her shoulders, Bret gave her a menacing look. "If you were a man, you wouldn't live to repeat that remark," he said quietly. "As it is, I suggest you shut up before you bite off more than you can chew."

Kitty could feel his fingers digging into her flesh and, sensing his leashed anger, experienced a moment of fear. Anger was a rare thing for Bret; yet provoked too far, his temper was menacing. This much she remembered from her childhood, though she had never backed down from him. Nor did she intend to do so now.

"Don't threaten me, Bret. I don't frighten easily." She jerked free of his grasp and stepped backward.

As fate would decree, she backed blindly into the net of a huge spiderweb that had been spun between two elm trees. Feeling the sticky, clinging threads ensnaring her hair, Kitty blanched with fright and leapt forward with a shriek. In the next instant, she was in Bret's arms.

"Get it off me—oh, please get it off me, Bret!" she squealed, trembling with the assumption that a spider was on her.

Bret had seen that the web was spiderless even as Kitty had backed into it, but understanding her phobia, he quickly brushed the cobwebs from her hair and back.

"Hush, Kitten, it's all right. Nothing is on you," he assured her with unusual tenderness, remembering how often he had held her thus as a child on the many occasions he had gotten her out of scrapes. In some ways she was still such a child, at least to him.

"Are you sure there's no spider on me?" she questioned doubtfully.

"I'm sure," he reassured her.

Feeling a bit foolish, she looked up at him. "I know you must think I'm a silly fool, but I just can't stand those ugly, creepy things," she said in an attempt to regain her dignity.

Bret's arm tightened around her, and his free hand stroked her dark, tousled hair. "I don't think you're silly nor a fool, though I'm a bit surprised you're still afraid of anything so small. Most spiders are not dangerous, you know. Their bite is hardly worse than that of a mosquito," he reasoned gently.

"I know, but I—I'm not really afraid of being bitten," she murmured against his broad chest, somehow dreading to leave the security of his arms. "I'm just afraid of one getting on me. I even have nightmares about them sometimes. It's always the same dream,'' she admitted hesitantly, almost certain he would laugh. When he didn't, she continued. "In my dreams, there's a huge spiderweb with a big black spider in the center. It comes down on me, and I can never move. I can't get away!" she said in a choked whisper.

When Bret did not answer, she felt embarrassed. "Oh, I know it sounds silly to you. You couldn't possibly understand. You've never been afraid of anything," she added defensively.

"Everyone's afraid of something, Kitty. Even me," he answered softly.

"You? I don't believe it! What could you possibly be afraid of?" she asked, her own fear forgotten.

He was amused by her naiveté. "Let's just say that everybody faces his own demons at one time or another."

Their eyes met and held. Suddenly conscious of his masculine body pressing against hers, molding her to him, she quivered. An awareness, a sudden tension, sprang up between them, yet Kitty did not attempt to move out of his embrace. She felt powerless to move at all, helpless to understand the tumultuous feelings his nearness was arousing in her. Unconsciously, her arms wound around his broad neck as he lowered his head to brush her lips with his. Then, as the kiss deepened, Kitty moaned and strained closer, feeling she could not get near enough to him.

She knew that he shared her longing when his arms tightened around her and his mouth became less and less gentle, possessively exploring the sweetness of her parted lips. She had never been kissed like this, not even by Miles, and an aching excitement stirred deep within her. Murmuring his name, she caressed the back of his head, her fingers feeling the crispness of the dark hair that grew low on his neck.

Consumed with a raging desire, Bret sensed if he did not stop now, he would not be able to control the situation much longer. The consequences would be regrettable, particularly when Kitty realized that he had no intention of marrying her. She would never forgive him, nor would Dave. Realizing this, he reluctantly released her.

For a moment neither spoke, but he saw her bemused expression a fleeting instant before she turned and walked quickly away from him. He did not attempt to follow but watched until she disappeared from view. Self-denial did not come easily to him, and as he sauntered toward the creek's edge, he vowed to keep Kitty at arm's length in the future. The thought was honorable, but not pleasing, and his mood darkened.

Chapter 4

The air was muggy, and great swirls of gray clouds were closing in fast, suggesting the threat of rain that was neither needed nor wanted. Dave sat astride his stallion and unconsciously listened to the field hands sing the rhythmic spiritual, "Ezekiel Saw de Wheel," while deftly picking the brittle cotton bolls clean and throwing the white fibrous balls into long cotton sacks that hung heavily around their glistening necks.

He was unmindful of the scene before him, however, his thoughts going back to happier days when his wife, Jody, had ridden beside him to inspect the fields at pickin' time. Lord, how he missed her, even though in his mind and heart she was never far away. At times, it seemed as if he could almost reach out and touch her, so that he often wondered about the life hereafter. Was it possible that God, in His infinite wisdom, permitted the dearly departed to return occasionally to the loved ones they left behind; to watch over them or, perhaps, share certain precious moments? It was a possibility he had considered, even hoped for, many times during the past two years.

Today, Jody seemed particularly close to him for some reason, and for a moment his vision clouded as a tightness filled his chest. Extracting a handkerchief from his hip pocket, he mopped the perspiration from his brow and the moisture from his tired eyes, then silently chided himself for being maudlin.

Yesterday was gone forever. He could always remember the past, but he could never recapture it. When Jody had been stricken with cholera in forty-nine, she had been given a reprieve from death. The following nine years had been filled with more happiness than most people experience in a whole lifetime. Now, it was only a question of time before he would be joining her in the life beyond, and this was the comforting thought that kept him going. In the meantime, he had to go on living, making the most of each day, for this was what Jody would want him to do. There was still Tad and Kitty, who needed him. Kitty—so vivacious and full of life, so much her mother's daughter. The love of his life, now.

His train of thought was suddenly interrupted as his overseer swore aloud and, lifting his shotgun, blasted the head off a rattler slithering over a nearby row of cotton. Tossing the hideous remains aside, he lumbered over to Dave.

"That's the third one I shot today. A darkie almost stepped on one this morning, and if'n them dang rivers don't stop swelling, the whole damn field is gonna be filled with them varmints," he stated morosely, pulling a twist of tobacco from his shirt pocket. After biting off a considerable chunk, he added, "Damned if it don't look like we're gonna git some more rain today!"

Dave glanced at the darkening sky and shook his head. "Seems like we've hardly had a dry day since spring. We sure don't need any more rain."

"That's a fact, fer sho'," Charlie agreed, pausing to spit. "Blamed if I ain't beginning to feel jes' like Noah!" He chuckled.

"Well, if this rain keeps up much longer, you're going to have more to worry about than snakes in those fields. That levee to the south of us can take just so much, and then it's going to give," Dave remarked.

"That's the truth," Charlie agreed. "Might not be a bad idea to check all the levees. Want me to go check on 'em after I call quittin' time?"

"No thanks, Charlie. You'd better be getting on back to your wife soon as you finish up here. I'll ride over and check some of the levees before this storm breaks. If it gets to looking much worse, you'd better call in the field hands and send them on home," he advised, turning his mount to go.

Charlie watched Dave until he disappeared from view. There were not many men like Dave Devan. No sir, he was one in a million, and a mighty good man to work for to boot! The faint rumbling of thunder in the far distance caused him to frown, and an inexplicable uneasiness washed over him. Maybe the boss should have waited

until tomorrow to check those levees; but then, who was he to be
telling him how to run his business?

Dave stood on the windy levee and thoughtfully watched the
angry water of the muddy Mississippi swirl past him only a few feet
below. The river was too high for this time of year. And as he had
feared, some sections were badly in need of repair. Normally the
levees were fortified each year, but five months of almost constant
rain had rendered such work impossible. High water in the spring
had weakened the embankments, and if the rain did not let up
enough for repairs to be made, it was almost certain that some
sections of the levees would not hold up much longer. Cotton crops
had been heavily damaged by the persistent downpours, but if the
levees broke, there would be no crops at all. With a worried sigh,
Dave walked back to his horse and remounted.

The wind was picking up, and though it was only midafternoon,
the sky was now almost gray. When the first huge raindrops fell, he
nudged his nervous stallion into a canter. Streaks of lightning zigzagged across the low-flying clouds, followed by loud claps of thunder.
Without encouragement, the horse charged into a full gallop, but
Dave did not try to rein him in. Again, his thoughts were on his
deceased wife, Jody, her face filling his mind so that he was unaware
of the drenching rain now coming down in a blinding torrent.

Minutes later, however, his mind was jerked back to the present
when lightning unexpectedly struck a huge oak tree just ahead of
him. A blinding light, accompanied by a deafening crack, caught
both rider and horse unprepared. The magnificent beast reared on its
hind legs, and Dave felt himself falling to the ground.

Pain seared through his thigh as the stallion's hoof came down on
him. He tried to roll away, only to be caught again by the huge limb
that had been severed by lightning. Pinned helplessly beneath the
heavy branch, he was dimly aware that his horse was galloping
away. A wave of dizziness descended upon him, yet as unconsciousness mercifully closed in on him, he was not afraid. The vision of
Jody filled his pain-drugged mind, and he was comforted.

Curled up on the sofa in the front parlor, Kitty bit into a succulent
peach, her eyes never leaving the dimly lit page of the book in her
lap, *Wuthering Heights*. Thoroughly absorbed in the story, she was
unmindful of the commotion coming from the back hall until Mammy

Lou scurried into the room, followed by Lemme. Holding her place on the page with a slender finger, Kitty looked up, frowning when she saw Mammy Lou's worried expression.

"Well, what is it, Mammy Lou?" she questioned impatiently.

"Miz Kitty—" The old woman floundered, at an unusual loss for words. "Lemme, heah, is got sum'thin' tuh tell you."

"Ah don' wants tuh wor'hy you none, but . . ." Lemme faltered.

"But what? For heaven's sake, Lemme, speak up," Kitty commanded.

"Well, yo' pa's hoss dun turned up, but dey wuz no sign ob Mist' Dave. Ah dun sent Zeke ober to Mist' Charlie's house tuh see if'n he mought know whar Mist' Dave is," he finished lamely.

Doshe, who had trailed in behind Lemme, rushed forward and put her arms around the girl. "No cause tuh gits all upset, chile. Ah'm sho' nuttin' bad dun hoppen't tuh yo' pa. Why, dem hounds in de back ain' howled all day, an' you knows dey a'ways duz if'n anybody's daid."

"Hesh yo' mouf, Doshe, an' let mah baby 'lone! Whut you tryin' tuh do, skeer de libin' deylites out ob her?" Mammy Lou admonished, shoving the well-meaning woman aside with an ample hip.

Hurried footsteps on the veranda caused the four of them to rush to the front door and fling it open.

"I got here soon's I could, Miss Kitty," Charlie informed them, knocking the mud from his boots before entering the spacious hall. "You say Mist' Dave's hoss came back without him?" he asked Lemme, who nodded affirmatively. "How long ago wuz that?"

"Jest now, Mist' Charlie. He sho' wuz winded, lak he mought hab been runnin' a fer piece."

"Do you think he might have been thrown from his horse?" Kitty asked, her voice quavering.

"Maybe," Charlie replied, rubbing his chin thoughtfully. "Do you think he could have stopped off by the slave quarters, Lemme?" he asked as the group made its way into the parlor.

"Naw, suh. Ah wuz jes' comin' back from ober dat way when Ah spotted Mist' Dave's hoss standin' in front ob de stables."

By this time Kitty was wringing her hands, but before she could ask questions, the front door burst open, and Tad, followed by Bret, came noisily into the hall, both of them laughing while they brushed the water from their clothes. The deafening rain and loud claps of thunder had apparently covered the sound of their approach, and their sudden appearance now caused everyone to jump and make a rush back to the hall.

"Hi, Sis. Look who I brought back for supper," Tad remarked, nodding toward Bret, who was still brushing the rain from his soaked clothes. Then, seeing the worried look on everyone's faces, he sobered and walked over to Kitty, gently placing his hands on her trembling shoulders.

"What's wrong, honey?" he asked.

"Oh, Tad—Pa's horse came back without him about twenty minutes ago, and we don't know what's happened to him or where he is. Lemme said his horse was winded, like he'd been running a good distance. He might be lying out there somewhere hurt, or even—" Her voice broke, and she covered her face with shaking hands.

Tad gathered her sister to him and tried to reassure her, while Bret turned his attention to the overseer.

"Did you see which direction his horse came from?" he asked.

"Naw, sir, but Mist' Dave did say he wuz gonna ride around the place and check on the levees this afternoon," Charlie replied. "The only trouble is that we got levees to the north, south, and west of us, and they ain't no tellin' which ones he wuz checkin'. Gawd only knows whar he mought be!"

"Oh, Tad, do something!" Kitty sobbed, close to hysteria. "We can't just let him lie out there in all this rain. He'll die! . . ." Her voice trailed off as she met Bret's disapproving gaze.

"Get hold of yourself, Kitty. Becoming hysterical isn't going to help Dave or anyone else," he remarked abruptly, then turned to the others. Realizing Tad was incapable of taking matters into his own hands, he took command of the situation.

"Gus, ride out and check all of the neighboring plantations. It could be that Mister Devan took refuge from the storm at one of their houses and his horse simply broke loose. Lemme, you'd better saddle up and search the area between here and the levee to the south. Charlie, you and Tad comb the area between here and the west, and I'll check to the north. Lemme, send Zeke to town and see if he can locate Doc Blanks or that young Dr. Johnson who's in practice with him. Tell him to take the carriage and bring one of them back with him."

"Then you do think Pa is hurt, don't you, Bret?" Kitty asked tremulously, fear clouding her lovely blue eyes.

"Not necessarily, but if he is injured, we'll need a doctor for him. We can't very well overlook that possibility, and it's best to be prepared," he answered gently.

"You an' Mist' Tad had best git on upstairs an' gits intuh sum dry clothes," Mammy Lou interjected.

"We'll be a lot wetter when we get back, Mammy Lou," Bret returned wryly. "Besides, there isn't time. Every minute might count." He turned to go.

Kitty rushed to him and caught his arm. "Let me go with you, Bret."

"Sorry, Kitty, it's best you stay here. Besides, if one of the others do find him, you'll want to be here when they bring him in."

That much was true, though deep down she felt Bret would be the one to find her father. Still, she could not argue the point, for if one of the others did bring Dave home, and if he were hurt, she would need to be here.

"Try not to worry, Sis. We'll find him and bring him home." Tad gave her a hug before turning to join Bret, who was just going out the front door.

Kitty watched dismally while the men rode out of sight, tears misting her troubled eyes as Doshe put a comforting arm around her waist. "Pa's got to be all right," Kitty whispered. "He's just *got* to be!"

It was dusk when Gus returned from the neighboring plantations, but with no news about Dave. A short time later, Zeke arrived with the elderly Doc Blanks, whom Kitty joined in the front parlor. The rain had settled down to a fine drizzle by the time Lemme, Charlie, and Tad returned, and still there was no news of Dave. That left Bret, and by this time Kitty was almost frantic with worry, though she camouflaged her anxiety well as she chatted politely with Doc Blanks while Tad washed up for supper.

As the time approached seven o'clock, Kitty suggested they adjourn to the dining room. Reluctantly, she had instructed Mammy Lou to serve the evening meal. She was not hungry and felt dubious that she could swallow a mouthful, but realizing Tad and the doctor must be famished, she tried to carry on as usual and at least be a dutiful hostess. Worry was no excuse for bad manners.

Almost the entire meal was eaten in silence, with neither Tad nor Kitty doing full justice to the delicious food. Shortly afterward, while they were sipping some elderberry wine, the sound of approaching hoofbeats suddenly caught their attention. Kitty rushed into the hall, the others right behind her, and flung open the front door just as Bret, cradling Dave in his powerful arms, made his way up the wide veranda steps.

"He's unconscious, but not dead," Bret informed them shortly, heading toward the stairs. "Doshe, run on upstairs and turn down the master's bed."

"Yassuh, Ah's almos' dere," came the joyful reply as Doshe quickly sped past him, Mammy Lou following closely behind.

Doc Blanks picked up his black satchel and, turning to Kitty, told her to get some hot water up to him as quickly as possible.

"Hot water?" Kitty croaked numbly, her half-relieved mind still in a muddle.

"Yes, girl, hot water—and plenty of it," the old man snapped. "We got to get him cleaned up and see what the damage is." With that, he turned and made his way up the long, curving stairs.

Kitty rushed down the back hall and encountered Uncle Thad, who was just coming in the back door.

"Dey foun' Mist' Dave, yit?" he asked worriedly.

"Yes, they've found him. He's alive, but hurt. Go tell Shasta and Daisy to heat up plenty of water and bring it upstairs. And *hurry*, Uncle Thad," she ordered.

By the time Kitty had rushed back upstairs, Bret and Tad were talking in hushed whispers just outside her father's closed door.

"Mammy Lou and Doshe are getting him cleaned up now so Doc can examine him," Tad informed her, then added: "Bret found him on the levee road, pinned under a big tree branch."

Kitty blanched, realizing that Dave might indeed have been killed and that there was still the danger he might be seriously hurt. Seeing her expression, Bret intervened.

"He'll be all right, Kitten. He's tougher than a coot," he said, repressing a shiver from the drenched clothes that stuck to his powerful body.

Observing his discomfort, Tad offered to get some clean clothes from Dave's room so that he could change, but Bret declined the offer and asserted he would much prefer a good, stiff drink.

"Doc will probably be with Pa for some time, Sis, so why don't you take Bret downstairs and rustle him up something to eat and a drink," Tad suggested. "I'll call you as soon as Doc tells us we can go in. Maybe he'll be conscious by then." He stepped aside to allow

Shasta and Daisy, both ladened down with buckets of hot water, to enter Dave's room.

Kitty hesitated, wanting to go to her father, yet knowing she would not be allowed to do so until Doc had finished his examination. At last she nodded, and as the two servants reappeared, she instructed them to set supper on the table for Mr. Bret, who had already started down the stairs.

When she reached the front parlor, she saw that he was pouring himself a stiff shot of whiskey from Dave's best stock, which he had undoubtedly retrieved from the gun closet beneath the stairs in the hall. Kitty bristled inwardly, resenting his familiarity with his surroundings, even though she realized that his actions were quite normal. Her father had treated him like a son, especially after Bret's father had died and he had moved in with them. It was natural that he felt at home, although she still resented his attitude.

As her eyes traveled over him, she became acutely aware of his sensuous appearance, the wet clothes clinging to every line of his tall, lithe body, accentuating his masculinity in a disturbing way.

Sensing her presence behind him, Bret turned and, meeting her resentful gaze, lifted his glass. "Care to join me? You look as if you could use one," he added, and before she could refuse, he picked up the decanter and poured a small amount of the amber liquid into another glass he had brought in from the dining room.

Kitty silently accepted the glass, her trembling fingers brushing his and making her uncomfortably aware of his nearness. Unused to anything stronger than a light wine, she hesitated before following Bret's example and tossing down the contents. Her throat, lungs, and stomach rebelled, and as she gasped and coughed, Bret patted her gently on the back and smiled.

"Lord, Kitten, don't you know not to gulp down whiskey?" he admonished once she had caught her breath.

"You—you did," came the somewhat resentful reply as she wondered for the hundredth time why she could never do anything right when he was with her.

"But I'm used to it. You, my love, are not." He chuckled, brushing a stray wisp of hair from her face. At the moment, she looked like a child. "Now stop pouting and pull yourself together like a good girl, or the entire household will think I've been mistreating you."

The September night was unusually warm, and with a weary sigh,

Kitty brushed a slightly unsteady hand across her moist brow. "I haven't thanked you for finding Pa before it was too late. I don't know what we would have done if you hadn't been here," she said with a slight smile.

Placing a large hand on either side of her waist, Bret looked into her upturned face. "I'm glad I was here, too, little one. You know you can always call on me whenever you need me."

"How can I call on you when I never see you?" she asked petulantly, remembering she had scarcely seen him all summer, other than the few times she had caught a glimpse of him in town.

"True, and for that I apologize." He grinned. "But as you might have heard, I've been rather busy this summer, rebuilding my warehouse and tending to other matters."

"Such as Selina Baxter, I suppose," Kitty remarked dryly.

"My association with Selina is none of your business."

"What you do is your own affair. I assure you I couldn't care less."

"Good. Let's drop the subject, shall we?"

Before Kitty could reply, Doshe appeared in the doorway, informing her that the master was awake and asking for her. Relief flooded over her upon realizing her father was truly going to be all right, and after reminding Bret that his supper was ready, she dashed upstairs.

Later, as she kept vigil over Dave while he slept and listened to the faint strains of "Deep River" that drifted to her from the slave quarters, Kitty's mind returned to Bret. It was fairly obvious that Bret preferred Selina's company to her own, which was undoubtedly the reason she saw so little of him. The realization was a bitter pill to swallow.

Chapter 5

Kitty adjusted her porkpie hat and listened to the Moore family chatting jovially as their carriage drew closer to the edge of Vicksburg. Ben and Buck, riding two magnificent bays just to the side of the carriage, had been singing at the top of their voices for the past thirty minutes and were now starting in on "Camptown Races." As they pulled into Washington Street, Mrs. Moore leaned over the side and reminded her sons that this was the Sabbath and to quiet down. Then she laughed good-naturedly and turned toward her husband, Sam.

"Good heavens, what will folks around here think, the boys pullin' up in front of the church and singing a song like that!"

Sam chuckled and shook his head, but before he could answer, his daughter, Mary Belle, quickly intervened.

"Just what they always think, Ma—that Ben and Buck are loud-mouthed and bad-mannered."

"Now, now, missy, you're being too hard on your brothers. I reckon they can be as mannerly as the next fellow, when they've a mind to," her father asserted with a broad grin, turning his attention to Kitty.

"By the way, do you think Bret will want to ride back to Belle Glen with us after church services?"

"I doubt it. In fact, I'm not sure we'll even see him in church," she replied.

"It certainly was neighborly of him to stay on and help Charlie run the plantation while Tad took your pa to New Orleans to see that

45

doctor who's so good at setting broken bones," Sam remarked, to which his wife quickly agreed.

"Yes, it was," Kitty admitted reluctantly, wishing the trend of conversation would change.

"It was mighty fortunate for Dave that he was around last week, that's for sure. If Bret hadn't been there to manage the slaves during pickin' time, I doubt Charlie would have had time to oversee the reparation of those levees," he added.

"Yes, it was kind of him to help," Kitty murmured.

"It's a shame he had to ride into town yesterday. He could have ridden in with us today," Mary Belle stated with obvious disappointment.

"Goodness, Mary Belle, you can hardly expect Bret to spend every minute of his spare time at our place while Pa's gone. Besides, he had to go into town on business, so that's why he wasn't back last night," Kitty informed her shortly.

"He will be returning to Belle Glen tonight, won't he?" asked Mrs. Moore. "If not, I really think you should come and spend the night at our place. I don't think it's a good idea for you to stay in that big house by yourself."

"Thank you, but I'm almost sure he'll be back tonight. If not, Mammy Lou and Uncle Thad sleep on the third floor, so I'll not be alone," she assured them.

Luckily Sam intervened, and the topic was closed, though inwardly Kitty was brooding over the fact that Bret had remained in town last night. Still, he had been most helpful for the past ten days, she reasoned, and perhaps he really had been too tired to return to Belle Glen last night. The past two weeks had been anxious ones, for Dave's accident had resulted in two severe fractures of the right leg, one below and one above the knee.

Realizing that such bad breaks could cripple a man for life, Doc Blanks had insisted that Tad put his father on the first riverboat heading toward New Orleans, where a well-known surgeon could set Dave's leg properly. The old doctor had set her father's leg as best he could and had prescribed liberal doses of laudanum to ease the pain during the trip, but as Tad and Lemme had carried Dave aboard the *Natchez*, it had been obvious to Kitty that her father was suffering. She doubted, however, that Dave would have agreed to make the trip had Bret not talked him into it, promising to stay on at

Belle Glen and supervise the running of the plantation until his return.

Though Kitty had tried to show Bret how grateful she was, it had not been easy, for he had nonchalantly brushed aside her thanks each time. Actually, she had seen very little of him these past ten days, other than at mealtimes, for he had utilized every moment to see that the plantation was running smoothly.

The carriage drew to a halt in front of the Christ Episcopal Church, and Kitty pushed all thoughts of Bret from her mind as Ben helped her to alight from the vehicle. After speaking briefly to several friends and repeatedly answering their well-meant questions about her father's health, she followed the Moores into the sanctuary. The church was crowded with familiar faces. As they made their way to the Moores' pew and sat down, Kitty heard Mary Belle gasp aloud.

"Kitty, don't turn around just now," she whispered excitedly, "but guess who's here this morning!"

"Who?" Kitty returned in a hushed voice, curiosity tempting her to disregard Mary Belle's command so she could see the object of her friend's excitement.

"Bret," Mary Belle informed her, then lowered her voice. "And guess *who* he's with!" she exclaimed in a shocked whisper.

Unable to restrain herself any longer, Kitty turned around. Selina! For a moment, her eyes locked with Bret's; then, with a haughty lift of her chin, she turned back to face the front. Luckily, the rest of Mary Belle's comments were stifled as the minister entered the pulpit and the service began. Seething with anger, Kitty was oblivious to the sermon, nor was she in a better frame of mind during the long ride back home, responding mechanically to the conversation only when necessary.

When finally in the privacy of her own bedroom, she ripped off her hat and flung it across the room, tears of frustration brimming in her dark blue eyes. He had deliberately lied to her! Well, perhaps he had not outright lied, but he had certainly not mentioned he would be seeing Selina. He had told her he had to return to town on business and might have to stay overnight. Jealousy seared through her as she realized that in all probability he had spent the previous night in Selina's arms.

By late afternoon, Kitty had worked herself into a frenzy planning her revenge. When Bret did not return for supper, she had reached one conclusion. Promise or no promise, he definitely was not spending another night under her roof. If he still wanted to help out at Belle Glen, he would simply have to stay in town and communicate daily. If this was not agreeable to him, then she would do without his help, even if she had to ride out to the fields and oversee the work herself.

It was a pity Miles was busy in court this next week, she thought. She was sure he would have been happy to stay on as a guest, though she doubted he was very knowledgeable about managing a plantation. It was just as well, she decided, for there was something intangible about Miles that sometimes made her uneasy. For this reason, she had managed to keep him at arm's length whenever it appeared that he might become ardent.

Night fell, and as the hour struck nine, it slowly began to dawn on her that Bret might not be returning tonight, either. Feeling thwarted, she sent the servants to their quarters, then blew out the remaining parlor lamp and made her way upstairs. It was a warm night for late September, and after changing into an almost transparent batiste nightgown, she slipped dejectedly into bed.

Sleep would not come as she tossed and turned, trying to block Bret from her tormented mind. The grandfather clock was striking ten when she heard the front door open. Remembering Dave had given Bret a key to the house, Kitty jumped out of bed and, without pausing even to don a wrapper, ran to the hall, her steps slowing as she reached the staircase. Bret was mounting the stairs, and from his disheveled appearance she surmised that he had been either riding hard, drinking, or both.

Sensing her presence, he looked up as he reached the top landing. Desire shot through him like a searing flame as his eyes appreciatively raked over her scantily clad body, lingering on the deep cleavage between her breasts before finally meeting her gaze. He groaned inwardly as a familiar ache stirred in his loins, yet his mounting lust and inner frustrations were carefully concealed as he smiled down at her.

"Waiting for me, Kitten?"

"Don't flatter yourself. I heard a noise and thought someone might be breaking into the house."

"Oh—and just how did you propose to overthrow this so-called burglar?"

Moonlight streamed through the upper hall window, revealing the unconcealed amusement in his eyes. Suddenly aware of her provocative appearance, Kitty flushed and stepped back into the shadows.

"I could have managed," she replied haughtily. "As a matter of fact, there was something I had intended to discuss with you last night, but of course you were in town attending to *business*."

"Which was concluded very satisfactorily."

"With Selina Baxter, no doubt."

"As I've told you before, whatever is between Selina and me is none of your business," he reminded her, his lips curving into a diabolical grin. "But since you're so interested, yes, I was with Selina—*after* I concluded my business in town."

"And then you flaunted your affair with her all over town by bringing her to church this morning. You're despicable!"

"You know, you're beginning to sound like a nagging shrew." He grinned. "Lord help the man who marries you!"

"Well, it certainly won't be you!"

"On that, at least, we agree."

"Hmph! I pity the fool who does marry you. She'll probably spend the rest of her days barefoot, pregnant, and waiting on you hand and foot."

His eyes sparkled with devilment. "Oh, I don't know," he drawled with mock seriousness. "I'll probably let her have shoes."

"I don't care whom you marry or how you treat her," Kitty shot back. "I just want you out of this house by morning."

"You do, do you? And just who do you suppose is going to keep things running smoothly around here until Dave returns?"

"I'll manage," Kitty replied with more confidence than she felt, then added maliciously: "In fact, I was already thinking of asking Miles to stay with me until Pa returns."

It was a lie, but she gloated as Bret's mouth tightened and anger flashed in his eyes.

"Like hell you will," he muttered grimly, no longer amused. "I'll go when Dave returns and not before, and if I ever hear of you asking Miles out here to stay, I'll give you a sound thrashing that's been long overdue."

"You—you wouldn't dare!" Kitty sputtered.

"Just try me," Bret returned, then chuckled. "I assure you it would give me the greatest pleasure to paddle you soundly. You need taking down a peg or two, either that way—or maybe this," he murmured, chivalry forgotten as he dragged her into his powerful arms.

Before Kitty could protest, his mouth was savagely covering hers, as though he were determined to punish her by forcing her to his will. She fought him instinctively, her clenched fists pushing ineffectively against his broad chest. Vainly she sought to free her lips from his, until at last she went limp against his unyielding strength. Feigning desire that she was far from feeling, Kitty forced herself to relax, her lips parting invitingly while her arms wound slowly around his neck. A sense of power filled her as, pressing closer to him, she felt the hard contours of his masculine body and was aware of his growing need for her.

Feeling his kiss soften and his hands caress her, she was almost tempted to yield completely, until the thought of Selina came to mind. Anger renewed, she viciously bit his bottom lip, causing him to release her with a muffled curse.

A satisfied smirk appeared on her face when Bret wiped the blood from his lip and glared at her. As she turned and started toward her room, fingers like steel grasped her small waist, forcing her around to face him.

"Oh, no, you don't," Bret muttered. Jerking her to him and pinning her arms behind her back, he secured her wrists with one large hand while the other caught hold of her hair, thrusting her head back until their lips were only inches apart.

"If you're going to act a hellion, you'll be treated like one," he stated coldly just before his mouth came down on hers.

There was no gentleness in him, only anger. Capturing her lips and forcing them apart, he explored her trembling mouth, tasting and devouring its sweetness until Kitty was almost faint from lack of breath. Still, she fought him, twisting her head as far as he would allow, but her resistance only added fuel to the passion he had held in check for so long. Against her will, she felt herself responding, her lips softening while she unconsciously pressed closer to him. Her nightgown was scant protection against the strong force of his body, and dimly aware of the extent of his arousal, she moaned with longing. His lips never left hers as, picking her up in his arms, he slowly made his way toward her bedroom, kicking the door open as he strode into the moonlit room.

Kitty had ceased to think. She could only feel, consumed by a hunger that overshadowed all reason, a hunger equal to that of the man who was carrying her to the bed. She wanted him and longed for the fulfillment only he could bring. Nothing else mattered. She would give him anything, everything, though a tiny voice inside warned her that she meant little more to him than Selina, if as much. The unbidden thought caused her to tense.

Sensing her slight withdrawal, Bret released her lips and looked questioningly into the depths of expressive eyes that mirrored desire and uncertainty. His sanity returned quickly, and for a moment conscience warred with lust. Then, with a muffled oath, he tossed her onto the bed and strode back to the door.

At first Kitty was too stunned to speak. Surely he was not going to leave her, not now!

"Bret?" she whispered in a quavering voice, wincing inwardly at the cold look he gave her when he paused at the door.

"Go to sleep, Kitty. It's way past your bedtime."

Kitty's mouth dropped open with surprise, for whatever she had expected of him, it certainly had not been this. Anger and embarrassment washed over her as she lifted her chin and glared at him defiantly. Before she could think of a suitable reply, however, Bret walked out, closing the door behind him.

Later, as sleep eluded him and he paced back and forth in the confines of his room, he chided himself for being a fool. He wanted Kitty more than he had ever wanted a woman. It was a simple fact, though the reason still eluded him. She was merely another woman—beautiful, yet no different from any other female, he reasoned—but his tired mind quickly rejected the lie.

She had always been different, and because she was Dave's daughter, she had always been beyond reach. Though Dave shared a certain closeness with him, Kitty had always been the love of his life. It was only natural for Dave to want the best for his daughter. Bret's own humble background, as the son of an overseer, would hardly make Kitty's father look favorably on him as a prospective son-in-law. Then, too, he had hardly led an exemplary life in the past, a fact of which he was sure Dave was aware.

The clock on the mantel struck twice. Damn, he thought, would morning never come? It was then that he heard the muffled cries coming from across the hall, followed soon by a piercing scream. Kitty! Without giving thought to his state of undress, he bolted for her room.

Bursting through the door, he rushed over to the bed where she was writhing, as though fighting unseen demons. She was drenched with perspiration, the dampness molding her nightgown to her body as she struggled to free herself from the twisted bedsheet. Bret, however, was unmindful of her appearance when he gathered her into his arms. Holding her in his lap, he brushed the damp tendrils of curling hair from her face, gently rocking her back and forth while whispering words of comfort. Finally her eyes opened, and she stilled, clutching the sheet to her breast.

For a moment she looked up at him in bewilderment; then memories of the nightmare returned, and she trembled, burying her pale face in the crisp, black hair of his bare chest.

"It was the same dream," she moaned softly. "There was a large spider on a web, and it was slowly coming down on me. I couldn't move. I couldn't escape!" She shuddered, and her arms tightened around his broad neck.

"Shhh—it's all right, Kitty. It was only a bad dream, nothing more. You're safe now," he murmured, gently kissing her brow.

"But—but I'm still afraid," she cried.

"You don't need to be. You know I wouldn't let anything hurt you," he assured her, placing her back in the bed and tucking the sheet around her before rising to his feet.

Kitty clutched at his hand, fear still etched on her upturned face.

"Don't leave me, Bret. I can't help it—I'm still afraid. I don't think I can go to sleep unless you stay with me," she said tremulously.

"That's impossible, and you know it. Good Lord, Kitty, have you forgotten what happened earlier?"

"Nothing happened. You're obviously not going to take advantage of me," she persisted. "Besides, if you sleep on top of the sheet, what could possibly be wrong with your staying with me?"

Bret knew it was a foolish suggestion, but as Kitty scooted over to make room for him, he lay down beside her. His muscles tightened as he waited impatiently for her to fall asleep so he could leave. Silently he cursed her naiveté, wondering how she could be totally unaware of the effect her nearness was having on him. He felt her move and knew she had turned to face him.

"Bret," she murmured.

"What?"

"Why do we always argue? Do you dislike me?"

With a resigned sigh, he gathered her into his arms. A wave of desire swept over him as he felt the outline of her body beneath the sheet, but he quickly repressed it.

"You know I don't dislike you, Kitten," he said, nuzzling her temple with his chin.

"But you don't like me, either. We're certainly not the best of friends."

Bret did not try to disagree. Kitty invariably brought out the worst in him. Now, she was tempting him almost beyond endurance, weakening his determination not to betray Dave's trust. Inwardly he admitted he could be an adversary or a lover to her, but never merely a friend. There was too much between them for that, a physical attraction that, being denied, sparked off an obvious antagonism.

Kitty sighed despondently at his lack of response. And, because she doubted she would ever understand him, a feeling of frustration swept over her.

"Miles asked me to marry him the other day," she said perversely.

"Oh? And what was your answer?"

"I said I needed time to consider. Pa doesn't like him, but—"

"But what? As an up-and-coming lawyer, Miles is probably looked upon as a good catch by many a doting parent," he remarked wryly.

With an astonished gasp, Kitty propped herself on one elbow and glared at him. "I suppose you want me to marry him!"

Bret jerked her down again, pulling her to him. "If I thought you were seriously considering it, I'd throttle you."

Feeling the provocative contours of her body against his own, he was dimly aware that his resistance was slowly crumbling, and for several feverish moments desire battled with conscience as her lips parted in silent invitation. He ached to take what she so naively offered, but he could not bring himself to take advantage of her youthful innocence, nor could he betray her father's trust and friendship. With a muttered curse, he put her from him abruptly and got to his feet.

"I think I'd better leave now—while I still can," he said.

Surprised and disappointed by his rejection, Kitty grabbed his arm. "Don't go, Bret," she softly implored. "Stay with me—"

"You don't know what you're suggesting, Kitty."

"I do!" she declared passionately, pulling him down beside her.

"God in heaven, do you know what you're doing to me? What the hell do you want?" he cried, taking hold of her shoulders.

Far from being intimidated by his gruffness, Kitty saw the raw desire in his eyes and knew his longing matched her own. She had little knowledge of what sexual fulfillment entailed, yet the curious hunger he had awakened in her made her ache to be a part of him. Heedless of the consequences, she responded instinctively.

"I want *you*," she whispered.

There was no resistance left in him, and with a low groan Bret crushed her to him, his mouth devouring the sweetness of her lips as he deftly removed her gown, then lowered her to the mattress, pinning her beneath him. Her arms tightened around his muscular torso as the kiss deepened. He was dimly aware of a soft moan of pleasure rumbling deep in her throat when his hands began moving over her feverish body, provocatively caressing her most sensitive areas while his tongue teasingly explored the inner recesses of her quivering mouth.

His touch was like fire, searing her flesh as his fingers sensuously stroked the fullness of her taut breasts, then trailed with lingering expertise over her waist, hips, and abdomen, coming to rest on the furry softness of her femininity. By now she was half out of her mind with wanting him. Everything about him excited her—the warmth of his masculine body molding her to him, the strange musky scent of him, but most of all, the hardness of his manhood pressing demandingly against her inner thighs.

As her legs parted of their own volition, his hand moved lower, and she felt the tantalizing movement of his fingers, touching and exploring the most intimate part of her until she was trembling violently. She wanted him, longed for some mysterious fulfillment that was seemingly just out of reach. Her tiny hands fluttered over his broad chest, lingering briefly on a jagged scar that, at any other time, would have aroused her curiosity. But not now. Nothing mattered now except the intense yearning that was devouring her like a flame.

Was this how men and women made love? she wondered dizzily. Was this all there was to it? It couldn't be! There had to more, much more, before her agonizing hunger for him could be satisfied. Instinctively her arms wound around his neck as she writhed beneath him with impatient abandonment. She was, nevertheless, taken by surprise when she felt his hardened member slowly entering her, and as a searing pain shot through her, she gasped aloud and stiffened.

Expecting her reaction, Bret immediately stilled himself, though his penetration had only just begun. A tender smile tugged at the corners of his mouth as he glanced down at her.

"Easy, little one," he murmured, brushing a damp tendril of hair from her cheek. "Just relax."

"But I can't," she replied tremulously. "You hurt me, Bret."

Her answer was childlike, endearing her to him all the more.

"I'm sorry, my darling, but it usually is painful the first time—at least, in the beginning. I won't hurt you again. I promise."

His words were reassuring, but she found it difficult to relax as he resumed moving against her, gently thrusting deeper and deeper until his throbbing maleness was completely embedded in her. There was no pain this time, but it took several minutes for her to relax enough to begin experiencing pleasure. Not until his mouth took possession of hers and his experienced hands resumed their masterful exploration of her body was her passion gradually rekindled. A strange urgency uncurled in the depths of her being, causing her to arch closer to him.

She was writhing now, instinctively keeping pace with his rhythm, which was accelerating. Her ardent response excited Bret even further, but, determined to make it perfect for her, he held himself in check until he was sure the moment was right. Only when he sensed that her passion could no longer be denied did he propel her over the brink, possessing her with an expertise that thrust them simultaneously into a whirling vortex of ecstasy.

Later, as Kitty nestled in the crook of his arm, she was filled with contentment. Never had she experienced such bliss, never had she felt as close to anyone as she felt to Bret. She had given herself to him heart and soul, and now she felt as though she were a part of him. She wanted to express her feelings, but it was difficult to find the right words. Shyly, she peeped up at him.

"Bret, is it always this wonderful?" she asked softly.

"No, my love, not always. Only when it's with the right person," he replied in a tender voice.

"Was it wonderful for you, too?"

"Do you need to ask?" he teased.

His answer pleased her, and she smiled up at him. "Well, I know there have been other women in your life, but was I . . . was it as special for you as it was for me?''

Pulling her even closer to him, he nuzzled the top of her head. ''Very special,'' he answered, kissing her temple. ''I've never felt for any woman what I felt for you tonight. Always remember that.''

Assured by his answer, she fell silent, and minutes later her eyelids closed. As Bret held her in his arms and gazed upon her innocent face, he felt a twinge of guilt. He had never expected to experience with any woman what he had experienced with Kitty—a total fulfillment he had never dreamed possible. It surprised and baffled him, and for a while he tried to imagine what it might be like to be married to her.

In the end, however, he rejected the idea. Too much stood in the way. The vast difference in their backgrounds was something he felt sure Dave would find objectionable, even though he was now financially secure. The fact remained that no one in Vicksburg was likely to forget that his father had once been Dave's overseer. Though he did not give a damn whether the socially ''elite'' accepted him, he had no intention of having Kitty subjected to ostracism because of him. This, however, was not the only stumbling block. Another obstacle was their inability to be compatible for any length of time, which led him to believe that living with her would be something less than harmonious.

No, marriage was definitely out of the question, nor did he intend to have a brief affair with her. Mulling the problem over in his mind, he came to what seemed to be the only solution. In order to prevent a repetition of what had happened tonight, he would have to avoid Kitty as much as possible. It meant that the remainder of his stay at Belle Glen was going to be sheer hell.

Luck was with him the next morning, however, when Dave and Ted unexpectedly returned home. It did not take him long to pack, and before Kitty had awakened he was already riding back to Vicksburg. But his hasty retreat brought him no peace of mind, for he realized he was merely gaining a brief respite from his dilemma. He could not expect to avoid Kitty forever, nor did he really want to.

Chapter 6

Sunlight sifted through the sparse foliage of massive oak, elm, and poplar trees, enhancing the multicolored beauty of the varying shades of gold, rust, and red leaves that clung tenaciously to their twisted branches. A pecan grove situated a short distance from the house was Kitty's favorite spot, for it was located on an elevated knoll that provided her with a picturesque view of Belle Glen.

Noted to be one of the largest plantations in Warren County, Belle Glen was totally self-sustaining, having everything from a small commissary to a grist mill and cotton gin near the Devans' private loading dock on the Yazoo River. Though a small portion was swampland, the plantation sprawled over several thousand acres of fertile river-bottom land, which in summer and fall produced cotton, rice, sugar cane, and corn as far as the eye could see.

The main house was spacious and one of the finest examples of Greek revival architecture in Mississippi. Tall oaks, dripping with Spanish moss, formed an arc over the winding carriage drive that led to the three-storied mansion. Dark shutters framed long French windows and contrasted becomingly with the white-brick exterior that was completely surrounded by graciously colonnaded galleries.

It was an imposing sight to behold, and as a rule Kitty could not look upon her heritage without feeling an overpowering sense of pride. Such was not the case today, however, for she was too occupied thinking about Bret to appreciate the grandeur that stretched before her. She had not seen him in weeks, not since the night of their lovemaking, nor had he asked for Dave's permission to court her, much less marry her.

At first she had felt completely bewildered, but as the realization of his intentions became obvious, anger supplanted her disappointment. He had simply used and discarded her, just as he had numerous other women. She despised her own permissiveness, which had, she feared, led to her ruination, but she hated Bret with a vengeance that was indescribable.

The days had stretched into weeks, and sleepless nights had produced dark circles beneath her large eyes, but it was not until her bout of nausea this morning that she actually realized the repercussion from that one night of folly. When she had missed her menses, she had attributed it to her fretful state of mind, though as a rule she was quite regular. Now, she could not dismiss this irregularity so lightly, and with sinking heart she faced the possibility that she was pregnant.

What should she do? Should she go to Bret and admit her fear, possibly subjecting herself to his pity? No, she would not beg. If she could not have his love, she would not accept his pity. The idea of his marrying her merely to protect her reputation was totally unacceptable to her. Then, too, there was the possibility that he might not be willing to marry her even if she were pregnant.

What, then, was the solution? She had received and rejected many proposals in the past, and even now she had numerous suitors visiting her on a regular basis. Though none of them particularly interested her, she considered several possibilities. The sound of hoofbeats interrupted her train of thought, and, glancing around, she saw Miles approaching the house.

After lightly dismounting, he handed his reins to Moses, the chubby ten-year-old son of Daisy and one of the field hands. Child-like, he reached up to stroke the magnificent chestnut's nose, yelping when Miles lashed out at him with his riding crop. Kitty jumped to her feet, upsetting the wicker basket that was half-filled with pecans she had gathered earlier. Though she could not hear his words, it was obvious that Miles was chastising the cowering boy, who, after a few moments, hesitantly took the proffered reins and led the horse around back to the stables.

Apparently Moses had told Miles of her whereabouts, for in the next instant he was approaching her, an amused smile on his aristocratic face. He was met with frowning censure and a pair of blazing blue eyes.

"Don't you *ever* strike another one of our servants, Miles!" Kitty commanded as he came to stand beside her. "If Pa had seen you do that, he would have thrashed you soundly with your own crop."

"I seriously doubt he could, even if he wanted to—not in his present condition, at least. Of course, he might try to break one of his crutches over my head, but that would be most unfortunate. Dave isn't the man he once was, nor is he getting any younger," Miles replied.

"He's man enough to handle you, crutches or no crutches, so don't take your temper out on our servants."

"The little beggar had no business putting his filthy hands on my horse," Miles snapped. Then, remembering the purpose of his visit, he attempted to change the subject. "But I hardly rode all the way out here from town just to quarrel with you, Kitty." With a chuckle, he added, "Come now, is this any way to greet a visitor?"

By no means appeased, Kitty picked up her basket. "It is if you're going to come charging in here like you own the place," she said, kneeling gracefully to gather another pecan she had spied.

Lifting the basket from her arm and placing it on the ground, Miles turned her to face him, mischievous laughter in his pale blue eyes. "You know, I never can decide whether you're prettier when you're happy or when you're angry."

In spite of herself, Kitty dimpled into a smile. It was impossible to stay angry with Miles for very long.

"Oh, Miles, why can't you be nice like this all the time?" she asked with a sigh. "Sometimes I think you don't even like colored folks," she added regretfully, remembering the many times she had seen Miles mistreat his own servants when, as a child, he had lived at the Blakes' neighboring plantation.

"I don't like them," came the short reply, "though I must say, some of the mulatto women I've seen are quite comely, particularly the octoroons."

Kitty frowned with disgust but realized the futility in arguing with him. No one was perfect, not even Miles, and this was simply a flaw in his character. Pulling away from him, she continued to search for the long oval nuts in silence.

"Isn't it a little early in the season to be gathering pecans?" Miles asked.

"I don't see why it should be. It's almost the last of October, and we've already had a couple of light frosts."

"Too light. That's why most of the pecans are still up in those trees.'' Miles pointed to the clusters of nuts still partially enclosed in their shells. "Wait a minute, and I'll see if I can find a stick or something to knock them down,'' he suggested.

A thought occurred to Kitty, and she suddenly giggled. "There was a time when you wouldn't have needed anything to throw. Remember how you and Tad and Bret used to climb up this tree and shake the limbs, so Beth and I could gather the pecans as they fell?''

"I also remember the time you talked Tad and me into helping you climb that blasted tree, as well as the difficulty we had in getting you down. Of course,'' he added with a wicked gleam in his eyes, "your climbing might have improved since then, and if you would prefer to do so—''

"No, thank you. A stick will do fine, I think. Ah, this one's just right,'' she informed him, handing him a small limb she had just found.

Miles gave her a mocking bow and, taking the limb from her hand, proceeded to draw back his arm and take aim.

"Wait!'' Kitty suddenly exclaimed. "There's a squirrel on that branch. You might hit it. Let's try another tree.''

As though he had not even heard her, Miles brushed aside her detaining hand and, taking aim, threw the short limb at that very spot. A soft cry was torn from Kitty's lips as she watched the furry animal drop noisily through the tree branches, landing almost at her feet with a dull thud. Kneeling beside the inert animal, she immediately saw that it was dead. Dismayed, she rose and angrily confronted Miles. "You deliberately aimed at that poor little thing, and now it's dead. How could you be so cruel, Miles?''

Feeling no remorse, Miles nevertheless feigned contriteness. "I'm sorry, honey. It was an accident. You know I didn't really mean to kill it.''

Kitty looked at him dubiously. She wanted to believe him, but somehow his words did not ring true. Still, it was difficult to believe he was heartless. Since childhood she had looked up to him, even though his behavior had struck her as being peculiar at times. Until now, however, she had never thought of him as being deliberately cruel. Or had she? Perhaps she had unconsciously shut her mind to the truth all along. Her distrust was mirrored in her eyes as she stared at him as if seeing him for the first time.

Aware of her doubts, Miles frowned. It was seldom that he

aroused Kitty's displeasure, and he certainly had no wish to do so now.

"Don't look at me like that, Kitty," he implored, pulling her into his arms. "You know how I feel about you. How much longer must I wait before you agree to marry me?"

Kitty looked up at him hesitantly. He was handsome and entertaining, and a brilliant future lay ahead of him. It occurred to her that, if she were pregnant, his proposal could provide her with an escape, though it would hardly be an honorable way to solve her problem. Inwardly she winced, for she was not normally a deceptive person. On the other hand, there was always the slim possibility that she was not pregnant. Confusion clouded her mind as she tried to reach a decision. Finally, she said:

"I don't know, Miles. I simply can't give you an answer right now."

Miles's mouth tightened with displeasure, but he held his temper in check. "There was a time when I think you would not have hesitated, but you've changed this summer—ever since Bret came back."

"Bret has nothing to do with it," she replied stiffly.

Miles studied her for a moment, his eyes narrowing as a sardonic smile twisted his lips. "I sincerely hope not, because if you're harboring any hope of his asking you to marry him, you may be in for a big disappointment."

"I assure you I'm hoping for nothing of the sort."

"I'm relieved to hear it. Bret's not the marrying kind, nor can he be trusted. He proved that with Louise Osbourne in Memphis."

"I was well acquainted with the Osbournes, and I hated to hear about their personal tragedy, but I fail to grasp what you're implying."

"You wouldn't, of course. Dave would defend Bret with his dying breath, even if he knew the truth, which I doubt he does. I hardly think Bret would confide that, even to him."

"Confide what? What on earth are you talking about?" Kitty asked uneasily, a perplexed frown marring her brow.

"Just this, my dear innocent. If it weren't for Bret—well, John Osbourne and his daughter would probably be alive today."

"That's not true! Bret was a competitor of Mr. Osbourne, but he was also his friend. In fact, Pa said Bret saved Mr. Osbourne from financial ruin when he bought his brokerage and paid him twice the amount it was worth."

"Which he shrewdly won back by provoking the old man into making a public bet at the races. That's why Osbourne shot himself."

"He was going to return the money to Mr. Osbourne, but he never got the chance," Kitty replied, staunchly defending Bret without reasoning why she should be doing so.

"And how do you know so much about it?"

"Because Bret wrote Pa about it, and I have no reason to doubt his word."

"Your loyalty would do you credit if it weren't so misplaced. I wonder how Bret explained Louise's death to Dave," Miles remarked smoothly, deliberately leading Kitty on.

"He wrote that Louise had been prostrate with grief and became irrational, blaming him for her father's death. He said she tried to shoot him at the funeral, and when some people attempted to take the gun from her, it accidentally went off and killed her."

"Ah, yes. Bret would say that, of course. Unfortunately, rumor has it otherwise. And just for the record, Louise didn't try to shoot Bret. She succeeded. Pity her aim wasn't better," was the malicious reply.

Kitty was momentarily stunned into silence. To avoid upsetting her, Dave had omitted this part of Bret's letter, which had been received some weeks after the tragedy had occurred. Now, Kitty wondered if Dave had deliberately withheld this information. The realization that Bret had been wounded, perhaps had been close to death, caused her stomach to churn and a tightness to fill her chest. Stepping away from Miles, she fought for self-control and determinedly lifted her chin.

"I know you've never liked Bret, but I had no idea you hated him. Louise Osbourne's death was an accident. Even you can't deny that. I'm not interested in hearing rumors, yours or anyone else's," she replied with a calmness she was far from feeling.

"Aren't you? I wonder." He hesitated momentarily, then added, "Louise was crazy about Bret. Everyone in Memphis was talking about the way she was throwing herself at him. Some say they were having an affair, that Louise was expecting a baby, and Bret refused to marry her. All rumors, of course, but where there's smoke, there's usually fire."

"I don't believe it!" Kitty cried. "Bret wouldn't, he just wouldn't." Her voice trailed off uncertainly as she remembered how ardently he had made love to her on that fateful night and how deliberately he had avoided her ever since.

"Wouldn't he?" Miles challenged with relish. "He has no scruples when it comes to Selina. Everyone in town knows she's his mistress. And half the town has heard about Louise and him and, I might add, are inclined to believe the rumor."

Kitty felt hurt and bewildered as Miles drew her to him. If the rumor were true, if Louise had actually been pregnant and Bret had refused to marry her, her own chances of extracting a proposal from him were slim indeed. Nor had she been certain, until now, that Bret had resumed his relationship with Selina, but from Miles's account, he had done just that. No wonder she had not seen or heard from him during the past weeks. She had been a diversion for him, nothing else. Bitterness engulfed her, and, burying her head against Miles's chest, she fought to hold back the tears that filled her lovely eyes.

"Ah, Kitty, forget about Bret. He'd never make you happy, believe me. Say you'll marry me. Say it," he commanded softly.

"Yes—yes, I'll marry you," she murmured at last.

Miles tipped her chin upward with his forefinger, smiling almost boyishly. "When?" he asked. "Don't make me wait too long."

Kitty forced a smile to her trembling lips. "I suppose I could have a wedding gown made in a couple of weeks. Shall we set the date for the middle of November?" she asked with a sinking heart.

By then, at least, she would know for certain whether or not she was pregnant. If she were not, there might not be a wedding. Underhanded it might be, but she could not bring a nameless child into the world. Miles was offering her a solution, a solution she would be a fool to reject.

"Perfect. We'll announce our engagement after the political rally Friday night, at the Kleins' barbecue," he declared. "I've waited a long time for this, Kitty. God knows how much I've wanted you." He pulled her to him passionately and claimed her with his lips.

His kisses evoked no response, but this he attributed to Kitty's lack of experience. Once married, he would enjoy teaching her the intimacies that particularly aroused him. She would be an apt pupil and, he hoped, a willing one.

The sun was setting as, arm in arm, the two of them walked slowly toward the house. Kitty dreaded telling her father of her decision to marry Miles, knowing he would try to talk her out of it.

She knew Dave would never accept Miles as a member of his family. She had seldom gone against her father's wishes, but now she would have to. Bret had seen to that when he took her virginity, then discarded her love. For that, she would never forgive him.

It was twilight, and the smell of wood smoke and freshly barbecued pork permeated the crisp fall air as Kitty sat idly beneath the large magnolia tree that faced the back of the Kleins' house, Cedar Grove. Miles had hovered possessively beside her throughout the rally at the courthouse and had insisted on accompanying her on the carriage ride to Cedar Grove, leaving little doubt in anyone's mind that he considered himself to be her escort for the evening. As a result, most of her admirers and beaux had not thronged to her as usual, though many had requested she reserve them a space on her dance card for the ball that would commence in a short time.

At her request, Miles had gone inside to get her a cup of punch. Replete from a delicious meal that had been served buffet style from long, wooden tables that dotted the spacious back lawn, Kitty leaned back against the tree and sighed. Almost everyone had gone inside, and for the first time in hours, she was given a brief respite from pretending she was having a lovely time.

Inwardly she was miserable, already regretting her impulsiveness in accepting Miles and dreading the intermission, at which time the engagement would be announced. Friends would smile and congratulate them, then later whisper among themselves about the unusual shortness of the engagement, though most had been expecting such an announcement for some time. Miles had been one of her most ardent pursuers for over a year. Still, they would wonder, and if she *were* pregnant, their worst suspicions would be confirmed, despite the standard excuse of the baby's coming prematurely. Eventually all would be forgiven, if never forgotten, her redemption being that Miles would have married her by that time, thus making his child legitimate. *His* child! Little would any of them suspect who the real culprit was.

The sudden remembrance of Bret caused her to frown. She had briefly seen him from a distance at the rally, but that was all. He had not come to the barbecue, either, and a feeling of disappointment washed over her as she realized he probably would not even show up for the dance tonight. The one bright spot that had carried her through the day had been her perverse desire to see his expression when her engagement was announced. Now, it seemed she was to be denied even that small satisfaction.

Hearing her name suddenly called, Kitty forced a smile to her lips and glanced at the upper gallery that crossed the back of the house. "My goodness, Kitty, what on earth are you doing sitting out there by yourself? Where's Miles?" Sally Collins asked, leaning over the railing.

"He's inside, getting me a cup of punch."

"Oh. Well, you ought to come inside, too, before you catch cold. Aren't you getting chilly?" Sally questioned.

"A bit, but I'll come in as soon as Miles returns. Here he is now."

Satisfied, Sally left as Miles handed Kitty a dainty crystal cup. Accepting his arm, she allowed him to usher her toward the house. The musicians were turning up for the first dance, a quadrille, and Miles led her into the small ballroom, which was filled to capacity.

"Where's Pa, Miles?" she asked, easing her arm from his grasp.

"He went to the study with Mr. Klein a few minutes ago. I daresay he's giving our host the details of our engagement so that it can be announced at intermission."

Kitty glanced dismally in the direction of the study, which was separated from the ballroom by a narrow carriageway. If only she could run to Dave and tell him to call off the betrothal now, before it was too late. She knew he would do so gladly, for during the past week he had used every argument to discourage her from marrying Miles.

"I somehow get the impression you're not altogether with me tonight. Is something wrong, my dear?" Miles asked as his eyes shrewdly scanned her face.

"Of course not," Kitty answered a little too quickly. Seeing that Miles was not convinced, she added, "It's just that it's a bit warm in here."

"Too many people for too little space. They've removed the furniture from the double parlors, and I believe they're forming another quadrille in there," he informed her, turning her in that direction and leading her from the crowded ballroom.

A slight breeze drifted through the open windows of the front and back parlors which, with partitioning doors pushed open, served as another large ballroom. Still holding Kitty's arm, Miles escorted her through the two lines that were being formed for the quadrille. As they made their way toward the front end of the parlor, Kitty caught her reflection in the long, gold-leaf pier mirrors that graced each end of the two parlors.

The lavender silk gown she wore was most becoming, a narrow flounce falling gracefully from her shoulders and meeting in a V where the décolletage exposed a modest amount of bosom. A wide sash of rich purple velvet nipped in her tiny waist. The voluminous three-quarter-length skirt was scalloped, the peaks adorned with small clusters of artificial violets that matched the sash, and the finishing touch was three tiers of white lace underskirt that floated to the floor.

Taking her place at the end, Kitty realized she had probably never looked lovelier, but the realization brought little comfort. Dance after dance was completed with a forced smile and heavy heart, and by the time intermission arrived, she was feeling quite depressed. She was also tired of Miles's company, and it was with a feeling of relief that she saw Dave coming toward them.

"Our host has graciously suggested that I make the announcement of your betrothal after the musicians have reseated themselves at the end of this intermission," he said with a gaiety Kitty sensed was forced.

Her deep violet eyes misted as, smiling brightly, she stood on tiptoe and planted a kiss on his cheek. "Thank you," she whispered. Then, turning toward Miles, she asked to be excused in order to go upstairs and freshen up a bit.

Once upstairs, however, she felt disinclined to join the ladies who were crowded into the bedroom that, tonight, was serving as a powder room. Instead, she slipped out to the long gallery that graced the front of the house. Had it not been dark, she undoubtedly would have enjoyed an excellent view of the river, for Cedar Grove was situated on a steep incline, and the river was only a short distance away. As it was, she could distinguish the flickering lights of a riverboat slowly making its way past the town. Suddenly, she wished she were on that boat, going as far away from Vicksburg as possible.

A horseman was making his way up the drive, and Kitty wondered disinterestedly who could be arriving so late. After dismounting and handing his reins to a colored boy, the man glanced up. When their eyes met and held, Kitty's heart froze, until at last she turned away and reentered the house.

So Bret had come after all. The knowledge that he would soon be learning of her betrothal to Miles bolstered her courage, and, forcing another smile to her lips, she slowly descended the stairs.

If Kitty expected Bret to show anger over her betrothal, she was sadly disappointed. He merely gave her a mocking smile, then turned his attention to the girl standing next to him, Lela Shelton, with whom he spent the rest of the evening. Even worse, he made no attempt to speak to her, not even to congratulate her or wish her happiness. That hurt more than anything else, for it showed how little he cared what happened to her.

Now, as the carriage headed for the Washington Hotel, where they would be staying until elections were held the following week, Kitty was barely able to hold back bitter tears. Tad and Dave discussed politics, in which she had little interest, and it was only when Tad mentioned Bret's name that she listened to the conversation.

"Don't you think we should consider Bret's offer to put some of our money in a European bank?"

"I don't know, Tad. If the wrong man is elected president, we could easily find ourselves in the middle of a long and costly war. Right now, it looks as if the election could go either way," replied Dave, pausing to light his cheroot. "The fact is that for the moment we haven't any capital to spare. The flood wiped out our crop last year, and all the rain this summer nearly took care of this year's crop. That's why I sold the mill in town, so the profit from the sale could go into the planting of next year's crop."

"It doesn't seem to matter to Bret how the election comes out. He's bound and determined to rent a warehouse in London and open up a banking account over there. In a way, I wish I could go with him. I've always wanted to see a little of England."

"Bret is going to England?" Kitty asked faintly.

"That's right, honey, right after the elections," Dave informed her.

Kitty turned her head and glanced out the window. I will not cry over a man who doesn't love me, she swore silently. *Not ever.*

Chapter 7

The courthouse hill was seized with pandemonium on election day. Men discussed, argued, and fought over the political candidates, for the final results of this election would determine the fate of the South. The night before, Jefferson Davis had helped to lead a rally that supported Breckinridge, and at the same time the Constitutional-Unionists had met at the courthouse in support of Bell.

There was no middle-of-the-line approach, and tempers that had smoldered the previous night now flared, the situation threatening to erupt like an ignited powderkeg. Hotheads shouted loudly for Breckinridge and secession, unmindful of their foul language, which carried to the women seated in nearby carriages, waiting for loved ones to cast their votes. Children rampaged through the streets and hillsides, setting off rockets and roman candles, which created even more havoc. Over the bedlam, the courthouse clock chimed twelve times, yet few seemed inclined to leave the scene in favor of the noonday meal.

Kitty, seated in an open carriage, tapped her red-slippered foot impatiently, waiting for Tad and Dave to cast their votes and rejoin her. They had been in the courthouse for almost thirty minutes, and though she had spent the better part of that time chatting with the four Hartz brothers, she was now eager to return to the hotel and have dinner. Her eyes scanned the crowd for some sign of her father, then narrowed when she spotted Bret leisurely making his way toward her.

As if he sensed her mood, his mouth quirked into a slight smile.

His eyes raked over her appreciatively, from the small red bonnet, smartly trimmed with a dark blue plume that curled over one shoulder, to the navy velvet jacket that provocatively outlined her well-shaped breasts, before dropping lower to take in the voluminous red-and-white-striped taffeta skirt that accentuated her tiny waist.

"Good morning, Kitty," he greeted her upon reaching the carriage. "I must say you're looking particularly fetching and patriotic today," he remarked with a devilish grin.

Instantly Kitty bristled. "And why shouldn't I? Pa says if Breckinridge wins, we still might not be forced to leave the Union."

"Don't you believe it." Bret chuckled mirthlessly. "*If* Breckinridge wins, which I doubt, it will make little difference to the South. I assure you, Northerners have no intention of condoning slavery."

"You're such a pessimist, and always a know-it-all," Kitty snapped. "Oh, I do wish Pa and Tad would return. Have you seen them?"

"Not only have I seen them, I happen to be bearing their message."

"Which is?"

"They've both been requested to help with the ballots, so Dave asked me to escort you back to the hotel."

"Why didn't Pa ask Miles to take me back?" she asked petulantly.

"Because, my sweet, Miles is also helping. Which leaves me," he answered. "Now, if you'll wait a moment, I'll retrieve my horse from across the street, then assist you back to the hotel."

"That won't be necessary. I can manage quite well on my own," she replied, picking up the reins and flicking them.

Unable to help herself, she glanced over her shoulder and saw Bret walking toward his horse. At that precise moment a youngster ignited a rocket that, a second later, went haywire, zipping wildly in front of Kitty's carriage. The next instant was chaotic as the two bays, already nervous, reared noisily, then bolted down the street. Caught off guard, Kitty felt the reins jerked from her hands and was suddenly paralyzed with fear. Familiar faces flashed by, and screams pierced the air as the runaway carriage careened down the crowded road toward the river.

Kitty clutched the sides and closed her eyes, praying to be delivered from an almost certain death. The sound of a horse thundering toward her interrupted the prayer, and as she turned her head and saw Bret racing past her, a feeling of relief swept over her. Then she saw his intent. A scream of protest was torn from her lips when he leaned over and caught one of the horses by the neck, slipping from his own mount in the process. For moments that seemed like hours, he hung suspended in the air before regaining his balance and mounting the horse's back. Fearful he would lose his tenacious hold and fall beneath the murderous hooves, Kitty watched with horror as, bit by bit, Bret brought the frightened animals under control.

Then it was over, and the carriage came to a halt. Several men rushed over and grabbed the harnesses while Bret dismounted. Without glancing at Kitty, he checked to see that the quivering animals were unharmed, then walked over to where his mount had stopped only a few feet away. Taking the reins in unsteady hands, he strode back to the carriage, where Kitty was assuring concerned onlookers that she was all right.

"Move over," he ordered her before entering the carriage and taking up the reins.

Seeing his murderous expression, Kitty slid over and wisely remained silent. Seldom had she seen him so angry, and a feeling of dismay washed over her as she realized she was in for a good tongue-lashing. As they rode one block up Grove Street and took a left turn onto Washington Street, she gave him a worried glance.

"Shouldn't you have turned right to get back to the hotel?" she asked uneasily.

"We're not going to the hotel. Not yet," came the short reply.

"Well, where are we going?"

"For a short ride, so just sit back and be quiet," he answered.

Kitty did as she was told, for one look at his face warned her that she was treading on thin ice. As they rolled past the northern outskirts of town, indignation slowly mounted within her. What right did Bret have to treat her in such a high-handed manner? she thought, biting her bottom lip to keep from verbalizing her feelings. By the time the carriage pulled to a stop on a knoll overlooking the river, her agitation was such that she pointedly ignored his proffered hand and alighted from the carriage without assistance.

Sweeping haughtily past him, she walked to the knoll's edge and looked unseeingly across the wide, muddy expanse of swirling water that separated Mississippi from Louisiana. She was too upset to speak, much less think clearly, as was evidenced by her grim expression and agitated breathing.

Bret's anger had diminished somewhat by this time, and an amused smile pulled at the corners of his mouth as he freed the reins that bound his mount to the carriage and allowed the animal to graze, then walked over to where Kitty stood. For seconds, he remained silent. Finally, his hands clasped the back of her stiff shoulders, propelling her slightly backward until she rested against the broad expanse of his chest.

"Kitty, Kitty," he murmured into her windswept hair, which was now free of the confining bonnet, "your impulsiveness will be the death of you yet."

The sudden realization that his anger had stemmed from fear for her safety acted as a balm to her pride.

"I suppose I should thank you for saving my life," she said wryly.

"That would be a welcome change." He smiled and turned her around to face him.

Looking up at him, she was suddenly reminded of what Miles had said about Bret's having an affair with Louise Osbourne while he was in Memphis. Heedless of the consequences, she was determined to know the truth.

"Bret, what happened between you and Louise Osbourne?"

His smile faded and was replaced with a slight scowl. "So you've heard," he returned grimly. "I suppose you want to know if I was having an affair with her—if I got her pregnant, then refused to marry her." When she did not answer, he asked, "Would you believe me if I said I never touched her, much less got her pregnant?"

The uncertainty in her eyes answered his question, momentarily filling him with bitter disappointment. "No, of course you wouldn't, so why should I bother to deny it."

"Don't, Bret," Kitty implored. "After what happened between us, I don't know what to believe."

"What happened between us was a mistake," he replied coldly. "God knows I've regretted it."

Kitty stiffened with indignation. "Is that why you're running off to Europe—to get away from me? Don't you even care that I'm engaged to Miles?"

"Oh, I'd care very much if I thought you were really going through with it, but you won't."

"And just what makes you so sure?"

"Because I happen to know you're not in love with him. I don't know *why* you got engaged to him, but I'm sure you'll think of some way to get out of it."

Too angry to speak, Kitty gave him a withering look as she stepped past him and got hastily into the carriage. Without waiting for him to join her, she picked up the reins and flicked the bays into a fast trot. It was not the first time Bret had humiliated her, but she vowed silently it would be the last. Once she was Miles's wife, Bret would have to keep his distance, which suited her perfectly.

The day after Abraham Lincoln won the election, Bret left for England. He had not waited to see if Kitty would actually marry Miles, nor had he bidden her good-bye. Two weeks later, Kitty and Miles were married in the Christ Episcopal Church, and an elaborate reception was held that evening in the Washington Hotel, where they planned to spend a brief honeymoon.

Now, as Kitty stared unseeingly from her hotel window into the night, she heard the last of their guests departing. Nervously she fingered the small satin bow that secured the opening of her lacy peignoir and waited for Miles to join her. He had obviously had too much to drink at the reception, and a sense of dread filled her as she realized he would soon appear to claim his husbandly rights. Would he realize she was no longer a virgin? If so, what would his reaction be—hurt, anger, or disrespect?

With an effort, she pulled herself together. Horseback riding had robbed many a virgin of her maidenhead, so there was no reason why Miles should ever have to know the truth. Why upset him needlessly? she reasoned, ignoring the voice of her conscience. She would simply have to devote herself to being a good wife and, in time, give him sons of his own. He need never know that the child she carried was not his. In fact, for the child's sake, he must never know. She knew instinctively that Miles would never accept another man's leavings, nor would he be inclined to forgive easily.

The door opened and Miles strode into the room, firmly closing the only exit behind him. For a moment he merely stood there, lust smoldering in his eyes as they traveled over the thinly clad girl who tremblingly awaited his next move. He saw the fear and uncertainty in her face and exalted in the knowledge that she was not going to be a willing bride. Her struggles would merely add to his excitement. He had never been attracted to women who were too willing, too eager to please, for only by using brute force could he become aroused enough to consummate the act.

Repressing a shudder, Kitty turned back to the window. "Have all our guests left?'' she asked to break the awkward silence, tensing when he walked over to her. She was barely aware of the affirmative answer as his hands clasped her shoulders, propelling her backward until her slender body rested against his hard length. The breath caught in her throat when she felt his arms encircle her midriff, imprisoning her and thus rendering her helpless as his steely grip tightened.

"You . . . you're hurting me," she whispered unsteadily, forcing herself to remain still when she felt his moist lips on her taut neck.

"Am I?" he asked with a soft, menacing laugh. Slowly he began stroking her neck, an evil smile twisting his lips as he sensed her increasing nervousness. "I've waited a long time for you, wanting you every time I saw you, dreaming of the moment when I could make you completely mine. Yes, I've wanted to hurt you, if only to show you the exquisite pleasure of pain," he murmured.

His hand tightened on her neck, squeezing the tender flesh until Kitty involuntarily moaned with pain. Fear shot through her as, feeling the length of him pressing against her, she realized the extent of his arousal and sensed his impatience.

She could not go through with it! Not even for the sake of her unborn child.

Somehow managing to extract herself from his grasp, she turned and faced him, momentarily dumbfounded by the malevolent gleam in his cold eyes. "Miles, I've decided I can't go through with this. I should never have married you, but I thought that in time . . ." Her voice faltered as she sought the words with which to explain.

"In time, what? That you'd forget about Bret?" Miles sneered, one hand grabbing her waist and jerking her to him while the other hand lifted her chin, forcing her to look at him. Seeing her surprise, he gave a mirthless laugh. "Oh, yes, my dear, I've known how you felt about Bret for a long time. Probably before you yourself realized it. But that's in the past, now. You belong to me, and I'll never let you go. *Never.* I don't give a damn who you love; I'm the one you're going to please—beginning now," he declared, her obvious alarm exciting him to a frenzy of desire.

Kitty's clenched fists pushed ineffectively against his chest as his mouth descended upon hers in a punishing kiss that forced apart her resisting lips. His fingers tightened cruelly on her chin, his foul breath filling her nostrils until she was gasping for breath. Twisting her head from side to side, she managed to free her bruised lips and tried to push away from him, but his arm only tightened around her waist, arching her to him.

"No, Miles, no!" she pleaded. "Not like this, please. Can't you understand? I don't love you, and I could never be your wife, not in the truest sense."

"To hell with love. I want you, and, dammit, I intend to have you—beginning now." His hand snaked out to grab the flimsy material of her peignoir, and, with a quick jerk, he tore it from neckline to hem. A glazed look appeared in his eyes when he gazed upon the lovely perfection of her exposed body.

He was breathing heavily, consumed with lust. Realizing that he was beyond reasoning, Kitty began to fight him in earnest, beating his chest with her fists and kicking him with her soft-soled slippers.

"That's right, you little hellcat, fight me. That's what I want," he cried, grabbing her hair and jerking her head backward as his mouth came within inches of her trembling lips.

Kitty opened her mouth to scream, but the sound never came. Sensing her intent, Miles slapped her again and again, until at last she lost consciousness. Then, picking her up, he strode over to the bed and tossed her on top of it. With quick, sure movements, he removed her arms from the remnants of her gown and wrapper, stepping back hurriedly to discard his own clothing.

Her eyes fluttered open, widening with horror when she discovered him standing beside the bed. Before she could roll away, he was on top of her, his weight pressing her down into the mattress, pinning her beneath him. His mouth hungrily devoured hers, and a whimper tore from her throat as she felt his teeth sink into her bottom lip and tasted the saltiness of her own blood. Twisting from side to side, she beat at him with clenched fists. Finally her nails clawed the side of his face, and he released her mouth with a vicious oath.

Kitty's head snapped sideways as his fist connected with her jaw, and for a moment blackness threatened to engulf her again. His weight was partially lifted from her when he reached over to extinguish the lamp on the bedside table, and relief soared through her. Surely he must be regretting his actions now. Surely he would let her go. In the next instant hope died as she felt his weight descending again. Unexpectedly, Miles jerked her arms above her head and imprisoned her wrists with one hand, his other hand kneading her breasts until she cried aloud. It was then that all hope deserted her.

He was going to rape her, and there was nothing she could do about it. He was mad, utterly insane, and totally beyond reasoning.

Her torment lasted for hours as he took her savagely time and again, too crazed with lust to realize that his bride was not a virgin. At first she resisted him with all her strength, but her strength diminished as his brutal assault continued relentlessly. Pain racked her bruised body, yet unconsciousness would not come. It was only when she became too weak to continue resisting him and lay limply while he had his way with her that his lust finally subsided and he rolled away from her.

As dawn approached and the first fingers of daylight sifted into the room, Kitty listened to her husband's even breathing and stared unseeingly at the ceiling. Her pain was too deep to be cleansed by tears, nor did she dare examine Miles's earlier actions too closely. Over and over she assured herself that his brutality had stemmed from his drunkenness, that he would regret his cruel treatment by the time he awakened. Yet, deep down, she knew this was not true. There was a dormant streak of cruelty in Miles that hinted of madness. All compunction regarding the secrecy of her pregnancy had been dispelled last night. She would never tell him that the child she carried was not his, for she shuddered to think of the consequences should he ever learn the truth.

Chapter 8

South Carolina seceded from the Union in December, and on January 9 Mississippi followed suit, becoming the second of eleven states that would soon constitute a new government—the Confederate States of America. Jefferson Davis resigned from the U.S. Senate and returned home via Vicksburg to his plantation, Brierfield, which was a short distance south of town. In February he passed through Vicksburg again, this time to catch a train for the Confederacy's capital, Montgomery, Alabama, where he was to be sworn in as president of the newly formed government.

People in Vicksburg turned out on a grand scale at the riverboat landing to bid their president a fond farewell. Overall, most Vicksburgers had not wanted to leave the Union, since the town's economy largely depended on river trade, but now that the dye was cast, they were loyal to the Confederacy.

Joyful cheers filled the air as the *Natchez* docked and Jefferson Davis walked down the boat's ramp toward the civic authorities who were on hand to greet him. Within minutes, Mayor Crump launched into a well-prepared congratulatory speech.

Kitty, with Miles at her side, stood at the outer fringes of the crowd, but her mind was not on the eloquent words she was hearing. Instead, she was thinking of how much Miles had changed since she had informed him she was pregnant. Deciding it would be unwise to prolong the news, she had made the announcement to him in the confines of their bedroom on New Year's Eve. Since then, he was always solicitous and surprisingly kind. His physical demands upon her had lessened too. On the few occasions when he visited her bedroom, he was unusually patient and gentle with her.

It would have been a great relief to have been able to confide in someone, if only to ease the weight of her feelings. But she had no intention of burdening her father with her unhappiness. At one time she would have turned to Tad for comfort, but since he had become engaged to Dede at Christmas, she had seen very little of him.

Mayor Crump turned the rostrum over to Jefferson Davis, who responded with a brief speech. His conclusion brought about an uproar of excited cheering and loud hurrahs, followed by the booming of musketry and the firing of a cannon. As the mayor escorted Davis to a waiting carriage, the crowd dispersed, many people hurrying toward the railway station.

Turning to go, Kitty saw Dave making his way toward them, and a feeling of relief swept over her. Perhaps she would not have to accompany Miles to the station after all. She tired easily now, partly because of her condition and partly because, in an attempt to keep her weight down so that her condition would not become apparent too soon, she had been eating as little as possible. So far the ruse had worked. With her loss of weight, plus a tightly laced corset, she scarcely looked pregnant at all.

"Hi, sugar." Dave greeted his daughter with an affectionate hug, nodding briefly to Miles. "I thought I might find you here, but now that I have, I'm not so sure you should have come. You're awfully pale, honey," he said, surveying his daughter with worried thoughtfulness. "You're not planning on going to the railroad station, are you?"

Before Miles could reply, Kitty tucked her hand into the crook of Dave's arm and gave him an appreciative smile. "Miles has his heart set on seeing Mr. Davis off, but I am feeling rather tired," she admitted, giving her husband an apologetic smile. "Would you be too disappointed if Pa drove me back to the house in his carriage, Miles?"

Miles, eager to be off, quickly agreed to this suggestion and departed. Seeing the look of relief in his daughter's eyes, Dave grew deeply concerned. He assisted Kitty to his carriage with the bitter conviction that her marriage had been a mistake, just as he had feared it would be.

His only hope for Kitty's happiness lay in the child she was carrying; but it was a very small hope, especially since Kitty seemed totally indifferent over the blessed event. Outwardly, Miles appeared to be making his daughter a good husband. His partnership with Judge Crane had proved to be a success, enabling him to purchase one of the nicer homes on Cherry Street, only a couple of blocks from the courthouse. Some of the older politicians deemed him to be a brilliant young lawyer, and it had even been rumored that some of these same men had entertained thoughts of running him as a Democratic candidate for the Senate during the last election. With the forming of a new nation, many still felt that there was no end of possibilities for a man of Miles's caliber. Most had forgotten his unpredictability in days of yore, but not Dave.

Despite his protest, Kitty talked Dave into stopping by Schuler's Grocery, assuring him that she felt well enough to procure a few items for the larder. The three-story building situated on the corner of Washington and Grove served a dual purpose: the bottom level was used as a grocery store while the two higher levels served as a living quarters for Henry Schuler and his family.

As Kitty browsed around the store, Dave walked over to the proprietor, who was donning a large white apron.

"G'afternoon, Henry," Dave said. "I take it you, also, have been down at the landing."

With a broad smile, Henry nodded affirmatively. "That was some welcome the mayor gave ole Jeff. Just wish Jeff's speech could have been a little longer, but I reckon he was in a hurry to catch that train for Montgomery."

" 'Spect so," Dave agreed. "And then again, he might have been all tuckered out. I understand his health hasn't been too good lately."

"I've seen him looking spunkier, but last time Joe was in, he said Jeff had been a little down lately," he said, referring to Jeff's older brother, who owned the large plantation Hurricane, conveniently situated next to Brierfield.

"Let's hope his health improves, 'cause he's sure stepping into a powerful lot of responsibility," Dave commented dryly.

Before Henry could reply, Kitty stepped up to the counter with her purchases. "I think that's all I need for the present, Mr. Schuler."

"Well, now, let's see—a pound of coffee, flour, sugar, and tea," he muttered thoughtfully, adding up the total.

Dave insisted on paying the small amount and, after exchanging farewells, assisted Kitty to the carriage. Once they had made the brief ride to Kitty's house, he helped her down and reached for the small sack of groceries.

"Oh, by the way, here's a little something Bret sent you from England," he said, handing her a small parcel.

"Bret sent me something?" she murmured, surprised.

"As a matter of fact, he sent us all something, including the house servants. Kind of a belated Christmas present for everyone."

Kitty smiled but refrained from opening the gift in front of her father. Instead, she asked if Bret mentioned when he would be coming home.

"Well, from the sound of his letter, I'd say pretty soon," Dave informed her. "It'll be good to have him home again, won't it?"

"I suppose so," Kitty replied noncommittally. Deliberately changing the subject, she invited Dave inside, but he declined, stating that Mammy Lou would be expecting him home for supper.

Kitty stood on the porch and watched until he had driven out of sight; then, with a sigh, she entered the house. Daisy, whom Dave had allowed her to bring from Belle Glen, met her in the hall.

"Miz Kitty, you ain't got no biz'ness out in dis cold weather, not in yo' delicate condition. You's gwine tuh ketch yo' death ob cold, dat's whut you is," the skinny girl fussed, attempting ineffectually to emulate Mammy Lou.

"Don't be a goose, Daisy. A little fresh air never hurt anyone." Shrugging out of her cloak, Kitty gave the frowning girl some last-minute instructions pertaining to supper, then walked into the parlor. She was eager to see what Bret had sent her, and seating herself on the sofa, she quickly unwrapped the small package. It was a leather-bound copy of Sir Walter Scott's *Waverley*. Pleased by his thoughtfulness, she was nevertheless disappointed that he had not included a note with the book, nor even inscribed the inside cover. The gift was anything but personal, yet it was some comfort to know he had at least remembered her favorite author.

Feeling tired, she decided to go upstairs and lie down for a while before supper. As she mounted the stairs, she wondered if Dave had written to Bret and, if so, whether or not he had mentioned her marriage to Miles. If he had not, Bret was certainly going to be in for a big surprise when he got home. He had been so sure she would not go through with the wedding, but for once she had proved him wrong!

Chapter 9

The month of April brought about new tension while the country waited nervously for the outcome of the Fort Sumter crisis. Would Lincoln order his Federal troops to evacuate the Southern fort just outside Charleston, South Carolina? If not, what action would be taken by the Confederate forces at Charleston Harbor?

Bret had heard little else discussed on the steamer that had carried him from England to the States, but though he was interested in the internal affairs of his country, his main concern had simply been to return home. After receiving a thank-you note from Dave in which Kitty's marriage to Miles had been briefly mentioned, he had concluded his business in England two weeks ahead of schedule and sailed for home. His reasoning for such haste eluded him, since the damage was already done. Kitty was married to Miles, and there was nothing he could do about it.

He arrived at Vicksburg feeling tired and out of sorts. Thinking to lighten his mood, he headed straight for Selina's house. As he reclined on her sofa and disinterestedly watched her unwrap the lace shawl he had brought her, his thoughts strayed to Kitty. He still could not envision her as Miles's wife, and for the umpteenth time he wondered what had possessed her to marry the scoundrel. Selina's voice suddenly brought him back to the present.

"Bret, I wish you'd stop scowling and pay a little attention to me. You haven't heard a word I've said for the past five minutes."

"Which was?" Bret asked, walking over to her.

"I said if there is a war, it'll probably be ages before I get anything as pretty as this shawl again," she answered, adjusting the

80

flimsy lace over her hair. "But if Miles is right, the war won't last long. He says no Northerner can hold a candle to a Southerner when it comes to fighting."

Bret's hands tensed on Selina's slim shoulders as, standing behind her, he gazed unseeingly at their reflection in the ornate mirror.

"You're still seeing Miles?" He frowned.

Selina gave him a puzzled look. Though she was selective about whom she entertained, it had never been any secret to Bret that Miles was one of the chosen few. Since Bret had only returned to Vicksburg that afternoon, he was hardly in a position to object, but the fact that he so obviously resented Miles's visits rather pleased her. Misunderstanding the reason behind his displeasure, she turned with a provocative smile and wrapped her arms around his neck.

"Yes, I am. Quite frequently, as a matter of fact. Do you object?"

"Have I ever?" he questioned smoothly in return. "I should think, however, that his wife might be less than pleased with such an arrangement. Or perhaps she's still unaware of it?"

"Quite probably. Though if she does know, I daresay that for the moment she's relieved." Selina chuckled, adding wickedly: "Most pregnant women prefer to turn a blind eye to the source of their husbands' pleasures, particularly during the last months."

"Pregnant!" Bret hissed, his fingers digging painfully into Selina's shoulders and causing her to gasp with surprise. Dropping his hands, he strode over to the bureau and poured himself a stiff shot of whiskey. After downing it in one gulp, he turned to face the woman who was staring dumbfoundedly at him.

"So, Kitty's pregnant," he mused darkly. "You're sure?"

"Of course I'm sure. I naturally assumed you knew, since you're a friend of the family and all. . . ." Her voice trailed off uncertainly as Bret reached for the jacket he had thrown carelessly on the bed.

"Bret, you're not going?" she asked incredulously.

"I'm afraid so," he replied, walking over to where she stood and forcing himself to kiss her. "I'm tired, too tired to give you much pleasure tonight. Another time," he promised with a brief hug, then strode from the room.

On the way back to his hotel, Bret's mind was in torment. Kitty pregnant! It could not be true; yet he knew Selina had no reason to lie to him. Kitty had only been married five months, and already she was carrying Miles's child.

Or was she? In that one moment of weakness when he had taken Kitty, could he have planted his seed in her? Could this, then, be the real reason she had chosen to marry Miles? But if this were the case, why in God's name hadn't she told him? And if the child Kitty carried were his, then what? What was more important, just how was he going to get her alone long enough to find out the truth?

The opportunity presented itself sooner than he had expected. Upon leaving the hotel the following morning, he walked aimlessly up Washington Street, which even for Friday was unusually crowded. Stopping at Collins's General Store, he purchased several long black Havanas and a copy of the newspaper. His eyes caught the day's date, *April 12*, before he briefly scanned the headlines. At that moment he saw Kitty coming toward him, her arms filled with parcels. She stopped abruptly, and when their eyes met and locked, he sensed her surprise and uncertainty.

A smile twisted his lips as he wordlessly relieved her of her packages. She was lovelier than ever, though her features had sharpened to a fine point of fragility, giving her an ethereal appearance. For a moment neither spoke, then Kitty broke the awkward silence.

"When did you get back?" she asked.

"Yesterday," came the terse reply, a sardonic gleam appearing in the depths of his green eyes. "None too soon, I might add. From the looks of you, married life isn't exactly agreeing with you."

Weakness, combined with sudden dizziness, washed over her as she glared angrily at the tall man who stood between her and her carriage.

"I might have expected you to say something like that," she snapped, trying to extract her packages from him.

"Not so fast," Bret muttered, and grabbed her arm. "You and I have a few things to discuss. Where's your carriage?"

Kitty nodded toward the parked vehicle and tried to ease out of his grasp. Before she could do so, however, he relieved her of the last package and, with his free arm, assisted her across the busy street. Seeing him again brought about mixed emotions, his nearness disconcerting her almost to the point of speechlessness. But not for long. As Bret helped her into the carriage, then climbed in beside her, past grievances welled up inside her, and she tensed.

"I fail to see what we have to discuss. As for your accompanying me, I think it would be best if you didn't. Miles wouldn't approve, and besides, people might talk."

"That's unfortunate, because I frankly don't give a damn what Miles or anyone else thinks. Now, where do you want to go?"

Kitty hesitated only for a moment; then, opening her parasol, she shot him an impish smile. "Well, I'd love to hear all about your trip to Europe, and I don't suppose there's any harm in letting you drive me to the depot. The artillery company is leaving town today, you know," she replied, thankful that the dizziness had passed.

Her conscience did not prick her in the least, since she had asked Miles this morning to take her and he had refused, saying he was too busy. Why, half the town was turning out to see the company off, and right or wrong, she was not about to pass up the opportunity to wave good-bye to friends who, in all probability, would be fighting on some battlefield in the near future. It would have been improper for her to drive down to the station alone, but Bret had just provided her with a solution.

Bret laughed softly and shot her an amused look as he picked up the reins, turning the carriage around in the direction of the depot.

"And just what do you think Miles is going to say when he hears I've escorted his wife to the depot? I daresay he's not going to be too happy about it."

"Serves him right," Kitty replied. "If he had put me ahead of business, I wouldn't be relying on you to take me to the station now. I suppose tongues will wag, but I don't care. Everybody in town will be there to see the boys off. I had been looking forward to going for days."

"Then by all means, you'll go." He chuckled. "Ah, Kitten, you'll never change, I'm afraid. There's little you wouldn't resort to in order to have your own way."

"That's not funny, Bret, and it certainly isn't true. I do care what people think, but I happen to want to go to the station even more right now. So many of my friends are leaving on that train today. David Shelton, Wade Waddell, Ben and Buck Moore . . ." Her voice trailed off wistfully as they approached the crowded depot.

Later, Kitty regretted having gone, for as the cannons fired salutes and the train pulled slowly out of the station, one of the cannons misfired and a man was seriously injured. The unexpected disaster sparked off a wave of hysteria, and for the first time Vicksburgers got a taste of war. It wasn't pleasant, for with it came the realization that there was more to war than glory. And with this realization came moans of anguish while men and women stood by helplessly and waved to their loved ones, some of whom they would never see again.

As people turned to go, a man burst out of the depot, shouting excitedly and wildly waving a telegram in the air for all to see. At first his words were obliterated by the noise of the departing crowd, but as their attention was arrested by the man's frantic gestures, a hushed silence descended, and his words could be heard clearly:

"We're at war, we're at war! Our Confederates fired on the Yankees at Fort Sumter at four-thirty this morning. This means war!"

Loud hurrahs and gleeful shouts intermingled with anguished cries of distress and fear as men and women expressed their reactions to the news. Some rejoiced, others wept unashamedly. Kitty watched for several seconds, sorting out her own emotions before turning to the man beside her.

"Oh, Bret, I can't believe this is really happening. If the Federals had just pulled out of Fort Sumter like they were told, the first shot never would have been fired."

"This has been building for a long time. War was inevitable," came the terse reply as he steered her back to the carriage. After assisting her into the vehicle, he gave a last, disparaging glance in the direction of the departed train. "Those poor fools. Those poor, gallant young fools. Many of them will never see home again, God help them."

A sense of foreboding swept over Kitty, because there was no denying the truth of his words. They were so young, most of them little older than herself. And if they did return, to what would they be returning? Would the South win? Could it win? They had to, they simply *had* to win, for it meant the survival of a particular style of living that would be impossible to change without ruination. The South's economics depended largely on the continuing success of the plantation system, but no plantation could function effectively without the use of slave labor. As she mulled over these facts, Kitty's resentment toward Northerners increased tenfold.

The ride back to her house was made in silence. When Bret ushered her to the front door, Kitty turned to bid him good-bye. "Thank you for taking me to the station, Bret. I know Miles will be sorry he missed seeing you, but perhaps you can visit us another time," she suggested coolly.

Bret scowled darkly. "Miles be damned! Why did you do it, Kitty? Why did you marry him?"

Kitty's gaze dropped, fastening blindly on the broad expanse of his chest. "Because I wanted to," she murmured, refusing to admit the truth.

Bret lifted her chin with his forefinger, forcing her to look at him. "I repeat, Kitty—why? You don't love him. You never have."

"What do you know about love? Why, you don't even know the meaning of the word. Lust is all you're capable of feeling for a woman," she retorted.

"Is it!" His fingers imprisoned her arm as he unexpectedly propelled her through the front door.

Alarmed, Kitty heard the front door close behind them, but before she could protest, he was pulling her to him, capturing her parted lips in a demanding kiss that caught her completely off guard. For a moment she tensed in his arms. Then, with a low moan, she pressed closer to him, returning his kiss with a hunger that could no longer be denied.

Her response aroused a savage yearning deep within him, yet seconds later he released her, a mocking expression on his face. "For someone who's supposedly in love with her husband, you have a peculiar way of showing it," he remarked wryly.

Kitty stiffened with humiliation, then lashed out angrily to slap his face. But her hand was caught midway to its target, her slender wrist imprisoned in a grip of steel.

"I wouldn't if I were you. I've never hit a woman before, but in your case I might be tempted. And that, my dear, would be unpardonable, especially considering your present delicate condition."

So, he knew! But did he suspect it was his child she carried? Kitty wondered. Unable to think of a suitable reply, she remained silent as Bret turned and strode through the front door.

Little did she realize how tempted he had been to ask her that very question. He had refrained from doing so simply because he had realized such questioning would have been futile.

If the child were his, Bret knew instinctively that Kitty would never admit it; yet if the baby were born in June, nothing she could say would ever make him believe that the birth was premature. Time would tell, but if the baby were his, he seriously doubted Miles would be fooled for long. And this, more than anything else, worried him.

Chapter 10

By June, the Confederate capital had been moved to Richmond, Virginia. Men from all over the South continued to enlist as the Confederacy organized its army and began developing a navy. Federal ships were successfully blockading much of the South's coastline. It had become imperative for the Confederacy to attain a strong navy in order to run the Yankees' gauntlet and reach Nassau, which had become a major supply port for the South.

Northern steamships had stopped docking at southern ports, and the loss of manufactured goods previously supplied by the North was being felt throughout the South. Though such action had been expected, it posed problems. How were Southerners to acquire manufactured goods that, until recently, had simply been taken for granted? Food was abundant, at least for the present, but how was the Confederacy to supply its expanding army with cannon, guns and rifles, ammunition, and uniforms? In Vicksburg, Reading and Paxton's foundries stopped making plows and began manufacturing war materials, as did many businesses throughout the South. But would these makeshift factories be capable of adequately supplying the Confederacy with its needs?

Such was the topic of conversation between Dave and Bret one afternoon as they sat on Kitty's front porch. Dave had driven into town on business and, later, had run into Bret, who joined him in paying Kitty an unexpected visit. Although not overly thrilled at seeing Bret, Kitty was determined to enjoy her father's visit, for she rarely saw him nowadays. Her pregnancy was nearing the final

stage, which prevented her from traveling to Belle Glen. She would
not have been all that eager to visit there, anyway.

After enlisting in the army in April, Tad had married Dede the
following week, and the woman now resided with Dave at Belle
Glen. Kitty did not dislike her new sister-in-law, but she found
Dede's constant chattering hard to endure. How anyone could talk so
much and say so little was simply beyond her comprehension. The
only thing she could find in common with the girl was a genuine
love and concern for Tad, whose company was tentatively stationed
at Meridian, Mississippi.

Miles had also enlisted, and his regiment had been ordered to
Kentucky early in May. Though Kitty worried that Tad might be sent
to the front, she was unable to arouse a similar concern for her husband.
She dutifully answered his infrequent letters, but her correspon-
dence was filled with news rather than longing, for it was impossible
to write of personal feelings that did not exist between them.

As for Bret, she rarely saw him, and then only at a distance,
which was fine with her. She was therefore dismayed when she
heard him tell Dave that he had just rented a room at Widow
Benton's house, only a block away.

As the cousin who had cared for Miles and his sister after their
parents' death, the widow looked upon Miles's wife as a close
relative and insisted Kitty address her as Aunt Phoebe, just as Miles
did. The fact that she lived nearby enabled her to drop in and check
on Kitty at regular intervals. In spite of the matron's well-meant
intentions, Kitty regarded these impromptu visits as something of a
nuisance, particularly when Phoebe was accompanied by Flora Drummond and her sister, Dolly, who were both spinsters—or worse, by
Doc Blanks's wife, Mattie, the town's biggest gossip.

Now she supposed she would have to put up with unexpected
visits from Bret as well, a possibility that hardly pleased her. With a
resigned sigh, she absentmindedly checked for signs of worms in the
peas she was shelling, then set the half-filled bowl beside the rocker.
Forcing her attention back to Dave and Bret's conversation, she said:

"I received a letter from Miles last week. Dennis Sasser has been
transferred to his company, and Miles thinks they may be ordered to
Tennessee before long."

"Have you heard anything from Tad?" Bret asked Dave.

"Not recently," he answered, "but I talked to Hal Hartz this morning. You know his oldest sons, Steve and Scott, are in Tad's company. He thinks the boys will be home on furlough soon.''

"Oh, I hope so.'' Kitty smiled.

Dave nodded his agreement, pausing to light his pipe before continuing. "Hal is pretty concerned about that middle son of his, though. Says Mike's thinking about joining up with the Union.''

"Surely not! Why, it'd just kill Miss Ginny if he did,'' Kitty exclaimed, referring to the boy's mother. "They should never have allowed Mike to attend West Point. Running around with those Northerners apparently addled his mind.''

They talked a few minutes more, and then Dave announced he had to be getting home. Kitty expected Bret to leave, too, but he didn't. Together, they watched as Dave's carriage disappeared from view. Wishing to break the strained silence, Kitty said the first thing that came to mind.

"I'm surprised Aunt Phoebe agreed to rent you a room. She was hoping to find a permanent boarder.''

"What makes you think she hasn't?''

"Why, I assume you're going to enlist *sometime*.''

"And just how did you arrive at that conclusion?'' Bret asked wryly.

"Well, you are, aren't you? I mean, all of our men are enlisting, except the ones who are too young or too old—and, of course, the cowards.''

Bret took hold of her chin, forcing her to look at him. "Do you think I'm a coward?''

"No, of course not. But if you don't enlist, it's certainly going to look peculiar.''

"Then I'm afraid it's going to have to look that way, because I have no intention of enlisting—at least, not at the moment.''

Kitty's eyes widened in disbelief. "And why not, may I ask?''

"Because I don't want to, for one thing, and for another, who would look after you if I weren't around? God knows somebody needs to.''

"I can take care of myself, thank you.''

"Since when?'' he returned. "You've been getting into scrapes ever since you took your first step. In fact, you have a definite talent for getting into precarious situations.''

"Don't go blaming me for your lack of patriotism, Bret. Either you're a coward, or else you're just waiting to see if the South can win before you throw in your lot with the rest of us. Like Pa once said, you've never been one to champion lost causes."

"No, I haven't, and I don't intend to now. In my opinion, the South is too poorly equipped to win this war. We may be able to outfight the Yankees, but I doubt we'll be able to outlast them. Even if by some miracle the war happens to end in a stalemate, what then? Do you honestly think Northerners are ever going to endorse slavery?"

"Why not? They're the ones who started slave trading in the first place. If Africans had been conditioned to the North's cold climate, and had they been able to adapt to working in factories, I daresay they would all have remained in the North instead of being sold to Southerners."

"Probably, but that doesn't change the fact that, whether we like it or not, slavery is doomed. It's only a question of time. Even Dave agrees with me about that."

"Maybe, but if *he* were a younger man, he'd be enlisting. As it is, he's already contributed a lot of money to the Confederacy, plus some of his best horses and mules."

"And I've contributed a lot of cotton. Several hundred bales, as a matter of face, and I intend to contribute more."

"Why? To appease your conscience or defend your honor?" Kitty asked.

His mouth quirked into a grin. "I assure you my conscience is quite clear. In fact, the cotton I donate will be far more useful to the Confederacy than my enlistment, which I'm sure most folks around here realize."

"I don't know why I bother discussing anything with you. You never listen to me."

"Oh, I listen"—he chuckled—"I just don't always agree."

Before she could argue further, he planted a light kiss on her forehead, then strode down the steps. As he walked away, however, a frown marred his handsome features. Other folks' opinions did not concern him, but Kitty's did. The realization that she was beginning to look upon him as a coward disturbed him.

He was no coward, but neither was he a fool. He had painstakingly built up a business that he had no intention of losing. If he enlisted and the South lost, his brokerages probably would be confiscated by the Federal government.

Still, there was one possibility he had been considering for some time, a means of supporting the Confederacy without necessarily leaving himself open to financial ruin if the North did win. Espionage, he realized, was a dangerous business, but that simply made it all the more appealing to him. Mulling the idea over in his mind, he headed briskly toward town.

Sewing was definitely not one of Kitty's favorite pastimes, but she had nevertheless been persuaded by Phoebe to join the Ladies Sewing Circle, a group comprised of all ages who congregated weekly at some member's home. This week, the meeting was being held at Kitty's, much to her dismay. It was bad enough to have to struggle with a pair of knitting needles, even worse to be forced to listen to the incessant jabbering of a bunch of women all bent on talking at the same time.

The exception was Judge Crane's wife, Cora, who was seated next to Kitty, for which she was thankful. The woman's gentle presence bolstered Kitty's determination to be a gracious hostess; thus, with a fixed smile she muttered, "Pearl one, stitch two," and feigned interest in the humdrum conversation that assailed her from all sides. By late afternoon, however, she was feeling the strain.

It was unusually hot even for the latter part of June, and as perspiration beaded her forehead, a dull, throbbing ache started in the lower part of her back. Attributing the persistent discomfort to the fact that she had exerted more energy than usual in preparing for her guests, she attempted to ignore it by concentrating on her knitting. The pain slowly intensified, causing her hands to tremble to the extent that she finally dropped a stitch. Cora immediately came to her rescue.

"Don't look so discouraged, my dear. You'll get the hang of knitting in no time," she encouraged, quickly sorting out Kitty's mistake, then placing the long needles back into the girl's unwilling hands. "By the way, have any of you ladies noticed that the cost of yarn has gone up recently?"

"Indeed it has," agreed Flora Drummond. "I bought a skein of yarn in your husband's store today, Effie. It cost a dime more than last week."

"Oh, my, yes! In fact, quite a few things have gone up at his store," Dolly twittered, casting a nervous glance at her sister for approval before continuing. "Of course, some things are getting mighty scarce since those awful Yankees have stopped bringing their boats to Vicksburg."

"We'll manage to survive without the Yankees' merchandise—provided, of course, our own merchants don't try to rob us blind," Flora stated dryly, her eyes never straying from her knitting.

"Really, Miss Flora!" Effie Collins sputtered indignantly. "I assure you my husband is not robbing anybody. He's merely trying to make an honest living. As your sister pointed out, some things are hard to come by nowadays, so they're naturally going to cost more."

"Oh, I'm sure Flora didn't mean to be critical of Mr. Collins," Dolly offered feebly, her plump face flushing with embarrassment.

"Hush up, Dolly. Effie knows exactly what I meant," Flora declared.

It was no secret that Henry Collins was profiting by the war, marking up everything in his general store to almost twice the original price.

"I'll thank you to remember that my husband has been most generous to the cause," Effie said. "Why, only last week, he paid one hundred dollars for Confederate bonds."

"Remarkable," Flora countered dryly.

"And just what do you mean by that?" Effie asked.

"Oh, I was just thinking about those two free Negroes, William Newman and Henry Lee, who each bought two hundred and fifty dollars' worth of Confederate bonds. I'm sure *their* money was earned the hard way and that their contribution was a genuine sacrifice—most generous, in fact."

An uncomfortable silence ensued, then Phoebe glanced up at the mantel clock and remarked with feigned surprise that it was almost five o'clock. Thankful that the boring afternoon had come to an end, Kitty smiled as the ladies thanked her for her hospitality and departed.

Closing the front door with a relieved sigh, Kitty walked back to the parlor, where Daisy was picking up dirty cups and saucers and placing them on a serving tray. After giving the girl some brief instructions about supper, she turned to go upstairs, then stopped as a sharp pain tore through her abdomen. Gasping softly, she clutched the door facing for support. Oh, no, she thought, surely the baby won't come now. First babies often arrived late, and she had been fervently hoping hers would come as late as mid-July. Then, neither Bret, Miles, nor anyone else would suspect the truth. Her worst fear was confirmed seconds later when she was seized with another contraction. This time she cried aloud, immediately catching Daisy's attention.

"What's de matter, Miz Kitty?" Daisy asked worriedly as she rushed over to her mistress. "Lawdy me, you's white as a sheet! Is de baby comin'?"

"I . . . I think so," Kitty panted. "Go get Doc Blanks, and—and *hurry*, Daisy!"

"Yes'm, but first let me hep you upstairs. You needs tuh be in bed."

Kitty nodded her agreement, but as they reached the stairs, there was a loud knock at the front door. Without waiting to be told, Daisy rushed over and opened it.

"Oh, Mist' Bret, thank de Lawd it's you!" Daisy wailed. "Miz Kitty's time dun come, an' Ah wuz jes' fixin' tuh go fetch de doctor."

Glancing past Daisy, Bret saw Kitty leaning weakly against the banister and realized the girl was not exaggerating the situation.

"You go on, and I'll get her upstairs," he said grimly.

Kitty had heard Bret's voice, but just then a wave of dizziness washed over her, and she was only dimly aware of being swept up in his powerful arms and carried upstairs.

"Where's your bedroom, Kitty?"

"First door on the right," she managed to whisper.

As Bret thrust open the door and walked over to the bed, one question was uppermost in his mind. Had Kitty's time come, or was the baby actually coming prematurely? If the latter were true, Kitty's life, as well as the baby's, could be in jeopardy. Gently he deposited her on the bed, then sat down beside her.

The dizziness was subsiding, and, seeing the concern in his eyes, Kitty forced a smile to her lips.

"I'm glad you're here," she said.

"So am I," he answered, taking her hand in his. "Actually, I rode over to Belle Glen this morning and had a visit with Dave. He asked me to drop by and check on you."

"I see," she murmured, her mouth drooping with disappointment. It hurt somehow to know her father had instigated his timely visit, though it hardly surprised her. She rarely saw Bret these days.

"I wish Pa were here now. I haven't seen him in two weeks, not since Tad was home on leave."

Bret assured her he'd send for Dave first thing in the morning.

Pleased, Kitty wanted to thank him but could only grimace as another contraction seized her. Her hand tightened on his, and she gave a soft moan.

"Oh, Bret, I'm afraid," she cried when the pain became almost unbearable.

"It's going to be all right, Kitten. Just try to relax until the doctor gets here."

"But what if he doesn't come in time?" she asked.

"Shhh—he'll get here in time," he answered, carefully masking his own anxiety as he brushed damp tendrils of hair from her face.

Her grip on his hand gradually relaxed when the pain began to recede, but he knew that the respite would be brief. God in heaven, where was the doctor? Perspiration beaded on his forehead, and for the first time in his adult life, he felt completely helpless.

Minutes later, Doc Blanks arrived. After first instructing Daisy to help Kitty into a fresh nightgown, he greeted Bret, then briskly ordered him from the room. Reluctant to leave, yet unable to witness Kitty's increasing torment, Bret gave her hand an encouraging squeeze before striding from the room.

The hours dragged by as he paced nervously back and forth in the hall, occasionally rushing over to the closed bedroom door whenever her intermittent cries became almost too agonizing to bear. Over and over he mentally cursed Miles, then himself, for bringing her such misery, for there was no way of knowing whose child she carried.

Exhausted at last, he walked over to the stairs and sat down on the top step, wearily resting his head between two unsteady hands. Did childbirth usually take so long, he wondered dismally, or was Kitty having complications? The possibility of her dying was something he was unwilling to face, and he repeatedly shoved it from his mind.

Suddenly, a piercing scream ripped through the air, bringing him to his feet like a shot. Without thinking, he raced to her bedroom and burst through the door. The sight of the doctor's holding a squirming object by its feet and swatting its small backside brought him to an abrupt halt, but when a tiny wail pierced the silence, he strode over to the bed. Kitty was unconscious and so still and pale that he immediately feared the worst.

"She's not . . ." His voice faltered helplessly.

"No, she's not dead. Just unconscious," the doctor assured him. "She had a hard delivery, but the boy's fine."

"A boy, huh," Bret repeated, pleased.

"Yep, a fine boy. A little on the puny side, but then most premature babies are." He had deliberately sought to mislead Bret with his reply, for there was no doubt in his mind that the baby was full term. Of course, Kitty had not confided in him, but he had no intention of betraying her secret. After suggesting Bret wait outside until Kitty regained consciousness, he instructed Daisy to bring him clean water and bedsheets.

By the time Bret was allowed back into the room, the baby had been cleansed and wrapped in a fresh swaddling blanket. Kitty, now awake and wearing a white batiste nightgown, was propped up in bed, gazing bemusedly at the child who nestled peacefully in the crook of her arm. She had never looked lovelier to him, and after the doctor had left he pulled up a chair and sat down next to the bed.

"Well, what do you think of him?" She smiled proudly.

As he glanced down at the child, his mouth quirked into a broad grin. "He's mighty fine, Kitty. Looks like he's going to favor you—black hair and blue eyes."

"Most babies' eyes are blue at first," she answered. "Later, they might be gr—" She stopped herself in time, then continued, "They might be any color."

Not noticing her frown, Bret gently took hold of the baby's hand, placing his large finger in the tiny fist. "Look at that grip, would you." He chuckled. "This little fella's going to be a real fighter, just like his mother."

"What's the date, Bret?"

"The twenty-seventh of June, I believe. Why?"

"I was just thinking how close he came to being a Fourth-of-July baby," she replied, then sighed. "I suppose it's just as well he wasn't, since we don't belong to the Union anymore."

Bret smiled. "I wouldn't let it worry you. By the time this young man is grown, the Civil War will be only a memory. With luck, Southerners may have an independence day of their own to celebrate."

"Do you really think so?"

"Well, I think we should hope for the best." Changing the subject, he asked what she was going to name the baby.

"I wanted to name him after Pa, but Miles wrote that he didn't like the idea," she replied, "so I finally decided on Scott Devan Blake." Her eyes slid briefly to the book on her bedside table, the one by Walter Scott that Bret had sent her from England. Her lips curved in a smile, for she was pleased that she had been able to connect the child's name with its natural father, if only in this remote way.

"Scott . . . yes, I like the name. It suits him," Bret remarked, though inwardly he winced over the last name. The boy should have been *his* son, not Miles'! In fact, he still wasn't convinced that Miles was the father.

"His father should be very proud of him," he said in a wistful voice, intently searching her face for the truth. Surely, if the baby were his, she would admit it now.

Kitty saw the question in his eyes and paled as an uncomfortable silence fell between them. Had Bret said then and there that he loved her, she would have told him the truth proudly, but he didn't. He probably never would, she realized.

Later, after he had gone, Kitty remembered the appeal in his eyes and sighed. She was so tired of pretending—tired of being one man's wife while yearning to belong to another. This should have been their happiest moment, hers and Bret's, but they had been able to share it only in part, for she had silently denied his unspoken question.

Part II

Chapter 11

April 1862

Shiloh—a small log cabin that served as a church, situated near Pittsburg Landing on the western bank of the Tennessee River. A seemingly insignificant spot, quiet and unobtrusive, until April 6. During the wee hours of that fateful Sunday morning, the Confederate army of General Albert Sidney Johnston encountered the unsuspecting Union army of General Ulysses S. Grant. Across the river and nine miles to the north was Savannah, Tennessee, and the Cherry Mansion, headquarters for General Grant, who, when the first shots were fired, had just sat down for breakfast. It was a meal he never finished.

By the time the general reached the front lines, bodies dotted the countryside. The fiercer battles occurred where the Yankees were holding their position in a wooden area along an old sunken road, nicknamed "Hornets' Nest" by the attacking Confederates, and in the flowering peach orchard where General Johnston was fatally wounded. Despite the loss of their revered leader, the attacking Rebels pressed on toward Pittsburg Landing, capturing all of the field up to that point. By nightfall, it appeared that southern forces had been victorious.

The next morning, however, the tide had begun to turn. The Confederates' failure to reorganize their scattered forces throughout the night had given the Federals an edge. Inch by bloody inch, the Yankees fought to regain most of the ground they had lost the previous day.

Disorganized and outnumbered, the Confederates were forced to withdraw from the field by late afternoon, then gradually retreat to Corinth, Mississippi, only a short distance from Shiloh. Both North and South claimed victory, yet losses on each side were extremely heavy.

Until now, the war had seemed far removed from the town of Vicksburg, since the fighting had been occurring much farther north. It was not until several days after the battle of Shiloh that the townspeople experienced the horrendous reality of war, when the wounded were evacuated from Corinth, loaded on trains, and transported to Vicksburg.

Kitty had been expecting a visit from Dave that afternoon, but as soon as she heard the news, she hurried down to the depot. By the time she arrived, some of the wounded had already been carted off to homes that were being renovated into hospitals. The weather was dismally cold and wet, with bolts of lightning cutting across the gray skies. As she stepped down from her carriage, brushing the rain from her face, her eyes widened with dismay at the scene before her. Line after line of wounded soldiers were lying helplessly in the rain, their bandages and blankets becoming soaked as they shivered and moaned in agony. Realizing some of these men could be from Vicksburg and that she might know them, she began to make her way through the wounded, carefully scanning each bearded face.

Most of the soldiers turned out to be strangers, but she occasionally discovered a familiar face and paused to offer reassuring words, the only comfort she could provide at the moment. As mothers, wives, and sweethearts found loved ones, wails of distress intermingled with anguished groans. Kitty looked about her wildly, wondering if Miles had perhaps been wounded and brought in on the train. If so, how was she ever going to find him in such a horrible mass of mangled humanity?

Seconds later, she saw one of the men in Miles's company lying only a few feet away from her. Fearfully, yet without hesitation, she made her way over to him, noting the pallor of his skin and the glazed, tortured look in his eyes—eyes that had witnessed the depths of hell and were changed forever.

"Hello, Dennis," she said with forced cheerfulness.

The boy looked up at her, a faint smile trembling on his lips. "Miss Kitty," he whispered with weak recognition. "Is it you, Miss Kitty?"

"Yes—it's me," she returned. Kneeling beside him, she brushed his damp hair from his face and tried to shield him from the rain with her umbrella. "Fine one you are, Dennis Sasser, letting those blue-bellies get the best of you. Why, I'm surprised at you!" She smiled, attempting to occupy his mind since there was no way she could ease his pain. "Where are you hurt?"

"Caught a minnie ball in the arm. Thought it was just a scratch at first, but it wouldn't stop bleeding. The doc said it was an artery. He put a tourniquet on it, but I forgot to loosen it ever' so often like he told me to. Now my whole arm is black and hurts like the devil," he said weakly.

Kitty could not bring herself to lift the blanket to see his arm. She did not want to see. There was a putrefying stench about him that was already causing her stomach to churn. Stretcher-bearers were carrying off a wounded man only a few feet away, and she called to them.

"Can you come back for this soldier next? He's badly wounded."

"They're all badly wounded, miss," came the gruff reply, but upon seeing her distressed look, the man grudgingly relented. "All right, lady, we'll try to get to your friend next."

Kitty breathed a sigh of relief and turned back to Dennis, who was moaning aloud with pain. Again, she sought to divert his mind and, at the same time, gain information.

"Miles was with you at Shiloh, wasn't he?"

Dennis nodded, then managed to say, "I sure hope he fared better than I did. The last I saw of him, he was fighting in the peach orchard. Lord, that was something to see! The shootin' was hot and heavy, bullets knocking the blooms right off the trees. There were so many peach blossoms fallin' that it damn near looked like it was snowing." He winced. " 'Scuse me for cussin', Miss Kitty, but that was the worst battle I ever saw. A small pond nearby turned red with blood, but even then men from both sides were trying to drink from it. Me, I couldn't do it. Reckon I just wasn't that thirsty."

"Don't, Dennis. Don't tell me any more," she protested faintly, relieved to see the stretcher-bearers returning. "A lot of people have turned their homes into temporary hospitals, so I don't know where you'll be taken. Don't worry, though, I'll find out where you are and send word to your folks." She bent to kiss his cheek and watched with a feeling of helplessness as he was carried to a nearby wagon that was already filled to capacity with wounded soldiers.

Her gaze was fastened to the makeshift ambulance until it finally disappeared from view. Turning away, she was surprised to find her father standing at her side.

"Oh, Pa, Dennis is hurt badly. I'm afraid he'll lose his arm."

Dave scowled and shook his head. "A lot of these boys are going to lose arms, legs, and in many cases their lives. They've already lost their youth," he muttered, guiding her back to the carriage. Once they were seated inside, he turned to her.

"Honey, I ran into Doc Blanks a few minutes ago. Miles was on one of the first boxcars. The hospital was full, so he was taken to Duff Green's house. It's being renovated into a hospital."

Stunned, Kitty strove to remain calm. "How seriously is Miles wounded?"

"He's in pretty bad shape. It's a stomach wound, and Doc thinks some of the shell fragments may have perforated his lower extremities. Either he or Mark Johnson will operate just as soon as possible. He thought you'd want to know so you could be there."

"Of course," she murmured.

They rode in silence the rest of the way. Riddled with worry and a sense of guilt, Kitty recalled the brief, unhappy months of their marriage. Remembering the perverseness of Miles's lovemaking caused her to shudder even now, and she chastised herself for recalling such incidents at this time.

Regardless of her feelings toward him, she did not want him to die. She had known him all her life, had idolized him as a child. If their marriage left much to be desired, Miles was not all to blame. He had given her his name and, in his own way, his love, but she had given nothing in return. If he lived, she vowed silently, she would be a better wife to him in the future. She must, for their marriage could not continue as it had in the past. It had been miserable for both of them, a fact she now bitterly regretted.

By the time they reached their destination at the corner of First and Locust streets, Kitty was filled with dread. Dave pulled the carriage to a halt in front of the three-storied, redbrick home that was now serving as a hospital. Several soldiers milled about on the upper verandas while others leaned against the beautiful iron banisters.

As Dave helped her down from the carriage, she suddenly clutched his arm. "I'm afraid, Pa," she admitted. "You'll stay with me, won't you?"

"Of course I'll stay with you—just as long as you need me," he reassured her, then led her up the porch steps and into the house.

Every room was filled to capacity with wounded and dying men, and she stood uncertainly in the foyer while her father went to search for the doctor. The monotonous drone of anguished suffering was all around her. Several ladies of her acquaintance were bustling around the soldiers in the front parlor in a futile attempt to ease their pain, and she marveled at their courage in a situation of such nightmarish proportions. Like herself, they had all led sheltered lives—until today. The wounded were not only unshaven, they were unclean as well, and a sickly smell of sweat, blood, and putrefying flesh filled the air.

By the time Dave reappeared with Doc Blanks, she was totally shaken, though she made every effort to appear calm. With unsteady steps, she walked down the foyer to meet them.

"How is Miles?" she asked.

The elderly doctor's bushy eyebrows drew together in a serious frown. "He'll pull through, child, provided there are no serious or unexpected complications."

"Complications? What kind of complications?"

"Infection, mainly. For that reason, he'll have to remain here several weeks. That way, I can check on him daily."

"But you do think he will recover?"

"Yes, with proper care, I believe he will," the doctor answered slowly. His frown deepened upon seeing her relief. "Kitty, under the circumstances, I feel I must be perfectly frank with you. If Miles lives, and there's every indication he will, his recovery might not be completely satisfactory."

"I—I don't understand," Kitty murmured.

"He was severely wounded. I did my best to remove all the shrapnel, but there's a possibility some of the minute shell fragments may still be embedded in the lower extremities. I've discussed my prognosis with your father, and I think he should be the one to explain the situation to you more thoroughly."

"May I see him?" Kitty asked, perplexed by the physician's explanation.

"Tomorrow, perhaps. In the meantime, Dave, I suggest you take Kitty home. There's no point in either of you staying."

Dave nodded his agreement and, after thanking the doctor, led Kitty outside. Somehow she managed to withhold her questions until they were seated inside the carriage. Then she turned to Dave with a worried look.

"Pa, what did Doc Blanks mean? Why is he so dubious about Miles's recovery?"

"Honey, the doctor thinks some tiny shell fragments may still be embedded in Miles's groin. If this is the case, the best we can hope for is that his . . . er, virility will be only temporarily impaired."

Kitty paled and waited for her father to continue. When he did not, she was forced to draw on the last of her courage, for she was determined to know the whole truth. Taking a deep breath, she asked:

"And if this condition isn't temporary, what then?"

"Miles will be impotent."

Miles was not the best of patients, nor did his disposition improve once Doc Blanks explained to him the seriousness of his condition and the possible consequences. Unable to accept the fact that he might be impotent, his irritability increased daily, often causing him to snap at Kitty for no apparent reason. When this happened, she managed to hold her temper in check, though her patience was wearing thin. She visited him daily and attempted to ease his boredom by discussing Scotty, the latest war news, or anything of interest that was happening in town. Occasionally she read to him, and when all else failed she sat beside his cot in silence and folded bandages.

By the end of April the people of Vicksburg had begun to recover from the shock of Shiloh. And then the impossible happened. New Orleans was seized by the Yankees, along with two other fortifications near the mouth of the Mississippi, Forts Jackson and St. Philip. There was nothing left between New Orleans and Vicksburg to hold back the Union gunboats. With New Orleans less than five days away by steamboat, it seemed probable that Farragut's flotilla would reach Vicksburg before the week was out. War was no longer far away, but at the town's very doorstep.

Kitty was at the hospital with Miles when the distressing news reached town. Pandemonium ensued; people closed their shops, boarded up their houses, and fled the town. Kitty always walked to the hospital, since Duff Green's house was only a short distance from her own. This particular afternoon, however, she wished she had brought the carriage, for the streets were in a state of chaos.

Wagons, carriages, horses, and even mules raced madly through town, occasionally running over unfortunate people who were rushing about on foot. Hysteria permeated the entire area, and as Kitty hesitated in front of the hospital, she wondered how on earth she would ever reach home safely. Minutes later, she was relieved to see Bret pushing his way through the crowd and heading toward her.

"Oh, Bret, thank goodness you're here!" she exclaimed.

"Miss Phoebe suggested I come. She knew you'd probably be at the hospital this afternoon, and she was afraid you might have difficulty getting home." He took her by the arm to steer her through the milling throng.

As they paused to cross the street, two wagons almost collided in front of them, and Kitty gave a startled gasp when Bret thrust himself forward as a measure of protection.

"This is awful, Bret. Everyone's in such a panic, you'd think the Yankees were here instead of in New Orleans."

"They probably will be soon," he answered matter-of-factly.

"How soon?"

"That's anyone's guess, but I doubt it'll be within the next few days. I've got a feeling Farragut will wait a week or so before he pays us a visit. Of course, I could be wrong. If he wanted to, he could get his flotilla here in five days, provided he could get past Natchez."

"Can't we stop him?"

"With what?"

Kitty fell silent, her mind in turmoil as she considered what action to take if the town came under attack. She wanted to go home, believing she would be safe at Belle Glen, but as long as Miles was not well enough to travel, she could not possibly leave town.

They had just reached her front gate when she saw Sally Collins hurrying toward them. With a brief smile, she acknowledged Bret's presence, then turned to Kitty. "Thank goodness Mr. O'Rourke brought you home, Kitty. I have never in all my life seen such madness. I do believe everyone has taken leave of their senses."

"It looks that way," Kitty agreed.

"Papa says they're even hauling cotton out of warehouses and carrying it outside of town to burn. Perfectly good cotton just going to waste. You're not going to burn your cotton, are you?" she asked Bret.

"Not unless I have to," he replied. "Of course, should the

Yankees succeed in capturing the city, none of us would want our cotton to be confiscated by the enemy, now, would we?"

"Certainly not." Sally gasped. "But you don't think they will, do you? Capture Vicksburg, I mean?"

"Well, I don't think we're in any immediate danger, though what the future holds for us is anybody's guess," he replied.

"That's what I've been trying to tell Mama and Celia, but they won't listen. They're bound and determined to tuck tail and run like a couple of jackrabbits."

"They're leaving town?" Kitty interrupted.

"Yes, they're going to the Robertson plantation near the Big Black River, at least until the scare is over. I don't want to go with them, though, which is why I ran over here. Could I stay with you, Kitty, until Mama and Celia return?"

"Of course. What about your father—is he leaving town, also?"

"No, he's moving a cot to the store, so he can sleep there and protect his merchandise. But he's packing up some of it, just in case the Yankees do attack and we have to get out of town. For someone who was so set against Mississippi's pulling out of the Union, Papa sure is a dyed-in-the-wool Rebel now." Sally grinned. "Well, I'd better sashay home and let Mama know I'll be staying with you. She'll have a conniption fit, but I wouldn't leave town now for all the tea in China! If Farragut does get this far, I don't want to miss seeing the fireworks," she tossed over her shoulder as she bustled away.

The girl's spunk amused Bret, but not Kitty. "Honestly, sometimes I think she hasn't the sense God gave a goose. You'd think she'd realize the danger we're in."

Bret did not answer but followed Kitty inside the house. Removing her bonnet, she hung it on the mirrored hall tree, then turned to see Daisy appear with Scotty. Spying his mother, the chubby ten-month-old gurgled happily and stretched out his dimpled arms. Before Kitty could take him, however, Bret had the boy in his arms.

"I swear, Daisy, this youngster gets bigger every time I see him," he remarked, lifting the delighted infant high into the air.

"Yas, suh, an' he's gittin' uh mouth full ob teeth, too," she replied with a wide grin. "He's been uh lil' fussy wid dem gums ob his being swole up lak dey is, but Ah gib 'im uh sugar tit dis af'ernoon, an' dat seemed tuh hep sum."

Bret lowered the boy, cradling him next to his broad chest in order to get a better look at him. "Well, we can't have those gums hurting, can we, Scott. We'll just tell Daisy to stop foolin' around with sugar tits, 'cause that's for sissies," he stated, brushing the dark, curly locks away from the cherubic face. Looking at Daisy, he smiled. "Rub his gums with a little whiskey. I guarantee it'll stop the itching and cut the pain."

Kitty's heart contracted as she watched Bret nuzzle the boy's soft cheek. "Since when have you become such an expert on babies?" she murmured, removing the child from his arms and handing him to Daisy.

"Oh, I've been around." Bret chuckled. "Don't forget what I told you, Daisy. No more sugar tits for that boy. Rub his gums with whiskey."

"Yassuh." She grinned, then looked at Kitty. "You wants me tuh put de baby tuh bed, or duz you wants tuh do it?"

"You go ahead, Daisy. I'm tired, and I have a fierce headache," she answered, planting a kiss on Scott's forehead. With a slight smile, she watched until Daisy had carried the child upstairs, then turned her attention to Bret.

"I think there's some leftover fried chicken and biscuits from dinner. Would you like to have a bite to eat?"

"No, I need to get back to the warehouse," he answered. "Before I go, however, there is something I'd like to discuss with you, Kitty."

Perplexed by his sudden somberness, she looked up at him questioningly.

"I don't want to alarm you, but as I said earlier, I think Vicksburg will be attacked in the very near future. Keeping that in mind, it would be advisable for you to take Scott and the servants back to Belle Glen as soon as possible. Preferably by the end of the week."

"I can't leave—not until Miles is well enough to travel, and that won't be for some time. Besides, I have no intention of running from the Yankees."

Bret took hold of her shoulders. "Now, listen to me, Kitty. If you're determined to stay here for the present, then do so. But when the Yankees steam up that river, you and Scott are going to Belle Glen if I have to carry you there myself, and that's final."

"I'll go when I'm ready to and not before," she replied firmly. Turning her back to him, she added, "You have no right to tell me what to do."

"Maybe not, but I'm telling you just the same. If you don't care about your own safety, at least think of the boy's."

Too tired and irritable to think sensibly, Kitty said the first thing that came to mind. "Your concern for our son would be touching if it didn't come so late."

"*Our* son?" Bret queried in a deep voice, turning her around to face him.

Unwittingly she had revealed the truth to him, but she was past caring. She was sick of lying to him about Scott, so, with a proud lift of her chin, she faced him squarely.

"Yes, our son—yours and mine!" she answered, wincing as his fingers tightened on her arms.

"God in heaven, why didn't you tell me?" he rasped. "Do you think I'd have gone to Europe had I known you were pregnant? Didn't you realize I'd have married you?"

"I didn't know how you'd react, but I had no intention of forcing you to marry me. Miles wanted me, and you obviously didn't."

"So you married him, knowing you were carrying my child."

"I married him to give *your* child a name," she returned emphatically.

"Had you told me, that wouldn't have been necessary," came the heated reply.

"I had no intention of telling you anything as long as Selina was your mistress."

"Dammit, did it never occur to you that I wouldn't have been sleeping with Selina if I could have had you?"

"As I recall, you *had* me—you just didn't want me."

"Want you! My God, Kitty, didn't you have any idea how I felt?"

"How could I? You never told me. You certainly never asked me to marry you," she replied in a choked voice.

Knowing she was on the verge of tears, Bret released her, turning away so that she would not see his own pain. "No, I didn't," he admitted softly. "Somehow I couldn't picture you being married to the son of your father's overseer."

"Do you honestly think that mattered?" she asked incredulously.

Again in control of his emotions, he turned and looked at her. "It mattered to me."

A brief silence ensued as they stared at each other, both realizing how their mutual lack of communication and trust had irrevocably destroyed what happiness they might have had. It was Bret who spoke at last.

"The question now is—what are we going to do about the boy?"

Steeling herself against the anguish in his eyes, she somehow managed to answer him in a level voice. "Nothing. You can see him whenever you like, but other than that . . ."

Her meaning was clear. There was nothing either of them could do. He did not want their child labeled a bastard any more than she did, nor did he want her name dragged through the mud by malicious town gossips. He could enjoy being with his son, but only to a limited extent and only as an outsider. At the moment, he was not sure whom he despised the most, Kitty or himself.

Bitterness filled him as he walked slowly to the front door. Pausing with his hand on the doorknob, he turned to face her, and his parting remark said it all.

"You had no right to deny me my son. I could have forgiven you anything—but that."

The door closed quietly behind him, but not before Kitty had witnessed the misery in his face. Tears streamed down her cheeks as she listened to his footsteps fading away, and it was all she could do not to run after him and beg his forgiveness.

Chapter 12

By the end of the week, the remaining townspeople had settled down and stiffened their backbones. Cannons were placed up and down the riverfront, and troops from Fort Jackson and Fort St. Philip began pouring into town, all reassuring measures that bolstered everyone's confidence. Positive steps were being taken to protect Vicksburg, and with this realization came fortitude. By the middle of May, most of the people who had previously fled to safety were returning to town, which now seemed to be bursting at the seams. The inconvenience this caused was willingly tolerated, safety being everyone's prime concern.

Brigadier General Martin L. Smith was sent to Vicksburg and placed in command of its defense. He arrived on May 12, the same day that Farragut's Union flotilla reached Natchez and obtained the town's surrender from its mayor. Distressed that Natchez had capitulated without any show of force, the people of Vicksburg were determined that their town would not be handed to the Yankees on a silver platter. They were quick to pledge support to their new commanding general, but few were actually willing to make personal sacrifices. As a result, General Smith's request for Negroes and tools to build up the city's defense was mostly ignored. A home militia was formed, however, and men between the ages of eighteen and fifty were mustered into an ill-matched group that was commanded by Charles Smedes, a grocer. The troops in this militia might be inexperienced, but patriotism was at an all-time high.

Six days after the surrender of Natchez, Farragut's flotilla, under the command of S. Phillips Lee, appeared at Vicksburg and demanded the town's surrender. The high bluffs overlooking the river were lined with curious and anxious onlookers, all waiting to hear what Mayor Lindsay and General Smith's reply would be to Lee's written ultimatum. Most were confident that Vicksburg would not be surrendered, but tension increased with each passing hour, becoming almost unbearable by late afternoon.

Like others, Kitty and Sally mingled with the crowd on the shadeless bluffs and nervously awaited the outcome. Their lacy parasols provided scant protection from the glaring sun, and there was no place to sit other than the ground. Hot and tired, Kitty resentfully eyed the seven odd-looking Union vessels anchored parallel to the bluffs. She had heard them referred to as gunboats and transports loaded with troops, but whatever they were, she failed to see how such small, squat objects could possibly pose any real threat to Vicksburg. She said as much to Sally, who quickly agreed with her.

Shading her eyes with one hand, Kitty strained to see the name of the lead ship. It was the *Oneida*.

"What a peculiar name!" Sally remarked.

"Not half as peculiar as the man responsible for this farce." Kitty snorted. "Farragut's a turncoat, you know. He was born and raised in the South."

Before Sally could reply, a loud shout ripped through the air and was immediately accompanied by a chorus of ear-splitting Rebel yells.

"We're not surrendering! Hallelujah—we're not surrendering!"

Kitty's lively eyes sparkled as she watched a steamer move out from the wharves to deliver the message to the Union gig. Vicksburg might fall to the Union, but not without a fight. They would *never* willingly surrender!

The Union vessels pulled away from the bluffs but anchored just below the city. They remained there for three days, during which time gunfire was exchanged once, though only briefly. After sending a warning to the mayor on the third day and receiving an unacceptable reply, Lee ran out of patience. On the fourth day, intense bombardment commenced.

Again, people fled from town, including many who had staunchly refused to join in the first exodus. Kitty stubbornly refused to budge. Dave and Bret combined forces and tried to make her see reason, but she was resolute. Miles's recovery had been impeded recently by a light case of pneumonia, and he was still not strong enough to be moved. She was not about to leave him behind, nor did she have any intention of running from Farragut's puny flotilla.

Before the week ended, however, she was regretting her decision, particularly when the bombardments repeatedly forced her to prod Daisy, Moses, and Scotty to the cellar. The loud shelling, combined with Daisy's hysterical wailing, set her teeth on edge, and each time, she clutched her whimpering son to her breast, silently cursed the ominous darkness of her dank refuge, and wished she were at Belle Glen.

As May slipped into June, Miles was finally released from the hospital and allowed to come home. His interest in Scotty was minimal, and though Kitty was thoughtful of his every need, his disposition became more disagreeable with each passing day. She was, therefore, surprised and relieved when he allowed her to plan a small, informal party for Scotty's first birthday.

As it turned out, refreshments were limited to cake and chilled cider, since there was a growing shortage of food in town. Planters were becoming more and more unwilling to risk their lives, as well as that of their slaves, by bringing their produce into town. The result was that many items, including butter, salt, and other necessities, were hard to find and extremely expensive. Remembering bygone days, when the smallest occasions had been celebrated with elaborate spreads of tantalizing food, Kitty did the best she could with what she had. She could have wept for joy when Dave and Dede arrived that morning and unexpectedly produced a smoked ham and a large watermelon from Belle Glen. Mammy Lou had also sent a sack of salt, which she had wisely scooped up and saved from the curing barrels in the smokehouse.

The party was scheduled to start at two o'clock, though Phoebe and Sally came over early to assist Kitty with the refreshments. The only other guests were Judge Crane, Cora, and their daughter, Bess. By late afternoon a good dent had been put in the food, and Scotty had blown out the one candle on his birthday cake. Then, with icing all over his cherubic face, he had watched with wide-eyed bemusement while Kitty unwrapped each gift and presented it to him. Afterward, Phoebe, Cora, and the menfolk remained on the porch while Kitty and the others sat beneath a tall oak tree and chatted.

Noticing how pretty Kitty looked in a pink-and-white-striped dress, Dede curiously asked if it were new.

"Heavens, no! Does anyone have new clothes nowadays?" she scoffed.

"I suppose not." Dede sighed. "It's quite a pity we've been reduced to such a sad state of affairs. Why, practically everyone's having to wear faded and worn-out clothes. In fact, even Papa Dave's shirts are getting frayed at the collars, and now he's down to one decent vest, which he saves for special occasions. If this war doesn't end soon, we'll all be in rags! Would you believe Mammy Lou made this dress I'm wearing from a piece of unbleached muslin she found in an old trunk in the attic?" Without waiting for a reply, she quickly continued. "Indeed, she did, and then she dyed it with blueberry juice. That's why it's a little streaked in places. New buttons were simply too costly, so guess what's holding my dress together in back!" she exclaimed, turning around so they could see the long row of oddly shaped buttons.

"Melon seeds!" Sally exclaimed.

"Precisely. Dried and dyed melon seeds," Dede answered smugly, obviously proud of Mammy Lou's ingenuity.

"What a quaint idea," Kitty mused. "I hope you saved some muslin and seeds for me. I'd love for Mammy Lou to make me a new dress the next time I come home."

"Of course we saved some for you. You know Mammy Lou would never forget you for a minute. Neither would I. By the way, when are you coming home? Papa Dave and I were hoping we could persuade you and Miles to spend at least a week or so with us. With you and Tad both gone, the house seems quite empty."

"I wish we could come and spend a week, but I'm afraid we can't just now. Miles has written to his commanding officer in Jackson and requested permission to rejoin his regiment. Until he receives a reply, wild horses couldn't drag him from town."

Minutes later, everyone was huddled around the punch bowl replenishing their cups. Unfortunately, the men were still engrossed in discussing the war. Memphis had fallen to the enemy on June 6 after a disastrous two-hour naval conflict, and this was the present topic of conversation.

"What happened at Memphis could easily happen here," Judge Crane solemnly reminded them. "The Yankees have started digging a canal right across the river. If they succeed in completing it, the Mississippi will be channeled to bypass Vicksburg, thus enabling their northern fleet to get past our guns on the bluffs and meet with Farragut's fleet just below town.''

"I don't think they'll be able to rechannel the river, but I must admit I'll feel a lot easier about the situation once General Van Dorn is appointed commander of our forces in southern Mississippi,'' Dave remarked, extracting a cheroot from his coat pocket.

Kitty realized his hope was shared by most folks in town, for although Van Dorn had often been criticized as an unprincipled rake, no one could possibly fault his courage as an officer. Not only had he attended West Point, he had gained valuable experience as a cavalry officer in Mexico, where he had been wounded by Comanches.

"Well, let's hope he can put a stop to this infernal shelling,'' the judge replied morosely. "It's getting where it's not safe for a body to walk the streets.''

"I quite agree with you," said Phoebe. "I can't imagine why those terrible Yankees started shelling us again yesterday. I almost wish I had left town, especially since the military authorities have clamped down on travel restrictions. Now no one can get out of town unless a pass is obtained, though I'm not sure how I'd leave even if I did get a pass. One can't travel by riverboat anymore, and I understand our train service is quite irregular and somewhat risky.''

"I think you're worrying unnecessarily," Miles commented. "Van Dorn arrived in town this morning, and like Dave, I think he'll be able to deal effectively with the Yankees.''

As if to defy his words, the bombardment, which had ceased earlier, suddenly resounded in the distance, thus bringing the party to an abrupt end. Dave and Dede remained awhile, but once the shelling had subsided somewhat, they departed for Belle Glen. Kitty hated to see them go, particularly since Miles had been unusually attentive to her all day. His thoughtfulness and the curious way he had regarded her this afternoon had made her uneasy.

All along, Miles had refused to accept the fact that he might be impotent, yet he had made no effort to test his virility. As in the past, they slept in separate bedrooms, which no longer appeared to bother him. He had seemed far more interested in rejoining his regiment than in asserting his husbandly rights.

That night, Miles came to her without warning, awakening her at two o'clock in the morning to satisfy his need, which was mental rather than physical. He reeked of whiskey as he bent over her, but before she could sit up, he was fumbling with the tiny buttons at the neck of her nightgown.

Fear clutched her heart, causing her hand to tremble when she reached out and grasped the fingers at her neck.

"Please, Miles, it's late. Besides, the doctor said we should wait a while," she reminded him.

"To hell with the doctor! The old fool says I'm impotent. My God, if I were impotent, do you think I'd desire you?" His angry expression lessened as he saw the fear and revulsion in Kitty's eyes, and a sinister smile twisted his lips. "No, dear wife, I'm afraid I must disappoint you. I assure you I'm as much of a man now as I ever was. Now, get out of that nightgown," he ordered.

Having no choice, Kitty slipped out of her gown, thankful the room was in darkness. It had been so long since he had taken her, and never once during those first months of their marriage had she come close to enjoying a relationship with him. The very idea was abhorrent to her. She felt totally repelled by his very nearness when, after discarding his robe, he lay down beside her and pulled her to him.

When his mouth clamped down on hers in a brutally punishing kiss, she was reviled by his foul breath, but it was when his hands began roughly exploring her body that anger and resentment consumed her. She felt defiled, unclean. Then, as the minutes ticked by and his breathing became audibly louder, a tiny flicker of hope welled up in her. He was desecrating her body, nipping at her soft flesh with his teeth and mauling her with ungentle hands. As yet, however, he had gone no further. Did that mean that, in spite of his words, he was physically unable to consummate the act?

She could feel him straining against her, but after a few minutes he released her with a pathetic whimper. "Help me, Kitty," he rasped. "For God's sake, help me!"

Pity stirred within her as she covered her nakedness with the sheet and sat up. "I can't, Miles," she replied softly. "No one can."

Rage contorted his features, and without warning his hand shot out and struck her across the face.

"Damn you! You'd like that, wouldn't you," he said furiously, standing up and tying his robe with a vicious jerk. "You've always been cold and unfeeling, and now you're trying to convince me that I'm impotent. Well, it won't work."

Kitty saw the manical gleam in his eyes as he turned to leave, and she was suddenly assailed with concern. "What are you going to do?"

For a moment he glared antagonistically at her, clenching and unclenching his fists. Then his hands stilled, and his lips twisted into a smile.

"I'll tell you what I'm going to do. I'm going to Mollie's Bordello and find myself a woman—a *real* woman who can satisfy me as you never could."

Kitty said nothing as he slammed out of the room. Too paralyzed to move, she sat trembling in the middle of the large bed and listened to his angry movements in the next room. Finally, she heard him going downstairs. He was incapable of reasoning, she realized, and she had no intention of trying to stop him from leaving the house. She no longer cared what he did or where he went.

A loud crash sounded from below, followed by the sound of shattering glass. Scooting from her bed, Kitty pulled on a dressing gown and ran to the door. Fear gnawed at her heart while she listened to him moving about in the front parlor. It was several minutes before he slammed out the front door, and with an audible sigh, she relaxed. Still, her fingers shook as she removed a lamp from its wall bracket beside the door, lit it, then cautiously made her way downstairs. Glancing in the parlor, she saw that a small table had been overturned, and the large mirror above the fireplace was completely shattered.

Anger washed over her, and with a determined lift of her chin, she walked over to the front door and bolted it. Miles would not get back into the house tonight, she thought with satisfaction. Tomorrow, she would instruct Daisy to pack their things, and they would go home.

Once at Belle Glen, she would be free of Miles, and with Dave's help she could plan what action to take. Divorce would be scandalous, particularly since Miles was recovering from a serious wound that had been inflicted in battle. No, divorce was out of the question for the present, but not indefinitely. In the meantime, she would just have to settle for a quiet and, hopefully, unnoticeable separation. If luck was with her, she could leave him a note and be gone before he returned home.

She seriously doubted he would follow her to Belle Glen. He was too intent on waiting for a reply from his commanding officer in Jackson, hoping to be reassigned to his regiment. She certainly hoped he would succeed.

Her mind was occupied with planning her departure as she walked into the dining room, picked up a decanter of elderberry wine from the sideboard, and poured a small amount into a glass. Seating herself at the dining table, she slowly sipped the dark red liquid, hoping it would have a calming effect on her nerves. She had not been seated long when a series of loud explosions ripped through the silence.

"Damn those Yankees, they're at it again," she muttered, jumping to her feet and running to the hall.

Her first thought was of Scotty. Luckily, Daisy had been sleeping on a cot in his nursery ever since the boy had been old enough to move from her own bedroom. Despite this fact, she now heard him screaming fearfully and rushed toward the stairs. Daisy was already at the top of the landing, clutching the howling infant to her breast.

"Oh, Lawd, Miz Kitty, dem Yankees mean biz'ness dis time. We's gwine tuh be kilt fo' sho'!" she wailed, scurrying downstairs.

"For heaven's sake, stop that caterwauling," Kitty snapped.

It was not until the girl quieted that she heard someone pounding on the back door and remembered Daisy's boy, Moses, who slept in a room over the stables. With a muttered oath, she rushed down the hall, unbolted the door, and jerked the wide-eyed boy inside.

"Ah sho' wuz scairt out dere, Miz Kitty. De whole sky's dun lit up wid fire. Whut we gwine tuh do?" the frightened boy whined above the horrendous din.

A feeling of dismay swept over Kitty as she glanced from Moses to Daisy and Scotty. For once, she was seized with uncertainty. The shelling was heavier and nearer than it ever had been before, but did that mean the Yankees had succeeded in running the town's batteries? If so, it might be possible for the enemy's shells to reach as far as her house. Would they be safe in the cellar? She seriously doubted it. If the house received a direct hit, they could be buried alive down there!

Another shell exploded, this time much closer. Daisy and Moses joined Scotty's howling, making it even more difficult for her to think.

"Moses, light another lantern. We're going to the cellar. We'll be safe down there," she said with false bravado. She could not give in to fear, not when they were relying on her for sound judgment and protection. How on earth was she going to protect them, though, when she could not even protect herself? A loud knock suddenly sounded at the front door.

"Gawd in heb'en, hit's de Yankees, Miz Kitty—dey's heah!" Daisy screamed hysterically.

"Don't be a goose, Daisy. If the Yankees had landed, they couldn't be shelling us from the boats. Now, hush, and get a grip on yourself!" Kitty commanded as she dashed by the trembling trio and headed for the front door. Fumbling with the bolt, she unlocked the door and flung it open, halfway expecting to find Miles. The breath caught in her throat when she saw who it was.

"Oh, Bret, thank goodness you're here!" she cried, flinging herself into his arms.

A tender smile tugged at his lips as he held her thus for a moment, then gently put her from him.

"Miss Phoebe and her servants have gone to the cave she had excavated. She thinks you should join her—and so do I," he said.

Kitty had seen some of the caves that had recently been hollowed out in the hills a block or so behind Cherry Street. A few had been large caverns, but most of the crude dwellings were little more than small holes in the hillside—muddy, damp, and totally uninviting, certainly not her idea of refuge. The shelling sounded ominously near, but she thought of the alternative and, deciding to take her chances in the cellar, shook her head.

"We can't go out there!" she exclaimed. "We'd be blasted to bits."

"Don't be a fool, Kitty. If a shell hits this house, you'll all be buried alive."

"Bret, I will not spend the night in a dark hole with all sorts of ungodly creatures crawling over me."

His eyes glinted angrily as his hands clamped down on her shoulders. "Now, you listen to me. I'm taking Scott to that cave, and you, dammit, are coming with me. Do I make myself clear?"

A mortar exploded directly in front of the house, cutting short any protest she might have made. Defiance gave way to fear, and she nodded her head.

"All right, but I can't go dressed like this," she agreed sullenly, glancing down at her dressing gown.

"This is no time to be modest. We're not going to a damn tea party." Turning to Daisy, who was clutching his son, he said: "Let's get a move on. Daisy, can you manage Scott?"

"Yassuh, but we ain' gwine out dere, is we?"

"We're going to have to. You and Moses follow right behind us. Do as I do, and above all, stay close to us."

Frightened out of her wits, Daisy muttered, "Mist' Bret, Ah's gwine tuh stick so close tuh you, dey ain't even gwine tuh be room for yo' shadow!''

Bret smiled slightly at the worried girl, then turned his attention back to Kitty. "Ready?"

She nodded, inwardly thankful for the steel grip he had on her arm.

The flight to the cave proved to be a nightmare she would long remember. The streets were filled with frantic men, women, and children, black and white, all running helter-skelter for safety. Hysterical screams intermingled with the eerie, high-pitched whines of shells that zipped constantly overhead, their fiery trails igniting the darkness only seconds before ending in earth-shattering explosions. Kitty's mouth dropped open in amazement when a man clad in his underwear ran past, but before she could say anything, Bret was urging her on at a faster pace. Winded and with a stitch in her side, she was almost relieved when Bret unceremoniously shoved her to the ground as a shell whistled dangerously near and exploded directly in front of them.

"Those damn parrot shells zip by you before you can hear them," he said. "By the time you do, it's almost too late. Remember that sound, Kitty. The next time you hear it, drop to the ground and pray it's well ahead of you."

Kitty jumped as a mortar found its mark at a frame house just to their right. Looking around, she saw that the servants and Scotty were right beside them—so close, in fact, that Bret almost collided with Daisy when he stood up. Grabbing Kitty's arm, he jerked her to her feet and prodded her on.

They were stopped in their tracks on several other occasions, when shells of every size and description zoomed over them, causing Daisy to wail louder each time. Scotty whimpered occasionally but did not actually cry. His attention was riveted on the colorful display of fireworks, which, under safer circumstances, would have been a spectacle to behold.

They sped on, Kitty's breath coming in ragged gasps as she strove to keep abreast of Bret. Another shell exploded, and a woman's agonized scream pierced the air. Shaken, Kitty wondered briefly if the woman had been hit or merely frightened. On and on they ran, until she felt that her legs would not carry her another step. A man darted past them, tears streaming down his cheeks as he clutched a limp and bleeding child to his chest. The sight unnerved her, and she cried aloud. In the next instant she felt Bret's arm around her waist, and he paused to let her catch her breath.

"Hush, Kitten. Don't cry, don't think—just keep going. It's not much farther now. Just over there." He pointed.

"All right," she quavered, her eyes focusing on the small hole in the hillside that offered some measure of safety. So near, yet so far . . .

It seemed an eternity before they reached the opening. Bret motioned for Daisy, Scott, and Moses to enter first, then turned to Kitty, who had stopped uncertainly before the cave. Slowly, she shook her head and stepped back.

"Bret, I can't go in there!" she declared.

"Well, you sure as hell can't stay out here!" Without wasting words, he pushed her forward, causing her to sprawl on her hands and knees just inside the entrance.

For a second Kitty was too dumbfounded to speak, until Bret sat down beside her and she heard soft laughter rumbling in his throat.

"And just what, may I ask, is so funny?" she sputtered furiously.

"You." He grinned. "Everybody in town is running like hell for cover, but you stand there like a ninny and argue about going into a cave. You're probably the only person in Vicksburg who's more afraid of the dark than of the Yankees!"

"I'm not afraid of the dark," she denied, "just what's in the dark! By the way, where's Aunt Phoebe? I thought you said she would meet us here."

"That was my understanding, but knowing Miss Phoebe, I imagine she opted for the Drummond sisters' cave. It's quite a bit closer to her house," he answered, brushing a long strand of hair from her face.

A shell exploded nearby, lighting up the entrance to the cave with such brilliance that Kitty's features were clearly revealed as she clung to Bret for protection. Farther back in the cave and well away from the entrance, Daisy squealed, but Scotty merely looked at the bright spectacle with bemusement, his eyelids growing heavier by the minute.

Regaining her composure, Kitty started to pull away from Bret, but his arm tightened around her waist. Gently, he fingered her cheek where Miles had struck earlier that night.

"What happened to your face?"

"I . . . I must have bruised it when you shoved me down out there."

"Don't lie to me. Miles hit you, didn't he? Why?"

"That's my business, not yours," she replied, looking away from him.

"When it concerns you, it *is* my business. Now, what happened? Tell me, or I swear I'll beat it out of Miles if I have to."

She was too tired to pretend, much less argue. With a resigned sigh, she said: "Miles wanted me tonight, but . . . but he couldn't. When nothing happened, he blamed me."

Bret said nothing but tenderly stroked her cheek, his touch more comforting than words. Hate, the desire to kill, was slowly eating away at him, and when Kitty finally looked up at him, she trembled at the unleashed fury in his face.

"Bret, don't do anything to him," she implored. "You mustn't. It would cause a scandal, and people might suspect Scotty is . . ."

"My son," he said with a trace of abruptness. His hold on her relaxed somewhat, but she did not attempt to move out of his embrace. "All right, I'll keep my hands off Miles for the time being. But I'm taking you and Scott to Belle Glen tomorrow. He won't stop trying to prove his manhood, and each time he fails, you'll be the one to suffer. That, by heaven, I won't allow!"

Feeling her shiver, he tightened his arms protectively around her. With a grim smile he said, "Have a valise packed for you and the boy, and be ready to leave at noon. Hopefully the Yankees will have pulled back by then, and it will be safe to travel."

Kitty murmured her agreement, relieved that he was taking matters into his own hands. A feeling of drowsiness swept over her, and she had to blink several times to keep awake. The shelling was still intense, with trails of color zigzagging across the black sky, always accompanied by menacing whines before the inevitable explosions rocked the earth.

Fire dotted the countryside wherever a missile of death had succeeded in hitting its unseen target. Kitty marveled that the entire town was not ablaze. Another explosion occurred directly above them, causing the ground to tremble so violently that particles of dirt showered down on their heads. There was no sound from the back of the cave, and Kitty correctly surmised that Scotty and the servants had finally succumbed to sleep. With a weary, contented sigh, she snuggled closer to Bret and closed her eyes. Minutes later she, too, was asleep.

Chapter 13

Most of Farragut's fleet succeeded in passing the town's batteries and steaming upriver shortly after dawn, thus proving it was not impossible for Union vessels to get past Vicksburg. Dazed and weary citizens crawled from their holes in the hills and returned to their homes. Despite the heavy shelling, casualties were few and property damage was surprisingly light.

Selina's house, however, was all but demolished. After seeing Kitty and Scott safely home, Bret ran into Sally Collins, who told him about Selina's misfortune. Realizing Selina could probably use his help, Bret asked Sally to stop by Kitty's and tell her he would have to postpone taking her to Belle Glen until that afternoon.

Kitty was already in the process of packing when Sally arrived with Bret's message and told her about Selina's house. Vexed at first that Bret would put Selina's welfare before her own, she grew calmer when Sally offhandedly remarked that Selina was catching the first train to Hattiesburg and apparently had no intention of returning—ever.

Soon after Sally's departure, Miles returned home and informed her he had finally received his orders. He was to report to his commanding officer in Jackson the next day, which meant he would have to leave immediately. Past differences were forgotten as Kitty followed him upstairs and helped him pack. He was obviously excited about rejoining his regiment, and she was relieved to see him go. The fact that he would eventually be coming home and she would again be faced with marital problems stemming from his impotency was something she pushed to the back of her mind. For the present, it was enough that he was leaving.

By the time Bret arrived that afternoon, she had changed her mind about going to Belle Glen. With Miles away, she was anxious to enjoy her new freedom, and the hustle and bustle of town seemed far more appealing than the quiet solitude of Belle Glen. Bret's argument that the town would be shelled again fell upon deaf ears. Her courage had returned, and in the light of day the Yankees did not appear nearly so menacing. Exasperated, Bret told her in no uncertain terms what she could do the next time there was a bombardment, then stormed out of the house.

Heavy shelling did continue for two more days before slackening somewhat, but Farragut's flotilla was always within sight of the town's bluffs. Their presence was definitely wreaking havoc on the community and causing numerous inconveniences. For safety, the railroad terminal, telegraph station, and post office had been relocated just outside the city. Even regular publication of the town's leading newspaper, *The Whig*, had been suspended, though Marmaduke Shannon, the editor, somehow managed to get copies printed at irregular intervals.

Since Vicksburg had become so overpopulated, food and water were growing scarce indeed. The weather was hot and dry, tempers were short, and there was an increasing resentment toward the soldiers who had been transported into town as a protective measure. The fact that some of them occasionally stripped a civilian's fruit orchard or raided a chicken coop hardly endeared the military to the citizens.

The Fourth of July arrived, but again there would be no celebration. Determined not to give in to melancholia, Kitty rose that morning, shrugged into a faded blue calico dress, and went downstairs. She had just plopped a wide-brimmed hat on her head when Daisy met her in the hall.

"Miz Kitty, you ain' gwine outside dressed lak dat, is you?" she asked with a disapproving frown.

"Good Lord in heaven, what difference does it make! I'm not going to a ball, you ninny, and I can hardly be expected to manage hoop and petticoats if I'm going to be picking figs and peaches this morning. I'd die of heat stroke if I tried."

"You don' need tuh be pickin' no figs an' peaches. Moses an' me kin do dat," Daisy asserted.

"No, I am. You and Moses are going to pick butter beans, okra, and whatever else is available in the garden. If we don't, there may be nothing left to pick by the end of the week. Why, only yesterday Ginny Hartz told me that all of her crabapple trees were plucked bare the other night, and last week Cora Crane's chicken coop was robbed. Not a chicken left, mind you. If this war lasts much longer, our own soldiers will have eaten us all out of house and home! Someone was meddling in our backyard last night. When I leaned out the window and threatened to shoot, he ran off. I'm not about to wait for a return visit, so we'll just pick everything we can today."

"But, Miz Kitty, hit jest ain' rat fo' you tuh go outside lak dat, mech less pick peaches 'n' figs lak some field hand. Hit ain' ladylak!" Daisy argued as she followed Kitty to the back porch.

"Ladylike be damned!" Kitty exploded. "We may be at war, but I, for one, do not intend for me or mine to go hungry. Now, quit fussin' and go fetch Moses to help you with the pickin'. I want to have some of those butter beans for dinner. I've asked Miss Cora to eat with us, since she's offered to help me make fig and peach preserves this afternoon."

"Uh-uh-uh, paradin' 'round widout her hoop an' petticoats, jes' lak white trash!" Daisy mumbled unhappily as she scuttled off.

Kitty merely frowned and headed briskly for the fig tree. So what if her skirts did cling to her legs and shamefully mold the outline of her figure? It occurred to her there were many things she was having to do now that at one time she would not have considered proper.

The South had better win or we'll all end up paupers, she thought an hour later, glancing over to where Scotty was playing in the dirt at Daisy's feet. But what if we don't win? If we lose, what in heaven's name will become of us? The possibility was too horrible even to contemplate.

"Damn the Yankees," she muttered, "coming down here and trying to run our business like a bunch of do-gooders! Hmph, they're all just a passel of low-down busybodies bent on making mischief."

By now, the lower branches had been stripped of figs. Hitching up her skirts, Kitty began climbing the tree in a determined effort to pick the ripe fruit from some higher branches. She had just succeeded in perching herself on a sturdy limb and had picked a few figs when Sally bounded through the back gate. Amusement twinkled in her large brown eyes as she stood almost directly beneath Kitty.

"What on earth are you doing up there?"

Not in the best of moods, Kitty made no attempt to be cheerful. "Picking figs, obviously. Good grief, you didn't see me up here from the street, did you?" she asked worriedly, carefully climbing down from her perch.

"No, your indecent exposure is hidden from view, so your secret is safe." Sally laughed, adding, "In fact, if I hadn't heard Scotty crying just now, I wouldn't have thought to look back here. I knocked on the front door but had just about decided no one was home."

Lost in her own thoughts, Kitty had not been aware of Scotty's fretfulness. Frowning, she took the whimpering child from Daisy.

"Shhh—it's all right, now. Mommy's got you, angel," she crooned, hugging the chubby infant to her and brushing the damp curls from his forehead while swaying back and forth.

The whimpering gradually subsided, and Kitty handed him back to Daisy. "He feels awfully hot to me," she murmured.

"Most lakly cuttin' another tooth, Miz Kitty," Daisy suggested.

"Maybe so," Kitty replied uncertainly, not totally convinced. Brushing aside her unease, she turned to Moses. "Take those butter beans up to the house for your mother, Moses, and shell 'em. Daisy, try to get Scotty down for a nap before you start on dinner."

The girl nodded and, still crooning to the fretful boy in her arms, followed Moses across the backyard and into the house. Kitty watched until they disappeared from view, then turned back to Sally, who was grinning broadly.

"And what, may I ask, is so amusing?" Kitty asked.

"You!" Sally giggled. "I'm afraid I'll never get used to your being a mother. Why, when we were growing up, you didn't like to play with dolls, much less babies."

"It's different when the baby is your own," Kitty replied as she sat down on a wooden bench beneath a shady oak tree.

"Yes, I guess it is," Sally replied, seating herself beside Kitty. "Oh, by the way, you should have heard the speech General Van Dorn gave in front of the courthouse this morning. Do you know what he had the nerve to do? He actually declared martial law!"

"What does that mean?"

"It means that he and his soldiers will be running the town, and we'll have to do whatever they tell us to do. A lot of tempers were riled, I can tell you, even though some of what he said made sense."

"Such as?"

"Such as saying that anyone who refuses to accept Confederate money or charges outrageous prices for necessities will be fined, imprisoned, or have their property confiscated. Maybe all three. You should have seen Papa's face." Sally chuckled. "I declare, I thought he was going to have an apoplectic fit!"

"Serves him right. One minute he's all for the cause, and the next he won't even accept Confederate money." Seeing Sally's distressed look, Kitty remembered her manners and apologized for speaking so bluntly. "Did anything else interesting happen this morning?" she asked, changing the subject.

"Indeed it did." Sally grinned, her distress forgotten. "I'll say this much for the general—he may be lacking in diplomacy, but he certainly has a lot of brass. You'll never guess what he suggested—*and* in mixed company, I might add!"

"Well, don't keep me in suspense, Sally. What on earth did he suggest?"

"Without batting an eye, he asked—no, *ordered* that every household save the contents of their"—Sally barely managed to get out the next words between spasms of giggles—"their chamber pots, and to donate such contents to the cause each morning. He said orderlies would come by to collect all such donations," she finished with a bubble of laughter.

Kitty's eyes widened in astonishment. "Whatever for?" she gasped.

Lowering her voice, Sally whispered, "The urine is to be used for making shells. It has nitrogen, or something like that, which goes into ammunition."

"Good Lord in heaven! Surely we're not so hard up that we have to resort to collecting chamber pots to make ammunition!" Kitty exclaimed.

"Apparently we are, or if we aren't, General Van Dorn thinks there may come a time when we might be. It's a shame we don't have the factories that the North does. We have so few down here, and I guess it's getting more and more difficult to supply those with all that's needed, thanks to the blockade."

"Damn those blue-bellies! How I wish I were a man! If I were, I wouldn't be sitting here now."

For a moment both girls were silent, then Kitty gave a soft laugh.

"I wish I had been there this morning, just to have seen the shocked look on everyone's faces. I bet there was quite a scene."

"Oh, my, yes. Ladies were swooning all over the place. I do believe Miss Phoebe would have fainted dead away had it not been for Miss Flora. She told her, 'Don't you dare have a fit of the vapors! If the general says he needs chamber pots for the cause, then chamber pots he'll get!' "

"Well, at least that's one thing there'll never be a shortage of," Kitty remarked.

"True," her friend agreed, then sobered. "I only wish David Shelton hadn't been standing beside me at the time. I swear he blushed all the way down to his toes! I think he would have offered to take me home if he hadn't been so embarrassed."

"Oh, so you're interested in David now," Kitty teased.

"Well, he is awfully nice," Sally admitted, "and he seems to be rather fond of me. I'm glad he's home on furlough." Having revealed more than she intended, she stood up to leave.

As they walked to the gate Sally's embarrassment abated, and she asked Kitty to supper that evening. Kitty declined, explaining that she had already accepted an invitation from Phoebe.

"Since we aren't celebrating the Fourth, Aunt Phoebe is having a small supper party in remembrance of the cause."

"I'll bet she's invited Miss Flora and Miss Dolly, too."

"Naturally, and, of course, Doc Blanks and Miss Mattie. I wish I didn't have to go." Kitty sighed. "I'll be the only young person there."

"Maybe not. Since Mr. O'Rourke boards with Miss Phoebe, don't you imagine she's invited him, too?"

"I have no idea," Kitty replied, though she secretly hoped so. She had not seen Bret since their disagreement over her remaining in town, and though she had resolved to put him from her mind, she had missed him these past few days.

Hours later she found herself seated next to Bret at Phoebe's long oval table in the dining room. The only one absent was Doc Blanks, who had been forestalled by a premature delivery. This had not prevented Mattie from coming, however, and as usual she was filling everyone in on the latest gossip. It was a relief when Flora changed the subject by asking Bret if he had any suggestions as to how the Ole Miss Club, a patriotic organization, could raise funds for the Confederacy.

"Well, there is one possibility that comes to mind, though I'm not sure you ladies would welcome such a suggestion."

"At this point, Mr. O'Rourke, I assure you we would welcome almost any suggestion. In a few months, winter will be upon us. Our soldiers in the North will be forced to endure a much colder climate than they're accustomed to, and I'm afraid many of them will be inadequately attired for such freezing temperatures. Sturdy boots, warm clothing, and blankets will be needed, but such necessities are costly. The purpose of our club is to see that such necessities are provided. As president, I speak for all of us when I say we are willing to go to most any lengths to further the cause. So, if you have a suggestion, please be good enough to state it," Flora commanded briskly.

"Very well." Pushing back his chair, he rose and looked slowly around the table, thus obtaining everyone's attention. "I suggest you have a keno party," he told them, referring to a popular game that resembled bingo. "You could hold it at one of the churches or, better still, the ballroom at the Washington Hotel. I believe it'd draw a big crowd, both citizens and soldiers, and if properly organized, it could bring in a lot of money."

"In case you haven't heard, there happens to be a shortage of money nowadays," Mattie reminded him. "Particularly hard cash. Besides, what you're suggesting happens to be gambling."

"Yes, but for prizes rather than money," Bret answered with a sobriety that belied his concealed amusement.

"What prizes?" Dolly asked with growing excitement.

"Cakes, pies, canned goods, or anything else the ladies in your club would be able to contribute."

Simultaneously, all heads turned toward Flora for her reaction.

"The idea certainly has merit," she admitted cautiously, "but I'm afraid many people could not afford to come. As Mattie pointed out, money is rather tight right now."

"True, but the admission price need not be limited to money alone. Other types of donations could be made, such as blankets, silverware, and jewelry," he pointed out.

"Well, I, for one, think it's a splendid idea," Phoebe asserted.

Dolly's rotund face fairly beamed. "Oh, so do I! Don't you agree, Flora?" she asked hopefully.

"I still don't like it," Mattie intervened.

"Then, perhaps you can offer a better suggestion," Flora returned, a tight smile playing on her thin lips as she looked at Bret. "You've certainly given us food for thought, Mr. O'Rourke. Our club meets this Thursday. At that time, we'll discuss your proposal and vote on it. Since you're staying with Phoebe, she can inform you of our decision."

A loud knock sounded at the side door, which was quickly opened by Phoebe's maid, Ella. Minutes later the young girl scurried into the room, a worried look on her face.

" 'Scuse me, Miz Phoebe, but Moses is at de do'r, wantin' tuh see Miz Kitty. He sez de baby dun tuk sick an' is mighty hot, lak he got a high fever."

Kitty jumped to her feet, but before she could rush to the side door, Bret intervened.

"Get your shawl, Kitty, and I'll walk you home," he ordered before turning to address Ella. "Tell Moses to find Dr. Johnson and bring him to the house."

The girl nodded and rushed out of the room just as Kitty reappeared with her shawl. The ladies expressed their concern, each voicing an opinion as to what might be causing Scotty's fever and each offering a remedy, though none of this penetrated Kitty's befuddled mind. Thankful for Bret's presence, she allowed him to whisk her from the room.

The walk to her house was made in silence, with Kitty almost having to run to keep up with Bret's long strides. A deep frown marred his handsome features, indicating the extent of his concern, but Kitty was too distraught to notice this until later, when the two of them bent over the whimpering child's crib. Placing her hand on Scotty's forehead, she cast Bret a worried look.

"He's so hot," she commented.

"Daisy, go down to the cistern and get a basin of cold water," Bret commanded, scooping the boy up in his arms and brushing the dark curls from his fevered brow.

Though Kitty rocked her son while Bret continuously placed cold compresses on his forehead, nothing seemed to help. Kitty's eyes brightened with relief when Moses returned with the doctor. After a brief examination, he assured them that Scotty was suffering from no more than a flare-up with his tonsils and extracted a brown bottle from his bag. After pouring a small amount of medicine into a spoon, he gently forced it between the boy's lips, then instructed Daisy to do the same every four hours.

"The medicine will soothe his throat and help him to rest easier. There's a little laudanum in it, so don't be alarmed if he sleeps a lot. I'll check on him again tomorrow night," he said, watching Daisy bathe Scotty with cool water as he had instructed. He motioned for Kitty and Bret to follow him out to the hall and, closing the bedroom door quietly, turned to them with a smile.

"His fever is beginning to break and he'll soon be asleep. There's nothing you can do for him that Daisy can't do as well, Miss Kitty, so I suggest you get some rest. You look as if you need it."

Kitty nodded and thanked him for coming. Relieved, she watched from the upstairs landing while Bret escorted the doctor to the front door and bid him good night.

"It was good of Mark to come," she said once Bret had returned to her.

"Yes, it was. He's right, you know. You do need to get some rest."

Touched by his remark, and especially by his gentleness with Scotty earlier, Kitty felt more relaxed with him than she had for some time. Mutual concern over their son's illness had drawn them closer, and if Bret still harbored a grudge because she had concealed the fact that Scotty was his son, Kitty saw no evidence of it now.

Happiness washed over her as his arm encircled her waist and he guided her down the hall to her room. Neither spoke, but as he released her and opened the bedroom door, she found herself wishing he would stay with her, make love to her as he had that one and only time—the night their son had been conceived.

Shaken by her adulterous thoughts and realizing her sudden vulnerability, Kitty stepped past him into her room, then turned to bid him a hasty good night. The words died on her lips, however, as their eyes met and something indefinable was ignited between them, an intense yearning that had long been suppressed and now threatened to erupt.

It was Bret who finally moved, stepping over the threshold and closing the door behind him. Mere inches separated them, yet he made no attempt to touch her, silently willing her to come to him.

"No, Bret, I can't," she whispered. "I won't commit adultery."

"You did that when you married Miles," he answered softly. "You've never belonged to anyone but me, Kitty. You never will."

In her heart, she knew it was true. She had always belonged to him, even as a child. There had never been anyone else for her.

There never would be. As if in a dream, she felt a magnetic force beckoning to her, drawing her to him, until, finally, his powerful arms enfolded her, pulling her to his hard-muscled body. A shaft of moonlight dispelled the darkness, revealing his hungering torment as he lowered his head until their lips were almost touching.

"God knows I've tried to forget you, but I can't—no more than I can stop breathing. Tell me you want me, Kitty. Say it!" he commanded passionately.

"Yes, I want you," she whispered, "with all my heart—"

With a low groan, Bret savagely took possession of her quivering lips as her arms wound around his neck. Lifting her effortlessly, he strode across the room and lowered her to the bed, his passion mounting while he removed first her clothing, then his own. He was racked with intense desire, by a raging need that was difficult to control as he lay down beside her and took her into his arms.

The unbidden remembrance of Miles's brutal lovemaking flashed in Kitty's mind, causing her to stiffen—but only briefly. As if sensing her hesitation, Bret instantly forced aside his own urgency and became gentle with her. He was determined not to hurt her, not to hurry, but to savor the sweet ecstasy of these precious moments for as long as possible.

Her hair, freed now of its confining net, splayed over her shoulders, partially concealing the perfection of her breasts. Brushing aside the dark tresses, he trailed his fingers over the firm mounds, stroking the rosy tips before sliding down to her flat stomach, then lower.

His touch was like fire, searing Kitty's sensitive flesh while, at the same time, his lips moved sensually over her face, feathering provocative kisses on her eyelids, ears, and the small hollow at the base of her throat. Her breathing became ragged as his hands and lips continued their tantalizing onslaught, ravaging her senses until she could bear no more. Pressing closer to him, she moaned with impatience, and it was then that he covered her trembling body with his own, his mouth slanting down on her parted lips while his hands moved to her hips, holding them firmly as his knee parted her thighs. Instinctively she arched toward him, her arms tightening around his neck when she felt the first deep thrust.

He took her slowly at first, his rhythmic movements quickening when her slender hips began undulating beneath him. They had been deprived of each other for so long, there was no holding back now.

Their need was insatiable, consuming them with a fiery passion that steadily intensified, then erupted, spiraling them into a rapturous paradise.

Their passion spent, they lay exhausted in each other's arms, reveling in the ecstasy they had just shared. It was Bret who finally broke the silence.

"You're not having any regrets, are you?" he asked, nuzzling her cheek.

"No," she whispered. "I only wish tonight would never end—that it could always be like this."

"Someday it will be, I promise you."

"How can it be as long as I'm married to Miles?"

Propping himself on one elbow, Bret looked down at her and, seeing her forlorn expression, sought to comfort her by offering the only solution he could.

"When the war is over, you can divorce him. Then, after a decent interval, we'll be married."

"But that may not be for a long time, and . . . and I don't want to wait. I don't think I can bear being away from you."

"Don't you think I feel the same? My God, Kitty, every time I see you, it's all I can do to keep my hands off you," he groaned. "I want you more than life itself, but not if it means dragging your name through the mud or jeopardizing our son's future."

"In other words, we can't keep taking chances like this, can we?"

"No, my darling, we can't. We can't risk your getting pregnant, especially not with Miles out of town. There'd be no way to explain it."

Replete with happiness, Kitty had not given any thought to this possibility. Now that she did, a worried frown creased her forehead.

"But what if I did get pregnant tonight?"

"I can't believe fate would be so unkind twice," he answered somberly, "but if you are, I'll think of something. Right now, all I want to do is hold you in my arms and forget about tomorrow. Tonight is all that matters."

Placing her hands on either side of his rugged face, Kitty forced a smile to her tremulous lips.

"Yes, tonight *is* all that matters. It's all we have for now. So, hold me, Bret. Love me . . ."

Chapter 14

All firing ceased a week later, giving the people of Vicksburg a brief respite from bombardment that lasted four blissful days. Farragut's fleet still hovered near town, but it was rumored that a newly constructed Confederate boat, the *Arkansas*, was steaming down the Yazoo River toward Vicksburg, coming to its defense. With the rumor came renewed hope for the townspeople.

On the morning of July 15, the rumor was confirmed. Despite leaky boilers, the motley ram left the Yazoo River and steamed into the Mississippi River, some twelve miles north of town. Farragut's fleet was ready and waiting, with more than thirty Union vessels positioned between the *Arkansas* and Vicksburg's batteries.

When the first sounds of distant shelling wafted over town, Kitty was in Henry Collins's general store, arguing over the price of a pound of butter.

"Three dollars! Why, I never heard of anything so outrageous!" she sputtered angrily.

"Now, Miss Kitty, just simmer down. If you can pay in gold or silver, it'll only cost you one fifty," Henry suggested in a placating voice.

"But I can't, and neither can most other folks, as you well know. You're robbing people blind, but you're not going to get away with it much longer. When I leave here, I'm going straight to General Van Dorn. I'm going to tell him you're taking advantage of your customers. You know what he said would happen to merchants who refused to accept Confederate money," she reminded him.

Henry nervously mopped his brow. "Hold on, now. I'm not

refusing to accept Confederate money. I'm just offering a fifty percent discount to those who can pay in gold or silver, like the sign up there says," he replied.

"It's the same thing, and I'm going to make sure the general knows about it."

"Look, I'm breakin' no laws, not so long's I accept Confederate money. Now I'll accept it, but it's gonna cost you more if I do. Shoot, the Confederate dollar's gone down so much, it's hardly worth the paper it's printed on. Sorry, Miss Kitty, but that's how it is. Them that has, gits."

Kitty sighed in exasperation. "Very well, Mr. Collins, let's stop beating around the bush. I need butter, and you have it to sell. What will you give me for the cameo I'm wearing?"

"Well . . . I reckon I could give you five dollars for it," he drawled with false reluctance, eyeing the exquisite pin at her collar.

"Five dollars!" she gasped indignantly. "Why, it's worth at least thirty."

"Tell you what, Miss Kitty, I'll up it to ten—just to be fair."

"Hmph! You, Mr. Collins, don't know the meaning of the word. I don't doubt you'd take a ticket to Hades if you could get it for half price!"

She would have vented her wrath further but was distracted by the distant sound of shelling to the north of town. Henry also heard the loud reports and, in the next instant, was quickly making his way around the counter. As he and Kitty simultaneously squeezed through the front door, they saw people scurrying toward the river.

"God Almighty, it must be the *Arkansas*," Henry shouted.

Her anger forgotten, Kitty clutched his arm. "Oh, I hope so," she exclaimed. "How I'd love to see those Yankees blasted out of the water!"

"Well, we can't see it from here. Come on, let's get down there," Henry replied, taking hold of her wrist.

Together, they ran toward the bluff situated nearest the wharves. The hilltops were already lined with onlookers trying to get a glimpse of the battle, which was still too far to be distinguishable. After a while the firing abated, and as the minutes ticked by, the townspeople held their breath while awaiting the outcome. Finally, the chocolate-colored *Arkansas* rounded the bend, limping toward Vicksburg with wheezing engines and leaky boilers. It was a far cry from the gallant vessel they had envisioned. For seconds a blanket of awed silence spread over the crowd, soon dispersed by a chorus of Rebel yells and joyous cheering.

By the time the odd-looking ram had docked, pandemonium had erupted. The throng rushed toward the wharf to get a closer look at the *Arkansas*, and everyone applauded the brave men who, despite unbelievable odds, had succeeded in running the Union gauntlet. Henry tried to discourage Kitty from going down to the dock, but to no avail. Following him closely, she scampered toward the docking vessel, pushing and shoving people aside until she stood beside the gangplank.

As she eagerly scanned the low deck that was almost level with the water, her eyes widened with horror. Blood was everywhere; the entire deck spattered with dismembered legs, arms, entrails, and brains. She swayed dizzily when she spotted the headless trunk of what had once been a man, and as nausea welled up inside her, she was only dimly aware that Henry was leading her away from the tragic scene.

Long after she had returned home, the stench of blood and death remained in her nostrils, the ungodly sight aboard the *Arkansas* firmly etched in her mind. Only ten men had been killed aboard the Confederate ram, and another fifteen had been seriously injured. To Kitty, however, it seemed like the most horrendous battle ever fought, and her hatred for the Yankees increased.

Still, the *Arkansas* had managed to get through Farragut's fleet and was temporarily anchored beneath the town's bluffs, offering some protection against the Union ships.

A week passed by uneventfully; then, on the morning of the twenty-second, three Union vessels made one last attack on the *Arkansas* and were repulsed. Two days later another bombardment erupted, with shelling so fierce that people were forced to flee to basements and caves for shelter.

It was to be the last attack on Vicksburg for several months. Union forces had been sadly reduced by malaria, and the canal they had dug on the Louisiana banks, hoping Federal boats could safely bypass Vicksburg, had proved to be a dismal failure. During the hot summer months, the river had fallen to such an extent that now there was only a trickle of water running through the canal. Deciding that Vicksburg could not be taken by the navy alone, Farragut pulled his fleet away from town. Some of the vessels, however, moved only to the mouth of the Yazoo River. After sixty-one days of almost

continuous bombardment, Vicksburg was safe—at least, for the time
being.

When it became apparent that the Yankees would not be returning
any time soon, living returned to normal in Vicksburg. The Ole Miss
Club voted to have a keno party at the Washington Hotel on the last
day of August, and for weeks the town stirred with excitement over
the proposed affair. Having tasted the bitterness of war, young and
old alike were looking forward to shedding their fears and enjoying a
rare night of festivity.

Though the idea for the benefit had originated with Bret, he was
one of the last to arrive. He'd spent the earlier part of the evening in
seclusion with General Van Dorn, an acquaintance of his from
before the war.

For some time now Bret had been giving serious consideration to
the possibility of volunteering to work with the Confederacy's wide-
spread espionage ring. His decision to act on the matter tonight had
nothing to do with the fact that Kitty was all but convinced he was a
coward. The intrigue and danger associated with espionage simply
appealed to him. It was a challenge, and he had long ago decided
that, if he served the Confederacy, it would be in this capacity and
none other.

Bret's offer had been immediately accepted by the general, who
recognized the merit of the younger man's proposal. It was no secret
that Bret had seemingly put business before patriotism, and Van
Dorn agreed it was unlikely anyone acquainted with him would
suspect he was a Confederate spy. The fact that he still owned a
cotton brokerage in Memphis, which was now occupied by the
Union army, would provide a believable excuse for his imminent
return to that city.

Once there, he would be in a good position to meet high-ranking
Union officers, work his way into their confidence—possibly at the
gaming tables—then eventually offer to spy for the Union whenever
business called him to Vicksburg. On such occasions, however, he
would actually be bringing invaluable information to Van Dorn,
who, in turn, would supply him with enough harmless information
for the Union to alleviate any suspicion. It was a neatly laid plan,
though dangerous.

Tomorrow he would leave for Memphis on his first assignment.
Tonight, however, he intended to have some time with Kitty. They

had avoided each other for the past two months, but now that he was leaving he had to see her—at least let her know where he could be reached in the event she needed him. It was a pity he was unable to tell her the real reason for his departure, but Van Dorn had sworn him to secrecy. It was just as well, he decided as he reached the Washington Hotel, since there was no doubt in his mind that she would be upset if she knew the danger he would soon be facing.

When Bret finally arrived at the benefit, Mattie and Phoebe were selling game tickets just inside the ballroom door. At one glance Bret saw that they were receiving more blankets, clothing, boots, and jewelry than actual hard cash, but that had been expected. The Confederacy could use any and all contributions.

"Good evening, ladies," he greeted them, extracting several gold coins from his vest pocket and dropping them in a basket on the table at the door. "It looks like the party is a big success."

"Oh, my, yes. Everything is going quite smoothly. Don't you agree, Mattie?" Phoebe ventured hopefully, remembering Mattie had been the only member of the Ole Miss Club who had been dead set against sponsoring the keno party.

"Splendidly," the wizened lady was forced to admit. Reluctantly she added: "In fact, tonight's festivities have been far more profitable than I ever would have imagined."

"Indeed, it has been profitable"—Phoebe smiled—"and we have you to thank for it, Mr. O'Rourke. After all, it was your idea."

"Ah, but it was you ladies who put the idea into motion," Bret countered affably before scanning the room in search of Kitty. He frowned slightly when he discovered her sitting with Sally and two officers at one of the keno tables.

Seeing his rather formidable expression, Phoebe was immediately concerned. "Uh—is anything wrong, Mr. O'Rourke?"

"No, not exactly." Hesitating, then shrewdly feigning just the right touch of concern, he said, "I was just wondering if Dave and Miles would approve of Kitty's presence here tonight and, especially, gambling with soldiers she hardly knows."

His words had the desired effect, and instantly concerned, the two matrons twittered indecisively for several tense minutes. Phoebe could not bear to think of Miles's being upset, and neither of them wanted to run the risk of arousing Dave's displeasure. Both finally concurred that Kitty should leave immediately. Their eyes turned hopefully to Bret, who, of course, gallantly offered to take Kitty home at the first opportunity.

The matter being settled, Bret excused himself and sauntered over to the refreshment table, where Flora was ladling out punch. Dolly was nearby rearranging a platter of finger sandwiches. Complimenting both ladies on the appetizing display, he chatted a few moments with them. Eventually Flora suggested to Dolly that the half-filled punch bowl needed to be replenished, and both women headed for the kitchen. An amused smile tugged at Bret's lips as he watched them leave. He seriously doubted that any two sisters could have been less alike. Whereas Dolly was lovably naive, short, and rotund, Flora was stern, her tall, buxom figure always held ramrod stiff so that few ever suspected she actually had a very soft heart. Nor did Flora attempt to change anyone's opinion, for she enjoyed her formidability. Bret, however, was not fooled.

Sampling a sandwich, he glanced up in time to see Henry Collins sidle up to the punch bowl and furtively extract a silver flask from his coat pocket. Quickly emptying its contents into Flora's punch, then filling his cup, he staggered off, unaware that Bret had caught him in the act.

The game in progress ended, and a short intermission was declared just as Flora and Dolly returned, both carrying full pitchers of fruit nectar that were soon added to the remaining spiked punch. Accepting a fresh cup from the unsuspecting Flora, Bret turned to find Kitty approaching the table. She came to an abrupt halt when she saw him, surprise and uncertainty mirrored in her eyes as she watched him close the gap between them.

"Hello, Bret," she said with a slight smile. "I didn't know you were here."

"I just arrived. Having fun?"

"Yes, though I haven't won anything all night," she admitted. "I was just about to have something to drink, but there seems to be quite a line forming. Miss Flora's punch must be exceptionally good tonight."

Bret chuckled. "It's exceptionally spiked."

"Spiked! I don't believe it," she scoffed. "You know Miss Flora is dead set against drinking. Why, she's the biggest teetotaler in town."

"True, but Henry Collins isn't."

"That old reprobate." Kitty chortled. "God help him if Miss Flora ever finds out!"

"That's his worry, not ours. Actually, Kitty, there's a matter I need to discuss with you, but not here. Would you mind leaving early?"

"I don't see how I can. I came with Aunt Phoebe, and she'd think it very peculiar if I left with you."

"Not after what I told her."

"Oh?" She shot him a curious look. "And what was that?"

"I'll tell you in the carriage." He grinned and steered her from the room. "Just take my word for it, she's relieved to have you off her hands."

When Bret informed her of his duplicity, Kitty was highly amused. She could well imagine the dither he had created with his false innuendos, which greatly appealed to her sense of humor. Laughter filled the carriage as they rode back to her house. It was not until he walked her to the front gate that he told her about his departure.

"But, Bret, the Yankees are in Memphis!"

"Yes, Yankees are occupying Memphis, but I happen to have a cotton brokerage there that needs my attention."

"Why? Even if you buy cotton, who are you going to sell it to . . . the Yankees?"

"If they can meet my price, yes."

"You wouldn't!" Kitty gasped, unable to believe her own ears.

"Oh, but I would, especially for gold."

"That's double dealing," she argued, "and it's also dangerous. If either side found out, you could be hung."

"Would you care?" he asked softly, wanting to take her in his arms.

"Not if you're going to do business with the Yankees," she replied, then turned on her heels and walked briskly away from him.

As was often the case, however, her words did not reflect her true feelings. She was miffed that Bret would stoop to dealing with the enemy, but she was also extremely worried about his safety. No matter how much she might disapprove of his actions, she could not bear to think of him in danger. If anything happened to him, how could she go on?

Chapter 15

By fall the South had taken the initiative in both the eastern and western theaters of the war. Two changes occurred in October that, in the months to come, would have a direct bearing on Vicksburg. General Ulysses Grant assumed command of the Union's Thirteenth Army Corps and Department of Tennessee, and General John Pemberton replaced Van Dorn as commander of the Confederate Department of Mississippi and East Louisiana.

The latter appointment posed a slight problem for Bret when he returned to Vicksburg four days before Christmas. Instead of reporting back to Van Dorn, he would now have to report to Pemberton, whom he had never met. Grant was about to launch an attack on Vicksburg, and it was imperative that he meet privately with the general and inform him of the details. The question was—how?

The opportunity presented itself on the night of his return, when Phoebe invited him to accompany her to an open-house celebration at Pemberton's headquarters. In a rare moment when the general was not surrounded by others, Bret cornered him and briefly explained his mission in Memphis. It was decided that the two men would meet secretly in the stable behind the house at half-past midnight.

Later, as Bret followed Pemberton up the ladder to the loft over the stable, he was somewhat surprised that the high-ranking officer had suggested a smelly stable as a rendezvous. Still, there was the utmost need for secrecy, and it was possible that Pemberton was unable to completely trust the staff that surrounded him.

After lighting a lantern and hanging it on a nearby peg, the general turned to Bret. ''Well, Mr. O'Rourke, I assume you're here to tell me that Grant is preparing to launch another assault on Vicksburg. When?'' he asked matter-of-factly.

"If all went as scheduled, Sherman left Memphis yesterday with three divisions of troops. Grant's plan calls for a two-pronged attack—an overland drive toward Jackson and Vicksburg and an amphibious move downriver. Sherman will lead his expedition down the Mississippi to some point between Milliken's Bend and Steele's Bayou. From there, he'll move into the Yazoo River and advance toward Haynes' Bluff and Walnut Hills, just north of town.''

"Hmmm. I've been expecting something like this ever since last month, when Grant took over Grand Junction and La Grange, Tennessee, then set up his headquarters and supply depot at Holly Springs, Mississippi,'' Pemberton remarked, stroking his long beard thoughtfully. "As a matter of fact, I've already notified President Davis that our situation here will be desperate in a short time if Grant does launch an all-out assault.''

"Just how supportive of defending Vicksburg is President Davis?'' Bret asked.

"Very. He feels Vicksburg must be protected at all costs. The Union now controls Memphis to the north, New Orleans and Natchez to the south, but unless they capture Vicksburg, they'll never have complete access to the Mississippi River. Davis is fully aware of the town's strategic importance. He realizes that if Vicksburg falls into enemy hands, so will Port Hudson, which would complete the Union's control of the Mississippi River. The South would then be split in half. God help us all if that should happen. It would be the beginning of the end for the Confederacy.''

"I understand General Johnston now commands all of our forces between the Appalachians and the Mississippi,'' Bret remarked. "I hear he's a good military man.''

"I won't argue that point, but Johnston is also a pessimist. He believes he has been given an impossibly large area to control, and that his armies are too small and too separated to effectively support each other. It's no secret he and President Davis seldom agree on anything, so it's hardly surprising that he disagrees with Davis about the necessity of protecting Vicksburg, particularly if it means employing more troops here. Says he can't spare them,'' Pemberton explained, pacing back and forth. Coming to a halt in front of Bret, he muttered, "Damn the man! Can't he see what will happen if Vicksburg falls to the Union?''

"So if worse comes to worst," Bret said, "you're not sure whether you can count on Johnston's support."

"Exactly." The general sighed. "I suppose I'll just have to cross that bridge when I get to it." Picking up the lantern, he motioned for Bret to precede him to the ladder. "Incidentally, how did you manage to work your way into the Yankees' confidence?"

"By being a graceful loser at poker—and, of course, selling cotton to them. The reason for my being in Vicksburg is that I am supposedly spying for them. They'd give their eyeteeth to know how well the town is fortified. It's my job to supply them with this information the morning after Christmas. What do you suggest I tell them?"

"Tell them we are well fortified and that you estimate we have approximately fifty thousand soldiers—which, of course, is far more than we actually have. I doubt such information will discourage them, but it will at least cause them to think twice about attacking. Nevertheless, if Sherman does attack as planned, he will be leading his men through swamps and bayous, which will be to our advantage."

"Definitely," Bret agreed, adding, "Few northerners are accustomed to wading through muck and skirting quicksand."

"Precisely, and when they do come out of the swamps, we'll be waiting for them. I'll have my men and artillery positioned on top of Chickasaw Bluffs, which should give us an edge."

"I understand Van Dorn destroyed Grant's supply depot at Holly Springs yesterday."

The two men had paused just outside the stable. Holding a lucifer to his cigar, Pemberton nodded. "That's right, and frankly I'm hoping now that Grant's depot is in a shambles, he may decide against joining Sherman in the assault. Even without his reinforcements, we're going to be badly outnumbered. Incidentally, where do you plan to rendezvous with the Yankees?"

"One of their scouts will meet me where Steele's Bayou intersects the Yazoo River at the edge of the Devans' plantation. I'm spending Christmas at Belle Glen, so it won't be difficult to make my connection the next morning."

"Will you return to town afterward or stay with the Devans?"

"Seeing as how the Yankees will be practically camping on the Devans' doorstep, I'll stay at Belle Glen for a spell—at least until the danger is past."

Pemberton nodded, then extended his hand to Bret. Thanking him

PROUD SURRENDER   143

for his help, the stately general turned and walked slowly back to his
darkened headquarters. It had been obvious that Pemberton, like
Davis, was determined to hold Vicksburg with or without Johnston's
assistance. The question foremost in Bret's mind was—would he
succeed?

There were more questions plaguing him, questions other than the
town's defense. With Yankees crawling all over Belle Glen, would
the Devans be safe? Despite his promise of secrecy, should he warn
Dave that the enemy would soon be encroaching upon his land? The
fact that Kitty would undoubtedly spend the holidays with her family
at Belle Glen was of no little concern to him. Invading armies not
only plundered and destroyed, they sometimes indulged in rape. The
thought of anyone desecrating Kitty's body caused his stomach to
churn, and he swore softly. No Yankee was ever going to lay a hand
on her, not if he could help it. God help any who tried!

Kitty snuggled into the soft feather mattress and pulled the thick
quilted comforter up to her chin. Christmas or not, it was too cold to
get out of bed just yet. With a small yawn, she shifted into a more
comfortable position and gazed absentmindedly at the frilly canopy
above her. She still felt tired from yesterday, which was only to be
expected. Christmas Eve was always a busy time at the Devan
household. Not only was the traditional fir tree decorated, but the
entire house was decked out in spruce, holly, and mistletoe, a task
that was shared by family and servants alike. This special day
always ended with a barbecue and barn dance for the slaves. After
most had tired from dancing the "turkey buzzard," Dave would end
the festivities by bestowing Christmas gifts on every slave at the
plantation—corn whiskey and tobacco to the menfolk, several lengths
of calico to the women, and a generous sack of licorice to each
child.

Kitty knew it had not been easy for her father to provide such
things this year and suspected he had had to deplete the plantation's
commissary in order to do so. With prices so high and no available
market for last summer's cotton crop, Dave's resources were dwin-
dling, and she wondered how he would manage to provide Christmas for their people next year. The prospects looked bleak.

Will the war never end? she wondered dismally. And will things
ever go back to the way they were? With a resigned sigh, she sat up
in bed just as Mammy Lou waddled into the room.

"Miz Kitty, heah 'tis Christmas mornin', an' you still in de bed!" she scolded, plopping both hands on her ample hips. "Whut's de matter—is you sick?"

"No, I'm not sick. Just tired," Kitty replied, swinging her legs over the side of the bed.

"Hmph! Dis ain' no time tuh be tired. Doshe's dun dressed de baby, an' Miz Dede's jes' waitin' fo' you so she kin go downstairs."

"Is Pa downstairs already?"

"Yas'm," the old Negro confirmed, handing Kitty a green velvet dressing gown. "He's in de library wid Mist' Bret."

"Bret's here?" Kitty questioned with surprise. She hadn't heard that he had returned from Memphis.

"Sho' is. He rode in 'bout an hour ago."

Excited at the prospect of seeing him again, Kitty beamed at Mammy Lou, who continued with a pointed look at her mistress.

" 'Course, hit's only nat'rul dat he wants tuh be wid de baby on Christmas."

Kitty's blue eyes widened with surprise, then narrowed in displeasure. "And just why, may I ask, should he want to be with *my* baby on Christmas?"

" 'Cause he's dat baby's papa, dat's why—an' dey ain' no use you tryin' tuh tell me diff'rent. Ah's knowed Mist' Bret eber since he wuz knee high to a grasshopper. Dat baby's de spittin' image ob him, an' dat's dat!"

Kitty's shoulders drooped with dismay. "Does Pa know?"

Mammy Lou bent over to make the bed. "Can't ratly say. If'n he don', Ah reckon hit's jes' as well," she answered noncommittally.

"Oh Mammy Lou, I'm so afraid Pa is going to find out. Bret and I . . . we . . ." Her voice faltered.

Finishing the bed, Mammy Lou straightened and gathered Kitty to her ample bosom. "Hesh up, honey. Ah don' knows whut hoppen't, an' Ah don' wanna know. Whut's dun's dun, an' all de frettin' in de worl' ain' gwine tuh change hit none. 'Sides, eben if Mist' Dave duz find out de truf, Ah 'spects he's gwine tuh love dat chile jes' de same."

Her words offered little comfort to Kitty, but when she finally descended to the parlor, her fears were carefully masked as she greeted her father and Bret. Skipping breakfast altogether, they gathered around the tree, and Dave handed out the gifts. Fewer presents were given this year, and most were practical necessities, except for Bret's gifts to the family. Dede received a bottle of cologne from him, Scotty a jack-in-the-box, and Dave a decanter of brandy—an expensive item, considering brandy was now selling for more than forty dollars a gallon. He presented Kitty's gift last, a pearl brooch set in delicate gold filigree. Since Bret's arrival had been unexpected, no gifts had been placed for him under the tree, but the oversight was quickly remedied by Dave. After excusing himself from the group, he soon returned with a rectangular, wooden box. Handing it to Bret, he said:

"Here's something I've always intended for you to have. Consider it as being from all of us."

Bret opened the lid and gazed with surprise at a finely crafted pistol that had come from Dave's prized gun collection. For a moment he was speechless, but when he glanced up at Dave, his eyes spoke volumes.

"Dave, I can't accept this. It's your favorite pistol."

"Of course you can. As I said, I've intended for you to have it all along." For a second the two men looked at each other in unspoken affection; then, clearing his throat, Dave softly added: "You can hand it down to your son one day."

For the first time, Bret realized Dave knew the truth, that Scotty was his son. Relief washed over him when he saw there was no condemnation in the older man's eyes, only understanding.

The moment passed as Mammy Lou appeared and announced that dinner was ready. Picking up a brown sack, Bret walked over to her.

"Just a minute, Mammy Lou. You don't think I'd forget you on such a special day," he said. "The wool caps are for Lemme and Uncle Thad, the bon-bons for Doshe, and the top parcel is for you." He grinned.

Setting down the sack, Mammy Lou extracted her gift from the rest, untying the string with trembling fingers. Her perplexed expression changed to one of sheer pleasure as she proudly lifted a multicolored, crocheted shawl from its wrapping.

"Ooo-eee, jes' luk at whut Mist' Bret dun gib me! Ain' dis de prett'est shawl you eber dun seed!" she exclaimed.

"Well, let's see how it looks on you, Mammy Lou." Bret chuckled, taking it from her and arranging it over her broad shoulders.

"Lawsy me, Mist' Bret, how'd you know Ah wuz needin' a shawl in de wurst way? You's mighty bodacious; yassuh mighty bodacious!"

As soon as the faithful old servant left the room, Dede turned to Bret and beamed with childlike pleasure. "I'm so glad you came today."

Kitty smiled in agreement, and Dave added, "It's been too long a time since you spent Christmas with us, and I, for one, would be very pleased if you would make it a habit from now on."

Before Bret could reply, Dede had changed the subject.

"Ummm—something smells mighty good. Are we having turkey?"

"No, we're having those two-year-old geese Lemme's been fattening up for the past six months," Dave said.

"You don't mean those two geese that've been penned up in that awful cage out back!" she exclaimed with dismay, then turned to Kitty. "I thought they were Lemme's pets. Why, the poor things have gotten so fat they can hardly move in that tiny cage."

"Honestly, Dede, you've eaten goose before," Kitty replied. "Surely you realize they have to be penned up and constantly fed so they'll get good and fat."

"That's right, sugar. The fatter the goose, the more cracklin's there'll be to eat," Dave affirmed, referring to the small, crisp morsels of golden-brown skin that was everyone's favorite part of the goose.

From Dede's forlorn expression, it was obvious she was not appeased, but Kitty doubted that the girl's squeamishness would hinder her at the dinner table. Goose was a rare treat nowadays.

After all were seated in the dining room, Dave said a short blessing, then Mammy Lou and Shasta served the first course, noodle soup. Hard times were forgotten, and conversation flowed freely, with Dede and Kitty chatting animatedly about Mary Belle Moore's marriage to Wade Waddell, which had taken place last week, and the forthcoming nuptials between Sally Collins and David Shelton. By the time the first course ended, Bret had been thoroughly briefed on everything he had missed during his absence.

As Mammy Lou was removing the soup bowls from the table, Kitty glanced out the window and saw Shasta shuffling along the dogtrot between the dining room and kitchen. She was carrying a large platter of cracklin's, and as she neared the house Kitty saw the plump girl pop one of the juicy morsels into her mouth. Unfortunately Mammy Lou also caught her in the act. Seeing the thunderous expression on Mammy Lou's face, Kitty smiled impishly and waited for the inevitable. As soon as the girl set foot in the dining room,

Mammy Lou angrily snatched the platter from her and placed it on the table.

"You see dat dogtrot 'twixt de kitchen an' de house?" she exploded. "Dat's called de *whistlin' walk*—an' when you cums down hit, you'd better be whistlin' an' not samplin'. If'n Ah ever ketches you snitchin' food agin, Ah's gwine tuh have yo' hide!"

Amusement was suppressed until Mammy Lou had marched Shasta out the back door, then laughter filled the room, ending when the old woman returned and, still grumbling, personally served the rest of the meal. The table was soon laden with delectable food, and true to Kitty's expectations, Dede put away her fair share of goose. Not until they had adjourned to the parlor for coffee and fruitcake was any reference made to the war. Quite unintentionally, Dede brought the matter up by asking Bret if he had attended the Christmas Eve ball last night.

Bret suddenly sobered. "Yes, as a matter of fact, I did."

"Oh, I do wish Kitty and I could have gone, but Papa Dave thought it was too cold to drive into town," Dede lamented. "Did you have fun?"

"Yes, it was very enjoyable—at least, for the most part."

Sensing something was being withheld, Kitty frowned. "What do you mean 'for the most part'?" she asked.

Bret hesitated, then decided there was no point in evading her question. "Shortly after midnight, the ball was interrupted by a messenger with news for General Smith that created quite a stir. Sherman's troops had landed at Milliken's Bend and Young's Point, just across the river. That ended the ball, of course, and General Smith suggested that all noncombatants leave town. I had hoped to spare you this news until Christmas was over, but since you asked—now is as good a time as any to prepare you for what we might be facing tomorrow."

For a moment no one spoke, and then Kitty asked: "Will the Yankees bypass us on their way to Vicksburg?"

"It's hard to tell," Bret answered. "In any event, I think it would be wise for everyone to stay at home."

"Yes, you're right," Dave agreed. "I'll talk to Charlie later and instruct him to pass the word that everyone is to stay close by tomorrow."

It was obvious that Dede was close to tears. Determined not to allow the Yankees to spoil the entire day, Kitty handed Scotty to Bret and walked over to the pianoforte.

"Let's have some music, shall we," she suggested with a forced smile. "After all, there's no sense in letting the Yankees spoil Christmas for us."

The men quickly agreed, and before long even Dede's mood brightened as they gathered around the pianoforte and sang familiar Christmas carols. The rest of the day passed enjoyably, ending with the traditional roasting of hickory nuts over smoldering logs in the fireplace.

It was not until Dede and Kitty had retired that Bret had a chance to speak privately to Dave. Adjourning to the study, the men had a nightcap and talked in earnest about the impending danger they might have to face in the days to come. Surprised, but not displeased, Dave listened while Bret informed him about his spy mission in Memphis, then explained the necessity of his rendezvous with the enemy tomorrow morning at the edge of Belle Glen.

"I'm glad you've told me the truth," Dave said. "It explains why you never enlisted, though I never doubted your courage. Does Kitty know?"

"No, and I'd rather she didn't. The less she knows, the better." Seeing Dave's perplexed look, Bret continued, "As you know, some of our agents have already been caught. Rumor has it that families and friends of known Confederate spies are being questioned and, in some instances, tortured or hung. Unfortunately, there's always a chance that the Yankees could get wise to me, and, of course, that Vicksburg could fall to the enemy. Should that happen, I don't want Kitty being dragged into an inquisition. In fact, I wouldn't have told you had it not been necessary."

"Don't worry about me, son. Just look after yourself." Dave smiled. "As for Kitty—well, like you said, the less she knows, the better."

Chapter 16

Kitty tapped her foot with impatience as she watched Doshe's son, Gus, tighten the cinch on her gray mare. His disapproval was obvious as, with a shake of his head, he took hold of the reins and led the frisky animal to where she was standing.

"Miz Kitty, yo' pa's not gwine tuh like hit when he finds out you's dun took off ridin'. You knows he dun tole ev'body tuh stay put dis mawnin', an' heah you is gallavantin' off wid dem Yankees rat at our do'step! Naw'm, he sho' ain' gwine tuh like hit."

"Oh, quit worrying, Gus. It'll take Pa and Mister Charlie all morning to ride around the plantation and get everything secured in case the Yankees do cut across our land. I'll be back long before they return. Just keep your mouth shut, and Pa will never know," she replied.

With another shake of his head, Gus reluctantly helped his mistress to mount, then stood back while she adjusted the folds of her red velvet riding habit.

"But whut's Ah gonna tell my mama an' Lou when dey asks whar you is?" he persisted.

"Just tell them the truth—you don't know," she retorted, then flicked the mare's flank with her crop and trotted off.

The morning air was brisk, and as Kitty nudged her mount into a canter, she felt relieved to be out of the house, particularly since news of the approaching Yankees had put the entire household in a state of turmoil. Every precaution was being taken to safeguard whatever was possible, and everybody was busy doing something. Mammy Lou and Doshe were taking smoked hams and canned goods to a nearby cave in one of the river bluffs in case the Yankees decided to plunder Belle Glen. Shasta had been instructed to pack clothing, blankets, and other necessities, which would also be taken to the cave. There was, after all, the danger that the enemy would set fire to the house, leaving them destitute. Lemme and his older son, Zeke, were out checking to see all livestock were secured in numerous barns scattered around the plantation. Only Dede and Kitty had not been required to do anything—and Dede had been closeted in her room all morning, having a fit of hysterics.

While eating breakfast, Kitty had asked Daisy where Bret was and had learned that he had ridden out about an hour before. She had naturally assumed he was with her father and Charlie, until Daisy innocently added that she had heard Bret say he was riding to Steele's Bayou.

Surprised and alarmed, Kitty had hurriedly dressed, then instructed Gus to saddle her horse. She calculated that the bayou intersected the Yazoo River almost due east of where the Yankees had been spotted at Milliken's Bend. She could not imagine why Bret would be riding directly toward the enemy, nor could she understand why her father had not discouraged him from doing so. From what Daisy said, Dave had raised no objections whatsoever, which led Kitty to believe that Bret was scouting the area with her father's approval. In her opinion, it was definitely a foolhardy risk to take. What if he ran into the Yankees? Even now he could be lying injured somewhere, perhaps even dead.

This unwelcome idea unnerved her. Inwardly cursing Bret for a fool, she urged her mare into a full gallop, heedless of her own possible danger. All that mattered was that she find him in time.

Breathless by the time she reached the narrow road that paralleled the Yazoo's levee, Kitty paused to collect her thoughts. There was a particular spot where the bayou ran into the river, and she decided this was probably where Bret had ridden. The slight knoll that sloped down to the river was densely wooded, providing adequate camouflage while offering an excellent view of the surrounding area. It was just around the bend, and as it dawned on Kitty that Yankees could be swarming all over the place, she dismounted and led her winded mare to a nearby thicket, hitching the animal to a sapling.

She extracted a small revolver from the waistband of her skirt, thankful that she had thought to bring it along, and proceeded to make her way through the woods. Upon rounding the bend, she spotted

Bret's horse, also tied to a sapling, but there was no sign of him. Pausing to catch her breath, she chewed nervously on her lower lip. There was the possibility that he was on the other side of the steep slope, safe and sound. If this were the case, it was unlikely he would welcome her presence. Still, she had come too far to turn back now.

Hitching her skirts up in one hand, she made her way up the wooded slope, the small revolver clutched tightly in her other hand. She had almost reached the top of the knoll when her foot slipped and she fell to one knee. Relieved that her weapon had not discharged accidentally, she started to tuck it back in her waistband, then stopped. The sound of voices drifted to her from the other side of the slope—men's voices. One she instantly recognized as Bret's, but the other was foreign to her, nasal in tone and clipped. A *Yankee!*

Believing Bret had run into trouble, Kitty began to tremble. Her hand tightened on the small gun as, crouching low, she made her way up the side of the knoll. Once she reached the top, she stepped behind a clump of spruce trees. Though a reasonably good shot, she realized that nervousness and fear for Bret's safety could cause her to miss this time, particularly at such long range.

The men's voices droned on but were too far away to be distinguished. Taking a deep breath, she carefully parted the prickly spruce branches and peeped down. Her eyes widened in disbelief when she spotted Bret and a Yankee sergeant standing by the river's edge where a small skiff was secured. Her concern for him faded as she watched him clasp the soldier's hand in a farewell shake and laugh at the man's parting remark. A feeling of helpless rage swept over her as she watched him help the Yankee shove off in the small boat, then wave good-bye. Suddenly it occurred to her that, beyond doing business with the Yankees, Bret was probably a *Yankee spy!*

Bitterly, she watched until the sergeant had paddled out of sight before stepping through the clump of spruce trees that had concealed her. Tears misted her eyes, but she held them in check. Planting her legs squarely apart in a determined stance, she waited for Bret to turn.

"Well, Kathryn, have you seen enough, or do you intend to stand up there all day?" he unexpectedly rapped out in a gruff voice, turning to face her. The glint in his eyes left little doubt as to the extent of his fury.

For a moment, Kitty was too dumbfounded to move or speak. He

had known all along that she was lurking nearby, a fact that should
not have surprised her, considering she had seldom put anything
over on him.

"Yes, I've seen quite enough," she stated. "Enough to see you
for what you really are—a low-down traitor!" She aimed the gun
directly at him. "How did you know I was here?"

"The next time you decide to spy on anybody, I suggest you wear
black instead of red. Luckily, the sergeant had his back to you," he
answered, sauntering up the hill.

Kitty bristled with anger. "Why were you talking to that Yankee,
Bret? Are you helping them—spying for them?"

He halted momentarily, one dark brow arching with arrogant
indifference—or so it seemed to Kitty. "Answer me, or I swear I'll
kill you!"

"Then I'm afraid you're going to have to kill me," he replied,
starting toward her again.

His apparent nonchalance, his seeming lack of fear in the face of
death, unnerved her, and her hand began to tremble slightly. He had
reached the top of the slope and was only a couple of feet from her
before she finally found her voice.

"Stop!" she commanded. "Don't come any closer or I'll shoot."

"Then do it! From this distance, you can't miss," he countered in
a steely voice, deliberately closing the space between them.

By now Kitty was visibly shaken and consumed with uncertainty.
If only he would explain or deny her accusation! But apparently he
did not intend to do either.

"Well, what are you waiting for?" he asked, halting in front of
her. When she failed to answer or carry out her threat, he reached
for the gun.

With a feeling of unreality, she allowed him to take the derringer
from her lifeless fingers, and it was then that the last of her control
crumbled. Tears ran down her pale cheeks as she stared at him.

"Why, Bret? Why are you doing this?" she cried. "How can you
turn against your own kind?"

Seeing the pain and confusion in her eyes, he longed to comfort
her but was unable to explain. He realized his silence was damning,
yet it was far better to risk her love than her life. With a tired sigh,
he gently placed his hands on her slender shoulders.

"I'm not. Believe me, I'm doing what I think is best. You're just
going to have to trust me."

"Trust you! How can I, after what I've seen? Do you honestly think I'm gullible enough to believe that your meeting with that Yankee was mere coincidence? God in heaven, there can only be one explanation. You're betraying us!"

"Stop it, Kitty, before you say something you'll later regret."

"The only thing I'll ever regret is having loved you—but that's over now. I'll never forgive you for what you're doing."

She started to turn away from him, but his hands tightened on her arms, dragging her to his chest.

"You little fool! Do you think this war or anything else is going to change what's between us? You may not like what you *think* I am, but by God, you'll always be mine."

"No, Bret. I could *never* belong to a traitor," she declared vehemently, pulling away from him. "But don't worry, I won't turn you in. After all, you're still the father of my son."

He made no attempt to detain her as she turned and walked away from him. There was nothing left for him to say—nothing he *could* say to ease her bitterness. Only the truth would do that, and the truth was the very thing he dared not give her. By the time it was safe to do so, it might be too late for them. There was always the possibility that he might be caught or that Kitty might even fall in love with someone else. Totally frustrated, he strode angrily toward his horse.

For several days Sherman's troops trudged across unfamiliar swamps and bayous, heading for the bluffs north of Vicksburg and near Chickasaw Bayou. Once their destination was reached, however, they were confronted by Confederate artillery that stopped them in their tracks. Unable to break through the Rebels' lines, Sherman stubbornly remained in front of the bluffs and explored different means of continuing his assault.

Hoping in vain that Grant would arrive with additional forces, the schoolmaster-turned-general finally decided to make one last thrust. On New Year's Day, he pushed his men around the Confederates' extreme right flank, a move that was doomed to fail. The advance had hardly begun when heavy fog rolled over the lowlands, throwing his troops into a state of confusion that quickly put an end to the maneuver.

The ominous sound of distant gunfire and cannons had echoed daily throughout Belle Glen, putting everyone on edge. Even Dave had shown signs of concern, the house servants had been jumpy, and

Dede had been reduced to frequent bouts of hysteria. Only Bret appeared calm, though he wisely suggested that a few rifles and several rounds of ammunition be buried behind the barn in the event Belle Glen was raided by the Yankees.

Dave acted on his suggestion and, realizing their vulnerable position, removed all valuables from the wall safe in his office, hiding the money and several pieces of his wife's jewelry behind loose bricks in the front and back parlor fireplaces. As an afterthought, he instructed the servants to wrap and pack the family silver so that Lemme could bury it out back.

Having put Scotty down for a nap, Kitty walked into the dining room, where she found Doshe, Thad, and Mammy Lou busily packing the family's elegant tea service and silver serving dishes in wooden crates.

"Miz Kitty, dis heah's de last box we's got, an' hit's 'bout full. Whar's we gwine tuh put de silverware?" she asked, pointing to the rows of gleaming knives, forks, and spoons that were laid out on the dining room table.

Kitty nibbled thoughtfully on her lower lip, then walked over to one of the dining room chairs and turned it upside down, running her hand over the burlap material that, tacked down, held the horsehair stuffing in place.

"Uncle Thad, remove the backing from these chairs and take out most of the horsehair," she commanded briskly.

"Miz Kitty! Dem chairs belong't tuh yo' mama an' her mama befo' her, an' we ain' about tuh tek 'em apart!" Mammy Lou exclaimed indignantly.

"Yes, we are, because that's where we're going to hide the silverware," Kitty answered, her dark look defying the old woman to argue with her.

Mammy Lou shot Uncle Thad a withering look as he began to disassemble the chairs. "Hmph! If'n de rest ob de year's supposed tuh be lak de furst day, den dis year's gwine tuh be mighty bad. Ah bes' git along tuh de kitchen an' put on a pot ob black-eyed peas and hog jowl fo' good luck."

"Honestly, Mammy Lou, you're enough to try the patience of a saint, always spoutin' off your silly superstitious beliefs. A lot of good black-eyed peas and hog jowl are going to do if the Yankees decide to pay us a visit," Kitty remarked.

"Don' git uppity wid me, missy. Ah's fixin' black-eyed peas 'n hog jowl fo' supper, an' you's gwine tuh eat sum, if'n Ah hafs tuh feed you m'self!'' Turning to Doshe, she added, ''An' hit's no use you settin' heah, wor'hying yo'self sick 'bout Zeke. Mought as well git in de kitchen wid me an' gib me a hand.''

For the first time, Kitty noticed Doshe's woebegone look, and a frown creased her forehead as she watched the woman follow Mammy Lou out the back door. With a tired sigh, she sank into a chair and looked on as Uncle Thad carefully removed the backing from another chair.

''What's wrong with Doshe? Why's she worried about Zeke?'' she asked.

''Dat boy ob hers is gibbin' her a peck ob trouble, talkin' 'bout how he wants tuh be free 'n how he's gwine tuh jine up wid dem Yankees so's de res' ob us kin be free,'' Uncle Thad replied with a disapproving shake of his gray head.

''Free! But—but this is his home,'' Kitty sputtered. ''Oh, Pa may own a scrap of paper that says he's a slave, but he certainly isn't treated like one, any more than any of the rest of you are. Why, all of you are a part of this family. You know that . . .'' Her voice faded as, for the first time, she wondered how Uncle Thad felt about being a slave.

As if sensing her uneasiness, the old man looked up and gave her a gentle smile. ''Don't worry 'bout Zeke. He's jes' young an' got itchy feet.''

Only partially reassured, Kitty walked over to the window and parted the lace curtains. The heavy fog was turning into a light drizzle, a depressing sight that did nothing to brighten her spirits, despite the fact that the distant cannonfire had all but ceased. ''It's certainly taking our mare a long time to foal. Mister Bret and Pa have been at the stable all morning.''

''Yas'm, they sho' have, but Ah reckon dey's sum things a body jes' cain't hur'hy,'' Thad replied, getting to his feet. ''All de backin's off dem chairs, Miz Kitty. You want me tuh wrap de silver in dat flannel befo' packin' hit in de bottom ob de chairs?''

''Yes, and I'll help you,'' she answered, turning to find the old man gently rubbing his left arm, an expression of pain in his kindly eyes. ''Are you all right, Uncle Thad?'' she asked with sudden concern.

''Aw, dis ole arm is actin' up a mite, but Ah reckon hit's jes' a tech ob de rheum'tism.''

Mammy Lou and Uncle Thad's sleeping quarters were on the third floor in the attic, and noticing that his face seemed suddenly tinged with gray, Kitty suggested he go upstairs and lie down for a spell.

"Naw'm, Ah be's all right direc'ly," came the reply as Kitty seated herself and began wrapping the silver in pieces of flannel. Seeing her look of concern, he sought to ease her mind. "Sho' is nice tuh have Mist' Bret back home. He wuz gone a moughty long time."

"Not long enough," Kitty muttered, tying a piece of string around a bundle of knives with a vicious jerk, then shoving it into the bottom of one of the disassembled chairs.

The very thought of Bret was enough to put her in a black mood. For days she had avoided him whenever possible, ever since the morning after Christmas when she had discovered he was a spy. Though tempted, she had not mentioned Bret's duplicity to anyone, simply because she doubted anyone would have believed her.

As for Bret, he acted as though nothing out of the ordinary had happened. If he noticed Kitty's coolness toward him, he chose to ignore it, except at mealtimes when his eyes occasionally locked with hers across the table. It was then that she despised him the most, as he sat there eating their food and enjoying their hospitality.

"Miz Kitty, you reckon Ah tuk too mech stuffin' outta dis heah chair?" Uncle Thad asked.

Kitty pulled her thoughts back to the present and nodded. "Yes, I 'spect you'd better put some of it back. The chairs mustn't be lumpy or uncomfortable."

Before he could act on her suggestion and restuff the chair, Dede came rushing downstairs, her face chalk white as she ran into the dining room.

"They're here—the Yankees are here!" she squealed in a high-pitched voice.

"How do you know? Did you see them?" Kitty asked, jumping to her feet.

"I saw them from the upstairs window. There's about twenty of them, and they're headed up the drive," she replied breathlessly.

Kitty's mind spun into action. "Dede, go out to the stables and fetch Pa and Bret."

"But—but they'll see me. They might shoot me!" Dede wailed in a terrified voice.

"Don't be a goose! They're not going to see you if you leave by the back door, and if they do—well, I doubt that even the Yankees would stoop so low as to shoot a defenseless woman,'' Kitty replied with far more assurance than she actually felt. When it looked as though Dede would protest further, Kitty's eyes narrowed in anger.

"Well, don't just stand there. Get a move on!"

Dede's eyes widened in astonishment at Kitty's unusual sharpness. Stiffling a sob with her fist, she rushed out the back door, almost colliding with Mammy Lou, who was just entering.

"Umph, umph, umph—whut dun' cum ober dat chile?"

"The Yankees, that's what's come over her. They're right outside, coming up the drive. Oh, dear, if they come inside and find all this silverware laying about, they'll rob us blind. Quick, Mammy Lou, help me. You, Uncle Thad, start tackin' the bottom of these chairs back in place just as soon as we fill 'em,'' Kitty ordered, thankful that most of the precious silverware had already been packed away in the dining room chairs.

They had just finished filling all but one chair when heavy footsteps sounded on the front veranda.

"They're on the porch,'' Kitty gasped. "Damn 'em to hell!"

"Miz Kitty, you watch yo' tongue!" Mammy Lou admonished. "Yankees or no Yankees, Ah ain' about tuh put up wid yo' cussin'. Hit ain't ladylak!"

"I wasn't cussin'—just wishin' mighty hard,'' Kitty muttered.

"Hmph! You wuz cussin', dat's whut,'' came the argumentative reply just as a loud knock sounded at the front door.

"Oh, for heaven's sake, just fill up that last chair. And if Miss Dede comes back inside, send her up to her room and tell her to stay there. We certainly don't need another fit of hysterics now. I'll go outside and try to hold them on the porch until Pa and Bret come.''

With a show of courage she was far from feeling, Kitty swept out of the dining room, closed the heavy double doors, and took a deep breath before proceeding to the front door. Filled with dread, she lifted her chin and slowly turned the knob.

An officer in a bedraggled blue uniform stood before her, his stern countenance emphasized by piercing, narrow-set eyes and craggy features. Rivulets of water dripped from his reddish-brown hair, coating his short-clipped mustache and scraggly beard. For a moment she froze, but her pluck returned as soon as the man spoke.

"Forgive this intrusion, madam, but my men and I have become separated from the rest of our company in this confounded fog.

Would you be good enough to tell me how far we are from the river?''

"You're lost?" Kitty asked, her eyes darting past him to rest on the small group of men who remained positioned in the driveway. As Dede had said, there were about twenty of them, all drenched to the skin, muddy, and wearing dour expressions.

"Temporarily, yes," came the clipped reply. "Now, if you would be good enough to answer my question . . ."

Kitty bristled, feeling he had addressed her as he would a small child. She was on the verge of denying his request when an idea suddenly struck her that held far more appeal. She would direct him to the river all right, but through the densest swampland!

Mischief danced in her expressive eyes, and her lips slowly curved into a deceptively sweet smile. "Of course," she answered. "Follow the drive out to the road and turn right, then go on for about a quarter of a mile until you come to a large willow tree. You'll find a narrow path to the left of that, which will take you to the river."

"I fear the little lady has a poor sense of direction, Cump."

The unexpected voice came from her left, and Kitty whirled to find her father and Bret rounding the corner of the veranda. Frustration swamped her upon seeing the latter's ill-concealed amusement as he strode over to the officer and extended a large hand in greeting.

"Bret, it's good to see you again," the officer remarked with obvious relief, taking his hand and giving it a hearty shake.

"I'd like you to meet a friend of mine, Cump," Bret answered. "This is Dave Devan. You've heard me speak of him."

"Of course," the older man replied, extending his hand toward her father.

"Dave, I'd like you to meet General William Tecumseh Sherman," Bret continued, "and this is his daughter, Miss Kathryn."

Kitty fumed inside as she coolly acknowledged the introduction. It was all she could do to keep silent when her father, with formal politeness, invited the general and his men to come inside and warm themselves by the fire. Had everyone taken leave of their senses? she wondered. These men were the enemy—low-down Yankee varmints who were bent on destroying the South. *Hospitality be damned!* They could stand out in the rain until they drowned. Her irritation dissipated slightly, however, when Sherman politely declined the invitation.

"It's imperative that we reunite with the rest of our company as quickly as possible," he said, pulling a map from his inner coat.

"Well, at least come inside long enough for us to spread that map out and show you your location," Bret persisted.

This was agreed upon, and Kitty's heart sank when she saw her father and Bret lead the general into the dining room. She prayed to God that Mammy Lou and Uncle Thad had finished packing the last of the silver. A sigh of relief escaped her when Dave slid open the double doors and she saw that the room was empty and in order, the dining room chairs arranged neatly around the long table.

She remained in the background while the three men bent over the map, which had been spread out on the table, and her eyes widened with horror when Dave suggested that they be seated. As luck would have it, the general selected the very chair that held the least amount of padding, and a moment before he seated himself, Kitty spied fork prongs protruding from the velvet cushion. A feeling of giddiness swept over her when he sat down on the piercing offender and stiffened visibly. A startled expression betrayed his discomfort, and easing himself forward in the chair, he shot her a knowing look. With a tight grimace playing about his thin lips, he turned his attention back to the map, but the next few minutes were a nightmare for Kitty.

There was no hope, no way to believe the general was unaware that his chair was filled with valuables rather than horsehair, and there was little doubt in her mind that he would have the entire house ransacked before he left. They would be destitute, left without anything. They might even be killed! Everyone except Bret, the low-down scoundrel. As a friend of General Sherman, he would undoubtedly be spared. Seconds later her fears increased tenfold.

"Hmmm, I see. This does, indeed, seem to be the quickest route to the river," the general said, thoughtfully stroking his beard. "Had I followed the little lady's directions, we'd have never gotten to the river through those swamps."

"Oh, you'd probably have gotten through, but you might have had to tangle with quicksand, gators, and moccasins along the way. As I said before, Miss Kathryn's sense of direction is sometimes a little confused," Bret answered with amusement.

"So it would seem. I would suggest, Mr. Devan, that you keep a close eye on your daughter in the future—for her own protection, of course." The words held a hidden warning, and Dave bristled visibly.

Before he could reply, however, Bret intervened. "Dave, did I ever tell you about the time Cump's horse almost beat Lightning in a race? As a matter of fact, that was where we met a few years ago—at the racetrack."

Though still aloof, Dave allowed himself to be drawn into a brief conversation about racing, and minutes later the tension had eased somewhat. Kitty sank down onto a chair and listened halfheartedly until the general mentioned that he had relatives living in Vicksburg, the Kleins. Then her resentment flared anew.

"I'm sure they must be quite proud," Kitty remarked scathingly, "being related to the man who's responsible for our present hardships." She gave him a withering look. "How can you live with yourself after trying to blast your own kinfolk out of house and home!"

"Young woman, I can assure you my relatives were in little danger, considering my men never got past the bluffs," he answered coldly.

"But they might have, and if they had, your own kin would have suffered as much as anyone else." Kitty rose from the chair and glared defiantly at the unrepentant officer.

Before Sherman could retaliate, Dave broke in with, "Forgive my daughter's straightforwardness, General. Like most southerners, she feels bitter when her homeland is attacked, particularly from such close range."

Sherman nodded and gave Kitty an understanding smile. "Which is no more than I myself would feel if the circumstances were reversed. I'm a soldier, an officer who is merely doing his duty and carrying out orders. The consequences are often unpleasant, more so when one's relatives are on the opposing side, but that's the price we have to pay. Understand, madam, this is no game. It's war."

"Well, it's a war you're *never* going to win. You Yankees will never rule the South, not as long as there's breath in our bodies!" Kitty cried.

The general was momentarily nonplussed, Bret was clearly amused, and Dave was speechless. An uncomfortable silence ensued, then Sherman rose from his chair. His formidable expression softened suddenly.

"Well, in any event, I want to thank you for your hospitality, Miss Kathryn. In return, I will offer you a valuable piece of advice. For your own comfort, I suggest you add a little more horsehair to those chairs, or else find a less conspicuous place to hide your silver!"

As understanding dawned on Dave, his laughter mingled with Bret's as they walked the general to the front door. Disgust washed over Kitty when she heard Bret offer to escort Sherman's men to the river. By the time Dave rejoined her in the dining room, she was pacing the floor like a caged animal.

"How could he? How could either of you be nice to that horrible man?" she exploded.

"Oh, he's not a bad sort, honey, even if he is a Yankee. And besides, he was a friend of Bret's long before this war started, so we could hardly be rude to him, could we?" he reasoned.

"I could, I was, and I meant to be," came the stubborn reply.

"So I noticed."

"Well, I did. As for Bret, I'll never forgive him as long as I live. Never!"

"For what? Being friends with General Sherman?"

"No, for being a traitor. A low-down Yankee spy!" Seeing her father's sudden frown, she rushed over to him and, throwing her arms around his waist, buried her head against his chest. "He is, Pa. I saw him talking with a Yankee soldier the day after Christmas down at Steele's Bayou, and when I accused him of being a spy, he didn't even deny it."

"He may not have denied it, honey, but that doesn't mean it's true. Being in the cotton business, Bret's become acquainted with a lot of people, some of them undoubtedly Yankees. Don't forget, he's spent the last few months in Memphis, and he's bound to have come in contact with quite a few of them there. That doesn't make him a traitor or a spy." Seeing his daughter was still not convinced, he continued: "If he met up with a Yankee he happened to know, I'm sure it was merely a coincidence."

"Way out at the bayou? Hmph, not likely," Kitty sniffed, looking up at her father. "Why won't you believe me, Pa? Bret's a spy. I *know* he's a spy!"

Dave frowned. "You're not thinking straight, honey. You've known Bret all of your life. Do you honestly think he would ever do anything to hurt us or betray our trust in him?"

"I didn't, but that was before I saw—"

"Look, sugar, things are not always what they seem." Forcing a smile to his lips, he strove for lightness. "Don't you know by now that you can believe little of what you hear and only half of what you see?"

Kitty sighed and shook her head. It was no use. Dave would never believe that Bret was capable of wrongdoing. She pulled out of his arms and was about to excuse herself and go upstairs to check on Scotty when Doshe came running into the room.

"Mist' Dave, Mist' Dave—cum out back, quick! Thad jes' keeled ober all of a sudden," she wailed, "an' he cain't hardly gits his breaf. Lou's wid him now, an' she's mighty wor'hied."

Kitty followed her father as, leaning heavily on his cane, he limped hurriedly down the wide hallway and out the back door. The sight that greeted them was not reassuring. Lemme and his family watched helplessly while Mammy Lou cradled Uncle Thad to her quivering bosom. Tears coursed down her stricken face as she murmured comforting words to the kindly old man with whom she had lived for some sixty-odd years. Even as they approached, Kitty noted Uncle Thad's ashen coloring and remembered he had been rubbing his left arm earlier, though he had claimed it was only a touch of rheumatism. She should have guessed then that something was wrong.

Unable to kneel because of his leg, Dave bent over the couple, concern etched on his face. Kitty sank down beside Mammy Lou and took the old man's gnarled hand in hers.

"Oh, Uncle Thad," she murmured, fighting back tears.

Hearing her voice, the old man slowly opened his eyes and attempted to smile. "Ah's real sor'hy tuh truble you, chile. Ah be's all right soon," he asserted weakly.

Wondering whether or not to move him inside, Dave asked, "Are you in much pain, Uncle Thad?"

"Naw, suh, not mech. Jes' awfully tired."

Dave turned to the other servants. "Doshe, run upstairs and turn down the covers on my bed. Lemme, can you carry Uncle Thad upstairs by yourself?" he asked the big man. Upon receiving an affirmative reply, he said, "Good. Gus, saddle up my horse and ride into town. Fetch Doc Blanks or that young partner of his back here on the double."

But before Gus could move, Uncle Thad was shaking his head.

"Don'—don' go tuh all dat truble, Mist' Dave. Hit t'wouldn't do no good," he murmured, closing his eyes as if it were an effort to speak.

Dave felt a lump rising in his throat, and when Mammy Lou tried unsuccessfully to stifle a sob, he placed a gentle hand on her shoulder. Before he could offer consoling words to her, Uncle Thad's wrinkled eyelids slowly reopened, and a loving smile illuminated his face as his eyes met Dave's.

"You wuz gwine tuh put me in yo' bed jes' lak Ah wuz real fam'ly."

"You *are* real family, Uncle Thad. Always have been," Dave assured him huskily.

"Yas, suh, dat's de way Ah's always felt, too. Me 'n' Lou's dun had a good life t'gether, an' we's been blest wid uh good fam'ly tuh take care ob us."

Kitty felt as though her heart were breaking as she watched the old man's strength failing.

"Don't talk, Uncle Thad. Just rest until we can get you inside. You're gonna be fine in no time a'tall. You *gotta* be! Why, what would we do without you?" Her voice faltered when the dying man gazed at her and she saw the knowing look in his ageless eyes.

"Don' fret, chile. Jes' take care ob Lou fo' me, 'til we be's t'gether agin in de promised land. Ah's had uh good life, but now . . . now Ah's gwine tuh be free . . . really free . . ."

A slight smile softened his wizened face, and, with a shuddering sigh, his eyes closed for the last time. For seconds no one spoke or moved, not even the numerous field hands who had drifted silently over from the slave quarters. Then, Lemme bent down and gently removed Uncle Thad from Mammy Lou's loving arms, cradling him next to his broad chest. Dave straightened and helped Mammy Lou to her feet. When Kitty saw her father's tears, she could no longer contain her own. Covering her pale face with quivering hands, she wept, only dimly aware of Lemme's deep, melodic bass voice breaking the silence as he carried Uncle Thad to the house. Gradually, the other Negroes joined in, expressing their sorrow in a spiritual that had been Uncle Thad's favorite:

Steal away, steal away,
Steal away to Jesus.

Steal away, steal away home,
I ain't got long to stay here . . .

Only Zeke remained silent, his face twisted in bitter sadness. "He wuz born a slave, an' he died a slave," he muttered. Turning, he walked slowly back to the slave quarters, his young shoulders drooping.

Chapter 17

Kitty hoped she had seen the last of Sherman, believing his failure to capture Vicksburg by land would surely discourage him from trying again. She soon realized, however, that the stubborn general did not give up easily. In less than three weeks he was back—this time across the river on the Louisiana banks. General Grant had finally joined him, and together they renewed the attempt to cut a canal through Swampy Toe, a lowland area across the Mississippi River and opposite Vicksburg.

When weather permitted, Kitty and Sally would go to Sky Parlor, one of the higher hills in town that afforded them an excellent view, and watch specks of Yankees laboriously felling trees and digging their canal across the river. At first alarmed, Kitty soon grew complacent, if not actually amused, by the enemy's puny efforts. Only Northerners would ever think of such a harebrained scheme, she often remarked to Sally, who was in complete agreement. After all, the Almighty had created the mighty Mississippi, so it wasn't very likely that any fool Yankee was going to alter its course! Their confidence was strengthened by the fact that few shells were being fired into town during this time.

Spirits continued to improve with the passing of time. Almost everyone was contributing to the cause, even emptying flower pots and window planters of their usual floral arrangements and refilling them with a species of poppies from which opium could be extracted. Groups met regularly to knit socks and mufflers, fill cartridges, or roll bandages.

Because she was not adept with a needle, Kitty had agreed to grow opium and volunteered to roll bandages, as had Sally. Now, as the two girls made their way up the steep hill to Cora Crane's house, where the Ladies Auxiliary was being held this week, Kitty paused to catch her breath.

"Can't you hurry, Kitty!" Sally exclaimed impatiently. "We're already ten minutes late. Honestly, I don't doubt you'll be late to your own funeral."

"Hmph, I hope so. I'd just as soon miss it altogether," she quipped. "You know, I believe your marriage to David has turned you into a disagreeable old matron."

"Well, it's no wonder if I am. David and I have been married a month, but we only had a week together, and then he had to return to his regiment in Jackson. We even had to spend our honeymoon at his family's house because there wasn't a vacant room to rent anywhere in town."

"Just be glad you had a honeymoon. At least David's family was considerate enough to retreat to their relatives' plantation outside of town so you two could have one week of privacy."

The conversation was terminated as they reached Cora's house. The buzz of feminine chatter reached Kitty's ears as Cora led the way to the double parlor, which was filled to capacity with women of all ages—married, single, and widowed, each occupied with the task of tearing strips of linen and rolling bandages. Kitty took a vacant seat beside Cora's daughter, Bess.

A small frown furrowed her brow when she realized that the usual topic was being discussed for the hundredth time, or so it seemed—the growing shortages caused by the war. Credit was now a thing of the past, gold was preferred, and the Confederate dollar was steadily declining in value. Everything was sky high. Even tea and coffee had become luxuries, the latter selling for no less than five dollars a pound, when it could be purchased at all. As a result, sassafras root and leaves were ground and used as a substitute for tea, and acorns or sliced, dried, and ground sweet potatoes acted as a poor replacement for coffee.

To Kitty, it seemed that in a short space of time the Yankees had succeeded in turning their world topsy-turvy. Postal service had stopped almost completely, communications were beginning to falter, and the Southern Railroad, badly in need of repairs, was now used mostly by the military. To make matters worse the ferryboat system between Vicksburg and Louisiana had been terminated. The

Yankees' noose was tightening, and everyone in town was feeling the pinch. Still, Kitty was tired of hearing the same topics discussed, especially when the older women usually dominated the conversation, as Flora was doing now.

"Well, if more planters had read Mr. Shannon's editorials in the *Whig*, instead of listening to our government officials, I daresay we wouldn't be in the fix we're in now," the dowager commented dryly. "All along he advised them to raise food rather than cotton, but few of them heeded his words. As he so aptly put it in one of his editorials, no provisions have been made to ensure our citizens' having the bare necessities in the event of a siege."

"Siege! Oh, Miss Flora, you surely can't believe that we'll ever be reduced to such horrible circumstances!" Lela Shelton intervened, for once taking interest in the older woman's opinion.

"I can and I do. The town's already overflowing with soldiers and camp followers, and every day more refugees pour in from New Orleans and other towns the Yankees have captured. How is everyone to be fed, watered, and sheltered? This dry spell we're having isn't helping either. Our cisterns are rapidly depleting, and even now soldiers and refugees are having to drink that filthy river water. It's no wonder tempers are short. It's getting to be unsafe to walk the streets in broad daylight," Flora finished, deftly ripping off another length of linen from an old bedsheet.

"Indeed it is," Celia Collins agreed. "Why, only yesterday I passed a group of soldiers in town, and I'm sure I heard one of them make an unseemly remark about my appearance that was quite lewd," she added indignantly, though the sparkle in her eyes belied her words.

"It's a shame more of our hometown boys aren't stationed here, then maybe we wouldn't have soldiers from all over the South infiltrating the town," Cora remarked. "The officers are nice enough, but I fear some of the enlisted men are sadly lacking in manners."

"To my way of thinking, these so-called nice officers show far more interest in pursuing our young ladies than pursuing the enemy. They entertain so much, one would think they were celebrating the war, not fighting it," Mattie Blanks commented waspishly.

Kitty stifled a yawn as the conversation droned on until, finally, Phoebe changed the subject to Jefferson Davis's brother, Joseph, with whom everyone in the room sympathized. The Yankees had ransacked his plantation, Hurricane, last summer and burned the house to the ground.

"Has anyone heard from Eliza Davis?" she asked, referring to Joseph's wife. Without waiting for an answer, she added, "I understand the poor woman is in exceedingly bad health. Of course, I'm sure the terrible rumor that's been circulating around town hasn't helped matters."

Normally not one to enjoy gossip, Kitty was for once curious, particularly when an uncomfortable silence fell over the room.

"What rumor, Aunt Phoebe?" she asked.

"Good heavens, Kitty, where have you been these past weeks?" Sally snorted. "Surely everybody in town has heard that ridiculous tale about President Davis and President Lincoln being half brothers!"

Kitty's eyes widened in astonishment, but before she could reply Mattie intervened.

"Considering the facts, I wouldn't call it ridiculous, Sally. For one thing, both men were born in the same vicinity in Kentucky. I understand that Jefferson's birth preceded President Lincoln's by only eight months," she finished smugly.

"A mere coincidence, which hardly proves that the two of them are half brothers," Flora retorted.

"Not by itself alone, perhaps, but don't forget that Jefferson's father, Sam, was a well-to-do landowner in Hardin County, Kentucky. Rumor has it that President Lincoln's mother was a domesticated servant at the same house where Sam Davis boarded one time. Rumor also has it that he was quite a womanizer and that his wife was in the last stage of confinement prior to Jefferson's birth when he stayed in Elizabethtown. It is believed that, during that time, Mr. Davis and Mrs. Lincoln formed an intimate relationship, which resulted in Mr. Lincoln's birth nine months later," Mattie finished with relish.

"Rubbish!" Flora snapped. "I doubt there's a word of truth to any of it."

"Maybe not, but there certainly could be," Effie Collins said, siding with Mattie. "If you've ever seen a picture of Mr. Lincoln, you must admit there is a striking resemblance between the two presidents, particularly from the nose up. Why, they're even similar in build—tall and lanky. Of course, all the Davis men are tall, or so I've heard."

Disgusted, Flora rose from her chair. "I, for one, find this entire discussion very distasteful, and I also think your assumptions are totally unfounded. It's growing late, so shall we adjourn?''

Since the room had become charged with friction between the two outspoken ladies, everyone thanked Cora for her hospitality and quickly departed. Sally left with her mother, so Kitty walked home alone. As she strolled up the front walk, Daisy rushed out of the house to meet her, informing her that Charlie had come into town to get medicine for his wife and was now waiting for her inside.

"Ah figured you'd wanna see him, so Ah talked him intuh stayin' a spell. 'Course de minute Ah brung out de hominy grits, black-eyed peas, and cawnbread frum dinner, he sot rat down!''

Kitty handed her shawl to Daisy and walked down the hall to the breakfast room. There she found Charlie seated at the round oak table, obviously enjoying the food Daisy had set before him. He stood up and, ignoring the napkin beside his plate, wiped his mouth with the back of his callused hand.

"Sit down and finish your supper, Charlie." Kitty smiled, pulling a chair away from the table and sitting down. "Daisy tells me you had to get some medicine for your wife. How is she?''

"She's doing por'ly, Miss Kitty. She jes' cain't seem to shake off that cough she's had ever since last spring. Now, she's spittin' up blood. Yer pa had Doc Blanks come out to see her last week. He thinks she's got a touch of lung fever. He give her somethin' fer pain, but she's done took it all, so I had to come into town to git some more.''

"I'm so sorry, Charlie. I hope she gets better real soon. By the way, how's Pa and Mammy Lou?''

"Oh, Mist' Dave's jest fine, and Mammy Lou—well, she's comin' along pretty good, I reckon. 'Course, she misses Uncle Thad somethin' fierce, but she never lets on much.''

"No, she wouldn't," Kitty murmured sadly, then forced a smile to her lips. "Won't be much longer 'til spring, from the looks of it. Will Pa plant mostly cotton again?''

Charlie took another swallow of buttermilk and shook his head. "Don't think so, since we ain't sold the bales we already got from last year. Nope, I reckon we'll be plantin' mostly cane and vegetables come spring. 'Course since that dad-blamed idiot in Washington took it upon hisself to free the slaves last month, mouthin' off somethin' 'bout 'mancipation procla—whatchama-call-it, a body cain't rightly tell who's gonna be around to do the plantin' this spring. The

Moores have already lost a passel of their field hands. So've the Waddells an' a few other planters.''

"That's a shame. Guess I'm not really surprised, though. Mr. Moore doesn't personally mistreat any of his people, but he's always turned a blind eye to the mean way his overseer handles their field hands. I think he just doesn't want to be bothered with the problems of running a plantation.

"Mister Waddell, however, is another matter altogether. He's just downright mean. I swear I believe that man beats his slaves just for the sheer pleasure of hearing them holler. Thank goodness people like that are in the minority!''

"Yas'm, but even so, that ain't gonna stop all of us from losin' some of our slaves, I'm afraid.''

Daisy had just set a place at the table for her mistress. Helping herself to the boiled pigs' feet and baked sweet potatoes, Kitty said: "I disagree. Pa's never been unkind to a slave in his life, and he's always treated our people fair and square. Belle Glen's as much their home as ours, so I doubt seriously that any more of ours will be running off, no matter what Mr. Lincoln says.'' She paused to ladle some greens into a bowl, then crumble her cornbread into the pot liquor.

"Some more of them already have,'' came the solemn and unexpected reply.

Kitty's fork clattered to her plate, and she shot Charlie a look of total disbelief.

"I—I can't believe it!'' she whispered incredulously. "How many have we lost?''

"Not many,'' Charlie assured her. "At least, not yet. All but one wuz field hands, so I doubt you'd know most of them.''

"And the one who wasn't a field hand—was it Zeke?''

Charlie ducked his head and nodded. "Yas'm. Funny thing about that. The week before he tuk off, he seemed happy as a lark. More'n once I heard him singin' that song slaves used to sing 'fore they'd take off for the Underground Railroad . . . er, 'Follow the Drinking Gourd.' Yep, that wuz the song all right. Reckon we should've knowed then whut he was aimin' to do, but we didn't. I tell you, pore ole Doshe an' Lemme wuz sho' broken up after he left. So wuz yer pa. Fact is, Mist' Dave's talkin' about freein' all his slaves once't the war's over an' he gits enough money set aside to pay wages to them that stays on.''

"Well, at least we haven't lost as many slaves as the Moores and the Waddells." Kitty sighed.

"Speakin' of the Waddells, did ya hear about Mist' Wade?"

"No. Is he coming home soon?" Kitty asked, taking another bite of cornbread.

" 'Fraid not, ma'am. Mist' Wade ain't ever comin' home. He wuz killed in a skirmish near Murfreesboro a couple of weeks back. His folks jest got the news last week. I thought you mighta heard already."

"No, I hadn't heard," she murmured, a sudden queasiness causing her to shove her plate aside. "Poor Mary Belle. Why, she and Wade have been married for less than two months. He only had two weeks' leave. They hardly had any time at all together."

"Miss Mary Belle's pretty torn up about it, but leastways she had a short spell of happiness with him."

"It needn't have been a short spell if Wade had just listened to Mary Belle. She had begged him to stay home and pay the five thousand dollars for a substitute to fight in his place, but he wouldn't do it."

"Naw'm—an' neither would any other man worth his weight in salt, not to my way of thinking. But then, I reckon everybody has to do whut he thinks best. Every bucket's gotta set on its own bottom, if'n you git my meanin'. If'n it warn't fer my missus doin' so por'ly, I'd be hotfootin' it up to Tennessee 'bout now. Shore would like to be fightin' side by side with them two boys of mine."

Finally replete from the ample meal, Charlie pushed back from the table and, after belching loudly, got to his feet.

"Beggin' yer pardon, ma'am," he muttered with obvious chagrin, then chuckled good-naturedly. "Like I'm always tellin' my missus, a good belch is a hungry man's best friend!"

Kitty returned his grin and walked him to the door. Standing on the front porch, she watched as he strode down the walkway. His horse was hitched to a black, wrought-iron statue situated in front of the white picket fence that enclosed the yard. Vaulting onto the saddle, Charlie turned to wave good-bye, then stopped with a snap of his fingers.

"Gosh darnit, I almost forgot! Mist' Dave said I wuz to tell you he got a letter from Mist' Bret yesterday. Says he's doin' fine, and he's still in Memphis."

Kitty stiffened. Bret had unexpectedly left for Memphis right after

Sherman had pulled away from Chickasaw Bluffs. He had not bothered to say good-bye, which had hardly surprised her. The deliberate slight still rankled, but it did not keep her from asking the question that was uppermost in her mind.

"Did Bret say when he'd be returning to Vicksburg?"

"Not exactly, but Mist' Dave said it sounded like he'd be comin' back pretty soon. You know Mist' Bret—he always turns up here sooner or later."

Long after Charlie had disappeared from view, Kitty remained on the porch, unmindful of the brisk nip in the air brought on by the descending twilight. The fact that Bret was a Yankee spy had not prevented her from missing him terribly these last weeks. She despised her own weakness but was powerless to do anything about it.

With a forlorn sigh, she turned to go inside, then stopped. Her eyes narrowed as she watched a soldier on horseback riding down the dusty street, coming closer and closer until, finally, he came to a halt in front of the house. Dusk made visibility poor, yet as the man dismounted and approached her, her eyes were already filled with dismay and her lips whispered his name with loathing.

"Miles!"

Chapter 18

The month of February ended with sporadic skirmishes occurring just north of Vicksburg while Grant's men continued to scout the area for some feasible means of capturing the town. The townspeople's spirit, however, had been bolstered by the Confederates' success in capturing two Union vessels in February—*Queen of the West* and the *Indianola*. These losses, plus that of the *Cairo* in December, had been serious setbacks to the enemy's river operations.

As a precaution, more Confederate troops had been pulled into Vicksburg. Among these troops had been Miles and David Shelton's regiments. Tad's company was still stationed near Jackson, much to Dede's distress. Kitty shared her disappointment and heartily wished that Tad, rather than Miles, had been ordered back to Vicksburg.

Since Miles had returned, his behavior had been totally unpredictable. Seldom was he congenial and then only briefly, his moods changing quickly and vacillating between lethargic sullenness and menacing irascibleness. During the few short weeks he had been home, Kitty's patience had been tried time and again while trying to placate him and restore harmony to their lives. They still occupied separate bedrooms, for which she was thankful. She was greatly relieved that his duties kept him away from the house for the better part of the day, but nights and weekends were becoming increasingly difficult.

During the past week, however, he had begun to shut himself in the study immediately after supper. She had been relieved at first, until last night, when she had entered the study to ask his advice on a matter pertaining to her household expenses.

The sight that greeted her had caused her blood to chill.

The room had been filled with a peculiar odor, one so pungent that she had almost gagged. Miles had been sprawled out on an overstuffed chair, intent on filling his pipe and lighting it. The obnoxious odor had become stronger, and as Kitty had spied a dried-out pot plant on the table beside him, she'd suddenly realized the identity of the sickening smell that was assailing her nostrils. Opium! Any doubt had been dispelled when Miles slowly turned his head and discovered her standing there.

For seconds neither had spoken. Then a malevolent gleam had appeared in his glazed eyes, and he'd begun to laugh, louder and louder, until Kitty had finally fled from the room.

She had not seen him since. In fact, she had stayed in bed later than usual this morning in order to give him the opportunity to have breakfast and report for duty before she made an appearance downstairs.

Now, as she stood in the dining room and counted the poppy plants she had been raising for the Confederacy, she discovered that three were missing. Was Miles suffering much pain from his old wound? She thought not, for he surely would have mentioned it. No, he was not smoking opium for medicinal purposes, but for sinful pleasure. Kitty realized she had to get rid of the plants, and the sooner the better. She had no sooner reached this decision than Daisy appeared. "Miz Kitty, duz you wants sum sas'fras tea an' biscuits fo' breakfas' dis mornin'?"

"No, I've something more important for you to do. Get Moses to hitch up the buggy, then the two of you load it with all these pot plants and take them over to Doc Blanks."

"You means jes' de dried-out ones?"

"No, I mean all of them. I want them out of here today before Mr. Miles returns home."

"But why, Miz Kitty? Dey ain' in de way, an' dey is kinda pretty."

Kitty sighed and, holding her temper in check, turned to face the puzzled servant. "Because we have to. My husband is using the dried-up leaves for his pipe, smoking them. That's why he's been acting so peculiar lately."

"Ah knowed sum'thing wuz de matter wid him, de way he's been lookin' at me, jes' lak he wuz thinkin' bad thoughts—mighty bad. Ah wuzn't gwine tuh say nuttin', Miz Kitty, but yest'day he tuk hold ob me in de hall, an' when Ah tried to git free, he hit me. He hit me hard,'' the girl informed her.

"Oh, Daisy, I'm sorry. You know our family's always tried not to mistreat anybody, especially our servants," Kitty apologized with obvious distress.

"Yas'm, Ah knows dat, but Mist' Miles . . . well, he's always been kinda dif'rent, if'n you knows whut Ah mean. Ah reckon sum folks is born wid a debil in 'em. Dem dat is . . . well, dey's jes' downright mean. Whut we gwine tuh do 'bout him, Miz Kitty? Hit ain' safe tuh be under de same roof wid him.''

"I don't know, Daisy, but you needn't worry," Kitty answered with a forced smile. "If things get too bad, we can always go home to Pa. In the meantime, get rid of these plants like I told you. Oh, and don't prepare any dinner for me. I'm eating over at Miss Sally's. Afterward, we're going to Sky Parlor Hill to see the new telescope that's been installed there.''

Later, as Kitty stood aside to allow Sally to look through the telescope, she wished she had not come. It was difficult to smile and pretend to be enjoying herself when she was so absorbed with personal problems. How she wished she could move back to Belle Glen and get away from Miles! But she realized this was not really possible. Miles would never allow it, and besides, she did not want to trouble Dave with her marital problems when he was already burdened with concerns of his own.

For one thing, Belle Glen was presently without an overseer. Charlie's wife had recently died, and last week he had joined the home militia. To make matters worse, many of their younger slaves had run away during the past few weeks, some of them hightailing it across the river to join the Union army. Besides being short-handed, she knew her father was also hurting for cash.

No, she hadn't the heart to add to his worries. She would just have to stick it out with Miles and hope for the best. Vaguely aware that Sally was speaking to her, she tried to take interest in what the girl was saying.

"I declare, this telescope is a real marvel. I've been watching those Yankees working on the canal across the river, and I swear I can almost count their whiskers!" Sally exclaimed.

"Yes, it does make them seem close. In fact, too close for comfort," Kitty answered. "I just hope they continue to stay on that side of the river.''

"They will if they know what's good for them. Did you know our soldiers are digging trenches two or three miles away that will completely surround the town? David says they're cutting down most of the trees and using the timber to shore up the trenches—or something like that. By the time they've finished clearing the woods and nearby fields, they'll be able to spot a Yankee a mile away!"

"Miles said something to that effect the other day," Kitty answered, "but, of course, he doesn't think the Yankees will ever get that close to us."

"Have you heard from Tad lately? There've been so many soldiers transferred from Jackson to Vicksburg that I keep expecting to see him marching into town with his regiment any day now."

"No, we haven't heard from him in weeks. I wish he would get transferred here."

Suddenly she noticed that Sally had become unusually pale. "Sally, what is it? Are you all right?"

"I—I am feeling a bit nauseated, but I'm sure it'll soon pass," she murmured as Kitty led her to a nearby bench. Sitting down, she managed to smile weakly and add, "It always does."

"What do you mean? Have you had these spells before? Have you seen a doctor?"

"Not yet. There's no need to, really. After all, having a baby isn't that unusual, is it." She grinned, her color returning as her queasiness disappeared.

"A baby! Oh, Sally, how wonderful!" Kitty exclaimed, taking her friend's hand in her own. "You are a sly puss! How long have you known?"

"Only a couple of weeks. You're the first to know, other than David, of course. We figured it happened on our honeymoon, but we didn't want to tell anybody until we were positive. Now, we are. Why else would I be having morning sickness every day for the past two weeks?"

They continued their conversation for another few minutes, until Sally glanced down at the dainty watch pinned to her bodice and exclaimed over the time.

"David promised to meet me here when he got off duty, but he's already twenty minutes late. I wonder what's keeping him," she said.

As if in answer, an officer suddenly appeared at the base of the wooden flight of steps that led to the top of Sky Parlor Hill. Kitty did not recognize him, nor did she pay him any attention until he unexpectedly approached them.

"Ah, Major Ritchly, how nice to see you," Sally greeted him, then turned to Kitty. "Allow me to introduce you to my friend, Mrs. Kitty Blake. Kitty, this is Major James Ritchly, David's commanding officer."

After briefly acknowledging the introduction, the major turned to Sally. "Mrs. Shelton, I'm afraid your husband is going to be slightly delayed this afternoon. When I learned he was supposed to meet you here, I offered to relay the message to you. However, with your permission, ladies, I'll be most happy to escort you both home," he offered, turning to include Kitty in the conversation.

Kitty caught the appreciative gleam in his eyes as his gaze rested on her face, silently impelling her to accept. Being the recipient of male admiration was no novelty for her, but there was a certain appeal about the major that made refusal impossible, and in the next instant both women found themselves being escorted down the treacherous steps.

To Kitty's dismay, after Sally had been left at the Sheltons' house, the major insisted on walking her the rest of the way home. She shuddered to think what Miles's reaction would be upon seeing her escorted to their front door by a total stranger, particularly one as attractive as the major. Within minutes, however, she found herself talking effortlessly with the young officer about one topic after another.

Not only was James Ritchly quite charming, he was also an extremely good conversationalist. By the time they reached her front porch, Kitty was in a relaxed frame of mind for the first time in many days, and without any thought of Miles, she invited him in for a cup of tea. Before he could accept, however, the front door was flung open.

When Kitty recognized the barely controlled outrage in her husband's eyes, her heart sank. She quickly introduced the two men, then pointed out that the major had been kind enough to escort her and Sally home from Sky Parlor Hill.

The atmosphere became charged with tension as Miles coolly thanked the puzzled major, then, after pointedly refraining from asking him inside, bid him an abrupt farewell. Seething with anger over his deliberate rudeness, Kitty turned and walked into the front parlor.

"How could you, Miles? How could you be so rude to a guest?" she demanded, turning to confront him with blazing eyes.

"Guest—or another one of your lovers, my dear?" he countered in a deadly calm voice that hinted of violence.

"I have no lovers," she denied.

"Haven't you? And what about Bret?"

Fear suddenly rippled through Kitty, and her reply was defensive. "I haven't seen Bret in weeks, though I fail to see what he has to do with any of this."

"Don't you?" Miles sneered, coming to stand before her. Encircling her throat with his hands, he gave her a malevolent smile as his thumbs began stroking her arched neck in a threatening caress. "Don't you, indeed?" he repeated in a quietly menacing voice.

Mustering all her courage, Kitty thrust his hands away and stepped back. "Don't change the subject by trying to intimidate me," she snapped.

Before she could continue, Miles's arms shot out, his strong fingers biting into her shoulders as he jerked her to him. Seeing the glazed look in his eyes, the venomous expression contorting his handsome features, she tensed with alarm.

For seconds that seemed like hours, Miles held her thus, and then a sinister smile twisted his lips. "Intimidate you?" he mocked. "I seriously doubt you've ever been intimidated by anyone, least of all me. I think that was what always attracted me to you. I've amused myself with many beautiful women, but none of them possessed your fiery spirit, your courage and determination. None were as unpredictable as you. Even when we were children, you were unattainable. You could never see me for Bret, but I swore then that you'd be mine someday. *All* mine," he murmured bitterly, adding with a mirthless chuckle, "Unfortunately, I underestimated you—or, rather, your ability to deceive."

Fear consumed Kitty, yet she refused to give in to it. "Don't be ridiculous, Miles. I married you, not Bret. If our marriage leaves something to be desired, I can hardly be blamed for that. I didn't force you to fight for the Confederacy. You chose to do so. I didn't shoot you, the Yankees did. They're the ones responsible for your . . . your inability to resume our relationship, and I refuse to take the blame for something that's beyond my control. We're just going to have to learn to live with it. In the meantime, I have no intention of letting you bully me, nor do I intend to put up with your suspicions and your rude behavior. Now, I suggest we end this conversation before we both say things we'll later regret," she finished coldly, removing his hands from her shoulders.

Before he could reply, Daisy appeared and informed them that supper was ready. Thankful for the interruption, Kitty swept past him and followed Daisy from the room, making a dignified exit that gave no hint of her fear and trembling. Without waiting for Miles to assist her, as was customary, she seated herself at the table and automatically gave instructions for the meal to be served.

An uncomfortable silence fell, and relief flooded through Kitty when the meal ended and Miles excused himself, then walked to the study. He apparently had not noticed the absence of the poppy plants—not yet. But there was little doubt in her mind that he would be livid with rage once he discovered they had been removed. Pray God, he won't miss them tonight, she thought nervously, for she doubted she could withstand another scene without going to pieces.

Feeling drained, she walked tiredly into the parlor. Too jittery to remain still, she picked up her sewing basket, now filled with several of Scotty's torn garments. Though she still disliked sewing, necessity had prompted her to learn how to mend her son's clothing.

Minutes later Daisy brought Scotty to her, a broad grin lighting up her face.

"Miz Kitty, duz you want me tuh come back in a lil' while an' put de baby tuh bed?"

"No, I'll tuck him in. I always like to read him a bedtime story," she replied, smiling fondly as her son toddled toward her outstretched arms. "And Daisy, I'd like for you to sleep on the trundle bed in Scotty's room tonight. If Moses is afraid to remain in the carriage house by himself, he can sleep on that cot in the attic. Since my husband isn't himself these days, I'd rest easier if you were nearby." Kitty hated to admit fear to herself, much less to the servants, but the situation had grown too dangerous to ignore.

Daisy nodded, then left the room. Shoving all unpleasantness from her mind, Kitty removed some blocks from a toy box in the corner of the room and sank down beside her son on the carpet. Within a short time she was totally wrapped up in building tall structures that, once completed, Scotty gleefully knocked down, then tried to help her rebuild. They were having so much fun that neither was aware Miles had entered the room until, seating himself on the sofa, he extracted a cheroot from his coat pocket and struck a match with his thumbnail. Surprised, Kitty glanced over at him, shriveling inwardly beneath his contemptuous gaze.

"Papa!" Scotty chortled, toddling over and holding out his chubby little arms to him. When Miles made no move to pick him up, the child's face clouded with disappointment. Suddenly the glowing tip of Miles's cheroot caught his attention.

"Light—pretty light," Scotty gurgled, his pudgy hand reaching out to touch the fascinating object.

Miles's eyes narrowed, and a cruel smile twisted his lips. Kitty's breath caught in her throat when she saw him reach out and take hold of Scotty's arm.

"So you want the pretty light, do you." He chuckled menacingly. "Well, it's time you learned a lesson."

"Miles!" Kitty cried, sensing his intent and rushing to her feet. But she was unable to cover the space between them in time.

"Pretty things can hurt, young man," he stated, and ground the glowing tip of his cheroot into the boy's tender flesh.

In the next moment Kitty was jerking the screaming child away from Miles, cradling him protectively and attempting to calm him with soothing words as she examined the burn on his arm. Her words, however, failed to comfort the frightened youngster, and as his howling grew louder, Daisy came running into the room.

"Whut hoppen't, Miz Kitty? Is de baby hurt?" she asked with alarm.

"There's been an accident," Kitty lied in a tremulous voice. "Scotty burned himself on my husband's cheroot."

"Ah'll fetch sum lard tuh put on hit. Dat'll take de sting out an' keep hit frum blist'ring," Daisy offered, already scurrying from the room.

"Bring it to Scotty's room, Daisy, and hurry," Kitty ordered, quickly following the servant even though she was aching to strike out at the man who, even now, was watching her with unconcealed satisfaction.

Much later, after she had tended to Scotty's burn and rocked him to sleep, she made her way back downstairs, consumed with fury. If she had heretofore been repelled by Miles, she now hated him with an intensity such as she had never before experienced.

Miles was still seated on the sofa when she reentered the parlor, a sardonic look on his handsome face as he watched her walk over to him. For a moment Kitty glared at him. Then, without warning she struck him across the face. His expression registered shock at first, then amused admiration as he got slowly to his feet.

"Why, Miles? Why did you deliberately harm your own son?" she demanded, her breasts heaving with agitation.

"My son?" he whispered, grabbing her by the shoulders and jerking her to him. "My son—or Bret's?" His eyes glittered with triumph when he saw her anger give way to alarm. "What kind of a fool do you take me for, Kitty? My God, I'm not blind! The little bastard is the spittin' image of Bret. Admit it, damn you!"

The last of Kitty's composure crumbled as she broke free of her husband's grasp. "Yes, he's Bret's son, and I'm glad he is. Glad, do you hear!" she cried. "Now, get out. Get out of this house!"

Too late she saw Miles's fist shoot out, then felt the full impact of his knuckles against the side of her face, snapping her head backward and sending her to the floor. Only half-conscious, she glanced up and found him standing over her but was too dazed to move. Horrified, she saw his foot come up and was powerless to stop its descent, groaning aloud when the tip of his boot thrust cruelly into her stomach.

"You damned bitch! You filthy little whore! Order me from my own house, will you," he snarled, kicking her again in the ribs.

Bruised and winded, Kitty moaned and clutched her middle, curling into a ball while he towered above her, clenching and unclenching his fists. It was with visible effort that he slowly regained his composure, his eyes glittering malevolently when he heard her whimper of pain.

"I have no intention of moving out," he stated, "not now or ever."

Relief flooded through her as she watched him turn and walk from the room, but not until she heard him slam out the front door did she attempt to get to her feet. She felt battered, and there was a dull ache in her side where she had been kicked, though she doubted any ribs had actually been broken. Biting her lip to keep from crying, she limped out of the parlor and slowly made her way up the stairs, clutching her bruised side.

Not bothering to undress, she sank down on the bed, lying crosswise on the soft feather mattress as her eyes stared unseeingly at the overhead canopy. One thought occupied her mind, one thought alone. She had to get away from Miles. She *must!* It was no longer safe for her, or her child, to live under the same roof with him. He was completely mad.

Accepting this fact, her nerves relaxed somewhat, and she began to plot a feasible course of action. Tomorrow morning she would take Scotty and the servants to Belle Glen as soon as Miles left for duty. A small buckboard would have to be hired from the livery stables, an expense that would simply have to be met.

Had Bret been in town, she could have gotten the buckboard from him, but he wasn't. It was probably just as well, she thought tiredly, for had he been here and learned of Miles's cruelty, particularly concerning Scotty, there was little doubt in her mind that he would have killed Miles. No, it was best that Bret was away. With a forlorn sigh, she closed her eyes and drifted off to sleep.

Some time later, a disturbing noise penetrated her dreams, gradually arousing her. Still half-asleep, she raised herself on one elbow and tried to distinguish the sound. She soon realized that someone was banging on a door and Daisy was calling to her in a distressed voice. Unmindful of the dull pain in her side, Kitty slid from the bed and made her way down the dark hallway toward the nursery. The door was slightly ajar, and the small lamp beside the bed cast eerie shadows over the room that, at first, appeared to be empty, until she heard Daisy's muffled voice coming from the wardrobe. The door had been locked, but luckily the key had not been removed.

"It's all right, Daisy, I'll have you out in a second," Kitty said reassuringly as she unlocked the door and flung it open. In the next instant Daisy stumbled from the closet, her eyes wide with fear.

"Oh, Lawd, Miz Kitty! Mist' Miles he dun tuk de baby," she wailed, wringing her hands with distress. "Ah wuz sleepin' on de trudle, jes' lak you sed, when Mist' Miles snuk up on me, put his hand ober my mouf, an' shoved me intuh dat closet. Den Ah heard him tell de baby dat he wuz gwine tuh take him out back, so's dey could play a game. Lawd, Miz Kitty, dat man ain' up tuh no good. Ah's skeered he's gwine tuh kill dat chile!"

Before the last words were uttered, Kitty was racing toward her own room. Not stopping to light a lamp, she jerked open the drawer to her nightstand and, groping blindly for a moment, extracted a small revolver.

"Lawd Gawd, Miz Kitty! You ain' gwine tuh use dat?" Daisy cried as her mistress brushed by her and headed for the stairs.

"If I have to, yes," came the curt reply. Upon seeing Moses, who had just come down from the attic and was sleepily rubbing his eyes, Kitty went into action. "Daisy, you come with me. Moses, go for help, and be quick about it," she ordered.

"Whar duz Ah goes fo' dat, Miz Kitty?" the boy asked, still not understanding the situation.

"The Altschuls and the Sheltons are our closest neighbors, so try them," Kitty answered over her shoulder as she rushed down the stairs, Daisy and Moses following quickly.

"But Miz Kitty, dey's asleep," Moses protested.

Kitty whirled around to face him. "Then wake them, but don't you dare come back here without bringing help. And for God's sake, hurry!"

"You duz lak Miz Kitty sez or Ah'll hab yo' hide when you gits bak!" Daisy added, then darted after her mistress, who was already opening the back door.

For a moment they stood uncertainly on the porch steps and peered into the darkness, both aware of the ominous smell of smoke that was faintly permeating the air. A child's frightened cry suddenly rent the air, causing Kitty's head to jerk toward the carriage house just as it appeared to burst into flames.

"Oh, no!" Kitty cried, already running toward the growing inferno.

Scotty's screams intermingled with the panicky neighing of the chestnut mare that was stabled just behind the carriage house; but Kitty was only dimly aware of this as she ran toward the blazing structure. She came to an abrupt halt as Miles rushed out of the carriage house, clutching a large can of coal oil in one hand and a torch in the other. Unaware of Kitty's presence, he chuckled villainously as he looked back upon his handiwork. Kitty's hand tightened on the revolver, and she stepped out of the shadows to confront him.

"Stand aside, Miles, or I'll shoot," she ordered in a deadly calm voice.

His evil mirth faded at the sound of her voice, replaced by a glowering frown. "Don't be a fool, Kitty. You can't go in there. You wouldn't stand a chance."

"I'm going in after my child, and you're not going to stop me. Now stand aside, or so help me, I'll kill you!"

Reluctantly Miles obeyed her command, his hand tightening on the handle of the coal-oil can. Silently he willed Kitty to come closer so that he could fling the half-filled container at her and throw her

off balance. As if sensing his intent, she halted and motioned for
Daisy to join her.

"I'm going in after Scotty, Daisy. Hold this gun on him, and if he
moves so much as an inch, shoot him," she instructed the wide-eyed
girl.

Without waiting for a reply, she dashed into the blazing building,
stopping just inside to get her bearings. The room was filled with
smoke and flames, but fortunately the fire was more intense toward
the rear of the building than the front. Of course it would be, she
reasoned, realizing Miles would have deliberately left open his own
means of escape. But where was Scotty? His screams had suddenly
died to a choked whimper. There was no sight of him anywhere.

"Scotty, where are you?" she cried, then was racked by a spasm
of coughing as smoke filled her lungs and burned her eyes.

"Mama!" wailed the child from nearby.

Holding one hand over her mouth and nose, Kitty stumbled
blindly toward the sound. A cry escaped her when she bumped into
the back of the carriage situated in the middle of the cobblestone
floor. Heat seared her skin and stung her eyes, causing her fear to
increase while she stood uncertainly by the vehicle and scanned the
room for some sign of Scotty. The tiny voice sounded again, and
relief washed over her as, glancing down, she spied her son lying
facedown underneath the carriage.

Jerking him to her breast, Kitty planted a kiss on his cheek and
backtracked to the door. Her progress was excruciatingly slow as she
picked her way through patches of fire. She was blinded by smoke,
which soon filled her lungs, making each breath more torturous than
the one before. A burning beam fell directly in her path, and for one
terrifying moment she feared they were trapped. Then she spotted a
small opening and managed to skirt her way around the blazing
obstacle. Pressing the boy's face against her shoulder to protect him
from the smoke, Kitty trudged on until at last she staggered outside
and fell to her knees, gulping in the fresh night air gratefully. A
short distance away, Daisy was still holding the gun on Miles,
whose clothes were spotted with coal oil that had sloshed from the
can when he'd dashed from the burning building.

"Thank de Lawd you's safe!" she exclaimed, glancing at her
mistress. It was an unwise move on her part, for in that instant Miles
dropped the half-filled oil can and lunged toward her.

Kitty's scream alerted the girl, and, whirling around to confront

Miles, she instinctively pulled the trigger. The bullet struck his shoulder, and for a moment he froze, unaware that he was standing in a puddle of coal oil from the can he had dropped seconds before. As pain seared through his shoulder, the torch he was clutching wavered, then dropped to the ground. Kitty and Daisy screamed simultaneously as flames engulfed him, quickly turning him into a writhing human torch. Too dazed to move at first, Kitty pressed Scotty's face against her shoulder, shielding him from the horrible scene as hysteria welled up inside of her.

"Oh, God—roll on the ground, Miles!" she shouted as, horrified, she saw her husband's hands flailing about, slapping at the burning clothes that were sticking to his scorched body.

The sickening stench of seared human flesh grew stronger and was accompanied by animalistic screams of agony as Miles darted about, then fell to the ground. The sight propelled Kitty into action. She thrust Scotty into Daisy's arms and ran forward but was stopped by the appearance of neighbors, who grabbed her, forcing her to stand back. It was David Shelton who beat out her husband's flaming body with his jacket, but by this time only a twitching mass of charred humanity remained on the ground.

Trembling, Kitty walked over to where several men were now kneeling around Miles. "He's alive, Miss Kitty, but I advise you not to come any closer," one of them warned.

Heedless of his words, she knelt down beside her husband and stared at his grotesquely burned face. As if sensing her presence, he opened his eyes and glared at her with undisguised hatred. He tried to speak, but she had to lean down to catch his words.

"*I would have killed you both if I could have!*" he rasped bitterly.

Then his head fell lifelessly to the side. Minutes later, as Sally gently guided her inside the house, his vicious words rang in her dazed mind. She had no tears to shed for Miles, nor was she sorry he was dead. His evilness would not be missed.

Chapter 19

Kitty sat on the floor in the front parlor, her black bombazine skirt billowing around her as she placed one of her worn slippers on a piece of black leather that had been cut from an old valise. Daisy stood nearby and shook her head disapprovingly.

"Miz Kitty, dat leather's too thin tuh make a good shoe sole," she remarked while she watched her mistress painstakingly cut into the tough material.

"Well, it's just going to have to do. All of us need shoes, and I can't afford to pay thirty dollars a pair for them," muttered Kitty.

"But whut you gwine tuh use fo' de top ob dem shoes?"

"There's a long, black satin cape in one of the trunks in the attic. Go upstairs and fetch it for me. After you've done that, go out back and pick about a dozen of those locust thorns."

Daisy looked at her mistress as if she had taken leave of her senses. "Locust thorns!" she exclaimed.

"Yes, locust thorns. I've heard they make passable needles. Oh, and while you're at it, take an ice pick and make a hole for the eyes of the needles."

"But why duz we need locust thorns? You hab sum needles."

"I have one needle. I broke the other one when I was mending Scotty's jacket. Like everything else, needles are as scarce as hens' teeth. I couldn't afford them even if I could find them, so I certainly don't intend to break my last needle sewing through this tough leather. Now just do what I tell you and stop arguing with me. Oh, how I wish Mammy Lou were here."

Minutes later, Kitty held the newly cut soles in her hand. Daisy was right, she admitted with disgust, the material was too thin to last more than a month, and then only if used sparingly. Whatever were they going to do for shoes? The idea of constantly having to make them was daunting to her, but she must conserve what little money she had left from Miles's once flourishing law practice. It would be gone all too soon, and then what? With a discouraged sigh, Kitty walked over to the window.

It had been only a month since Miles's death, and already she was worrying about money. At least while he lived they had been receiving a small monthly payment from the Confederacy. Now there was nothing coming in. The very mourning clothes she wore had been loaned to her by Cora Crane—clothes she despised wearing. She felt like a hypocrite, for she certainly did not miss Miles, nor did she pretend to mourn his loss in the company of those who were closest to her.

Thanks to Daisy's hysterical caterwauling to the neighbors on the night of the fire, everyone in town knew the sordid details concerning Miles's death and what had happened beforehand. Kitty had their complete sympathy, if not their understanding of the situation. Most felt that Miles's previous injury, coupled with battle fatigue, had brought on a nervous breakdown. Those closest to Kitty knew the unvarnished truth—that Miles had always possessed a streak of cruelty that had bordered on insanity. Only Sally and Phoebe had been shocked by this revelation, but after seeing the evidence of Miles's cruelty, the burn on Scotty's arm, and Kitty's bruised face, neither of them doubted Miles's malice. When Kitty had reluctantly answered Sally's questions the day after Miles's death, giving her some insight into her unhappy relationship with her husband, Sally had been horrified.

Throughout the ordeal her father had been a source of strength for her, and even Dede had been a comfort during the few days she had stayed with Kitty. Nothing, however, could persuade her to return with them to Belle Glen. It simply would not have been wise for her to leave her house vacant, not with so many soldiers and refugees roaming the streets. To have done so would have been inviting vandalism. In all probability, by the time she returned from any extended visit, her house would have been stripped bare.

Bret did not return to town until the day after the funeral. Accompanied by Phoebe, he had briefly paid his respects to Kitty, as was customary. Once he saw her bruised face, however, leashed anger had glittered momentarily in his eyes, belying his outward calm. Other than that, he had shown no greater concern for her than what would have been ordinarily expected. He was a master at masking his feelings, and Kitty had been secretly irked by his polite but distant attitude. It never occurred to her that his remoteness had stemmed from a desire to protect her from unsavory gossip.

That same week he had left for Natchez, and she had not seen him since. Unlike others, it seemed that he could come and go as he pleased, though how he managed to do so baffled her. She supposed he was making the trip to bid for the coming year's cotton crops in the vicinity. The fact that he would put business ahead of Scotty and her welfare infuriated her, particularly when some of his business would undoubtedly be conducted with the Yankees who still occupied Natchez. It amazed her that no one had suspected this, and she often wondered why nobody ever questioned his movements. Little did she realize that, while posing as a cotton buyer in Natchez, Bret had actually been on another spy mission for Pemberton.

Now, as she stared out the window, a feeling of depression washed over her. It all seemed so hopeless. There was little money left in her account at the bank, and she knew her father no longer had the resources to help her. If and when Bret returned, she might ask him for a loan, but after mulling this possibility over in her mind, she quickly discarded it. She had no means of repaying such a loan, were he willing to make one, and she had no intention of asking him for a handout, not even for the sake of their child. Besides, she was convinced that whatever money he might have had been made from his business ventures with the enemy. No, she would not accept help from a traitor!

An idea suddenly struck her, and she squared her shoulders. *Water!* Why not sell water to soldiers who passed by her house? Not very patriotic, perhaps, but certainly practical. There were two cisterns in the backyard that, despite the recent dry spell, provided her with an ample supply of water. The cisterns at the courthouse were dry half the time from constant use; consequently, soldiers and refugees were forced to drink muddy river water. Lord knew they would be glad to get clean water, and she was going to provide it—for a price!

"Heah's de cape an' de thorns, Miz Kitty," Daisy drawled upon reentering the room.

Kitty whirled around to face her, excitement dancing in her eyes.

"We'll get to those later, but right now there's something else we're going to do. Go fetch those boxes of fruit jars out of the storehouse and give them a good washing. While you're doing that, have Moses draw me a couple of buckets of water from the cistern."

"Whut you gwine tuh do?" Daisy asked.

"I'm going to sell water, that's what!"

"Who's you gwine tuh sell it to?"

"Soldiers, refugees, or anybody else who's willing to pay for it. Now let's see," Kitty mused, tapping her cheek with one forefinger, "we'll charge a dime per cup, fifty cents a pint, and a dollar for a quart."

"Miz Kitty, hit ain' rat tuh sell water to dem po' soldiers. Hit jes' ain' patriotic!"

"Patriotism is fine for those who can afford it. We can't. You and I are going to sell water to anyone who wants to buy it, and like Mr. Collins, we'll double the price if they pay us with Confederate money."

"Miz Kitty, you oughta be 'shamed ob yo'self!" Daisy exclaimed. "Whut's folks 'round heah gonna think?"

"I'm not ashamed of myself, and I don't care what anybody thinks," came the angry retort. "I've got to have money if we're going to keep on eating, and this is how I'm going to make it. Now quit arguing with me and get a move on."

Daisy made a hasty retreat, but Kitty could hear her grumbling all the way down the hall. Thank goodness Mammy Lou isn't here, she thought, or I wouldn't get to sell the first drop of water. Nevertheless, Daisy's disapproval had dampened Kitty's spirits somewhat and pricked her with shame.

"Hmph! The soldiers will spend their money anyway. Better to spend it on water than whiskey," she muttered, shoving conscience aside.

By late afternoon four pails of water had been emptied, sold by the cup, pint, or quart to soldiers and refugees who had lined up in front of her picket fence. Keeping tab of the sales in her head, Kitty estimated that she must have made twenty dollars or more, and all in less than three hours. Not bad for a day's work, she thought with satisfaction. As long as her cisterns held water, she would manage. Surely it would rain soon—but not too much, she hoped. An over-abundance of rain would keep the courthouse cisterns plentifully supplied, and that would hurt her own little business.

Too tired to try and sell another bucket of water, Kitty turned away the last few customers and picked up the cigar box that held the money from her numerous sales. Turning to walk back to the house, she stopped, her eyes widening with surprise when she saw Bret walking briskly toward her. One glance at his stormy expression told her he was livid with rage. Without so much as a greeting, he took hold of her arm and quickly escorted her to the house.

"Just what in the hell do you think you're doing?" he growled. "I'm not in town five minutes before Miss Phoebe is telling me that you're selling—actually selling water. God in heaven, what'll you do next?"

"Anything I have to in order to survive." She tried and failed to free her arm from his unmerciful grasp. "Whatever I do is none of your business, not that you've seemed particularly concerned about our welfare since Miles died. In fact, you couldn't wait to leave town as soon as you found out I was a widow. Now, take your hands off of me!" she insisted as he half shoved her through the front door.

Bret slammed the front door and propelled her into the parlor. He tossed a neatly wrapped parcel on the sofa and turned to face her.

"Just why is it necessary for you to sell water in order to survive? Surely Miles left you well provided for. Or didn't he?"

Pride made Kitty hesitate before answering, but upon seeing the determined gleam in Bret's eyes, she sighed in defeat.

"No, he didn't. Like everyone else, he turned everything we had into Confederate bonds and currency, which is hardly worth the paper it's printed on. Now, there's even little of that left in my account at the bank. But I'll manage, and I'll do it on my own," she finished defiantly.

"How? By selling water like some common street vendor?" Bret snapped.

Before Kitty could reply, Daisy appeared, leading Scotty by the hand. Tugging free of the servant's hand, the child toddled over to his mother. Gurgling "Mama" several times, he lifted his chubby arms and demanded to be picked up, which Kitty did.

"Miz Kitty, duz you want me tuh feed de baby, or duz you wants tuh do hit?" Daisy asked after extending a brief greeting to Bret.

"Mama feed, Mama feed, pwea-se," Scotty implored, gently patting Kitty's face with his small hand.

"All right, Mama will feed you shortly, precious," Kitty murmured, planting a kiss on his rosy cheek before handing him back to Daisy.

For a moment Bret's features softened as Kitty held his son, but when the child was passed back to Daisy, he spied Scotty's bare feet, and his expression hardened.

"Where are his shoes?" he demanded as soon as they had left.

Kitty turned from him and nervously nibbled on her lower lip. It seemed that Bret was not going to be satisfied until he had stripped her of the last vestiges of her pride.

"It's warm, and all children enjoy going barefoot when the weather permits," she lied smoothly with a pretense of nonchalance. Then she added maliciously: "Having been raised as the son of an overseer, surely you can remember going barefoot yourself."

Bret, however, was not to be sidetracked by her cattiness. Jerking her around to face him, he fastened his hands on her shoulders. "I repeat, where are his shoes?" he asked. "Or doesn't he have any?"

"Yes, he has some. One pair, which I'm saving until winter, when he'll really need them," Kitty snapped.

Bret swore softly and released her. It was then that he saw the cut-up valise that had been tossed on a nearby chair. He picked up the leather soles Kitty had laboriously cut out earlier that afternoon. His frown deepened, and, dropping the pitiful-looking objects with obvious disgust, he strode back to Kitty.

"Let's have a look at your shoes," he ordered in a voice that prohibited argument.

"No! My shoes are fine, thank you."

"Good. Then you shouldn't mind my seeing them," he retorted, kneeling and yanking the hem of her gown up to her ankles.

Kitty felt she could have died with embarrassment as he knelt before her, for she was painfully aware that the slippers she wore, her last serviceable pair, had holes in the toes that exposed the first appendage of each foot. A slow flush crawled up her neck when he got to his feet and gave her a withering look. Reaching inside his coat, he extracted a wallet and emptied its contents, then grabbed her wrist and shoved the sizable amount of money into her hand.

"No, I won't take money from you!" Kitty cried.

"Yes, by God, you will!" Bret fired back at her. "If you think I'm going to have my son going barefoot, you have another thought coming. Nor do I intend to allow his mother to look like a street urchin, much less behave like one."

"Why should you care?" Kitty persisted. "Nobody knows Scotty is your son."

"*I* know, dammit! I won't tolerate you or the child doing without. I hope I make myself clear."

Kitty fumed inwardly but fought down the impulse to throw the money back at him. "Very well," she replied stiffly, "for Scotty's sake I'll accept your money, but I won't use one penny of it for myself. I'd rather be without than accept charity from a Yankee spy."

The last of Bret's patience snapped, and he hauled her roughly to him. "I don't give a damn what you think of me. I will not have you *or* the boy doing without. Not now, not ever. Don't fight me on this, Kitty, because it won't do you a damn bit of good. Either you do as I say, or I'll drag you downtown and personally see to it that you're outfitted from head to toe. Needless to say, that *would* cause a scandal."

Kitty glared at him but knew better than to continue the argument.

"All right," she muttered at last.

"That's better." Bret smiled. "I understand the Collinses are giving a ball tomorrow night and you're planning on going."

"Yes, Sally insists that I come with her and David, though I'll only be helping her serve the punch. As a widow, I can hardly participate in the dancing."

"Cheer up, Kitten, your period of . . . er, mourning won't last forever," he reminded her, amused. Then, placing his fists on his lean hips, he insolently appraised her from head to toe and shook his head with mock despair.

"Lord, you look like hell!" he remarked devilishly. "Black has never been your most becoming color. Still, I daresay you'll look a trifle more presentable in what I brought you from Natchez."

Kitty watched curiously while he sauntered over to the sofa, where he had earlier tossed the parcel. Breaking the string and shoving aside the brown paper, he lifted a black lace gown from the tissue wrapping, shook out the creases, and, holding it up, turned to face her. In spite of herself, Kitty's eyes danced with pleasure as she quickly closed the space between them. With eager fingers, she gently touched the exquisite garment.

"Oh, Bret, it's lovely," she said, lovingly fingering the lacy material. "You don't think it's too daring?" she asked with sudden concern, all previous declarations of refusing his help now forgotten in her excitement over owning a new gown.

"I don't think so. That scalloped neckline may be a trifle low, but I think the sleeves will detract from that," he remarked, eyeing the long, narrow sleeves that were V-shaped at the wrists. Yes, it was definitely the right gown for Kitty. He had known it the moment he'd spied it in the dressmaker's window.

Quivering with pleasure, Kitty took the gown from him and, rushing over to a gold-leaf pier mirror, held it up for size. Black or not, it was a beautiful creation. Pressing the material to her body, she turned first one way, then another, oblivious of Bret's pleased expression.

"Oh, it'll fit perfectly!" she exclaimed. "How on earth did you ever guess my size?"

"How could I possibly forget?" he countered meaningfully with a wicked grin.

Kitty's smile faded, and she petulantly met his gaze in the mirror. "If you were a gentleman, you wouldn't keep mentioning the past."

"Had I been a gentleman, there would be no past for me to mention," he reminded her, amusement tugging at the corners of his mouth. "And had you been a lady, there would be nothing for you to be regretting now, assuming you do regret our past . . . er, relationship."

Kitty whirled around to confront him, anger sparkling in the depths of her blue eyes. "You're a blackguard and a scoundrel, and I don't know why I let you set foot in this house!" she cried, still clutching the gown to her.

"Because, my pet, you had no other choice—at least, not today," he replied wryly. Sobering, he took hold of her chin, forcing her to look at him. "Don't ever try to lock me out, Kitty, and don't ever underestimate me. I always get what I want, one way or another."

"You'll never have me. Never!"

"Perhaps. But I will have my son, and when the time is right, he *will* bear my name, with or without your consent," he informed her coldly.

Kitty's anger was replaced by apprehension as she watched Bret stride out of the room, slamming the front door behind him. What had he meant? she wondered. Scotty could never bear his name unless she married him, and that was something she would never do. She would not marry a traitor, so marriage was definitely out of the question.

Still, Bret was not one to make idle threats, and this realization caused her no little concern. As she turned back to the mirror and held the gown up for another appraisal, she was already regretting that she had accepted his money and halfheartedly regretting her acceptance of the gown.

"It *is* lovely," she whispered, fingering the black silk underskirt. "Too lovely to return." Her anger and fears were soon forgotten as she continued to preen in front of the mirror.

The ballroom at the Collinses' house sparkled with gaiety while laughing couples whirled around on the dance floor or clustered in small groups and chattered amicably. Occasionally the topic of war was touched upon, particularly Sherman's continued efforts to reach Vicksburg via inland waterways. This was hardly surprising, considering the numerous attempts that had been made.

The first two weeks in April, however, had seemed relatively inactive. The Yankees were still just across the river, but many people were beginning to believe that the attack on their town had finally ended. Wrapped in false security, they began entertaining officers in their homes, even allowing the dashing soldiers to escort their daughters on moonlight rides in the quiet and pleasant evenings.

Like others, Kitty was all too willing to believe the worst was over. She was particularly relieved that the Union gunboats were no longer lurking on the Yazoo River, which bordered her family's plantation. During the weeks the enemy had surrounded Belle Glen, she had worried incessantly about her family's safety.

Now, as she stood beside Sally and ladled punch into crystal cups, her lips curved in a forced smile. Having stood behind the punch bowl for hours, she was tired and her legs were aching, particularly her feet. Everyone was having a good time—except her. Sally had periodically left her side to dance with David or one of the other soldiers, but Kitty had not been asked to dance once. Even Bret had not asked her, though he had perfunctorily danced with just about every other female in the room, young or old.

Still, there had been a bevy of handsome officers gathered around the punch bowl most of the evening. Knowing she was looking her best in her new gown and slippers, she had been aware of their unconcealed admiration, especially Major Ritchly's. Had she not been a widow and dressed conspicuously in black, there was no doubt in her mind that soldiers would be standing in line to dance with her. But this realization only added to her depression.

Glancing at the clock on the mantel, she saw that it was almost eleven o'clock. Another hour to go before this blasted party ends, she thought dourly as she watched Sally mingling with the guests. Minutes later, however, Sally returned to the serving table, a perplexed frown furrowing her brow.

"Kitty, did you know there's a rumor going around town that Mr. O'Rourke is selling cotton to the Yankees?"

"No, I hadn't heard."

"Well, there is, and I think it's shameful. Just because Mr. O'Rourke has to go out of town on business from time to time doesn't mean he's selling cotton to the Yankees. Folks seem to forget he's contributed a lot of money *and* cotton to the Confederacy. Why, there's not a man in Vicksburg who's more patriotic," Sally declared.

Although Kitty was unwilling to betray Bret, she was certainly not about to defend him. Sally's blind loyalty to someone so undeserving was almost more than she could bear at the moment. Wishing to escape before her tongue got the best of her, she was on the verge of asking to be excused from the refreshment table when a loud commotion broke out in the hall. In the next instant, a disheveled soldier rushed into the ballroom.

"General Pemberton, Admiral Porter's fleet is approaching the city!" the messenger loudly reported.

"How many vessels in all?" Pemberton asked bruskly.

"Eleven or twelve. There's no moon tonight, so it's hard to make out what's going on for sure. It looks like they're going to attempt to make a run past the city. If they make it, they'll probably try to help Grant's troops cross over the river just south of us!"

Hysteria filled the room, and several ladies fainted on the spot. Henry Collins walked over to General Pemberton, who was already surrounded by anxious guests. Kitty watched as her host pulled the general aside, conferred with him briefly, then strode over to the musicians' platform.

"Ladies and gentlemen, please!" he shouted several times before getting everyone's attention. Nervously mopping his brow, he continued. "Please remain calm. Some of you may want to return to your homes. Those who wish to remain—my cellar is at your disposal. This house is well away from the river, however, so none of you will be in any immediate danger even if the Yankees do fire upon the town."

As if on cue, a loud explosion erupted, soon followed by numerous others. As the thunderous sounds intensified, windows rattled and chandeliers tinkled eerily, blending with alarmed gasps and occasional screams. Some of the guests scurried outside, determined to reach the safety of their own homes. Others stood around in confusion, afraid to stay, yet rooted to the spot. When the musicians unsteadily struck up a tune, some of the couples even resumed dancing with forced gaiety in an attempt to ignore the continuous sound of shelling, which seemed to grow louder and louder by the minute. All were aware that the Union fleet must be abreast of town and was being greeted with fierce resistance from the town's batteries.

One question was uppermost in everybody's mind. Would Admiral Porter succeed in getting his vessels south of Vicksburg? He must not, for then there would be nothing to keep Grant's troops from crossing the river just below Vicksburg and assaulting the city from the south. Should this happen, it was not inconceivable that the town could eventually be encircled by the enemy.

Though Kitty fully realized the seriousness of the situation, her main concern was for Scotty, whom she had left at home. Determined to get to her child, she turned to Sally, who was clinging fearfully to her husband's arm.

"I must leave, Sally. I've got to get to Scotty."

Sally nodded reluctantly, realizing that since they had brought Kitty with them, her husband would have to take her home.

"If you'll get your shawl, Miss Kitty, I'll escort you," David offered with solemn politeness.

"That won't be necessary," said a familiar voice. "I'll see her home as soon as the shelling lets up some."

Kitty whirled around to find Bret standing at her elbow.

"Oh, Bret, thank goodness you stayed!" she exclaimed with obvious relief. "I can't wait until the shelling stops. I must get home to Scotty."

Bret frowned and shook his head. "I'll take you home, but not just now. In the meantime, don't worry about Scott. I'll see to it he's safe."

"But if you're going to the house, why can't I go with you?" Kitty persisted.

"Because I won't have you exposed to unnecessary danger. Just stay put. As soon as the bombardment ends, I'll come back for you."

Without giving her a chance to argue, he walked briskly away. Kitty's chin trembled with vexation and worry as she watched him leave. What if he did not make it to her house? What if he were struck by a shell, perhaps even killed? "Damn him," she whispered. "Now I have Scotty *and* him to worry about!"

Sally overheard and compassionately put her arm around Kitty's shoulders. "Don't worry, Kitty, Mr. O'Rourke knows what he's doing. Nothing's going to happen to either of them, so try to relax."

That was easier said than done, and as the minutes ticked by, Kitty's tension mounted to such proportions that she felt like screaming. The shelling lasted over an hour, during which time all but one of Porter's vessels succeeded in maneuvering past Vicksburg and heading south to Hard Times on the western banks of the Mississippi. By the time Bret finally returned for her, Kitty's nerves were so jangled that she almost felt nauseated.

Thanking Sally and her family for their hospitality, she allowed Bret to steer her outside, unmindful of what anybody might say or think about her permitting him to escort her home. Both Bret and Scotty were safe, and that was all that mattered.

As she allowed him to guide her to the open carriage he had borrowed from Phoebe, her gaze swung west to the river that was faintly illuminated by a mysterious pink glow. The cause of the ominous glare did not register on her tired mind, however, until they drew nearer to Washington Street and she spied several wooden buildings ablaze along the waterfront.

"Bret, the town's on fire!" she exclaimed.

"Only a few buildings near the river, which our own soldiers set fire to, so simmer down."

"But why would they do such a thing?"

"To light up the river. It's almost impossible to hit a moving target if you can't see it. As a matter of fact, we only managed to sink one transport."

"Hmph! Lucky for them the moon wasn't out tonight. If it hadn't been pitch dark, our boys would have blasted them out of the water," Kitty remarked staunchly.

"Luck had nothing to do with it. Grant planned it this way, figuring if Porter made the run on a moonless night, the fleet would stand a better chance of making it past our batteries. The ol' coot may drink a lot, but he's undoubtedly one of the shrewdest generals Lincoln has."

"You would admire him," Kitty said peevishly.

"I might not admire him as a man, but I certainly respect him as a general. He's as cunning as a fox and determined as hell to capture Vicksburg. God help us if Pemberton makes a mistake. Just one slip and Grant's army will encircle this town like a noose."

Kitty frowned but said nothing. Bret might not be for the South, but neither was he a fool. If Grant was as smart as Bret believed, then she fervently hoped Pemberton was capable of coping with him.

As the end of April rolled around, the townspeople waited expectantly for Grant's arrival. The city's churches held regular services, and attendance was at an all-time high, with everyone praying for deliverance from the Yankees. The brief lull they had enjoyed was over, replaced by total chaos as the streets teemed with soldiers and refugees from neighboring parts of the state, all fleeing from Colonel Grierson's raiders, who were making a startling sweep through Mississippi in an attempt to detract attention from the planned assault on Vicksburg. Ear-splitting Rebel yells added to the turmoil as soldiers dragged more cannons through the streets and placed them strategically on the bluffs.

Sleep was becoming almost nonexistent as Union gunboats attempted to run past the town's batteries. North of Vicksburg, Sherman led another assault against Drumgould's Bluff and Haynes' Bluff, a diversionary tactic to draw attention from Grant's movements. The next day, April 30, the first of Grant's troops crossed over the river, landing at Bruinsburg. The Yankees were now just below Vicksburg and ready to move inland. The trap was set.

The following day a small town about thirty miles south of Vicksburg fell to the enemy—Port Gibson. Instead of marching on to Vicksburg, however, Grant made a surprise move and prodded his troops toward Jackson. If the townspeople were momentarily relieved, they were also tense with anticipation. What would the scheming general do next? Some of the citizens fled from town; most stayed, fearful to leave lest they collide with the Yankees while attempting to flee to safety.

Though Kitty had desperately wanted to return home to her father, she had remained in town. Now, as she prepared to attend an evening prayer meeting, she again wondered if her decision had been wise. As she made her way downstairs, a knock sounded at the front door. A smile tilted the corners of her mouth when she glanced up at Bret.

"Going somewhere?" he asked with a quizzical lift of one brow.

"I'm going to a prayer meeting with Sally and David."

"Prayer meeting! Since when did you become so pious?" he teased.

"Since the Yankees have perched themselves on our doorsteps. Wouldn't hurt you to go, either. It's going to take all we've got to keep those blue-bellies from taking over the town, not that I think they will, mind you. Like our preacher says, God is always on the side of the righteous. So, the more prayer meetings we have, the better." Her smile faded upon seeing the ill-concealed amusement in Bret's eyes.

"I'm afraid it's going to take more than prayer meetings to stop the Yankees, but far be it from me to discourage you from going."

Kitty yanked her black bonnet from the hall tree and tied the black satin bow under her chin with angry jerks.

"Why don't you just say what you came to say, then leave," she demanded.

"Very well. I had hoped to spend a little time with you and the boy, but since that's impossible, I'll come right to the point. It's been rumored that slaves are leaving plantations in droves, some joining up with the Yankees and others filtering into town. That, plus the fact that the town is already overcrowded with soldiers and refugees, makes it unhealthy for any unescorted woman to venture out on the streets. So if you want to go anywhere, send word to me and I'll take you."

"I hardly think that will be necessary. As always, you're being overly pessimistic."

Bret took hold of her shoulders and gave her a little shake. "Wake up, Kitty. This is war. Nothing is like it used to be, and you're going to have to learn to live with that fact. People are no longer safe even in their homes. God knows how many houses and businesses have been broken into within the last week alone. Refugees are going hungry, so they resort to plundering and taking whatever they can get their hands on, as are some of our own soldiers."

"To hear you talk, home is no safer than the streets. Just what do you suggest I do?" she asked, checking the hem of her skirt in the table's "petticoat" mirror.

"Keep all of your windows and doors locked, and above all, don't wander out on the streets by yourself at any time, day or night. You'd also be wise to keep Daisy and Moses inside as much as possible. I don't think they'd run off, but they could be mistaken for runaways and be picked up by the authorities, should you send them into town on an errand."

"Surely not!" Kitty exclaimed, then, seeing his somber expression, she gave a small, dejected sigh. "Oh, Bret, I'm so tired of all this. Why won't the Yankees go and leave us in peace? I'd give anything if things could be like they used to be and we didn't have to worry about what tomorrow might bring."

Bret drew her into his arms, and she instinctively rested her face against his broad chest, drawing comfort from his nearness.

"There's no sense in wishing for the past or worrying about the future, Kitty. Live one day at a time and make the most of it, because no day, no moment, can ever be relived. Forget your yesterdays and your tomorrows. Just live for the present."

"I suppose you're right," she said, "but living in the present isn't easy. Right now, I'd give anything in the world to be home with Pa. He always seems to make things right."

For a few seconds neither spoke as Bret held her and soothingly caressed the nape of her neck with his strong fingers. It was then that an idea struck her. Why remain here, when she could just as easily return home? Let the soldiers and the refugees ransack the house if they wanted. Small price to pay in exchange for her child's safety and her own peace of mind. No more worrying about making ends meet. Pa would see to it she had whatever she needed and that she and her son were protected, come what may. Her blue eyes widened and danced excitedly as she contemplated the move. Nibbling her lower lip, she glanced up at her only means of escape.

"Bret," she began uncertainly. "Bret, I want to go home. Scotty and I will be much safer at Belle Glen than here, and I miss Pa so much. Will you take us?"

"No, Kitten, I won't." Releasing her, he let a smile play on his lips while he watched her expression grow mutinous.

"And just why not?"

"Because it's highly unlikely that we could get through. Don't forget, the Yankees were skirmishing around Haynes' and Drumgould's bluffs only last week, which happens to be a short distance from Belle Glen," he reminded her.

"I haven't forgotten, but that was last week. Besides, seeing as how you're on such friendly terms with the Yankees, if anyone can get us through their lines, it's you," she countered.

"Perhaps, but I have no intention of trying. If the Yankees make an all-out assault on Vicksburg, do you honestly think you'd be any safer at Belle Glen? Good Lord, Kitty, don't you realize, if Grant continues his overland campaign, it's only a question of time before his troops are crawling all over the place, including Belle Glen. When that happens, I want to make damn sure you and Scott are where I can keep an eye on you. In the meantime, I suggest you do what everybody else around here is doing—have a cave dug."

"Caves happen to be expensive," she snapped. "Sally and David paid twenty dollars to have a simple room excavated, and the larger caves cost even more. It's a ridiculous expense, and I have no intention of squandering what money I have on something like that."

"Very well, then I'll have a cave excavated for you," Bret declared.

"Don't bother. I'd never use it," she replied, wincing when Bret's fingers suddenly bit into her arms.

"If and when the Yankees attack us, you'll live in a cave just like everyone else. I won't have my son exposed to any more danger than is absolutely necessary. He's been exposed to too much already. So make no mistake about it, if this town comes under another bombardment, you and Scott *will* take refuge in a cave."

"No!" Kitty stomped her foot in defiance. "I won't live in a hole in the ground like some . . . some mole! Caves are damp, buggy, and degrading. Yankees or no Yankees, I will not hide in a cave!"

"When the shells really begin to fly, I think you'll reconsider. In any event, I'm going to have a cave excavated for you and the boy."

"And just where will you be?"

"In a hole right next to yours," he said with amusement.

Kitty fumed as she watched him depart, arrogance and self-confidence in every line of his bearing as he strode down the walk.

"All he thinks about is Scotty," she muttered waspishly. "If I got blasted from here to kingdom come, he wouldn't care!"

Chapter 20

The South's costly victory at Chancellorsville and the loss of General "Stonewall" Jackson was about the last bit of war news Vicksburg received. Soon after, telegraph and railroad lines leading into town were cut. Tension increased while everyone wondered what was happening on the battle fronts, particularly those nearby. A feeling of hopeless isolation blanketed the town as people waited to see what Grant's next move would be.

The seventeenth of May was a sunny and pleasantly quiet Sunday. The streets seemed almost deserted as Kitty and Sally walked to church. The night before, one of Vicksburg's two remaining military divisions had been ordered to Big Black River just east of town. David's regiment had been the first to leave, and Sally now expressed her concern to Kitty.

"I wish we knew what was going on. It's terrible not having any news at all," she complained, adding, "Why, we haven't had any real information about the war all week. It's like we're completely shut off from the rest of the world."

"You can thank the Yankees for that, though it does seem like General Pemberton could have prevented our lines of communication from being completely cut," Kitty answered.

"That's just it. We don't know what he could have prevented, because we don't know what's happening. Surely David's regiment would not have been ordered to the Big Black River had it not been urgent, which means that Grant's army must be getting nearer to Vicksburg."

Since the Big Black was only a short distance from town, Kitty was inclined to agree with Sally, though she refrained from saying so. Both women fell silent until they reached the church. Briefly greeting several friends, they seated themselves in the Shelton's pew beside David's parents and his sister, Lela.

Minutes later one of the deacons approached the pulpit and announced that their regular pastor had accompanied the troops to Big Black the previous night and a visiting preacher would deliver the sermon. Worried, Kitty tried and failed to concentrate on the preacher's words, which seemed to drone on and on. Halfway through the service, her attention was arrested by the sound of fast-approaching horses and, soon after, a crescendoing commotion just outside the church. Despite the growing noise the minister continued, even though the worshipers had begun to shift nervously in their seats. Anxious eyes turned toward the back of the sanctuary when a disheveled soldier burst through the door and made his way up the aisle. The preacher stopped midsentence, anxiety mirrored in his eyes as he stepped from the pulpit and faced the distraught runner, who whispered something to him. Lacy fans clicked shut, and all movement ceased while everyone strained to hear what was being said. Seconds seemed like hours before the minister slowly straightened and faced the congregation.

"If I may have your attention, please," he began uncertainly. "I have just received word that on Thursday, the Yankees seized Jackson."

Moans and distressed cries erupted, then faded when the preacher raised his arms and recaptured their attention.

"Yesterday, our troops were beaten at Champion Hill near Edwards' Station. Grant's army now stands between us and General Johnston. General Pemberton withdrew to the Big Black and has been in fierce confrontation with the enemy, but is unable to hold the position. He's ordered the bridge to be destroyed and our troops to fall back to Vicksburg. The enemy will be upon us by evening. I suggest we have a brief benediction, then everyone return to the safety of your homes."

Kitty fidgeted while the pastor prayed fervently, if somewhat hastily. What did prayer matter at a time like this? she thought impatiently. Everyone had been praying for weeks for deliverance from the Yankees, for all the good it had done. Was this how God answered prayers? Was this how the Almighty protected the righteous? She felt like shaking her fist at heaven itself.

By the time the congregation was dismissed, the streets were already teeming with the first wave of troops who were retreating helter-skelter back to town from the Big Black. Eager to be free of Lela's unpleasant company, Kitty declined Sally's invitation to accept a ride in the Sheltons' carriage and started for home. She soon regretted her decision when she struggled to push her way through the throng of frantic soldiers and townspeople. She had barely escaped being trampled by an officer on horseback when a supply wagon tore around the corner and almost ran her down as she attempted to cross the street. Rebel yells intermingled with angry curses and hysterical screams, pandemonium intensifying with each passing moment.

Feeling almost giddy with fear, Kitty covered her ears with trembling hands to block out the horrifying sounds, but to no avail. The distant sound of cannon fire from the east rumbled with ominous intensity as she proceeded to push her way through the melee of dirty, hollow-eyed soldiers who were pouring into town in a steady procession, some in ragged uniforms and often unarmed, others bloody and limping with weakness, all haggard and defeated. A gun carriage ripped past her, followed soon after by a horse-drawn ambulance filled to capacity with the wounded, the stench from their dirty, blood-soaked bandages assailing her nostrils so that she almost gagged. Were these poor, miserable creatures the laughing, handsomely uniformed soldiers who had occupied Vicksburg only weeks before? Were these wretched, footsore men all that stood between Vicksburg and Grant's monstrous army?

A young soldier limped past her, tears streaming down his haunted face as he muttered vehemently to himself, "The damn coward betrayed us!"

Without thinking, Kitty grabbed hold of his scrawny arm. "Who betrayed us?" she shouted above the din.

"That lily-livered, Yankee-born general of ours—Pemberton! Took him forever to make a decision, and when he did, it was always the wrong one. We'd have stayed and fought 'em down to the last man before giving those blue-bellies an inch, but Pemberton kept ordering us to retreat. Always retreat," he muttered brokenly, shrugging off her hand and walking away.

Kitty blinked back the tears that misted her vision as she crossed over the street to her house.

"It can't be true," she whispered to herself. "Pemberton won't let us down. He *can't* betray us! His own wife is a Southerner. We're not licked, and we're not going to be!''

Her chin lifted with determination as she reached for the latch on the gate; then, hearing her name called, she stopped. She turned, frowning perplexedly when she saw a filthy, bewhiskered soldier rushing toward her. Her eyes suddenly widened with recognition, and in the next instant she was running to meet him.

"Oh, Tad, thank God you're here!" she cried joyously, hugging him to her fiercely.

For seconds they embraced each other, until finally Tad held her from him. "I see my little sister is all grown up now, and prettier than ever." He smiled fondly.

Brushing tears from her eyes, Kitty sniffed and smiled up at him. "I can't say the same for you, but you're a mighty welcome sight," she quipped. "Come on in and we'll get you cleaned up."

"I can't, sugar. There isn't time. The captain sent me in for supplies, so I can't stay long, as much as I'd like to. How's Pa and Dede?"

"The last time I saw them, they were fine. Of course that was several weeks ago, before the Yankees began skirmishing around Belle Glen. Since then I've had no word."

"I pray to God they're all right," he said huskily. "I heard about Miles, Kitty. I know it wasn't easy for you."

Unsure of exactly how much Tad had heard, Kitty was unwilling to waste precious moments giving him the details. "No, it wasn't," she replied simply, then changed the subject. "Tad, it isn't true what some of the soldiers are saying about General Pemberton, is it? I mean—he isn't a coward, is he? He wouldn't betray us?"

Tad frowned and sighed. "No, Pemberton is no coward, nor is he a traitor. He's a good man, but indecisive and overly cautious at times. His worst fault is that he lacks aggressiveness, but there's no doubting his loyalty."

"Are things as bad as they look? Could the Yankees break through our lines?"

"I don't think so, sis. Trenches have been dug to completely surround the town. When they come, we'll be ready for them. Besides, haven't you heard Vicksburg is known as the 'impregnable city'?" He grinned.

"Hmph! Maybe somebody should tell General Grant, so he'll go away and leave us alone."

"Oh, he's been told, but he apparently doesn't believe it. I reckon we'll just have to show him, won't we." He chuckled. "By the way, Steve and Scott Hartz are in my regiment. I guess you've heard their younger brother, Michael, joined up with the Yankees."

"Yes. Poor Miss Ginny hasn't gotten over the shock even now," Kitty replied.

"God, this is a helluva war! Brother fighting against brother, maybe killing each other . . ." His voice trailed off.

"Tad, I heard the Yankees have taken Jackson, and General Johnston can't get through to Vicksburg. Does that mean we can't expect any reinforcements from him?"

"I'm afraid so, at least for the time being. But reinforcements are already pouring into town from Warrenton, so don't worry. Vicksburg will be well fortified."

"But the men look so tired and beaten," Kitty pointed out with a worried frown.

"A lot of them haven't slept in over forty-eight hours, much less eaten. A good night's rest and some decent food will get 'em back on their feet. Don't worry, honey. Our boys may not look like much, but whatever they lack in appearance, they more than make up for in courage. The Yankee hasn't been born who can outfight a Southerner, and don't you forget it."

Kitty felt greatly relieved by his confidence, and the next few minutes were spent in talking of things other than the war. Then Tad bent to kiss her cheek and reluctantly told her he must get back.

"Where will you be?" Kitty asked, dreading to let him out of her sight.

"Our regiment will be at the Third Louisiana Redan on Jackson Road. At least, that's where the captain told me to report."

"But you're with a Mississippi regiment," Kitty said, not understanding why Tad's outfit was being thrown in with one from Louisiana.

"Honey, we're all fighting the same war, and we'll all be fighting from the same trenches." He smiled. "A redan can have more than one company covering it."

"Oh, I see. Will all eight roads leading into town be covered?"

"You can count on it. Now, I've really got to leave, Sis. I'll be in touch with you as soon as possible,'' he promised, giving her one last hug.

Kitty watched until Tad disappeared from sight before she turned to go to the house. Once inside, she sank tiredly onto a chair and removed her bonnet. The shutters had been closed to block out the midday sun, and the dark parlor was stiflingly hot.

A moment later Daisy came rushing downstairs and into the parlor. ''Miz Kitty, Ah didn't heah you come in. Ah wuz puttin' de baby down fo' his nap, but wid all de noise out dere, hit tuk a powerful lot ob rockin' tuh git him tuh sleep. Whut's hoppen't?''

''The Yankees are at Big Black, and our troops have retreated to town.''

''Lawd Gawd! Duz dat mean we's whooped?''

''No. We're not whipped, and we're not going to be. What's for dinner?''

''Moses cotched a mess ob crawfish down at de creek early dis mornin', so Ah fixed a big pot ob gumbo an' rice, and a polk salad. Ah used de last ob de cracklin's tuh make up a nice batch ob cracklin' bread.''

''I'm not very hungry, so I'll just have a little of the salad and a piece of cracklin' bread. Tell Moses to set up a table out front, and we'll give the rest of the food to the soldiers. Oh, and be sure to have a pail of water on the table. I 'spect they're all thirsty as well as hungry. After we get through feeding them, I guess we'd better find some place to hide the good silver and a few other valuables just in case the Yankees do manage to break through our lines,'' Kitty said wearily. What had started out to be a pleasant day had turned out to be quite different, and the prospect of personally serving dirty and disillusioned soldiers did nothing to bolster her flagging spirits.

Later, as Kitty was handing out the last of the cracklin' bread, Mattie Blanks came bustling down the sidewalk, obviously headed for Phoebe's house just down the street. Tight-lipped, she gave Kitty a curt nod, then proceeded to walk stiffly through the small gathering of soldiers who blocked the sidewalk. One soldier had fallen asleep against the picket fence, his long legs sprawled across the walk so that passersby were forced to step over or skirt around him. Mattie, however, had no intention of doing either. Nudging him in the ribs with her foot, she watched distastefully as he yawned and stretched, then slowly opened his eyes to encounter her steely gaze.

"Young man, if you can move for General Grant, you can move for me," she snapped.

The soldier grinned and got to his feet. "Sorry, ma'am. I reckon I'm just tuckered out to fall asleep that way."

"Hmph! I can well imagine after all the running you've done. Shame on you! Shame on all of you for giving in to the Yankees and running back here like a bunch of sniveling cowards." Turning on her heel, she continued huffily on her way.

Embarrassed beyond words, Kitty looked on with an expression of sheer dismay. Some of the soldiers chuckled, while others glaringly watched the outspoken dowager disappear from view. All of them looked disheartened.

"Shucks, we should've had her at Champion Hill—then Grant would've tucked tail and run!" one of the soldiers said good-naturedly.

Everyone agreed, and the tension was broken as the men thanked Kitty for her hospitality and departed. Their friendliness, combined with the admiring glances she had received from them all afternoon, had done much to lift her spirits.

The next morning Sally dropped by before breakfast and informed Kitty that she had volunteered to help at one of the hospitals. Disinclined to follow her friend's example, Kitty remained silent while Sally named some of the other young women in town who were doing the same, including her sister-in-law, Lela.

"*Lela* volunteered!" Kitty exclaimed.

"Yes, last night," Sally affirmed. "I must admit I was surprised at first, particularly since Lela's so flighty, but I suppose one can't always judge a book by its cover. She volunteered for surgery, and anyone who does that has got to have a lot of grit."

"Or curiosity," Kitty retorted dryly. "If Lela offered to assist in surgery, I daresay it was because she wanted to see what a man looks like without his clothes on!"

Sally doubled over with laughter, for, like Kitty, she somehow could not picture her pretentious sister-in-law as a ministering angel. In fact, she doubted Lela would last the day—especially in surgery. Kitty, however, was another matter, and remembering the purpose of her visit, Sally sobered.

"You know, the doctors are going to need all the help they can get. Would you like to come with me?"

Not eager to face the suffering and death that was sure to confront her at the hospital, Kitty hesitated a moment before slowly nodding in agreement. After all, she reasoned, if someone as shallow as Lela would volunteer, could she do less?

By midmorning, however, she was already regretting her decision. One by one the wounded were brought in on stretchers, many of them only boys. It came as no surprise when Lela fainted at the first sight of blood and had to be carried out of the operating room. Realizing the doctor was short-handed, Kitty offered her assistance, administering chloroform while shell fragments were extracted and gaping bayonet wounds were stitched. The smell of anesthesia and the sight of so much blood caused her stomach to churn, yet she was determined to remain as long as she was needed.

Rumors were rife throughout the day, and on more than one occasion she heard soldiers accusing General Pemberton of being a traitor. Another disturbing rumor was that General Johnston had refused to send reinforcements and had ordered Pemberton to evacuate the town, but that Pemberton had refused to do so.

Gunfire was sporadic throughout the morning and only faintly audible, increasing in intensity when Grant's army crossed the Big Black River, took Haynes' Bluff, and proceeded to surround Vicksburg by late afternoon. As dusk descended, more alarming news reached the hospital. All roads leading out of town had been closed to civilians, and it was believed that a major battle would erupt around daybreak.

It was past seven o'clock when Dr. Johnson noticed Kitty was swaying with fatigue. Thanking her for her invaluable assistance, he ordered her home. Bret had been in and out all day, each time bringing in new casualties, but Kitty had been hardly aware of his presence. Now, as she walked out the front door, she was surprised to discover him leaning against the porch railing.

"I was beginning to think you were going to spend the night in there," he said with a slight smile.

"Oh, Bret, I'm so worried. Someone said the Yankees took Haynes' Bluff this afternoon. That's mighty close to Belle Glen."

"I don't think they'll bother with Belle Glen just now. Their main objective is Vicksburg," he answered solemnly, taking hold of her arm and assisting her down the steps.

"I hope you're right," she returned, not at all convinced.

They walked in silence for a while, neither of them in the mood for light conversation. The streets seemed almost empty compared with what they had been earlier, and an eerie hush now encompassed the town. Fireflies flickered about in the darkness as crickets chirped in the distance and were joined by a chorus of tree frogs croaking for rain. As they crossed Jackson Street, Kitty noticed an ominous glow faintly illuminating the sky to the east of town.

"Look!" she exclaimed.

"Our engineers are burning some houses and fields on the out-skirts of town," he told her.

"Why?"

"They're clearing the area for observational purposes. When the fighting begins, Pemberton wants to make sure his men can see what they're shooting at, plus remove all possibility of the Yankees sneaking up on them through the surrounding underbrush," he answered, opening the picket gate and following her up the walk to her house.

For several minutes they stood on the porch and watched the pulsating glow, then Kitty slowly shook her head.

"Last month, buildings along the riverfront were burned, and now it's houses on the outskirts of town. I wonder what General Pemberton will decide to burn next," she said bitterly. "Maybe folks are right. Maybe he is a traitor."

"Pemberton is no traitor, Kitty. He's doing what he has to do. Vicksburg is under siege."

"Somehow I never dreamed it would come to this. Can we win, Bret? Can we hold out?"

"Time will tell," he replied evasively, for there was no doubt in his mind that the odds were against them.

His words stuck in her mind long after he had gone. Standing dejectedly on the porch, she once more turned her gaze to the east. A rosy glimmer still flickered at the edge of town, faintly illuminating the inky night and hinting ominously of what was to come. There was no place to run, no place to hide. Yankees now surrounded the town. The siege had begun!

Part III

Chapter 21

Kitty yawned and lazily stretched her arms above her head while she watched Daisy scurrying around the room opening the shuttered windows. The sound of distant gunfire reached her ears, causing her to frown and sit up in bed.

"What time is it, Daisy?"

"Hit's almos' nine. Umph, dey's been shootin' off dem guns eber since daybreak. Hit sho' makes a body jump." Turning back to Kitty, she asked, "Is you hongry, Miz Kitty?"

"Starved. What's for breakfast?"

"Dey's sum coffee, grits, an' Ah dun made you a nice lil' hoecake," Daisy beamed. Hoecake was a large, flat biscuit about half the size of a small pie.

"Potato coffee?" Kitty asked distastefully.

"Yas'm. You knows we ain' got no real coffee."

"And I don't suppose we have any butter to go on the grits, either," Kitty grumbled.

"Naw'm, we sho' ain', but we got sum milk an' a bit ob sugar."

"Oh, all right." Kitty sighed. "Hand me my brush and mirror, then bring my breakfast tray up here."

Daisy followed her mistress's orders and scurried out the door. By the time she returned Kitty was in a better mood, as was evidenced by the soft tune she hummed while she brushed the tangles from her long, curling tresses.

Her voice was suddenly drowned out by a succession of loud

213

explosions that rattled the windowpanes. With a piercing scream, Daisy dropped the breakfast tray on the floor and stood rooted to the spot, her eyes as large as saucers.

"Don't stand there like a ninny," Kitty shouted above the uproar, jumping out of bed and running over to the clothes closet. "Get the baby and Moses and go down to the cellar."

In the next instant Daisy was flying down the hallway, squealing hysterically each time another shell exploded. Kitty's hands trembled as she jerked a black bombazine dress from its hanger and dragged it over her head, not bothering with crinolines, hoops or stays. The mortar fire was coming from the Yankees' gunboats on the river, the blasts growing nearer and nearer by the minute. Fumbling with the tiny jet buttons that hooked up the back, Kitty heard heavy footsteps coming up the stairs. Relief flooded through her when Bret burst unceremoniously into her room.

"Come on, we've got to get out of here. Where's Scott?" he asked, breathing heavily.

At that moment Daisy appeared with the boy in her arms and Moses in tow. "Heah he is, Mist' Bret. Ah wuz jes' fixin' tuh take him down tuh de cellar."

"The cellar's not safe, not with the shelling this close. We'll try to make it to the cave."

"What cave?" asked Kitty, grateful when Bret abruptly turned her around and fastened the remainder of her buttons.

"The cave I had dug about a block away from here," he answered, turning to take Scotty from Daisy's arms.

Barefoot, Kitty started toward the door, then stopped, her hand shaking as she swept a long strand of hair from her face. Making her way back to the dresser, she grabbed up a black hair net, then dashed over to the rumpled bed and scooped up her hand mirror and brush, unmindful of Bret's exasperated scowl.

"For God's sake, Kitty, come on!" he thundered, taking hold of her arm and jerking her down the hall.

There was no time to argue, nor was Kitty inclined to do so. The bombardment was growing louder, and scarcely a second separated one blast from another. Once outside, she was dimly aware of her unshod feet as she limped beside Bret, though several times she stepped on sharp, unseen objects that caused her to wince. The howling of dogs intermingled with the screams of women and children who were frantically making a dash for safety. Twice Kitty tripped on the hem of her skirt, and it was only Bret's firm grip that kept her from falling flat on her face.

Though only a block from the house, the cave seemed much farther away as she stumbled across the deeply rutted street and allowed Bret to steer her toward the clay hill that was dotted with dark yawning caves. She was relieved when he pointed to one, and without waiting to be prodded, she scampered inside and stepped toward the back, glancing over her shoulder to make sure the rest were following her. Each time a shell exploded, the ground seemed to tremble beneath their feet. As Daisy and Moses wailed with alarm, Scotty became fretful.

"Stop it! Both of you hush right this minute. You're scaring the baby with all that caterwauling," Kitty snapped, determined not to show her own mounting fear.

Though the cave was devoid of furniture, a torch had been left behind by the excavator, and as Bret ignited it, Kitty blinked and refocused her eyes.

The hollowed-out room was larger than she had expected, and she soon spied another opening at the back that led to a similar room with an exit of its own. Several niches had been dug out of the clay walls, obviously to be used as makeshift shelves. All in all, it was a spacious, if crude, dwelling. Surprised, Kitty slowly surveyed her unusual surroundings, her fear momentarily forgotten until a shell burst loudly near the mouth of the cave, jerking her back to the present.

"Oh, Lawd, we's gwine tuh be buried alive!" Daisy screamed, clutching a whimpering Moses to her breast.

Her hysteria did nothing to soothe Scotty's bewildered uneasiness. With a small sob, he buried his head against Bret's heaving chest. "Wanna go home," he muttered tearfully.

"Not just yet, son," Bret answered in a reassuring voice. "Did you know I had this cave dug just for you? Now you have a big playhouse all your own. Why, when I was a boy, I used to play in caves all the time. You and Mommy are going to have a lot of fun here."

"Daisy and Moses, too?" Scotty questioned with sudden interest.

"Sure." Bret grinned.

Unlike her son, however, Kitty's anxiety merely increased as the hours dragged by. By midafternoon, Sherman's men had advanced on Stockade Redan, a Confederate fortification guarding Graveyard Road, which led directly to town. As the bombardment grew louder, Kitty cowered beside Bret and tried to block out the servants' intermittent wails of distress by watching Bret entertain their son. How he could remain calm enough to launch into a telling of "Jack and the Beanstalk" was beyond her comprehension, though she was thankful for his inner strength. At least Scotty was no longer afraid.

Gradually the firing subsided, ending altogether by late afternoon, when Grant called off the assault. By that time everyone was totally exhausted.

"Miz Kitty, is we going home?" Daisy asked hopefully.

"Yes, and we're *not* coming back," came her mistress's firm reply. Seeing Bret's frown, Kitty glared at him. "I mean it, and nothing you say is going to change my mind."

"Don't be a fool, Kitty. This cave is a helluva lot safer than your house, and you know it," he countered. Seeing she was unconvinced, he took another tack. "Look, tomorrow morning I'll get over here bright and early and fix this place up. I'll put in some cots and maybe a small table and a couple of chairs, plus whatever else you need."

"Do what you like, but I repeat—I will *never* set foot in this place again," Kitty replied. Handing Scotty to Daisy, she stalked out of the cave and headed for home.

Two days later Admiral Porter's fleet began continuously to bombard the beleaguered city with such accuracy that it became unsafe for anyone to remain at home. Shells ripped into houses and often left them in fragments, and it was rumored that several citizens had been seriously injured. At first Kitty was adamant about not returning to the cave, but she quickly changed her mind when a cannonball crashed through the parlor around noon and embedded itself in the wall. Fortunately it was a dud, but the frightening incident forced her to realize that her house offered little protection from the deadly missiles that were zipping all over town.

With grim resentment, Kitty sent Moses to fetch Bret to help her move to the cave, then ordered Daisy to start packing food, cooking utensils, and other essentials. While this was being done, she pulled a small trunk from the attic and hastily packed some of Scotty's clothes and her own. Taking three of her coolest dresses from the wardrobe, she laid them on the bed. Two were calicoes, one red and the other yellow. The third was a simple cotton gown of periwinkle blue, and it was this one she slipped over her head. She had just fastened the last button when Daisy scurried into the room.

"Ain' you gwine tuh pack none ob dem black dresses?" she asked with a disapproving frown.

"No, they're too hot."

"But Miz Kitty, whut's folks gwine tuh think if'n you wears dem bright-colored dresses? Hit ain' fittin' for a widow woman tuh wear nuthin' but black."

"I don't care what anybody thinks," Kitty retorted, folding the two calicoes and placing them in the trunk. "Caves are damp and hot, and I'd smother to death wearing black. At least I can thank the Yankees for providing me with an excuse to dress the way I want. I'm sick and tired of looking like an old black crow!"

Before Daisy could reply, there was a loud crash, causing them to swing around to where Scotty had been playing with his soldiers on the bedside table. The hand-painted vase that Kitty had always cherished now lay in pieces around the child's feet. Her nerves, already stretched to the breaking point, suddenly snapped. Without thinking she jerked up the distraught boy and paddled him soundly on the behind, then sent him to his room. Daisy's pouting expression clearly revealed her disapproval of the spanking as she left the room.

Hot, tired, and thoroughly dispirited, Kitty sat down on the bed and strove to regain her composure. Her conscience pricked at her when she heard Scotty crying softly to himself. At last, with a resigned sigh, she made her way to his room. The door was ajar, and as she paused on the threshold, her lips curved in a tremulous smile at the sight in front of her. His knickers pulled down, the boy was studying his chubby backside in the long cheval mirror, his eyes brimming with tears while he gingerly rubbed the reddened area with his hand.

"Bwoke—Mommy bwoke it," he sniffed pathetically while surveying the crevice that separated his tender buttocks.

Rushing over to him, Kitty scooped him up in her arms and hugged him. "It's not broken, honey—only a little pink. I'm sorry I hurt you, but you must be more careful. Now, let's go down and see if we can help Daisy."

They had just reached the bottom landing when Daisy came rushing back through the front door.

"Mist' Bret's heah, an' he dun brung a wagon wid him."

"Thank goodness." Kitty sighed, letting go of Scotty's hand. "Get Moses to help you carry my trunk to the wagon. Oh, and be sure to pack a couple of chamber pots and plenty of candles," she

tossed over her shoulder as she grabbed a couple of the wall lanterns, and rushed out to the porch.

She immediately spied their means of transportation, a rickety
wagon drawn by a mule that had obviously seen better days. Still, it
was a welcomed sight, as was the man who was striding up the walk.

"Well, I'm glad to see you've finally come to your senses." Bret
grinned, relieving her of the lanterns and placing them in a crate.

"Only because I had to. How on earth are we going to get
everything into one wagon?"

Eyeing the crates Daisy had pulled out on the porch, Bret shook
his head. "We're not, but don't worry. I'll come back for the rest as
soon as the shelling stops."

Kitty watched as he lifted one of the larger crates and started for
the wagon, then she turned and went back inside to hurry the
servants along. Once the vehicle had been loaded to capacity, she
locked the front door and rushed back to where the others were
waiting, then scampered into the wagon and seated herself beside
Bret.

The streets were again in a state of chaos as soldiers and citizens
rushed about on foot or careened by in overloaded wagons, all
making a mad dash for safety while the shelling persisted. In no
mood to talk, Kitty remained silent until they reached the cave.

As Bret helped her down, she saw that a tent fly had been
stretched over the mouth of the cave, which would undoubtedly
offer shade as well as some degree of privacy from passersby.

"I see you've fixed up the cave," she commented with reluctant
appreciation. "Did you get some cots?"

"Yep. I put one in each room, plus a couple more in the lean-to
behind the cave." Seeing her puzzled look, he continued, "You'll
occupy one room and Scotty the other. Daisy and Moses will sleep
in the lean-to," he explained, nodding to a crude structure of wood
and canvas that had been erected several yards behind the back
entrance of the cave.

"Will they be safe back there?" Kitty asked.

"Safe enough, except during bombardments. Then, of course,
they will have to stay inside the cave."

"Well, at least I'll have some privacy part of the time."

Once inside, she realized that Bret had, indeed, made numerous
improvements. Mosquito netting had been hung from the wooden
beams that supported the front and back entrances, and two ladder-

back chairs and a small, square table were now situated against one wall.

While they were unpacking the last crate, Bret informed her the town was now almost totally surrounded by the enemy. Sherman and Steele were reportedly camped to the north, McClernand to the east of the Southern Railroad, and McPherson was situated in the middle, near the Jackson Road.

By dusk the firing had lightened enough for Bret and Daisy to return to the house for the rest of Kitty's belongings. Apparently even the Yankees had to pause long enough to eat, she concluded, swearing inwardly when the bombardment resumed a short time later. Her own fear had to be put aside while she tried to appear calm, keep Scotty from becoming alarmed, and assure Moses that his mother was safe with Bret and would soon be returning. Moses, however, was not easily convinced, and each time a shell exploded nearby, his eyes widened with fright.

Too frightened to attempt to reason with the boy, Kitty tightened her arms around her own son. By the time Bret returned, she could have wept with joy. Instead, she handed Scotty to Moses and hurried out to the wagon. Among other necessities, Bret had thought to bring her small rocker and an oval bathtub, for which she was exceedingly grateful.

As Daisy rushed by with an armful of bedding, a missile exploded only yards away. Grabbing the rocker, Bret told Kitty to get back to the cave. She turned to obey but stopped upon hearing the sound of thundering hooves coming right toward them. Perplexed, she glanced toward Jackson Road, her frown deepening when she saw soldiers on horseback mustering hundreds of horses and mules down the road and away from town.

"They're driving most of the town and militia livestock out to the Yankees' lines. There's a shortage of feed, and rather than let the animals die from starvation and smell up the place, it was decided to turn them loose outside of town."

"Aren't we keeping any horses and mules?" she asked.

"Only the ones we can feed. Those being mustered out will graze on the land or be fed by the Yankees. Pemberton's probably hoping that by dumping so many animals on the Yankees, their feed supply will become as critical as ours," Bret explained.

"Well, I hope he's right for once," Kitty muttered, and followed Bret inside the cave.

Chapter 22

As the first week passed, Kitty slowly became accustomed to living in the cave. Meals, such as they were, had to be cooked outside but were prepared only when the enemy stopped bombardment long enough to eat. Earlier that week, General Pemberton had requested and been granted by the Yankees a brief truce so that the dead and wounded could be removed from the fields of battle. Still, the sickening stench of death hovered in the air.

Outbreaks of measles, malaria, typhoid, and dysentery were becoming a source of concern in town as well as in the trenches. People longed for news from the outside, and when the Federal gunboat *Cincinnati* was sunk the day before, many had thrown caution to the wind and rushed to the river to retrieve newspapers from the floating debris. These were generously passed around, as was the rumor that General Robert E. Lee might soon be laying siege to Washington. Another encouraging rumor was that Bragg's Tennessee army and Johnston's forty thousand men were now marching toward Vicksburg. If such relief came, they reasoned, Grant would surely have to retreat. Waiting for such help, however, became increasingly difficult as the hot days dragged by.

Kitty derived strength from the fact that everyone was enduring the same hardships and managing to survive. If Sally could cheerfully attempt to make her cave into a home, then she was determined to do no less.

Though the hours passed slowly, Kitty tried to keep herself occupied by entertaining Scotty, visiting friends in neighboring caves when the shelling permitted, and working at the hospital. When the evenings were quiet and free from bombardment, she and Bret would sit by a small campfire and talk while she rolled bandages or filled cartridges. Often as not, they were joined by others, and it was these pleasant interludes that she looked forward to.

The night before, several officers had joined their campfire, among them Major Ritchly and David Shelton, who had been given a few days of leave from the front lines. The major had somehow managed to acquire a sack of dried corn, which Sally and Kitty had used to make popcorn over the smoldering embers. It was obvious that the major was captivated by Kitty, as were most of the other unattached officers, and for the first time since her marriage to Miles, she felt femininely carefree. She had forgotten how satisfying it was to be so openly admired and how much fun it was to actually flirt. The fact that Bret looked on with obvious disapproval merely added to her pleasure.

Her spirits remained unusually high the next morning when she rose from her cot and slipped into her yellow calico gown. She had just finished arranging her long raven hair into two coils at the back of her neck when Daisy rushed into the cave.

"Miz Kitty, you oughta see who's movin' intuh dat cave cross't de road!"

"Who?" came the mumbled reply as Kitty took another hairpin from her mouth and finished securing the last coil.

"A painted Jezebel, dat's who. Ah ain' neber seed no woman lak dat. She's got a maid wid her, too, an' she's brung mo' clothes wid her den you kin shake a stick at. She sho' am a sight fo' sore eyes!"

Curious, Kitty walked outside and looked across the road. A rickety wagon was parked in front of the newly dug cave, and as a thin, dark-skinned servant struggled to remove a small trunk from the vehicle, a tall female appeared at the cave's entrance. Though gaudily dressed in a low-cut, chartreuse-and-black-striped taffeta gown, the auburn-haired woman was strikingly attractive, her height and erect carriage giving her an air of flamboyant regality. Kitty took in the newcomer's unusual appearance with some amazement and realized that Daisy had not exaggerated in describing her. She was, indeed, wearing lip rouge!

Her low décolletage was trimmed with black satin ruffles that complemented the creamy texture of her skin. Several strands of jet beads adorned her neck and matched the earrings that dangled halfway to her exposed shoulders. A heavily jeweled hand plucked impatiently at a feather boa draped carelessly over one arm, then reached up and patted the elaborate coiffure that was ostentatiously adorned with a cluster of black plumes. She was certainly a sight to behold!

As if sensing she was being observed, the woman gazed across the road to Kitty, and then, giving her a dazzling smile, she walked over.

"Hello there," she began in a well-modulated voice tinged with a British accent. "Since we're to be neighbors, we might as well get acquainted. I'm Dixie Darlin—at least, that's my stage name. My real name is Agatha Gallagher, but I much prefer to be called Dixie for obvious reasons. I can't imagine a worse name than Agatha, can you?"

Nonplussed, Kitty stammered an acknowledgment and gave her own name. Decent women did not associate with actresses, but the woman's friendly personality somehow broke down all barriers of propriety. Minutes later Kitty was feeling perfectly relaxed with the strange newcomer, whom she judged to be in her early thirties. There was certainly nothing reserved about the actress, who insisted that a first-name basis was called for among "friends." Remembering her manners, Kitty offered Dixie a cup of sassafras tea, and as they sat under the tent fly and sipped the beverage, the two women became better acquainted.

"You seem so young to be widowed, but then I suppose we've all had our share of burdens to bear since this beastly war began. When I came over to this country, I never dreamed I would be caught up in such a ridiculous situation. It took me years to build up my establishment, which happened to be one of the finest in New Orleans. And then that horrid "Beast" Butler marched in as if he owned the town, and the next thing I knew, I was being closed down. Imagine the gall of the bas—of the man!"

"It must have been dreadful for you," Kitty murmured. "What . . . er, kind of establishment did you have?"

"Not the type you would set foot in." Dixie grinned devilishly. "I suppose I should prevaricate and tell you it was a perfectly respectable establishment, but I never lie to my friends, and I should like for us to be just that. I owned a recreational hall which catered to a high-class clientele. The downstairs' attraction was the gambling tables and a small stage upon which yours truly occasionally performed. The upstairs provided . . . er, a different kind of entertainment, if you get my meaning.''

"Oh!" Kitty mouthed, deeply shocked.

"Don't worry, pet, I'm not contagious—just wickedly honest!''

Feeling completely out of her depth, Kitty sought to change the subject. "What have you been doing since General Butler closed you down?''

"I suppose I am what is commonly referred to as a 'camp follower,' much to my distress. I've followed our troops and earned my keep by performing for them, in a manner of speaking. Actually, I arrived here about ten days ago, along with the soldiers from Warrenton. One of the officers managed to get me a room in the Washington Hotel before he was sent to the front. After enduring a few nights of bombardment, I quickly decided to have a cave dug, but I'm not at all sure I've made a wise decision. Ye gods, I can't imagine living in that hellish hole!''

Kitty smiled in understanding and was on the verge of offering her visitor another cup of tea when Bret sauntered out of his cave. To Kitty's utter amazement, Dixie jumped to her feet and rushed over to him.

"Bret!" she cried joyfully. Wildly flinging her arms around his neck, she proceeded to kiss him soundly on the mouth.

Seeing the pleased recognition in Bret's eyes, Kitty watched with helpless frustration as his arms tightened around the voluptuous woman and he enthusiastically returned her kiss. By the time the embrace ended, Kitty was seething with jealousy, which she hid with a tight smile.

"Well, it would seem you two are old friends," she said.

"Hmmm—indeed we are," Dixie replied in a husky voice filled with implication.

Bret cleared his throat and, for once, appeared somewhat uncomfortable. "Yes, I've visited Miss Darlin's establishment on occasion while doing business in New Orleans.''

"*Miss* Darlin!" Dixie exclaimed. "Don't be such a prig, Bret. After all, we *are* old friends, so I'm sure Kitty will understand if we dispense with formality.'' She chuckled provocatively.

"Oh, I quite understand," Kitty replied. "Now, if you'll both excuse me, I must get my son up and dressed.''

"Yes, of course you must. In the meantime, Bret, I insist you come over and help me get settled in that dreadful cave," Dixie said. Thanking Kitty for her hospitality, she strode off with Bret in tow.

By the time Scotty was dressed and fed, Daisy, who had left earlier to help Dixie's maid unpack, was just returning. Kitty handed the boy to her, then walked outside and glanced sourly toward the opposite cave. Her scowl deepened as she watched Bret and Dixie secure a tent fly over the entrance.

Swamped with jealousy, she finally tore her eyes away from them and was on the verge of walking over to Sally's cave when she spotted Major Ritchly heading toward her. Pride came to the fore as she waved and gave him her most fetching smile, her enthusiastic greeting deliberately pitched so that it would carry across the road.

The major was obviously delighted by her warm reception, unaware that Kitty was casting furtive glances toward Bret from time to time. It seemed, however, that Bret was completely absorbed in his conversation with Dixie. Vexed, Kitty dragged her attention back to the major.

"David and I will be returning to the trenches tomorrow. I wouldn't want to wear out my welcome, Miss Kitty, but I was wondering if I might drop by tonight."

"Why, of course. In fact, last night was so much fun, why don't you bring some of your friends along, too?" she suggested brightly.

Though disappointed he would not have Kitty to himself, the major agreed and promised to bring another bag of corn to pop and, if possible, a jug of cider. They talked for a few minutes more, then the major left.

"Daisy, tell Moses to mind Scotty for a few minutes," Kitty said. "I'm going over to Miss Sally's, and while I'm gone, I want you to wash and iron my blue dress. Major Ritchly and some others are coming over again tonight."

Daisy frowned disapprovingly but refrained from arguing. "Tongues sho' gwine tuh wag," she grumbled as her mistress turned to leave.

The same thought occurred to Kitty, but she stubbornly brushed it aside. She was tired of being a recluse, of never having any fun simply because she had made a bad marriage. She was not sorry Miles was gone, and she resented having to act the part of a dutiful widow. Tonight would put an end to the whole farce, for she intended to make it quite plain to everyone that she no longer considered herself to be in mourning.

By the time evening approached and everyone gathered around the campfire, Kitty was in the best of spirits. Again, Sally helped her pop the corn, and true to his promise, the major produced a jug of cider. Kitty laughed and flirted outrageously with the officers who flocked around her, reveling in their open admiration, particularly the major's. Bret had not made an appearance, and she could not help but wonder if he was with Dixie. Determined not to allow anything or anyone to mar her fun, she managed to put him from her mind.

It appeared the soldiers could not do enough for her as they vied for her attention and good-naturedly squabbled over who would refill her cup with cider. Compliments flowed freely, but though Kitty did not doubt the sincerity of their admiration, she knew some of their doting stemmed from homesickness and a lack of female companionship. Still, their attention acted on her like a heady wine, filling her with confidence as she charmed her way into their hearts. Kitty was having a good time, and so was everyone else, laughing and joking, eventually joining together to sing "Oh! Susanna."

The war was temporarily forgotten until one of the soldiers pulled out a harmonica and began softly playing a familiar tune, "Shenandoah." By the time the haunting melody had ended, a melancholy silence had fallen over the group.

Clearing his throat, Mark Johnson glanced over at Kitty and smiled. "Miss Kitty, you've got a mighty pleasing voice. How about singing something for us?"

The others quickly echoed his request, and with blue eyes twinkling, Kitty launched into a tune that quickly dispelled all nostalgia: "Song of the Mississippi Volunteers."

As the song progressed, Kitty rose and, moving gracefully among them, motioned for everyone to join her again on the chorus. They did not have to be coaxed to sing with her on the last verse, for their lighthearted mood was now fully restored. Jubilant laughter echoed around the campfire until, finally, it grew late and they were forced to disband. Major Ritchly hung back while Kitty cheerfully bid everyone good night, then helped her to clear away the dishes.

As they walked back to her cave, it occurred to Kitty that the major's expression had become unusually somber, and a ripple of uneasiness swept over her. Though she was fond of him and certainly flattered by his attentiveness, she was not romantically attracted to him in the least. She only hoped he felt the same.

They had almost reached the cave's entrance when Kitty stepped in a rut and stumbled. Her escort's arm steadied her immediately, then drew her to him. At that precise moment, she spied a tall form silhouetted in the moonlight, leaning against a nearby tree. A match was struck, briefly illuminating the man's face as he lit a cheroot. Bret! Recklessness combined with spitefulness as Kitty lifted her face and gave the major a provocative smile, her eyes silently inviting him to kiss her.

Needing no further encouragment, he slowly lowered his head and claimed her lips in a shy kiss that gradually deepened when her arms slipped around his neck. She felt his body quiver with longing as he struggled to keep his passion under control, yet his kiss left her unmoved.

Inadvertently, she recalled how Bret's kisses always aroused her, igniting a desire that left her trembling and weak. No one else had ever affected her so, certainly not the man who was reluctantly releasing her.

She at least had the satisfaction of knowing Bret had witnessed their embrace, and she hoped he was experiencing the same jealous despair she had felt earlier that morning when he had brazenly returned Dixie's kiss right in front of her!

"Kitty, I know it's too soon for me to declare my intentions, but you know how I feel about you," the major began huskily.

"Please don't, James. We've known each other only a short time. I'm very fond of you, but I'm not in love with you," she told him, her conscience now pricking her for having used him as a means of getting even with Bret.

"Well, at least you're fond of me, and that's something." He smiled ruefully. "May I see you again?"

"Of course," she replied. "Now, I really must say good night."

Once he had gone, Kitty gave a sigh of relief and went inside the cave. The night was stifling hot, and, thinking to take a sponge bath before retiring, she walked over to the water barrel, only to find it empty. Irritated that Moses had forgotten to fill it earlier, she snatched up a wooden bucket and stomped back through the entrance. A startled cry escaped her lips when she unexpectedly collided with Bret.

He grabbed her shoulders to steady her, and his mouth quirked into an amused smile as he saw her look of dismay. "Going somewhere?"

"Only around back. I was going to tell Moses to go over to the house and get some water from the cistern."

"No sense in waking him at this hour, not when we can get it ourselves. Come on," he said, "it's a nice night for walking."

Before she could think of an excuse, Bret relieved her of the bucket and took hold of her arm, steering her toward the large meadow that led to the back of her house. It was several minutes before he broke the silence between them.

"Have a good time tonight?"

"Yes, I did. In fact, I think everyone had fun. You should have come."

"Maybe I should have," he drawled without humor, "if for no other reason than to keep you in line."

Immediately on the defensive, Kitty halted and turned to confront him. "And just what do you mean by that?"

"I mean that I think you're seeing too much of Major Ritchly. In fact, that little good-bye scene was quite touching. For a minute, I thought he was going to spend the night with you."

"Don't be ridiculous. I can assure you James wasn't trying to seduce me. He merely kissed me."

Placing the bucket on the ground, Bret straightened, a sardonic look flitting across his handsome face as he took hold of her arms.

"Even you aren't that naive, my sweet. A kiss like that is uptown shoppin' for downtown business!"

Sensing his anger, she defiantly refused to be intimidated by him. "You're being deliberately crude, and I don't like it. Now, will you please take your hands off me?"

Ignoring her demand, he tightened his grip. "I suppose you find the major's touch more to your liking."

"Whatever I feel for him is none of your business."

"Like hell it isn't!" he said, jerking her to him. "I won't have other men pawing you, nor will I have you encouraging them."

There was no gentleness in his kiss as his mouth slanted down on hers, cutting off her angry retort. Taken by surprise, Kitty was infuriated, and for several seconds her tiny hands pushed against his broad chest while she struggled to escape his steellike embrace.

Her resistance, however, was short-lived. As the kiss deepened and she felt the hard length of him pressing against her, her lips parted and her traitorous body began responding to him, her firm breasts jutting against his chest as she molded her body to his.

Aroused by her response, Bret tightened his embrace. Fire shot through his loins, consuming him like a flame. Lifting Kitty in his arms, he stepped through the branches that offered total seclusion, enclosing them in a world of their own. Nothing mattered to him now, nothing except the woman he was slowly lowering to the ground. Never had he wanted her more, nor could his hungering passion be contained for long.

Lying down beside her, he pulled her to him, his excitement escalating when her arms encircled his neck and she arched closer to him. The sweet smell of her, the warmth of her flesh, added to her sensuality, increasing his need to unbearable proportions; yet he held himself in check, savoring each precious moment.

A magical quietness surrounded them. As shafts of moonlight broke through fleeting clouds and briefly illuminated the star-studded sky, Kitty saw the raw hunger in Bret's eyes and silently waited for him to reclaim her lips. Instead, his mouth began seductively tracing the contours of her face, then trailed down the long column of her neck. Her breathing quickened as she felt the delicious touch of his lips on her sensitive skin, his hand probing beneath the bodice of her gown to brush lightly over the crest of one creamy breast. The exquisite torment continued until she was half out of her mind with wanting him. Impatient for total fulfillment, she began unfastening the buttons of his shirt, her hand slipping inside to explore the wide expanse of his muscled chest, then gradually sliding lower to where the crisp dark hair tapered to a V at his narrow waist.

"Lord, it's been so long," he groaned.

"Too long. It's so hard being near you, yet not able to—"

Her words were cut short as a loud volley of shelling erupted, destroying the mystical spell and hurling her back to reality. Instinctively she stiffened with self-reproach.

"Relax, sweetheart," he told her. "The bombardment's coming from the river. We're safe."

"It's not that."

"Then what?"

"You once said you wanted to marry me," she replied hesitantly. "Did you really mean it?"

"Of course I did. I still do."

"Then—oh, Bret, if you care for me at all, please don't have anything else to do with the Yankees. Don't help them anymore. Can't you see it's wrong? You belong on our side, not theirs."

"Dammit, Kitty, forget the war!" he exploded. "It has nothing to do with us."

"It has everything to do with us. Don't you understand? We have no future as long as we're on opposite sides."

Releasing her, he rose and turned his back, but not before she had witnessed the angry torment in his eyes.

Bret was torn by conflicting emotions—the temptation to confide in her and restore her faith in him, and the desire to protect her by keeping her ignorant of the facts. The latter won out, and as he heard her approach him from behind, his expression hardened.

"I once thought you loved me, though you never actually said so," she said stiffly. "I see now that I was mistaken."

Turning to face her, he deliberately gave her a sardonic look. "Love, my dear, happens to be built on trust. Unfortunately, that's the one thing that seems to be lacking in our relationship."

"That *and* respect—which is something you'll never have from me," she vowed.

Without waiting for him to reply, she started back to the cave. Once inside, however, she flung herself down on the cot and sobbed bitterly for what might have been. Without Bret, how could she go on? No matter how much she might despise him, she could never stop loving him.

Chapter 23

May rolled into June, and still there was no relief in sight for the beleaguered people of Vicksburg. Grant's batteries now covered all eight roads leading into town, and earth-shattering bursts of artillery increased daily with terrifying intensity.

To make matters worse, there was an alarming shortage of food. Like most folks, Kitty had been reduced to eating rice, boiled cane sprouts, and "pea bread"—a poor substitute for cornbread made from rice and pea meal. The only available meats were salt pork and bacon, and both were scarce. On one occasion Bret had been able to procure a small sack of weevily flour, but without baking soda the biscuits Daisy had turned out had been barely edible.

Since Bret provided their meager food supply, he usually shared their meals. Apart from mealtimes, however, Kitty rarely saw him. Ever since the night they had almost made love, both had carefully avoided any situation that might instigate intimacy between them. Tension increased, and as a result Kitty's temper grew shorter with each passing day, as was apparent this morning when she abruptly instructed Daisy to reheat the leftover split-pea soup from last night's supper.

Eyeing the congealed liquid that had been left under the tent fly all night, Daisy shook her head. "Ah don' knows 'bout dat soup, Miz Kitty. Hit mought be soured by now."

"Sour or not, it's all we have to eat. Is there any pea bread left?"

"Sho' is. Maybe Ah kin warm hit up ober de coals. Ah's gwine tuh need some water tuh thin down dat soup, though."

"Isn't there any left in the keg?"

"Yas'm, but Moses forgot tuh put de lid on hit last night, an' now de water's full ob bugs."

"Then Moses can just trot back over to the house and get some more," Kitty snapped. "Where is he, anyway?"

"He dun took de baby fo' a walk."

Kitty frowned and strode over to the campfire Daisy had just managed to ignite. "Here, give me the spoon, and I'll stir the soup while you fetch some water from the house."

"Lawd, Miz Kitty, whut if de Yankees start up dat shellin' agin?"

"Then you'll just have to run a little faster," Kitty replied unsympathetically. "Now, quit piddlin' and go on."

Watching until Daisy had darted across the road, Kitty sighed and turned back to the fire. She had just banked the skillet of pea bread on the outer coals when a gaunt-looking soldier sauntered over and hesitantly addressed her.

"Mornin', ma'am. That's some mighty tasty-lookin' bread you got heatin' over them coals. I, er . . . I'd be mighty obliged if'n you'd see fit to sell me a small piece."

There was barely enough to serve her family, yet Kitty's reply was automatic. "I won't sell you any, but I will give you a piece." She smiled, ladling a large hunk onto a spatula and handing it to him.

"That's awfully nice of you, ma'am, but I couldn't rightly enjoy it less'n I paid you a little something," he argued in a friendly manner, gently taking hold of her hand and thrusting some coins into her palm.

Kitty's eyes widened with surprise. "Why, there's three dollars in gold here!" she exclaimed.

"Yes'm, that's a fact. I took it off a dead Yank the other day, that and this here belt buckle," he boasted.

Seeing the man wolf down the last of his bread, then hungrily lick his fingers, Kitty impulsively emptied the skillet of the remaining pieces of pea bread and handed them to him. He accepted only after she had insisted that he do so.

"Thank you kindly, ma'am. This here's the best food I've had in weeks. Ain't much food to be had in them trenches."

"Surely our men are being fed every day?"

"Yas'm, we all git a daily ration, usually 'bout a half cup of green field peas and a speck of rice, plus a strip or two of bacon."

"That's all?" Kitty cried in distress.

"Well, hit ain't much, but s'nough to keep a body going. Reckon I'd better be movin' on, now. Thank you agin for your kindness, ma'am."

Tears misted Kitty's eyes as she watched the soldier shuffle off, but she brushed them away when she spied Bret coming from the direction of Dixie's cave.

"Who was that?" he asked.

"Just a hungry soldier. I gave him what was left of the bread," Kitty answered, still distraught. "Bret, our boys out in those trenches are going hungry!"

"I don't doubt it."

"But how can they possibly fight on empty stomachs? They can't go on like this much longer."

"True, but while I understand your concern, I would advise you not to become overly friendly with strangers."

"Strangers!" she exclaimed. "I would hardly call our own soldiers strangers. Besides, you were so busy with Dixie that I'm surprised you even noticed what I was doing."

"Oh, I noticed. I always notice," came his amused reply. "I'm going down to the warehouse and make sure it's still standing," he informed her, deliberately changing the subject. "While I'm gone, be a good girl and stay out of trouble." He turned to go before she could think of a suitable reply.

Vexed at Bret's eternal amusement at her expense, Kitty began stirring the soup with a vengeance. A loud explosion told her that the bombardment had resumed, and minutes later, Daisy appeared, breathless and minus the water keg.

"Where's the keg?" Kitty yelled above the din.

"Ah drapped hit," gasped Daisy.

"For heaven's sake, why didn't you pick it up and bring it back?"

"Miz Kitty, dem minnie balls started flyin' all ober de place, zippin' rat ober my head lak dey wuz jes' lookin' fo' me. Lawd, Miz Kitty, dey'd found me fo' sho' if'n Ah'd stopped fo' dat bucket!" the frightened woman exclaimed, her eyes as large as saucers.

"So, now we're minus a keg. Oh, come on, we'd better get inside the cave." Kitty was slightly mollified when Moses returned safely with Scotty a few minutes later.

They had just entered the dark cavern when a shell unexpectedly ripped through the tent fly and rolled into the cave, coming to a halt just inside the entrance. Only vaguely aware of Daisy's hysterical scream, Kitty reacted instinctively. Rushing over to the deadly missile, she picked it up and heaved it outside. The ensuing explosion was ear-splitting, and for a moment, everyone was too paralyzed to move.

"You aw'rat, Miz Kitty?" Daisy asked, trembling with fear.

Kitty nodded, her gaze glued to the spot where the shell had exploded. The haze of dust eventually settled, exposing a hole where the campfire had been only moments ago. There was no sign of the pot of soup, other than bits and pieces of cast iron that were scattered around the campsite.

"Oh, well, I didn't want soup anyway," Kitty said with a wry smile.

The shelling lasted most of the afternoon, and as soon as it ended people were flocking around Kitty's campsite and gawking at the hole that had been left by the menacing shell. All were relieved that they had not experienced similar hazardous experiences, but the realization that a shell could roll right into one's cave was hardly reassuring. After they had gone, Kitty and Sally sat beneath the patched canvas and talked.

"Have you heard anything from David?" asked Kitty.

"No, not since last week. Every day I hope I'll see him, even if it's only for a few minutes, but I guess every available man is needed out there," Sally answered.

"Sally, why don't you move in with me? There's no point in your living alone in that cave."

"I'm not exactly alone. Tilly keeps me company," she said, referring to her young maid. "Besides, my folks' cave isn't too far from mine. Hardly a day passes that Mama, Papa, and Celia don't drop by to check on me, and so do the Sheltons. I manage to keep busy during the day. It's the nights that I mind. I do feel lonely then."

"I still don't think anyone in your condition should be helping out at the hospital," Kitty remarked. "When is your baby due?"

"Early October. I do hope all of this is over by then. I would hate for my baby to be born in a cave like poor Mrs. Green's child was."

"I'm sure we'll all be safely back in our own homes by then."

Kitty smiled reassuringly, though deep down she was feeling far less confident. "Have you decided on a name yet? If it's a girl, I certainly hope you won't name her Dixie," Kitty remarked, scowling with obvious displeasure upon discovering that Bret was visiting with the actress in front of her cave.

Sally frowned. "I thought you liked Dixie."

"Well, I don't, and I certainly don't approve of her conduct. Clothes don't make a lady."

Sally's perplexed look changed to one of sheer surprise as the truth suddenly dawned on her. "Why, Kitty, I believe you're jealous!"

"Why would I be jealous?" Kitty returned a little too quickly.

"You know why. Mr. O'Rourke spends a great deal of time with Dixie, and you resent it," Sally mused. "You're in love with him, aren't you?"

When Kitty nibbled on her lower lip and refused to answer, Sally shook her head in amazement. "You've always loved him, haven't you? Even before you married Miles. And all the while I thought you looked on him as a brother. Good heavens, how blind I've been!" She gasped, turning sympathetic eyes to her friend. "How does he feel about you?"

"I haven't the faintest idea." Kitty shrugged. "Now, could we change the subject and talk of something more pleasant?"

"I'm sorry. I didn't mean to pry, and you know I won't say anything about this conversation to anyone else. My lips are sealed!" Sally promised.

They talked of less personal things for several minutes, and all traces of tension had disappeared by the time Sally stood up to leave. A low rumbling in her stomach reminded Kitty that she had not eaten since the previous night, yet the thought of having another supper of field peas and rice was anything but appetizing. She was about to call for Daisy and instruct her to lay another campfire when she noticed Bret approaching her.

"Dixie told me what happened this afternoon. You had a damned close call. I should have been here," he muttered with a dark scowl.

His apparent concern brought a slight smile to Kitty's lips. "I managed," she murmured, eyeing the brown paper sack he held in one hand.

"Yes, and thank God you used your head for once," he remarked, handing her the brown sack.

"What's this?" she asked, somehow disappointed that his praise had been tinged with sarcasm.

"Buzzard," he informed her matter-of-factly, grinning when she wrinkled her nose and frowned distastefully. "Don't be hard to please, Kitten. I'll have you know it cost me an arm and a leg, but it was either that or green pork and molding rice."

"Where did you get it?"

"The commissary officer is a friend of mine, and a very poor poker player who happens to owe me a tidy sum of money. I, er . . . persuaded him to sell me the bird, plus a dozen ears of corn."

Kitty's expression brightened, for though she doubted she would be able to swallow more than a bite or two of the unsavory meat, she dearly loved corn on the cob. Supper might not be bad after all.

Daisy shucked and boiled the corn, while Bret skewered the buzzard and instructed Moses to turn it on a spit over the fire. Kitty busied herself grinding sassafras roots and leaves for tea.

Though it was almost dusk, the air was hot and muggy, yet there had been no sign of rain for weeks. Slapping a mosquito from her arm, Kitty carried the ground sassafras over to the fire and dropped it into a kettle of boiling water, then dusted the remnants from her hands. She felt grimy and sticky with perspiration. Bret often bathed at night in a nearby creek, but she was only permitted the luxury of bathing whenever the bombardment subsided long enough for Daisy and Moses to fetch numerous buckets of water from the house. She was hoping that such would be the case tonight. Brushing a damp tendril of hair from her face, she was roused from her thoughts by the sound of Scotty's voice.

"Mommy, Mommy—look! Big worm!" he called gleefully, pointing to a dark, coiled object lying on a flat rock only a couple of feet away.

Kitty gasped, her eyes widening with horror as she heard the ominous rattle of the deadly snake that was already coiled to strike.

"Bret!" she cried in a hoarse voice.

Bret had already drawn his revolver from its holster. Even as Kitty started to rush toward the unsuspecting child, a loud shot rang in the air and the reptile writhed, then stilled. In the next instant Kitty reached the boy's side and knelt down beside him, hugging him to her fiercely. She was unmindful that Bret had come to stand beside them until moments later when he gently took Scotty from her and handed him to Daisy. Only when he helped her to her feet and took her in his arms did her courage crumble.

"Oh, Bret, I want to go home. We've got to get away from here, or we're all going to die!" she cried, burying her face against his chest and clutching the front of his shirt in her fists.

"Don't you think I'd get you and Scotty away from here if I could?" he muttered against the soft cloud of her hair, despising his own helplessness to relieve her of the hardships she was suffering. He continued to hold her thus until she stopped trembling, and then he lifted her chin with his forefinger and smiled down at her.

"I know you've been through a lot today, more than anyone should have to bear, but try to be brave for just a little longer. All of this will be over soon. When it is, I'll take you home—back to Belle Glen."

Kitty sniffed. "You . . . you promise?"

Bret nodded, then extracted a handkerchief from his pocket and wiped her dirt-streaked face. Their eyes locked in a silent embrace, and neither was aware that Dixie had rushed over after hearing the shot. Quickly summing up the situation, she thoughtfully ushered Scotty, Moses, and Daisy to her cave to afford the couple a moment of privacy.

By the time supper was ready, Kitty's nerves had calmed to some extent, and the terrifying events of the day faded as she bit into a golden ear of corn and savored its sweetness. Even the buzzard proved to be edible, though tough and stringy.

Later, Dixie visited with them for a short time, producing a jug of corn beer that had been brewed by one of the soldiers who frequented her cave. The odd-tasting concoction was too strong for Kitty's liking, but by the time she had finished her second cup, the flavor seemed to have improved and she was feeling pleasantly relaxed. Daisy had already put Scotty to bed, and when she and Moses retired, Dixie also stood up to leave. Seconds later Kitty and Bret were alone.

The night was peaceful, and the sweet fragrance of honeysuckle and night-blooming jasmine drifted on the air as Kitty watched Bret pour the last of the corn beer into his cup. Neither spoke when he sat down beside her on the fallen tree trunk that now served as a bench.

Tree frogs and crickets chirped nearby, reminding her of the many summer nights when the two of them had joined her parents on the veranda at Belle Glen and enjoyed quiet evenings together as a family. Tad had also been present then, and everyone had laughed and talked, often listening to the happy singing that had reached them from the slave quarters. Such a peaceful way of life, one that no longer existed.

"Bret, do you think the Yankees will leave when General Johnston comes?" Kitty finally asked.

"I'm afraid there's no guarantee that Johnston *is* coming," he answered.

"But he must! He must bring reinforcements, or the Yankees will never leave."

"No, they won't, but even if Johnston is prepared to risk his troops in Vicksburg's defense, it's doubtful that he can break through the enemies' lines now. So I don't think we can expect much help from Johnston, not now or in the future."

His opinion was one that others were beginning to express, and Kitty felt there was no point in discussing it further. Only time would tell.

"Well, at least some people don't seem to be unduly alarmed about our situation," she said, casting a disparaging look toward Dixie, who was entertaining several soldiers seated around her fireside. "I'm surprised you're not over there with them," she added without thinking.

"Meaning what?"

"Oh, nothing," Kitty replied with a slight shrug. "It's just that you do seem to enjoy her company."

A hint of merriment twinkled in his eyes. "If you're wondering whether or not I'm having an affair with her, the answer is no."

She shot him a dubious look. "Are you saying there's never been anything between you?" she asked.

"No, I'm not saying that, but I am telling you that whatever our relationship was in the past, it's over and done with now. Dixie and I are friends—nothing more."

Relieved, Kitty smiled as he rose and assisted her to her feet. His next words, however, quickly dispelled her happiness.

"Incidentally, I'm going to have to leave you to your own devices for a day or so. While I'm gone, I suggest you and the others stick close to the cave."

"You're leaving town?" she asked with obvious dismay. "When?"

"Tonight—in a couple of hours. Don't worry, though, I'll be back tomorrow or the next day."

Kitty's expression was one of incredulity. Surely he did not intend to embark on a business trip now, not when it meant that he would have to risk life and limb to sneak through enemy lines? Or would it? Her eyes narrowed as, cocking her head, she regarded him suspiciously.

"I suppose you're going to tell me it's a business trip," she remarked sarcastically.

"As a matter of fact, I am."

"Don't lie to me!" she shot back. "You're not going on any business trip."

His expression was unreadable as he gazed down at her. "Oh? Then just where do you think I *am* going?"

"I think you're going to sneak over to the Yankees and tell them everything you know about our position and God knows what else. Isn't that what spies usually do?"

"So, you still think I'm a spy."

"What else can I think?"

He made no move to detain her as she turned and entered the cave. It was ironic that she was so close, yet so far from guessing the truth. He was, indeed, embarking upon a spying mission—but for Pemberton, not the Yankees!

Chapter 24

Bret reached for the lantern that hung from a peg at the cave's entrance, lighting and placing it on a crude square table that was situated in the middle of the room. The last twenty-four hours had been tense and tiring, and his shoulders drooped wearily as he sat down on the cot and unbuttoned his shirt, then shrugged out of it. His mission had been only partially successful. Other than confirming that Grant's supply lines had been firmly established and General Johnston was still operating unsuccessfully in the rear of Grant's army in a vain attempt to break through to Vicksburg, he had learned very little. The information Pemberton had given him to relay to Grant had, of course, been meaningless but tinged with enough validity to lend credence to his masquerade. The dangerous part of the mission had been sneaking past Confederate and Yankee pickets.

Realizing it would soon be daybreak, Bret rose wearily to his feet, shaved, and dressed, then set out for Pemberton's headquarters. The shelling had not begun as yet, and the town seemed unusually quiet. As he walked down the deserted streets, a feeling of uneasiness assailed him, causing his footsteps to quicken.

Unaware of Bret's return, much less his concern for her welfare, Kitty rose in good spirits. After first dressing her son, she slipped into her faded red calico dress. She was thoroughly tired of wearing the same clothes day after day but realized that finer clothing would be out of place in a cave, not to mention uncomfortable.

After having secured her long curling hair in a black net, she snatched up a tattered parasol and informed Daisy that she was going over to Sally's cave to visit for a spell. It was too lovely a morning to stay cooped up inside, and she was longing for the exercise of a short stroll. It seemed that others shared her feelings, and as she walked down the narrow dirt road, she stopped and chatted with several women before finally reaching her destination.

Sally was hanging some wet clothes on a line that had been strung between two trees, and though she greeted Kitty with a smile, her frail shoulders drooped with weariness. Kitty briefly scolded her for overexerting herself, then helped her to finish the task.

"Where's Tilly?" she asked.

"I sent her to town for some provisions," Sally replied, hooking her arm through Kitty's as they walked toward her cave. "Come on, I want you to try some tea I brewed this morning. You'll never guess what I put in it!"

"What?" Kitty laughed.

"I made it from blackberry leaves," came the reply. "It's not half-bad, and at least it's a change from sassafras tea."

The women sat beneath the tent fly and sipped the tepid brew, which had an odd, bittersweet flavor. It seemed to Kitty that Sally had become adept at discovering ingenious ways of substituting oddities for necessities, such as adding hot water to charred wood to produce ink and making soda from corn cobs. They were having a second cup of tea and happily exchanging tidbits of information when a volley of loud explosions sent them scurrying inside the cave.

"Oh, for heaven's sake! It looks like they could let up for just one morning," Kitty muttered.

Sally lit a candle with trembling hands. Seeing her friend's sudden pallor, Kitty became immediately concerned.

"Are you all right?" she asked.

"Yes, I'm—I'm fine, really," she answered, her lips curving in a tremulous smile that could not camouflage the tears brimming in her eyes.

"Why, Sally, you're almost crying!" Kitty exclaimed worriedly. "What is it? Are you ill?"

Sally shook her head. "No, I'm all right. Just a bit edgy, that's all."

A Parrott shell zipped overhead and exploded a short distance away, causing both women to jump with an audible gasp.

"Hell's bells!" Kitty swore hotly. "Why doesn't General Pemberton do something? If Van Dorn were here, he'd do something! Pity he had to get killed over some silly woman," she snorted, remembering that the daring general had been recently assassinated in Tennessee by an irate husband who had learned of his wife's alleged affair with him.

When Sally did not reply, Kitty stopped pacing back and forth and regarded her with concern. It was not like Sally to succumb to hysterics. The fact that she was struggling to remain calm was evidenced by her somber expression and the way she was holding her clenched fists rigidly at her sides.

"Sally, tell me what's troubling you. Perhaps it will help to talk about it," she suggested, gently pulling the girl into her arms.

In the next instant Sally was sobbing on Kitty's shoulder. Surprised by her friend's unusual behavior, Kitty stroked her head and murmured comforting assurances. After several minutes Sally slowly regained her composure. Brushing her tears aside, she smiled weakly.

"I know I'm being fanciful, but I—I have this awful feeling I'm never going to see David again, that I'm never going to have his baby."

"Oh, Sally, you mustn't think things like that. Of course you'll see David again, probably any day now. As for the baby, childbirth really isn't that bad, especially when a woman is young and healthy, which you certainly are. You're just tired and nervous, that's all. Look, why don't you lie down for a while, and I'll sit over here by the entrance and make sure no stray shells wander in for a visit," Kitty suggested brightly.

Sally sank wordlessly down on the cot situated against the rear wall. With a worried frown, Kitty stationed herself just inside the entrance and peered out, praying they would be safe. The shelling seemed worse than usual and much closer. It occurred to her that Sally's cave was a block nearer than hers to the river, the source of the shelling. This was hardly reassuring. Nearby trees were being splintered by the deadly mortars that were bursting all over the place. And then she heard the distinct whine of a Parrott shell, seemingly headed directly toward them.

Terrified, she jumped to her feet and shouted Sally's name in warning, but before she could move, the missile found its mark. An earth-shattering explosion ripped through the air, knocking Kitty to her knees as overhead beams gave way and the walls caved in on her. As she threw up her arms in a futile attempt to ward off the landslide, her last conscious thought was of Sally. Then, pain knifed through her, and she knew no more.

Minutes later she stirred and slowly opened her eyes. Pitch darkness greeted her, and for a moment she felt bewildered and stunned. She tried to sit up, but something heavy was pinning her down across the ribcage. The slight movement caused her head to throb, and a feeling of suffocation washed over her as she gasped for air and tried to focus her blurred vision. Her eyes became riveted to a small opening directly overhead, and it was then that she recalled the terrifying cave-in. She was buried alive! Panic swamped her as she realized her predicament and remembered that she was not alone.

"Sally! Sally, are you all right?" she called feebly.

There was no answer, and she tried again.

"Sally, where are you?" She paused for breath, but still there was no reply. Surely Sally had heard her, if she were conscious—if she were alive! Fear clutched at Kitty's heart, and she cried out hysterically, "For God's sake, answer me, Sally!"

Then the hum of anxious voices sounded from above, one voice in particular. "Kitty, can you hear me?" Bret shouted hoarsely.

"Yes, yes, I can hear you," she sobbed.

"Are you hurt?"

"I don't think so, but I can't move. Something is pinning me down." The sight of his anxious face peering down at her through the small opening offered a small measure of comfort, and she fought to contain her mounting hysteria.

"Listen to me, Kitty. We're going to get you out of there, but don't move. From what I can see, you're trapped beneath a beam, but if it shifts—"

Bret did not have to finish the sentence for her. Kitty fully realized that the beam was all that stood between her and instant death.

"Hurry, please hurry, Bret! Sally's in here, too, but—but she must be unconscious. She didn't answer when I called to her," she told him in a broken voice.

"Just hold tight," he answered reassuringly. "We'll have you both out in no time."

It was difficult to breathe, so she did not attempt to answer. There was little doubt that Bret would reach her in time, particularly since others were helping him to free her from the debris. Her main concern was for Sally, buried in the back of the cave.

Within fifteen minutes the beam was being lifted from her and Bret was pulling her out into the open. Her legs felt as though they would not support her when he helped her to stand, and she fell against him, coughing and gasping for air. His arms wrapped protectively around her, and she was surprised to find that he, too, was trembling, that his heart seemed to be racing as madly as her own.

"Thank God you're all right," he muttered huskily.

For once, his feelings were unmasked. Glancing up at him, Kitty read the anxiety in his eyes, saw his grim expression, and was comforted by his deep concern. His hand was shaking when he tenderly brushed particles of dirt from her hair and face, and for a moment they shared a world of their own, a world in which no words were needed. The shelling seemed to be abating somewhat, drifting toward the south end of town, and when other people crawled from their caves and rushed over to them, the intimate spell was broken. Suddenly Kitty remembered Sally. Turning away from Bret, she stumbled over to where a group of men were grimly shoveling through the debris.

"Have you found her?" she asked. There was no reply, and she was only vaguely aware that Bret had come to stand behind her as her eyes clouded with tears. "She was in the back of the cave, somewhere over there." She pointed to where several men were digging.

"Kitty, let me take you back to your cave. There's nothing you can do here," Bret suggested.

His words horrified her. "No, I can't leave! Not until they find Sally. She might need me. She might be hurt." Her tremulous voice hinted of the rising hysteria she was fighting to subdue. She would not, could not, begin to face the frightening possibility that Sally might not be alive.

No one spoke as the long minutes ticked by, but Kitty saw their dour expressions and knew what they were thinking. Suddenly she felt alienated from everyone and was filled with rebellious anger.

"You think she's dead, don't you?" she accused. "Well, you're wrong. You're all wrong! She's alive—alive, I tell you!"

The words had hardly been uttered when one of the men spotted Sally and shouted for help. The next ten minutes were a nightmare for Kitty while she stood helplessly by and watched the frantic attempt that was being made to reach her friend. It was Bret who finally lifted Sally's limp form from the yawning hole and gently laid her on the ground. An eerie silence had fallen over the group, and Kitty chewed nervously on her lower lip as she made her way over to where Bret was kneeling beside the still figure, so covered in dirt that she was almost unrecognizable.

Sinking to her knees, Kitty brushed the caked dirt from the girl's closed eyes. "Sally, wake up," she implored softly, then reached for her friend's hand, which had already grown cold. With a perplexed frown, she began chafing it, slowly at first, then faster, determined to get a response from Sally, any response at all. Fear gnawed at her when she realized the futility of her efforts, yet she could not face the agonizing truth.

"Sally, don't die. Please don't die!" she whispered in anguish, taking hold of the girl's shoulders.

Gently Bret captured Kitty's hands in his own and pulled her to her feet, ignoring her attempt to resist as he drew her to him and cradled her head against his chest. "Don't, Kitty," he whispered tenderly. "Don't torture yourself like this. You can't help her now. No one can. Do you understand what I'm saying? Sally is gone, and there's nothing you or anyone else can do to bring her back. We just couldn't reach her in time."

A strangled sob escaped her lips when Bret scooped her up in his arms and carried her away from the tragic scene. Tears coursed down her cheeks as she buried her face against his neck and tried to erase the horrible memory of Sally's pathetic body from her mind. It seemed unreal, like a nightmare from which she must surely awaken; but if this were true, why couldn't she awaken now? And why were others weeping as Bret headed solemnly toward her cave? Nothing seemed real, other than the throbbing pain in her head. Numbed by grief, she had succumbed to inertia by the time Bret reached her cave and laid her down on the cot. As if in a dream, she heard the excited voices of Daisy and Moses, then Bret quietly instructing them to fetch several pails of water from the house so that she could be cleansed.

Her glazed eyes stared unseeingly at the overhead beams when, moments later, Bret dipped his handkerchief into the basin that had been used earlier that morning and began washing the dirt from her face.

What did it matter whether or not she was clean, unless—unless she was in the same grotesque state that Sally had been when they had finally dragged her from the debris? But Sally had been dead even then, so still and lifeless that she had seemed almost a stranger. Did Bret now look upon her in the same way?

No, of course not. The Yankees had not succeeded in killing her as they had Sally. She was alive and breathing, but most of all she was filled with a burning hatred so intense that she began to shake convulsively.

She did not resist when Bret gathered her into his arms, but her hands clutched at his shirtfront as his deep voice pierced her dazed mind. "Ah, Kitty—I wish to God I could have spared you, protected you from all this. I know how much you loved Sally, how deeply you feel her loss, but at least you can be comforted in the knowledge that she didn't suffer. I doubt she even knew what happened."

"But she knew what was going to happen," Kitty cried. "She was afraid she would never see David again, nor have the baby. She said so only seconds before it happened, but I didn't understand. I thought she was imagining things, but she wasn't. Don't you see, it was a premonition, and I ignored it. If I hadn't told her to lie down, if I had brought her to the entrance with me, she'd be alive now!"

Bret took hold of her shoulders and shook her gently. "Stop it, Kitty. You're tearing yourself to pieces, and I won't have it. I won't have you blaming yourself for something you couldn't help. We all have to go sometime. Nobody lives forever."

Tears streamed down Kitty's face as she tried and failed to find solace in Bret's words. Slowly, she shook her head.

"Sally was so young and full of life. She so desperately wanted to live, to have David's child. Now she's dead. Why? Why did God allow this to happen?"

"I wish I could give you an answer, but I can't. It's not always easy to understand His ways, but I am sure of one thing. God never does anything without a reason. You know, it's easy to have faith when everything is going your way. The real test comes when the going gets rough. You mustn't stop believing."

Kitty jerked away from him, her face contorted with bitterness. "Oh, I believe all right. I believe God has stopped caring *what* happens to us. Why else would we be suffering at the hands of the Yankees now?"

"Well, if you're determined to be bitter, at least direct your bitterness in the right direction. The Yankees are the enemy, not God," Bret answered, relieved to see her spirit returning.

"Yes, and I hope every last one of them burns in hell! I'll never forget what they've done to us. Not ever. I'll hate them till the day I die!"

Bret shook his head but did not argue the point. It was enough that she was beginning to recover from the shock she had received. Later she would see things with a clear prospective. For her sake, he hoped her bitter despair would be short-lived and her normal optimism quickly restored. Hate was a lonely companion, warping one's outlook on life and, in the end, destroying its victim. He was determined that such would not be the case with Kitty. Not if he could help it.

Chapter 25

The hot, dry days dragged by with no sign of relief from pestilence, hunger, or Grant's relentless assault on Vicksburg. Of General Johnston there was still no news, and as the end of June approached, people began fearing the worst, that the general might not reach them in time.

They could not hold out much longer. Starvation was a terrifying reality that was being painfully experienced in town as well as in the trenches. Children whimpered with hunger and were periodically terrorized by hordes of rats that scurried boldly through the campsites in a forage for food. The struggle for survival was becoming a full-time occupation, leaving Kitty with little spare time to dwell on Sally's death.

Bombardment seldom ceased, the worst times being in the early morning when shells were lobbed into town from every direction. While Grant's artillery pounded them from three sides, the navy blasted them from the river. Hardly a house or building escaped damage, but while civilian casualties mounted, surprisingly few were actually killed.

The twenty-seventh of June marked the fortieth day of the siege, and Scotty's second birthday. Though the cannons had rumbled early that morning, the afternoon was proving to be pleasantly quiet. Having decided that it would be safe to venture out, Bret escorted Kitty to town to buy supplies and a present for Scotty.

As they walked leisurely toward the business district, Kitty was appalled by what she saw, for in the few short weeks since she had last visited the downtown area, everything had changed. The streets were virtually deserted except for the few soldiers they passed who were lounging beneath shade trees or sprawled out on benches in front of the scantily stocked stores. All streets leading into town had been barricaded, and as they strolled down Washington Street, Kitty spied a sentinel keeping lonely guard over the artillery that blockaded the far end of the avenue. The residential section had been bad enough, with fine homes shell-marked and deteriorating, their once picturesque lawns and flower gardens uprooted and overgrown with weeds; but the sight of the ghostlike business district was even worse, hinting of doom to come.

Twice they were forced to sidestep a pack of rats that had scurried directly across their path. Though Kitty managed to suppress her revulsion each time, her nerves were on edge by the time they finally reached Henry Collins's store.

Most of the items on Kitty's list were out of stock, but they were able to purchase a small amount of pea meal, a few candles, and a couple of licorice sticks for Scotty. Pleased that she now had a birthday gift for her son, Kitty was able to turn a blind eye to the town's deteriorating condition and enjoy Bret's company on the walk back to the cave. By the time they reached the campsite, she was feeling fairly light-hearted, but the mood was soon dispelled when Daisy informed her that the pot of peas she had been simmering over the campfire had been stolen by a passerby.

"Who on earth would do such a thing?"

"Hit wuz one ob dem soldiers, dat's who," Daisy replied. "Ah'd jest stepped in de cave tuh check on de baby, an' when Ah got back, Ah seed dat low-down varmint makin' off wid de peas. Ah's sor'hy, Miz Kitty."

Kitty sighed and patted the girl's arm. "It's all right, Daisy, you couldn't help it. I'm kind of tired of peas, anyway, so I guess we'll just settle for pea bread and cane sprouts tonight," she said dejectedly.

"Like hell we will!" Bret muttered. "Daisy, have you ever cooked mule meat?"

The girl's face lit up in a grin. "Naw'suh, but Ah'd sho' be willin' tuh gib hit a try. If'n Ah b'iled hit fo' a spell, hit mought not be too tough, an' sum meat sho' would be tasty."

"My feelings exactly," he agreed, his eyes twinkling with amusement when he saw Kitty's dubious expression. "I'm going back to town and pay Henry another visit, then stop by the warehouse for a few minutes."

"Why are you going to the warehouse?" Kitty asked. After all, today was Scotty's birthday, and it seemed to her that Bret could forget his interests this one day.

"You'll see." Bret smiled and turned to go.

Shortly after his departure, Bess Crane stopped by to visit, and for a while the two women exchanged tidbits of gossip; eventually, of course, the conversation swung around to the siege.

"Bess, why don't you stay home tomorrow and let me take your place at the hospital?" Kitty suggested.

"Oh, I can't do that. They need all the help they can get, especially since the Yankees set off that mine explosion day before yesterday."

"What mine explosion? Where?"

"You haven't heard? Why, the Yankees tunneled up to the Third Louisiana Redan and blew the top right off the hill, then they attacked and tried to capture the redan. Thank goodness they failed, but I understand it was a fierce battle. Several Mississippians were buried alive. Major Ritchly was one of them, Kitty."

Although stunned by the news of James's death, Kitty was also concerned about her brother. "Tad is at the Third Louisiana Redan," she murmured.

"I didn't realize—" Bess faltered, regretting that she had delivered such a shocking blow to her friend. "But I'm sure Tad is all right, or you would have heard otherwise by now."

Far from comforted, Kitty shook her head. "Not necessarily," she answered, a far-off look in her eyes. "What time will y'all be leaving in the morning?"

"We're supposed to meet in front of Duff Green's house at six o'clock," she answered, referring to the closest hospital in the vicinity.

With a determined lift of her chin, Kitty said simply, "I'll be there."

They talked for a few minutes more, then Bess departed just as Kitty spied Bret coming across the road, laden down with a large parcel under one arm, a bulging burlap sack beneath the other, and several lengths of heavy rope coiled over his shoulders.

"It looks like you've bought out the town," she remarked.

Bret shot her a pleased grin. "Not quite, unfortunately. This, my love, is for supper," he informed her, handing her the heavy parcel of mule meat.

"What's in the sack?"

"You'll see directly. In the meantime, why don't you give Daisy a hand with preparing supper," he suggested with a hint of laughter in his deep voice. Before Kitty could question him further, he headed toward the back entrance of the cave and disappeared from view.

By the time Daisy had cut the tough strip of meat into hunks and dropped them into a kettle of boiling water, Bret had finished his mysterious task in back. Kitty was in the process of arousing Scotty from his nap when she heard him calling to her. Consumed with curiosity, she scooped the child up in her arms and dashed outside, almost colliding with Bret.

"Come on, I've something to show you," he said cheerfully, taking Scotty from her and leading the way.

Kitty followed him around to the rear of the cave, her face alight with excitement as she waited for him to reveal his secret. Her mouth dropped open in amazement when he pointed to a large oak tree only yards from the rear entrance. A long burlap bag stuffed with cotton had been fastened securely at one end with a long length of rope that was looped over one of the lower, sturdier branches.

"A bag swing—just like the one we had when we were children!" she exclaimed. "Remember how Tad and I used to get you to push us, so we could swing higher?"

Bret grinned and nodded. "I also remember the time you got Tad to throw the swing up to you in the hayloft. I got there just in time to see you reach out for it, then fall all the way to the ground. You were damned lucky you didn't break your neck," he remarked dryly.

"Well, I did sprain my ankle," she reminded him with a pout.

"Yes, but that didn't stop you from trying again. If nothing else, you were a hardheaded little minx."

Kitty laughed, realizing that Bret had had every reason to consider her a nuisance when she was a child. "Let's hope Scotty doesn't take after me in that respect. Oh, Bret, he's going to have so much fun with that swing! It was so thoughtful of you to get it for him." She clasped her hands with delight, looking for all the world like a little girl.

Still holding Scotty in the crook of his arm, he smiled down at her. "You didn't think I'd forget our son on his birthday, did you?" he said softly.

Their eyes met and held for a brief, tender moment, until Scotty started wiggling with impatience to be set down. Almost reluctantly, Kitty watched while Bret walked over to the swing and placed the boy on it, instructing him to grasp the rope with both hands and wrap his legs tightly around the bulging bag. This done, Bret began gently to swing him to and fro. In a short time Scotty was squealing excitedly and begging to go higher, just as his mother had done long ago. A lump rose in her throat as bittersweet memories of their childhood flitted through her mind. But her nostalgia had to be put aside when Bret laughingly insisted that she pitch in and help him swing the elated tyke.

The remainder of the afternoon passed all too soon for Kitty, who felt as though she were almost reliving the past. Only one incident marred her happiness, when Scotty unthinkingly called Bret "Papa." A sadness appeared in Bret's eyes when she quickly corrected the child, reminding him that *his* papa had gone away. But when Scotty innocently asked if Bret could be his papa now, it was she who averted her eyes in confusion. Sensing her discomfort, if not her pain, Bret smoothly ended the subject by swinging the boy up on his shoulders and letting him ride piggyback.

The sun was already sinking into the west by the time Daisy announced that supper was ready. Kitty discovered that mule meat was just as tough as Bret had predicted, but at least it stopped the gnawing in the pit of her stomach. She did not complain, nor did anyone else.

Using a fallen tree trunk for a bench, she sat beside Bret and cheerfully consumed the tasteless food as though it were a meal fit for kings. She knew that in years to come she would always look back on this day as one of the few pleasurable times during the siege, and for this rare happiness, only one person was responsible. Bret.

Filled with contentment, she watched him pull their son onto his lap, and a smile curved her lips as she listened while he told the sleepy child several bedtime stories—the same ones he had told her during her youth, usually to divert her from mischief.

Later, as she lay on her cot and recalled the closeness they had shared that afternoon, she found herself wishing she were Bret's wife and they were a real family. Past differences, even his disloyalty to the South, suddenly seemed not to matter. She loved him more than life itself.

Unable to put Bret from her mind, she didn't succumb to exhaustion until more than an hour later. Even then she slept fitfully, tossing and turning as a kaleidoscope of dreams invaded her, dreams climaxing in the same nightmare that had plagued her for so many years. Again, there was a threatening web hovering directly above her, descending slowly, coming closer and closer until, finally, it was almost upon her. Feeling almost smothered, she sought to escape, only to discover that she could not move. She was trapped, paralyzed with indescribable terror, while her eyes searched frantically for the hidden danger that was certain to come, the menacing horror that lurked somewhere in the dark shadows beyond. And then it appeared. A huge, black spider, centered in the web above, was flexing its long, gruesome legs in a macabre movement as it crawled nearer to her, ready to pounce and devour!

In past dreams she had always awakened at this point, but this time the nightmare continued with terrifying clarity. Unexpectedly, the spider's thick body was supplanted by an image of the town's courthouse, and all eight legs suddenly turned into the roads that led to Vicksburg—roads thast were lined unendingly with thousands of brightly uniformed soldiers, all jubilant as they marched victoriously into town.

Yankees!

Chapter 26

It was stifling in the tent that served as one of the field hospitals. The buzzing of flies intermingled with the continuous sound of agonizing moans that Kitty tried to block from her mind. Exhausted, she waved a palmetto fan over a delirious young soldier whose leg had been amputated earlier that afternoon.

There had been no anesthesia, nothing at all to ease the pain. Kitty had been filled with pity and revulsion, relief washing over her when the youth's terrified screaming had ended and he had fainted from shock. Now, as perspiration trickled down her back, plastering the blue dress to her sticky body, she wished she had never volunteered to come out here today. It was a nightmare she would never forget.

A strange rattling sound reached her ears. Glancing down at her patient, she saw that he was having difficulty breathing. Alarmed, she got to her feet and, catching Mark Johnson's eye, beckoned urgently to him.

"Isn't there anything we can do, anything to ease his pain?" she asked.

Mark bent his head in despair, bitterness etched in his face.

"I wish to heaven there were," he answered with defeat. "I've no way of counting the ones we've lost today. If we'd just had the necessary medical supplies, more than half could have been saved. I'd give my right arm to have one-tenth of the supplies the Yankee surgeons are using right now, less than a mile away from us. God knows I've never felt so helpless."

Realizing the soldier could not last much longer, Mark stayed with Kitty until the end. Then, seeing her pallor, he suggested she step outside for a short break. Kitty did not argue. She was eager to get away from it all.

The afternoon had all but faded, and the firing between the rifle pits was beginning to subside somewhat as she stood beneath the tent flap and stared unseeingly across the battlefield.

Two weary soldiers were talking a few feet away, their raised voices drifting to Kitty and finally capturing her attention. One of them had apparently spotted General Sherman a few minutes ago.

"You're crazy!" his companion exclaimed. "What would Sherman be doing in the trenches?"

"Maybe inspectin' the men. Hell, I dunno, but I damn sure saw him, right over yonder!"

Kitty's mind immediately went into action. Without pausing to consider the consequences, she rushed over to the two soldiers. "You say you saw General Sherman over there?" she questioned.

"Yes'm, that's a fact." The youth grinned.

"How long ago was that?"

"About ten minutes, I reckon. Last I saw of him, he was walking away from that trench over yonder, but then I lost sight of him. Took me so by surprise, I didn't even take a bead on him. Shucks, it ain't every day you see a general right on the front lines!"

"No, I don't imagine it is," Kitty replied absently, her thoughts in a whirlwind as she contemplated the possibility of getting through the lines and catching up with the general. Once, her father had granted him a favor, the hospitality of their home. Now, she wanted a favor in return, and she was determined to get it. But how?

The answer came to her in a flash, and in the next instant she gave the two perplexed soldiers an appealing smile. "Would there be any way I could get through to see the general?"

Both soldiers guffawed, their expressions quickly sobering upon seeing the stubborn glint in her eyes. " 'Fraid not, ma'am," one of them answered in a slightly patronizing voice. "It ain't likely you could git through our lines, much less theirs, not unless you wuz under a flag of truce."

"I see," Kitty mused, deftly untying her white apron and holding it up for inspection. "If this were attached to a stick, could it be regarded as such a flag?"

The amusement faded from their faces. "Maybe," the older man drawled, "but I hope you ain't thinkin' what I think you're thinkin'.

You wouldn't have it in mind to try an' pay ol' 'Sherm' a visit, now, would ya?''

"Yes, I do. Of course, if the two of you would be willing to escort me as far as the picket lines, I'd feel much safer," she answered shrewdly, hoping to appeal to their sense of chivalry. "General Sherman is an acquaintance of mine. If I could reach him and talk to him, I believe I could persuade him to provide us with some medical supplies," she ended breathlessly, looking from one to the other while waiting for an answer.

When none was forthcoming, she stomped her foot in sheer frustration. "You've *got* to take me! There are men in that tent dying this very minute simply because there's no medicine—no chloroform or quinine, nothing to ease their pain. Don't you understand? I've got to get through to General Sherman. We must have medicine, and there's no other way to get it."

"I dunno, ma'am," the first man finally drawled, scratching his bearded chin thoughtfully. "It'd be mighty risky, mi-ghty risky."

The younger soldier, however, was not so reluctant. "The Yankees wouldn't hurt her, Tom, not if'n she's a friend of Sherman's. 'Sides, there ain't much firing going on now. The blue-bellies always take a break 'round suppertime, so this'd be the best time for us to sneak her up to the picket lines."

"You're mighty all-fired quick to be riskin' somebody else's neck, Dan. Hell, don't'cha know we could git busted for pullin' a damn-fool stunt like this?" Tom growled.

"Can't think of a better reason to git busted, can you?" Dan grinned. "Like the lady says, we gotta have medicine, so what are we waitin' for?"

The older man took out a plug of tobacco, chomped off a piece, and put the remainder back in his hip pocket. After chewing it a bit, he glanced down at Kitty, whose face was set in a determined look.

"Seein' as how your mind's made up, I reckon it'd be downright ungentlemanly fer me to refuse. Mind you, I ain't sure we can git you through, but leastways we can try," he said. "See that there hill over yonder? That's a redoubt, and directly beyond that's the Yankees' trenches. Like Dan said, most everybody's knocked off to grab some vittles, so they ain't likely to be more'n a couple of men up there now. We'll jest mosey on over, kinda like we're showin' you 'round the place.''

Somehow Kitty managed to contain her excitement as she smiled up at the tall, lanky sergeant. "And then what?"

"Then, we'll jest have to play it by ear." He winked.

As they sauntered toward the redoubt, both soldiers conversed with Kitty as though nothing out of the ordinary were happening, occasionally stopping to explain certain points of interest as if they were actually taking her on a sightseeing tour. In spite of her impatience to reach the redoubt, Kitty went along with the charade and dutifully asked questions.

It was not until they reached the redoubt that Kitty became slightly apprehensive. Her footsteps, however, never faltered, nor did she have any intention of turning back at this point.

"Well, this is it," the sergeant informed her, "and it looks like luck is with us. Nobody around, 'ceptin' them that's eatin' and snoozin'," he added, nodding at a small group of men to the right, who, after eyeing Kitty curiously, returned to their meager meal.

An occasional rifle shot could be heard, but apart from that the area was almost quiet. To Kitty, it seemed strange that these men, so close to the enemies' lines, could relax long enough to eat, but then she supposed the Yankees were doing the same. Her thoughts were dispersed as Dan motioned her over to an opening that had been cut in the parapet, which he briefly explained was an embrasure, a gap from which their artillery fired upon the enemy.

"Sure you want to go through with this?" the sergeant asked.

Kitty nodded and held out her apron. "What can we tie this to?"

"What about this, Tom?" Dan asked, picking up a rifle that rested against the parapet.

The older man nodded his approval. Taking the apron from Kitty, he proceeded to secure it to an ominous-looking bayonet at the end of the weapon. "I'll wave this thing back and forth a few times, and if'n they wave one back at us, we'll know it's safe fer you to go."

Kitty's heart began to race as she watched her apron being raised above the parapet, then waved back and forth. Would it be seen? she wondered anxiously. And if it were, would it be accepted as a flag of truce?

"Look, Tom, there it is!" Dan whispered excitedly, pointing to a white scrap of material that suddenly appeared less than a hundred yards away.

"Yep, that's it." A look of respect appeared in his eyes when he glanced down at Kitty. "I'll take you a piece of the way," he said simply.

She gave him a slight smile, inwardly thankful she would not have to face the enemy alone—at least, not at first. If and when she met with Sherman, she only hoped he remembered her.

Taking a deep breath, Kitty stepped through a narrow opening in the parapet and followed her companion down the hill, keeping close to his side as they marched toward the opposite trenches. Her knees felt wobbly, and her heart was racing like a triphammer when a blue-uniformed soldier carrying a white, makeshift flag came into view. Within seconds they came face to face with the man, who, like her companion, was a rough-looking character.

"Howdy, soldier," Tom greeted him in a friendly manner. "I got a little lady here who'd like to see General Sherman. Says he's a friend of hers."

"The general's already left, Reb," the Yankee answered, then cast a dubious look at Kitty. "You really friends with him?"

"I'm an acquaintance of his, yes," Kitty replied, lifting her chin as if defying him to deny it. "In fact, he's been a guest in my home."

It was obvious that the soldier was not sure how to handle the situation. "Well, if that's the case, I guess I could escort you to him. I think he went over to Grant's headquarters, which is only a short distance away."

"I'd be most grateful for your assistance," she said crisply, adding wryly, "I'm sure the general will be surprised to see me."

After suggesting it would be best if Tom waited there for her, the Yank proceeded to escort her to General Sherman. As they walked past the pickets and across the trenches, Kitty ignored the whispers and guffaws she heard, though she was acutely aware that, despite her disheveled state, many of the gawking Yankees were staring at her with open admiration, if not actual lust. The realization that many of them had not enjoyed female companionship in months did not arouse her sympathy one iota; had they stayed at home where they belonged, celibacy would not have been forced upon them. As far as she was concerned, no hardship was even half what they deserved!

The battlefield looked barren, almost totally devoid of trees and undergrowth. All that remained were the well-fortified hills and trenches, all ravaged by war. It was a gruesome sight, and bitterness welled up in Kitty as she recalled the beauty of this particular area in days gone by.

Hating the Yankees as she did, it was only by exerting every shred of willpower that she was able to appear calm while she followed her escort to a tent that, he informed her, was Grant's headquarters.

A boy lounged beneath the tent flap. Seeing Kitty's interest in him, the sergeant explained the youth's presence. "That's General Grant's boy, Fred. He's been with us throughout this whole campaign."

"But he's so young," Kitty remarked with surprise.

"He's twelve, but I'll tell you something, lady—that boy handles himself like a real trooper." He nodded to the boy and asked, "Have you see General Sherman, Fred?"

"He's inside with my pa. You want me to tell him you're here?" asked the youngster, sending a curious glance in Kitty's direction.

"I'd be much obliged," the sergeant replied with a wink. "Tell him there's a lady out here to see him, a friend of his. Might help to give Fred your name, miss," he suggested.

Kitty hesitated. "I doubt he would recognize my married name, so perhaps you'd better introduce me by my maiden name, Miss Devan of Belle Glen," she instructed him with an aloof smile.

With a brief nod, the boy entered the tent, reappearing a few moments later with General Sherman and another officer whom Kitty correctly assumed to be General Grant. The breath caught in her throat as she watched the two high-ranking officers approach. It was obvious that Sherman did not immediately recognize her, but his puzzled look was soon replaced by one of surprised recognition. With a polite smile, he stretched out his hand to her.

"Ah, yes, now I remember," he said, taking hold of her elbow. "You're the young woman who tried to steer my men back to the swamp when we came across your father's plantation last winter. Miss Kathryn, isn't it?"

There was a hint of amusement in his voice, though his expression was unreadable. For a brief moment Kitty was nonplussed.

"Your memory does you credit, General," she murmured with a slight incline of her head, "particularly since you have undoubtedly enjoyed the comforts of many southern plantations during the past months," she added with a trace of sarcasm.

If she had nettled him, he gave no evidence of it as he turned to

introduce her to his fearsome commander, the man who had master-
minded the Vicksburg campaign—General Grant himself. More than
anyone else, she hated this man with an intensity that defied description. It was he who had instigated the siege, who was primarily
responsible for the misery she and her loved ones had been subjected
to over the past months. She wanted to shoot him on the spot.
Instead, she allowed Sherman to steer her inside the tent, his touch
on her arm filling her with a revulsion that was difficult to hide.

Once inside, she coolly refused the offer to be seated. She was
strongly disinclined to accept their hospitality and eager to introduce
the reason behind her visit so that she could leave as quickly as
possible. It was Sherman who opened the way for her.

"Well now, Miss Devan, to what do we owe this unexpected
pleasure?" he asked without preamble.

Kitty ran her tongue over her bottom lip, then, lifting her chin,
boldly returned his gaze. "I need your assistance—your's and General Grant's, of course."

"Forgive me if I seem somewhat surprised. As I recall, you are a
loyal Southerner who staunchly supports the Confederacy," Sherman
remarked dryly.

"General, I am not asking a favor as a Southerner, but as a human
being who is appalled by the needless suffering which is occurring
only a short distance away. Our doctors have run out of medical
supplies. We have nothing left to administer to the wounded—no
medicine or bandages, nothing with which to ease their pain."
Turning distressed eyes to Grant, she continued in a tremulous
voice, "Today, I have seen arms and legs amputated and heard
men's agonizing screams because there was no chloroform. Many
were only boys, not much older than your own son, General Grant."

Both men frowned, their expressions unreadable as Kitty looked
from one to the other and prayed that her request would be granted.
Finally Grant cleared his throat and called to the orderly posted just
outside the tent. The man quickly appeared, and Grant asked him if
the supply wagons had arrived, to which the orderly nodded
affirmatively.

"Good. Take this young lady to the medical supply tent and tell
the officer in charge to provide her with whatever we can safely
spare—laudanum, chloroform, quinine, and anything else that's available. She'll need some assistance in taking it back to the Rebel lines,
so get a couple of men to help her."

Kitty blinked and stared at the general, amazed that her request was being granted. She had been prepared to beg, to grovel if necessary, but Grant had magnanimously consented to provide her with whatever she needed, sparing her the ordeal of further humbling herself. A feeling of gratitude rendered her momentarily speechless. Then Grant closed the space between them and smiled down at her.

"I doubt these supplies will be enough, but they'll help some, at least."

"Thank you, General," Kitty answered politely. "I am grateful indeed."

"I hope you will feel the same in a week," he remarked dryly.

"A week?" she repeated.

"Yes. When my men and I enjoy the hospitality of your town. You see, I have every intention of celebrating the Fourth of July in Vicksburg."

Kitty stiffened, her blue eyes darkening with undisguised anger as she lifted her chin and looked him squarely in the eye.

"You'll have to get there first, General!"

Chapter 27

Kitty returned from the camp hospital that evening to find Bret waiting inside her cave. Whatever elation she felt over procuring medical supplies from the Yankees quickly faded when she saw the thunderous look on his face. He was furious with her for leaving, and with good reason. The town had been under heavy bombardment most of the day, resulting in more civilian casualties than usual. Not only had the Catholic Church been hit during mass, but some of the hospitals had also been shelled. The fact that he had been worried sick about her did not lessen her own growing anger as he upbraided her. For the next three days she barely spoke to him.

On the fourth day, however, Bret dropped by to tell Kitty he would be transferring some of the more critically wounded soldiers from the battlefield to the town's original hospital. She was surprised to learn that he had actually volunteered to drive the ambulance wagon, a cumbersome vehicle that was often an easy target. Considering he was a Yankee sympathizer, she was amazed he was willing to go on such a dangerous assignment in their behalf. Was his offer some kind of a ruse, she wondered, or was his conscience finally getting the better of him?

It was enough that he was going, for the situation had become desperate at the field hospitals. The Yankees had succeeded in blowing up a mine at the Third Louisiana Redan yesterday, and this time the casualties had been numerous.

Realizing that every available hand would be needed to nurse the wounded, Kitty asked him to escort her to the hospital before he left. Later she regretted that she had come, for the multitude of mangled bodies that were continuously brought in was not a pretty sight. On more than one occasion, Kitty abruptly left the operating room, violently ill.

For the most part, however, she worked tirelessly beside Mark Johnson, ignoring the fact that her face, apron, and yellow calico dress were splattered with blood. There was no anesthesia, and it often took the combined strength of Kitty, Bess, and two orderlies to hold down the wounded soldiers, who jerked and screamed beneath Mark's scalpel until unconsciousness, or death, released them from their torment.

"How can anybody survive in this hell?" she muttered to herself after seeing a young boy of fifteen lose both his legs.

Bess had finally fainted and been taken home, but it was not until late afternoon that Mark noticed how pale Kitty was and ordered her to take a short breather outside. Too exhausted to argue, she made her way to the front porch, where she sank down on the wide steps. There was little doubt in her mind that she had taken about all she could, yet she hated to leave Mark short-handed. She rested for a few more minutes, then stood up with a dispirited sigh. She was on the verge of returning inside when she saw Bret driving up in the ambulance wagon. At least he was safe, and her lips curved into a smile while she watched him striding toward her. Her smile faded, however, when she saw his somber expression. Even before he spoke, she guessed the reason for his grimness.

"Tad?" she whispered when he stopped before her.

Bret nodded and took hold of her hand. "He's in the wagon. It's his arm."

Getting a firm grip on herself, Kitty asked, "How bad is it?"

"I don't know, but it doesn't look good."

It took a great deal of self-control not to break down and cry when she saw Tad being carried into the hospital on a stretcher, but at least he was conscious and able to give her a weak smile as she walked along beside him. The stretcher-bearers set him down just outside the operating room, and she knelt beside him and took hold of his good hand.

"Guess I was in the wrong place at the wrong time," he joked feebly.

Kitty forced a slight smile to her lips and gave his hand a tight squeeze. "I guess you were, but then you never were fast at ducking," she quipped in an unsteady voice.

Tad's mouth tightened with pain. "There was no way to duck that explosion. Seemed like the whole damned ground blew up right under us."

"Don't think about it, Tad. You're safe now, and you're going to be all right. Ah, here's the doctor," she said, thankful that Bret had been able to persuade Mark to leave the operating room long enough to take a look at her brother's wound.

Mark quickly examined the mutilated arm, which oozed with blood once the dirty bandages were removed. Kitty leaned weakly against Bret for support when she saw the extent of Tad's injury. It came as no surprise when Mark finally shook his head and told them that gangrene was already setting in. The arm would have to come off immediately. Kitty blanched and glanced down at Tad, pride washing over her when she saw his brave, determined look.

"Then let's get on with it, Doc, 'cause the damned thing's hurting like hell," he muttered. His eyes sought Kitty. "Now, don't you start getting teary on me, Sis. After all, it's just my left arm, and I hardly use that one anyway."

"Don't worry, I won't cry all over you, and I won't leave you, either. You may not realize it, but Mark and I make a pretty good team in surgery. I'll be right beside you."

"You don't have to assist me this time, Kitty," Mark informed her.

"I know I don't have to, but I want to," she answered firmly.

Bret had remained quiet but now he intervened, pulling her aside as the stretcher-bearers carried Tad into the operating room.

"Don't be foolish, Kitty. It's one thing to help out with strangers, but quite another when the patient is your own brother."

"Don't you see, Bret, it's *because* he's my brother that I have to help. I can't desert him now, not when he needs me. I just can't!"

Bret frowned but did not try to deter her when she followed Mark into the operating room.

It was a terrifying experience, and as Kitty stood beside the operating table and took hold of Tad's good arm, she fervently prayed for her brother's life. Above all, she prayed he would not suffer, that unconsciousness would quickly release him from the agony he was sure to experience once the scalpel cut into his flesh. Oh, God, if only there had been a few drops of chloroform left! But there was nothing—no merciful way to put him to sleep and nothing for the pain he would be forced to endure.

Dusk was falling, and Mark had ordered several lamps to be lit and placed around the table. Kitty was dimly aware that Bret was standing beside her. It was stiflingly hot, despite the fact that the shuttered windows were half-open, and as the stench of rotting flesh assailed Kitty's nostrils, beads of perspiration popped out on her forehead. Did anyone ever become insensible to the smell of decay? she wondered, automatically waving a fly away from Tad's face. His eyes had been closed, but now they opened, and he glanced up at her.

"You shouldn't be in here, Sis, but I'm mighty glad you are. I'll try not to put up much of a fuss."

"Don't worry about that, Tad. You yell all you want to." She swallowed hard to force back a sob.

Mark approached the table, saw in hand, and it was then that Bret eased Kitty out of the way and bent over Tad.

"I wish to heaven there were some other way, Tad, but there isn't," he said grimly. Before anyone could guess his intentions, he smashed his fist into Tad's jaw, knocking him unconscious.

Kitty gasped with surprise but said nothing. She had prayed for a miracle, and Bret had provided one. Tad would not consciously be aware of pain, at least not until the operation was over and he awakened.

Later, as she sat by Tad's cot and intermittently bathed his feverish face with cool water, she knew she would never forget seeing her brother's arm hacked off and discarded, just as she would never forget his tormented expression when he had awakened briefly and discovered the limb was missing. Despite his effort to be brave, it soon became evident that his pain was almost unbearable; yet only an occasional moan escaped his cracked lips. Finally he fell into an exhausted sleep. Only then could Bret persuade her to let Cora Crane take over so she could return to the cave and get a good night's rest.

When she returned to the hospital early the next morning, she was relieved to discover that Tad's fever had lessened. Mark assured her this was a good sign, as was the fact that Tad's coloring was improving and his pulse returning to normal. He slept most of the day, but each time he awakened, Kitty spoon-fed him sassafras tea and a thin broth made from boiled mule meat. Soon after, he would drift back to sleep, but the sound of intense bombardment occasionally awakened him with a start, causing him to moan aloud.

Twice during the day the hospital was struck by shells, but luckily no one was injured. Nerves were frayed, however, and when the firing ended around five o'clock that afternoon, sighs of relief could be heard throughout the hospital. An hour later Cora relieved Kitty and told her Bret was waiting for her in front of the hospital. After kissing Tad on the cheek and assuring him she would return early the next morning, Kitty skirted around the numerous cots and wearily made her way to the porch.

Storm clouds had rolled in from the northeast and now loomed over the silent town like a bad omen. Kitty shivered in spite of the oppressive heat and, tearing her eyes away from the dismal sky, walked quickly down the front steps and wordlessly accepted Bret's proffered arm. He inquired about Tad's condition, but soon they lapsed into a silence that lasted until they were almost back at the campsite. By then a feeling of uneasiness had mounted in Kitty, though she was not sure why. Perhaps exhaustion was putting her on edge, or perhaps it was because Bret seemed unusually quiet and somber this evening. Hoping to lighten her spirits, she began to talk.

"Bret, I was thinking about moving back into the house so Tad can have a comfortable bed to sleep in while he's recovering," she said, glancing up at him. When he did not answer, she quickly continued. "After all, some people have remained in their homes, and they seem to have made it through this just fine. I'm sure we can manage somehow, particularly since this siege can't possibly last much longer. Everyone says General Johnston is bound to get here any day now."

Bret stopped and turned Kitty around to face him. "General Johnston isn't coming, Kitty. There's no way in hell he can possibly break through the Yankees' lines and reach us, and I seriously doubt he intends to risk his men by attempting the impossible. Had he moved sooner, the outcome might have been different. But it's too late now."

"What do you mean, it's too late?"

"I mean that an armistice was called this afternoon so that terms of surrender could be discussed."

"How do you know?"

"I saw General Pemberton, General Bowen, and another officer ride out toward the battlefield shortly before three o'clock. Rumor has it they met with General Grant and his staff, and that Grant and Pemberton discussed the terms at length, but arrived at no solution.

Grant wants an unconditional surrender, and Pemberton is insisting his men be granted paroles. The meeting ended in a stalemate. Since Bowen is an old friend of Grant's, Pemberton allowed him and Montgomery to remain behind and try to arrive at a satisfactory solution with Grant's staff. We should know something by tomorrow.''

"But General Pemberton can't surrender! He can't betray us like that, not after all we've been through, and especially not tomorrow— not on the Fourth of July!" Kitty argued passionately.

"Especially on the Fourth of July," Bret disagreed with a wry smile. "You see, Pemberton realizes Grant is anxious to end this siege. Then he would be able to move his troops out of here and deploy them elsewhere. I think he's probably hoping that, by surrendering on the Fourth, Grant will be more lenient with the terms of surrender."

"And I think you're wrong. No matter what's happened, I refuse to believe we're going to tuck tail and run like a bunch of scared jackrabbits. We're not about to surrender, not tomorrow or any other day. The Yankees haven't licked us yet, and they're not going to!''

Bret watched as Kitty turned on her heel and marched inside her cave.

"No, my little Rebel, the Yankees haven't beaten us," he murmured, "but starvation has."

Chapter 28

Surrender!

The Rebels scoffed at the rumor that rippled up and down their dusty trenches, but as the pale fingers of dawn stretched over the ominously quiet battlefield, anxiety mounted. By midmorning the worst was confirmed: General Pemberton had conceded defeat. The fact that Grant had reluctantly abandoned his terms for unconditional surrender, agreeing to paroles and an exchange of prisoners, did little to lessen their anguish.

Disillusioned, the gaunt soldiers in tattered butternut uniforms crawled from their trenches, stacked their firearms, then sullenly lined up to be inspected by their conquerors. To their surprise, they were met not with exultant cheers or boastful taunts, but with quiet deference. A hard-fought battle had waged between them for months, ending in a forty-seven-day siege. Now, it was over. The Confederates, though ill-equipped and half-starved, had persisted against all odds, fighting with valiant determination that had long ago commanded respect. They had been worthy foes, and if there was one thing the Yankees respected, it was courage.

In town, the oppressive silence could almost be felt while nervous civilians waited to learn if the distressing news they had heard was rumor or fact. Had General Pemberton surrendered, they wondered anxiously, and if not, why were the guns now silent? For once, the sound of the big cannons would have been almost a relief.

Kitty said as much to Daisy while she paced back and forth in front of her cave and impatiently awaited Bret's return.

"Oh, why doesn't he come back? Where can he be?" she muttered irritably.

"He sed he wuz gwine tuh make sho' de warehouse wuz locked good 'n tight, den try tuh find sum food fo' us," Daisy reminded her.

"That was over an hour ago. It's almost noon."

The words were barely out of her mouth when one of the men in the Home Guard came galloping down the road, shouting:

"We've surrendered! The Yankees are coming!"

Within seconds, pandemonium erupted, and hysterical wails of distress and anger permeated the air. Women fearfully gathered their bewildered youngsters to their breasts and cried, while the few remaining men in the area cursed and accused Pemberton of being a traitor. Refusing to succumb to panic, Kitty forced herself to think of options, alternatives, and she soon came to a decision.

"Daisy, we can't wait for Mister Bret any longer. We're going home. You and Moses pack up as much as you can carry, and I'll bring Scotty. Hurry, now," she ordered.

"But, Miz Kitty, most lakly de Yankees gwine tuh cum marchin' rat by de house. Whut if'n dey d'cides tuh cum inside?"

"The only way they'll get inside is over my dead body," Kitty answered grimly.

In ten minutes their few belongings had been packed, and they started for home. As they passed Dixie's cave, Kitty paused long enough to inform the actress where they were going and ask her to pass the word on to Bret as soon as he returned. Dixie, at least, seemed calm and informed Kitty that one way or another she fully intended to have a comfortable hotel room by nightfall.

Unwilling to waste time chatting, Kitty said good-bye and, motioning Daisy and Moses to follow, hurried down the dusty road that led to Jackson Street. It only took a few minutes to reach the house, but not until they were safely inside did she breathe a sigh of relief. Realizing the best way to keep everybody calm was to stay busy, she told Daisy to put Scotty down for a nap, then help Moses unpack their belongings and remove the dust covers from the furniture. Too nervous not to take her own advice, she proceeded to check all the downstairs windows and doors to make sure they were securely bolted.

She had just finished this task when a loud knock sounded at the door, accompanied by the sound of excited voices that she quickly

identified as belonging to Phoebe, Dolly, and Flora. Shooting back
the bolt, Kitty flung open the door with the intent of inviting them
inside, but Flora's autocratic voice forestalled her.

"Kathryn, Pheobe has decided to stay at our house today, and we
thought you might be persuaded to do the same. It simply isn't wise
for you to remain here alone, particularly since the Yankees will
undoubtedly come right by your house any time now. We feel you
would be much safer with us," she said firmly.

"I appreciate your concern," Kitty replied just as firmly, "but I
can't leave right now. I'm expecting Bret any moment, and I'm
hoping he'll take us to Belle Glen this afternoon, provided Tad is
strong enough to travel."

Phoebe intervened, frowning worriedly. "But, my dear, what if
Mr. O'Rourke doesn't arrive in time? There's no telling what those
barbarians will do to an unprotected woman! Oh, do reconsider and
come with us."

Kitty had no wish to upset them further, but neither had she any
intention of changing her mind. For one thing, she was afraid her
home would be ransacked by the Yankees while she was away,
particularly when they marched into town in what she imagined
would be a disorderly manner.

"I'm sorry, I really can't, Aunt Phoebe. I don't want to miss
Bret. Besides, Scotty is taking his nap, and I hate to wake him. As
long as the doors and windows are locked, I'm sure we'll be quite
safe."

Before Phoebe could reply, Dolly squealed with dismay. "What's
that? Isn't it drums?"

All four ladies glanced up Cherry Street, straining to hear the faint
roll of drums that first came from the north of town, then seemingly
from all directions.

"Oh, dear, it's *them!*" cried Dolly, nervously wringing her hands.
"What shall we do? Where'll we go?"

Flora shot her a withering look. "We shall go home just as we
planned."

Dolly wiped perspiration from her plump face, but for once she
was not silenced by her sister's disapproval. "But, Flora, maybe we
should do what Kitty's doing and leave town while we can," she
whimpered.

"We'll do no such thing," Flora retorted. "We were here long before the Yankees came, and we'll be here long after they've gone! Now, for heaven's sake, Dolly, pull yourself together.''

''I do think we should hurry, ladies, or we'll be caught in the streets when they arrive,'' Phoebe reminded them, then turned to address Kitty. ''You're sure you won't come with us?''

''I'm quite sure. Now, don't fret about us. We'll be all right,'' she said, walking them to the gate.

An amused smile played about her lips as she watched the agitated dowagers scamper down the street and disappear around the corner. Her amusement soon faded, however, as she was brought back to the present by the cadence of drums coming closer and closer. Though some residents were sufficiently intimidated by the enemy to hide behind locked doors, others were not. Already, curious onlookers were lining the streets to see the Yankees when they marched victoriously into town. Tempers had cooled somewhat by now, though a resigned bitterness was evident as the crowd watched and waited for the inevitable.

Though Kitty could see the courthouse from where she stood, she realized she would get a better view of the surrender from the top of the east hill just opposite the courthouse. Temptation overcame caution, and in the next instant she dashed back to the house. Daisy was standing at the door, obviously terrified.

''Now, listen to me carefully, Daisy,'' Kitty said, motioning for the young woman to follow her as she walked down the hall to the study. ''I'm going to the courthouse so I can see what's going on. After I've left, I want you and Moses to bolt the front door.''

''Oh, Lawd, Miz Kitty, you ain' got no biz'ness runnin' off tuh de courthouse,'' Daisy wailed.

Kitty did not bother to look at the disturbed girl as she marched over to the grandfather clock, opened the glass door, and extracted a revolver and derringer from a secret compartment. Realizing the futility of arguing further, Daisy sullenly followed her mistress back to the front hall and watched while Kitty put the revolver in the drawer of the marble-topped table and slipped the derringer into the pocket of her apron.

''I'm leaving the revolver with you, and I want you to use it if anybody tries to break into the house,'' she ordered crisply. ''But for heaven's sake, make sure you don't shoot Mr. Bret. He ought to be here any time. When he arrives, tell him I've gone to the courthouse. If he can't find me there, tell him to go to the hospital.

That's where I'm going after the surrender. And Daisy, if Scotty wakes up and you bring him downstairs, be sure to keep him away from this table. I don't want him touching that gun.''

"Yas'm, but Ah don' lak hit, an' if'n Mammy Lou wuz heah, you t'wouldn't be gittin' out dat door. Jes' wait 'til we gits home an' Ah tells how you dun' run off tuh see de Yankees dis afternoon. You's sho' gwine tuh be in a peck ob tru'ble.''

"Oh, hush and just do what I tell you," Kitty said irritably, then sailed out the front door.

More people had flocked to the sidewalks, which were now completely jammed. The loud intermingling of drums and fifes accompanied the sound of approaching horses and soldiers, and Kitty knew she must hurry. Quickening her pace, she managed somehow to push and shove her way through the nervous crowd until she had reached her destination. She immediately saw the Collinses and Sheltons standing nearby. Weaving her way through the mass of onlookers, she came to stand beside her friends just as Mr. Shelton was hotly labeling General Pemberton a traitor. He paused long enough to greet Kitty, then continued with his tirade. For once, Henry was listening rather than talking, nodding his head occasionally in agreement. His wife, Effie, was more verbal, however.

"You're quite right, Mr. Shelton. And to think I made General Pemberton a sash for his uniform, which Celia embroidered with our insignia. Why, he's probably wearing it this very minute! If I get the chance, I shall certainly ask him to return it," she declared.

Lela and Celia were carrying on their own excited conversation, ignoring Kitty after a brief greeting. Noticing that the girl was not being included in anyone's conversation, Mrs. Shelton turned to her with a kind smile.

"We were so sorry to hear of Tad's misfortune. I hope he's recovering satisfactorily," she told Kitty.

"Thank you. I believe he is. Of course, he'll have to adjust to having only one arm, but he seems to be in good spirits."

"I'm sure he'll adjust just fine, especially after he's reunited with that pretty wife of his," the older woman returned gently.

Kitty wondered how Dede would react to Tad's disability but refrained from saying so. God forbid that Dede faint or show any sign of being squeamish when she saw Tad's stump. The possibility worried her, and she frowned. She was almost relieved when Effie peevishly commented on the numerous Negroes who were lining the sidewalks.

"Just look how they're laughing and carrying on, like they can't wait for the Yankees to get here," she remarked waspishly. "Why, isn't that one of the Cranes' house servants?" she said with surprise.

"Yes, I do believe it is," Mrs. Shelton replied with equal surprise. "I think her name is Lilly. And there's our stableboy, Isaac, standing just behind her." Turning to her husband, she asked, "Do you think many of our servants will desert us, Mr. Shelton?"

Smiling sadly, he patted her small hand. "It's quite possible, my dear. Now that the enemy is here to liberate them, I'm afraid quite a few families will be losing their servants."

The possibility had not actually occurred to Kitty before now, and an uneasy feeling swept over her when she recalled that she had left Scotty in Daisy's charge. But surely she could count on Daisy's loyalty. Or could she?

She was almost tempted to return home to check on them, but at that precise moment, shouting rent the air. Grant's army had arrived.

"Here they come down Cherry Street!" one man yelled.

"Look at 'em coming up Jackson and Clay roads!" hollered another.

As the conquering invaders drew near the courthouse, the anxious crowd became silent. Officers wearing gold-trimmed uniforms and brightly plumed hats rode proudly at the front of long columns of dusty, blue-uniformed soldiers who were filing in from every direction. All were in step, marching first to the fifes' tune of "Yankee Doodle," then harmoniously singing "Hail, Columbia!"

The hot sun glared down on Kitty's bare head, but she was unmindful of the sweltering heat as she stood on tiptoe to get a better view. The sight was awesomely familiar, reminding her of her recurrent nightmare—the menacingly huge spider that had hovered over her, then changed suddenly into eight roads leading into town, each road filled with victorious Yankee soldiers. Now the dream had become a reality from which there was no escape. Vicksburg had been captured.

The winding columns of troops reached the courthouse almost simultaneously, their solemnity giving way to exuberance as they tossed their hats into the air and raised their voices in a chorus of loud hurrahs. For months they had tried to get into Vicksburg, and now they had succeeded! Many would soon be fighting on other battlefronts, but none would ever forget the siege or this particularly memorable day, July 4, 1863. Nor would they forget the formidable Confederate soldiers and the courageous townspeople who had thwarted them for so long.

Minutes later the nation's flag was being raised above the cupola of the courthouse, and as a slight breeze stirred, the stars and stripes slowly unfurled and fluttered into plain view. An electrifying silence ensued, and, like many of her compatriots, Kitty was inexplicably moved. It was a beautiful flag, she thought reluctantly, *almost* as beautiful as the beloved Confederate flag. The silence continued for several more seconds, though restrained sobs rippled intermittently through the spectators. Then, in the distance, a lone bugler began to play the first melodic strains of "The Star-Spangled Banner." Soon, other bugles joined in, gradually accompanied by a faint rolling of drums that, along with the bugles, crescendoed to a spine-tingling climax at the end of the chorus.

Suddenly misty-eyed, Kitty glanced self-consciously about and saw that her emotions were shared by many Southerners, for few eyes were dry at the moment. What was happening to her, to all of them? she wondered. How could they possibly feel nostalgic when experiencing such bitter defeat? These men in blue were enemies, not friends. They were Yankees, the same people who had killed Sally and many of her friends and who were responsible for Tad's losing his arm. They had shown no mercy in battle, killing and mutilating men and boys alike, and the knowledge that Confederates had done the same did not lessen her animosity. The North was bent on destroying the South, and though she did not believe they would ever succeed, they had certainly wrecked her own way of life. No, she would never forgive them, and when General Grant mounted the courthouse steps, she turned away. Bitterness grew in her heart while she shoved her way through the crowd and headed for the hospital.

By the time she reached the hospital, Kitty's depression was so great that she found herself dreading her visit with Tad, who would naturally be curious to know about the surrender. It would be difficult to recount the day's events without breaking down, yet she knew that for his sake she must strive to be as cheerful as possible.

With determination she kept her lips curved in a smile throughout the next hour, even when Doc Blanks refused to consider her suggestion that Tad be moved to Belle Glen within the next day or so. Not only was Tad too weak to travel, she was told, but he would probably have to take an oath of allegiance before the Federals would permit him to leave town.

This bit of news put Kitty in a real dilemma. She did not want to leave Tad behind, but neither did she want to stay in Vicksburg. She was anxious to go home and see her father. How on earth could this be managed, particularly if she had to be granted permission to leave town?

If only Bret were here, she thought, he would come up with a solution. Mulling the problem over in her mind, she sat beside Tad's cot and rolled bandages, thankful that her brother also seemed disinclined to talk.

The atmosphere was noticeably tense while doctors, nurses, and patients waited for the Yankees to appear, as they most assuredly would. Kitty had just finished rolling here sixth bandage when the front door swung open and several officers in Federal uniforms strode briskly into the hall. In spite of everyone's resolve to remain calm, a certain amount of commotion did erupt. Several nurses cried out in startled alarm, and one actually fainted. Across the room from Kitty, a young woman let a porcelain water jug slip from her fingers and shatter on the hardwood floor. Seeing the girl's sudden pallor, Kitty jumped up and rushed over to her.

"Sit down before you faint."

"Oh, I've made such a mess," the girl murmured weakly, but did not protest when Kitty guided her to a nearby chair.

"Don't worry about it. I'll clean it up," Kitty assured her.

Kneeling between two cots, she began to gather the broken pieces of glass, dumping them into the apron tied around her waist. She had almost completed the task when a shadow loomed over her and she became aware of a pair of neatly polished boots directly in front of her. An angry frown creased her forehead when she glanced up and saw a middle-aged Union officer observing her.

She would not greet him politely as though he were a welcome visitor, nor would she quiver and quail before him. With a defiant lift of her chin, she returned his kindly look with a belligerent glare and groped for another piece of porcelain, gasping aloud when its jagged edge cut the palm of her hand. The officer immediately knelt beside her and gently took hold of her injured hand, which was bleeding profusely.

"Forgive me for distracting you, madam," he apologized before instructing an orderly to fetch a basin of water and the medical satchel he had left in the hall. Turning back to Kitty, who had just noticed that he was wearing a medical insignia on his lapel, he went on, "I regret my presence precipitated this unfortunate accident, though I do not regret staring at you. I happen to have a daughter who is about your age, and you reminded me of her."

Nonplussed, Kitty cleared her throat and tried to think of a cutting reply, but none came to mind. "You don't sound like a Northerner, sir," she finally said rather foolishly. "Where is your home?"

"Virginia," he answered, nodding his thanks to the orderly who was setting his satchel and a wash basin beside them. "A small town near Richmond called Meadow Bridge. You've probably never heard of it."

"No, I haven't." Kitty winced when the doctor, after washing the cut, carefully examined the wound for slivers of glass. This done, he extracted a bottle of whiskey from his bag and positioned her hand over the basin. Seeing his intent, Kitty quickly resumed the conversation in an attempt to take her mind off what he was about to do. "I'm surprised any self-respecting Virginian would fight against the South, particularly since y'all have slaves up there, too."

"Yes, Virginians have their fair share of slaves. I even owned a couple myself—before the war, that is—but that didn't make it right. Some of my kinfolks don't see it that way, though. Fact is, I've a brother and two nephews who are fighting for the Confederacy," he informed her matter-of-factly while he poured the fiery liquid over her cut palm.

In spite of herself, Kitty gasped softly, feeling chagrined when the doctor gave her a kind smile as he wrapped her hand in a clean strip of linen. After checking to see that her palm was not bound too tightly, he assisted her from the vacated cot where he had seated her only minutes before.

"There now, that should do nicely, provided you keep the bandage clean. It's only a small cut and should heal in no time."

"It doesn't feel like a very small cut," Kitty sniffed, half inclined to thank the doctor for his trouble.

"No, I don't imagine it does right now, but I think I can safely assure you that you'll soon be fit as a fiddle and ready to dance at the next ball."

"Not if it's a Yankee ball," she replied saucily, though for the

life of her she could not help but return his smile. As much as she
hated to admit it, the portly physician was a gentleman and quite
likable—at least, for a Yankee. When he chuckled good-naturedly
over her impudent retort, the last of Kitty's reserve crumbled. After
all, this man had probably never killed anyone in his life. He saved
lives rather than destroyed them.

"Anyway, my quarrel isn't with you, I suppose," she said, "and
I don't want to be ungracious. Thank you for taking care of my
hand."

"It was a pleasure, my dear. In fact, if I can assist you in any way
while I'm stationed at Vicksburg, please don't hesitate to ask."

Just then the woman who had broken the pitcher returned. "Kitty,
Mr. O'Rourke is waiting for you outside. He can't come in because
he's afraid someone will steal his wagon."

After assuring Tad that she would find some way of moving him
to Belle Glen as soon as possible, she kissed him good-bye and
rushed outside to meet Bret. The smile died on her lips when she
saw the scowl of displeasure on his face.

"Why in hell can't you stay put?" he growled as he helped her
into the rickety vehicle. "This is hardly the time to make me have to
track you down."

Kitty's temper was immediately aroused. "You're a fine one to
talk. Just where have you been all day, or shouldn't I ask?"

"I haven't been celebrating with the Yankees, if that's what you
mean. I spent most of the morning down at the warehouse, trying to
repair the wheel on this wagon so I can get you and our son back to
Belle Glen."

Only partially mollified, Kitty gave him a dubious look. "Why go
to the trouble of repairing this old thing when you have others that
are in better condition?"

"Correction, my dear. I did have others until last night. Someone
broke into the warehouse and took every wagon I had with the
exception of this one, which, as you can see, is none too sturdy."

"Oh," Kitty murmured. "Did they take anything else?"

"No, they didn't bother the safe in the office, nor did they take
any of the bales of cotton that were stacked in the back. Whoever
did it seemed interested only in the wagons, which at the moment
happen to be very much in demand. Unless I miss my guess, quite a
few people will be hightailin' it from town now that it's been
captured."

"I don't see how, not unless they take the oath of allegiance. And frankly, I can't imagine anybody doing such a cowardly thing," Kitty asserted.

"They'll have to take the oath unless they plan to sneak out of town, and that would be risky at the moment. Of course, taking the oath and actually abiding by it are two entirely different matters."

"Well, I certainly have no intention of swearing allegiance to these low-down varmints, so just precisely how do you intend to get me out of town?"

"By using the passes I got from General Sherman, which happens to explain my whereabouts this afternoon. My own was no problem, but I had to do some mighty persuasive talking to get him to issue one for you."

"Well, I'm not surprised *you* got a pass, considering you're one of their spies, but I can't imagine how you talked him into signing one for me."

"He did it as a personal favor. I told him we were engaged."

"Engaged!" Kitty gasped. "Bret O'Rourke, you're the biggest liar I ever met. You know very well we're not engaged. Had we won, had we beaten the Yankees, I might have forgiven you for betraying us, but now I'll never marry you."

"Oh, I think you will in time."

"Then you're very mistaken. The day I marry a Yankee sympathizer will be the day hell freezes over!"

Bret frowned but did not reply. This was neither the time nor the place to tell her the truth. His first concern was to get her to Belle Glen, which was not going to be easy. The town was bursting at the seams with Union and Confederate soldiers, refugees, and citizens. Former slaves, giddy with their first taste of freedom, thronged the boardwalks, conversing happily and, in some instances, taunting white civilians, referring to them as "dem high an' mighty Rebels."

Glancing at Kitty, Bret saw her mouth tighten as they passed a cluster of Yankees boisterously singing "The Battle Cry of Freedom." They had obviously had more than a little to drink, and one of the white soldiers had carelessly draped his arm around the waist of a gaudily dressed mulatto. As the pair broke away from the group and staggered across the street, Kitty stiffened with indignation.

"Just look at that!" she muttered. "His behavior is positively indecent."

"I daresay it's going to be a lot more indecent by nightfall," Bret replied dryly. "In fact, the sooner we leave for Belle Glen, the better. This town's going to be in a helluva state before sunset, with Yankees celebrating their victory and Negroes celebrating their freedom. I'll feel a lot easier once I've gotten you and Scott away from here."

His point was emphasized as several rockets went off near the river, where civilians were now flocking to the wharves to receive food and provisions that had been brought by the Union fleet and were being generously dispersed among the crowd. It angered Kitty to see some of her friends kowtowing to the enemy just to get a free handout, and she fumed about it all the way back to her house.

An hour later Bret was hurrying her down the front walk to the wagon, which was now so crammed full of her belongings that there was hardly a place for Scott, Daisy, and Moses to sit. Despite Bret's insistence that they take only the bare necessities, Kitty had packed a crate of her most treasured belongings and a small trunk of serviceable clothing. She hated to leave their finer garments behind but realized there simply wasn't room in the small wagon for another trunk. Seeing her dismay, Bret promised to return for the rest of their clothing tomorrow, though he seriously doubted anything would be left by then. With so many Yankees, Negroes, and refugees roaming the streets, the house would probably be stripped of everything by morning. At the moment, however, his main concern was getting Kitty and Scott out of town before dark.

As they made their way up Cherry Street and drove away from Vicksburg, Kitty observed the disorderly procession of refugees, Negroes, and camp followers that was heading toward town. Some appeared to be half-starved, and a few wept openly while they plodded down the dusty road. These were undoubtedly the refugees who, thinking to escape the Yankees, had forsaken their own homes throughout Mississippi and Louisiana and fled to Vicksburg for safety. By contrast, the Negroes and camp followers of the Union army walked jubilantly in their midst. Their vicious taunts were almost more than Kitty could bear.

She stared unseeingly at the high bluff they were approaching, a Confederate defense line overlooking the river. As the dilapidated wagon drew level with the steep incline, it gave an unsettling lurch, which caused Bret to swear aloud and pull the wobbling vehicle to an abrupt halt.

"What is it, Bret? Why have we stopped?" Kitty asked with a worried frown.

"It's that damned wheel again. It's about to come off," he answered, striding around to the back of the wagon to examine it. He instructed them all to alight so the damaged wheel could be repaired and secured again to the rusty axle.

Kitty left the others behind and tiredly made her way up the steep hill. Her gaze focused on the endless column of Confederate soldiers who hobbled past the foot of the hill, heading wearily toward town. Some were limping or being half carried by friends, and a few wept quietly, unashamedly. All looked grim, haggard with defeat, and as Kitty witnessed their raw misery, her throat constricted.

"This can't be happening. It can't be!" she whispered, unaware that Bret had come to stand behind her.

"But it is. Unfortunately, it's only the beginning."

Startled, Kitty whirled around to face him, her expression one of bewilderment. "The beginning?" she repeated.

"Yes—the beginning of the end."

Anger flashed in the depths of her blue eyes. "You'd like that, wouldn't you," she replied. "You'd like to believe we're losing. Well, we're not!"

"What you've just witnessed could hardly be called a victory," he reminded her.

"Maybe not, but starvation beat us, not the Yankees. Just because Grant's captured Vicksburg doesn't mean we've lost the war."

Her refusal to face reality caused him to lose patience. Taking hold of her shoulders, he dragged her to him. "Dammit, Kitty, wake up and face facts. The South is beaten. Vicksburg fell today, and by the end of the week, so will Port Hudson, the last Confederate garrison on the river. When that happens, the Yankees will have complete control of the Mississippi. The South will be divided, crippled."

"Stop! I don't want to hear any more," she cried, jerking away from him and retreating to the edge of the bluff.

Turning her back to him, Kitty gazed down at the mighty river that churned below, her heart wrapped in despair. She stiffened when she felt Bret's arms encircling her waist, drawing her against him. To the west the sun was slowly sinking behind low, billowy clouds, emblazoning the overhead sky in blood red and silhouetting their bodies as one. In the distance, the beaten soldiers marched on,

some of them mournfully singing a familiar song that brought tears
to her eyes:

> *Oh, I wish I was in the land of cotton,*
> *Old times there are not forgotten,*
> *Look away, look away,*
> *Look away, Dixie land.*
> *In Dixie land where I was born,*
> *Early on one frosty mornin',*
> *Look away, look away,*
> *Look away—*

The rest of the words became indistinct, gradually fading away
altogether. With a defiant lift of her chin, Kitty stared unseeingly
across the river, her delicate features hardening with determination.

"Someday, the Yankees are going to pay for this. They can starve
us, burn our homes, and take our land, but they'll never break our
spirit," she vowed. "As long as there's an ounce of pride left, the
South will never surrender, nor shall I—to the Yankees or you."

Bret's arms tightened around her. As he glanced down at her erect
head, his lips curved in an enigmatic smile.

"We'll see, my love," he murmured. "We'll see."

Part IV

Chapter 29

August 1863

Nothing was the same, nor would it ever be again. The Yankees had come, conquered, and left a path of destruction in their wake that was evident throughout the countryside. Plantations had been divested of livestock, food, money, and other valuables, their gracious homes ransacked and, in some instances, burned to the ground. Crops had been trampled by bands of the marauding invaders, who pilfered wherever they went, emptying corn cribs and storage houses and maliciously burning bales of stored cotton. Many slave quarters now resembled ghost towns, most occupants having joined the Union army as they passed through or else simply disappearing without warning.

Such had been Belle Glen's fate. What had once been a flourishing plantation was now stripped, an empty shell. Kitty had feared the worst, but even so she was not prepared for the devastating sight that greeted her when they reached the plantation at dusk. The house still stood, but numerous windows had been broken, and the east wing, used for balls and formal entertaining, had been badly damaged by fire. She learned that the fire had occurred when the last group of Yankees had bivouacked on the front lawn.

The quick thinking of Zeke, Lemme and Doshe's son, saved the house from being deliberately burned to the ground. Led by a young, surly officer, the soldiers had been bent on destruction. Zeke had fully realized their intent and distracted them by leading them to the cave where he had helped Dave stash away the family valuables months ago, including a couple of cases of expensive brandy.

Discovery of the latter had almost been disastrous. By nightfall the last drop of brandy had been consumed, and soon after, the rowdy soldiers had set fire to the barn. A gusty wind had carried sparks from the blazing inferno over to the roof of the east wing, and it had taken every hand on the plantation to put out the fire before it spread to the rest of the house. The once white exterior was now tinged with gray from smoke, as was the elegantly wallpapered interior.

Those first few weeks after her return had been a difficult period of adjustment for Kitty, yet she was determined from the beginning to help Dave in his struggle to put the plantation back on an even keel. Tad had returned home, but despite his willingness to assist them, he was still too weak to be much help. Dede fluttered around him constantly, but to her credit, she had not fainted when she'd first seen his stump.

The prime concern was food, which was almost nonexistent. The Yankees had taken all edibles from the smokehouse and larder, trampled down most of the vegetable garden in back of the house, and raided the henhouse. Nothing was left, nor was there any money with which to buy more.

The situation at Belle Glen was grim, but not utterly hopeless. Nearby forests were filled with wild game, and though the lack of ammunition made hunting difficult, rabbits and small animals were occasionally snared and cooked for supper. Because of the dry spell throughout the summer, the rivers and lakes were too low for good fishing, but sometimes Lemme or Gus would bring in a few catfish that had been caught on trotlines set the night before or, in rare instances, a small gator.

With so few field hands left, the cotton and cane fields lay fallow, but everyone, including the family, worked in the small portion of vegetable garden that had survived. It was not an enjoyable task, but it was necessary if vegetables were to accompany their meager food supply throughout the coming winter months.

Only Dede complained about having to work side by side with the servants. She particularly resented the fact that her procelain complexion was becoming freckled. Her attitude had improved somewhat during the past week, however, when Tad had begun accompanying her to the garden. Though unable to do hard manual labor, he was quite capable of picking peas and beans with his good hand, and this he did in such a jovial manner that Dede's resentment diminished.

Now, as Kitty knelt in the August heat and deftly pulled weeds from a patch of cucumbers, she wondered how much longer any of them could endure such hardships. Every muscle in her body ached, as did her cut and blistered hands. Even the floppy, wide-brimmed hat and long-sleeved blouse she wore did little to protect her sensitive skin from the midmorning sun.

Although slightly giddy from the oppressive heat, she continued with her task and tried to look on the bright side. After all, if Bret had not provided them with more seeds for the garden, plus a mule and a milk cow, their plight would have been much worse. Unfortunately, he had not had much cash on hand to spare, since most of his ready capital was tied up in his cotton brokerage. Still, the supplies he had given them had been a blessing, she reasoned, even if they did come from a Yankee sympathizer!

On his last visit he had even brought them an old edition of a New York newspaper, dated July 11, 1863, which he had somehow managed to obtain from a Federal officer. The front page had been full of war news, one of the longer articles describing General Lee's defeat at Gettysburg, Pennsylvania, on July 3—the day before Vicksburg's surrender. At the bottom of the page there had been a short article about the siege and Pemberton's capitulation to Grant on July 4. No reference was made to the last Confederate garrison on the Mississippi, Port Hudson, which had surrendered on July 9, just as Bret had predicted.

After reading the detailed article about Gettysburg, then the much shorter one about Vicksburg, Kitty had been livid with rage. After all, the battle at Gettysburg had lasted only three days, whereas Vicksburg had been besieged for over six weeks! It seemed to her that, once again, the South had been slighted.

Dragging her mind back to the present, Kitty decided that she had done enough weeding for one day. She stood up and rubbed the small of her back, her dour expression brightening when she remembered that Gus had caught several large catfish on the trotline that morning. For the first time in days they would have something to eat other than boiled cabbage, potatoes, stewed tomatoes, and onions. With luck there might even be enough fish left from the midday meal to go into a thick gumbo for supper. Thinking to suggest as

much to Mammy Lou, Kitty walked briskly over to the kitchen, her
mouth curved in a pleased smile. Her smile faded, however, when
she heard the old woman's voice raised in anger and saw Gus
backing out of the kitchen onto the dogtrot that led to the house.
Fear and dismay were etched on his face as he tried to duck a
succession of blows Mammy Lou was leveling at his head with her
broom.

"Good heavens, Mammy Lou, what's all the ruckus about?"
Kitty asked.

"Dem fish, dat's whut hit's about."

"What's wrong with the fish? Are they spoiled?"

"Naw'm, dey ain' sp'iled. Dey's been et by dem two cats ob Miz
Dede's," Mammy Lou snorted with outrage.

Comprehension suddenly dawned on Kitty with sickening clarity
as she spied the two culprits lying beside Gus's fishing pail a few
feet away, contentedly licking their paws.

"Oh, no!" she groaned, her expression furious when she finally
turned to Gus. "How could you have let those dirty, flea-bitten cats
eat our dinner!"

"Lawd, Miz Kitty, Ah's powerful sor'hy. Ah sot down tuh clean
de fish, an' Ah reckon Ah jes' dozed off."

Gus's remorsefulness, though sincere, was wasted on Mammy
Lou. Plumping her fists on ample hips, she shot him a withering
look. "Hmph, how many times is Ah tole you—when you's snoozin',
you's losin'? Trouble wid you, boy, you's got dia'reah ob de mouf
an' constipation ob de brain! Jes' whut we gwine tuh hab fo'
dinnah—dem cats?"

Gus stared woefully down at his dusty, bare feet, and for a
moment silence ensued. Little did he suspect that Kitty was seriously
considering Mammy Lou's words. She had eaten rats, so why *not*
cats? She simply refused to go without meat for another day. Surely
there must be some way the detestable animals could be cooked so
they would be edible, if not actually palatable. Her eyes suddenly
widened with enthusiasm as she faced the scowling cook.

"Mammy Lou, wouldn't you say those cats weigh as much as a
couple of hens?" she asked innocently, knowing the old matriarch
was not going to be very agreeable to what she was about to suggest.

"Dem cats is de fattest animals we's got on *dis* plantation. De
way Miz Dede fusses ober dem an' feeds 'em scraps frum de table,

hit's no wondah dey's so fat an' sassy. If'n ah had mah way, dey t'wouldn't be heah t'all.''

"My feelings exactly," Kitty agreed sweetly, picking up the unsuspecting felines and handing them to Gus. "Better ask Lemme if he's got a good skinning knife, Gus."

It suddenly occurred to Mammy Lou what her mistress had in mind. "Miz Kitty, you ain' thinkin' whut Ah think you's thinkin', is you?" she asked uncertainly.

"Oh, yes, I am. Gus, take these varmints behind the stables and skin them. Clean 'em good before you bring them back to the kitchen."

"Miz Kitty, Ah ain' about tuh cook no cats, mech less hab you eatin' 'em," Mammy Lou sputtered indignantly as Gus sauntered off.

"I've eaten worse, Mammy Lou, so there's no need for you to be squeamish on my account. Besides, if you fix them right, say, in a thick stew, they'll probably taste quite good."

"An' jes' whut's Miz Dede gwine tuh say when she finds out?" Mammy Lou shot back.

"Miss Dede isn't going to find out, nor is anybody else. Make it like you do squirrel stew, with plenty of onions and herbs. Nobody will know the difference."

"Ah'll know de diff'rence, an' Miz Dede's gwine tuh be moughty upset when she cain't find her cats. How's you gwine tuh explain dat?"

"I'm not. After all, cats have been known to wander off and disappear for good, which is precisely what she'll think has happened. Anyway, with Tad home, I doubt she'll miss them long," Kitty reasoned. "Just you and Gus keep your mouths shut, and no one will be the wiser."

"Well, dey ain' no way Ah kin git dem cats cooked fo' dinnah, 'cause dey's gwine tuh haf tuh be b'iled a good spell befo' dey's tender."

"Then we'll just have to eat them tonight, I guess," Kitty retorted. "But do try to have an early supper. I'm starved."

Kitty's conscience was not bothered in the least as she happily anticipated the evening meal. Dede's feelings be damned. Tonight, meat would be served on the table!

That evening, the first part of the meal went off smoothly, the overall atmosphere being quite congenial as everyone entered the dining room. After Dave had murmured thanks for the bountiful nourishment they were about to receive, light-hearted conversation accompanied the first course, potato soup.

Unmindful of Mammy Lou's worried look as she brought out the large tureen of stew, Kitty smiled with pleasure while everyone helped themselves to ample portions. Well seasoned with herbs, the aromatic concoction tasted surprisingly good, and, refusing to dwell on its unusual contents, Kitty ate with gusto.

Mammy Lou had just refilled the tureen and was setting it in the middle of the table when Dave remarked, "You've outdone yourself this time, Mammy Lou. This is mighty fine stew, mighty fine! For the life of me, though, I can't quite place the taste of the game."

Kitty's fork halted in midair. With a small frown, she cast a warning look at the dumbstruck servant. To her dismay, the subject was not dropped. After echoing Dave's sentiments, Tad even went a step further.

"Well, it sure doesn't taste like rabbit or squirrel. Is it possum?" he asked with a grin.

The old woman's face was a picture of guilt as she uncomfortably shuffled from one foot to the other and clasped her hands beneath her heaving bosoms.

"Naw'suh, hit ain' possum," she drawled.

"Then it must be raccoon," Dave suggested uncertainly.

"Naw'suh, hit ain' dat, neither."

Kitty nervously scooped up another bite onto her fork and crammed it into her mouth. Damn, she thought furiously, why doesn't Mammy Lou leave instead of just standing there like she's rooted to the spot!

"Well, whatever it is, it's simply delicious," Dede mumbled with her mouth full. "Be sure to save the scraps for the cats, Mammy Lou. You know how partial they are to stew. By the way, have you seen them this evening?"

The porcelain pitcher Mammy Lou had just grabbed to whisk out back and refill dropped from her shaking hands and shattered on the hardwood floor. Clearly distraught, she slid her gaze to Kitty, who appeared to be having some difficulty swallowing her last bite of food. A bewildered silence ensued, soon dispelled by Dave.

"Just exactly what *is* in this stew?" he asked in a slow, determined voice.

"Lawd, Mist' Dave, don't ask!" Mammy Lou moaned, casting another distraught look in Kitty's direction.

Dave followed her telltale glance, his brow creasing in a frown upon noticing his daughter's unmistakable discomfort.

"Since Mammy Lou seems to have temporarily lost her memory," he said, "perhaps you would be good enough to answer my question, daughter. What's in the stew?"

Kitty cleared her throat and attempted to appear calm. "Heavens, how should I know, Pa? It tastes like any other ol' stew to me."

Dede blanched and rose slowly to her feet. Glancing from Kitty to Mammy Lou and seeing their mutual guilt, she began to tremble. "You didn't answer my question, Mammy Lou. Have you seen my cats?" she asked fearfully.

"Yas'm, Ah's seen 'em," came the reluctant reply.

"Well, where did you see them?" she persisted, gasping aloud when the distraught servant woefully nodded toward the bowl of stew.

"You mean that you . . . that we've just eaten—" She stopped, too horrified to continue. Nausea welled up inside her, forcing her to clap a hand to her quivering mouth as she turned and, with a hysterical wail, fled from the room.

Tad had also risen from his chair and was now looking at Mammy Lou with a stunned expression. "Why did you do it?" he asked incredulously.

"Because I told her to," Kitty intervened.

"I might have known. My God, Kitty, have you no decency!" he exclaimed.

"Don't you talk to me about decency, Tad Devan," Kitty retorted as he strode swiftly from the room to find Dede. "Just be glad it was cats and not rats!"

"Enough!" Dave thundered. "Mammy Lou, send Daisy in to clean up this mess. I'll have a word with you later." After she had waddled from the room, muttering to herself, he eyed his daughter with cold disapproval. "Well, Kathryn, I'm waiting for an explanation."

Embarrassed, but not at all remorseful, Kitty shrugged and gave a small, dejected sigh. "Dede's cats ate the fish Gus caught for our dinner, so I told Mammy Lou to put the cats in a stew for supper. We haven't had meat on the table for days, and . . . well, it seemed like a good idea at the time," she finished lamely.

Her father's displeased expression did not alter as he rose and stared down at her. "In the future, Kathryn, you would do well to think before you act. Times may be hard, but by heaven, I'll not have another domestic animal served at this table. Do I make myself clear?''

"Yes, Pa," Kitty whispered, blinking back tears as she watched him stalk from the room.

It was not until she retired for bed that her conscience began to prick her. Sleep did not come easily, and as she tossed and turned on her feather mattress, she could not put Dede's distress or her father's disapproval from her mind. Neither of them would ever understand her aversion to hunger. Other than Tad, none of them had ever been faced with the threat of starvation on a day-to-day basis. She hoped they never would.

Tomorrow, she would simply have to make amends, she decided, even if it meant apologizing to Dede. Above all, she wanted to placate her father. Loving him as she did, she could not bear his disapproval. Having so decided, she was able at last to sleep.

By the time she awakened, the household was already stirring. Daisy informed her that Tad had driven Dede into town to visit friends and would not be returning until late afternoon. There was no need to ask where her father was, since the first thing he did each morning was to pay a brief visit to her mother's grave.

The family cemetery was not far from the house and, until this year, had always been well kept. Now, as Kitty walked down the winding path, her heart constricted as she spied weeds growing rampant where flowers had once flourished. The sight was depressing, and her footsteps quickened until she drew abreast of the low, wrought-iron fence that surrounded the small cemetery. A large magnolia tree overshadowed the few gravesites, and at first Kitty did not see her father kneeling beside her mother's resting place. She was about to turn back when he slowly rose and turned to leave.

Seeing her, he smiled, but not before Kitty had seen the sorrow in his eyes. The carefully rehearsed apology she had earlier prepared in her room was forgotten. With a choked sob, she rushed into his open arms.

"Oh, Pa, I'm sorry," she murmured against his chest. "I didn't mean to upset everybody last night."

Dave patted her back and gazed lovingly at her bent head. "I know you didn't, honey. I realize things haven't been easy for you lately. It hasn't been easy for any of us, and I'm afraid our situation isn't going to improve any time soon. No matter who wins this war, we're all going to experience a difficult period of adjustment once it's over. We may be facing new hardships, but none that we can't handle so long as we hang on to two things—common decency and faith."

Kitty's chin quivered, and her eyes were filled with doubt as she glanced up at him. "Faith?" she echoed. "How can any of us have faith after all that's happened?"

Her words caused him to frown, yet his reply was gentle. "How can you not? You believe in God, don't you?"

Unwilling to hurt him, yet unsure of her answer, Kitty stepped away from him and stared unseeingly at the house.

"I believe in God," she finally said, "but I don't think He really cares what happens to us." Swinging around to face him, she uttered her next words with passion rather than restraint. "How can I believe otherwise after having seen so much death and misery? How can I believe God is a kind and loving Father, when He allows the Yankees to come down here and destroy everything we love?"

Tears dimmed her vision as she took a deep breath and continued in a lower voice filled with impassioned bitterness. "I used to think that if I prayed, my prayers would be answered. Now, I know it doesn't work that way. I prayed the Yankees wouldn't come, but they came. I prayed we wouldn't have to surrender, but we did. I prayed our hardships would end, but they haven't. Oh, Pa, I've done nothing but pray these last months, yet not once have my prayers been answered. How can I have faith in a God who's never there when I need Him?"

Compassion and wisdom were etched on Dave's face as he placed his hands on her shoulders. He longed to comfort her, to assure her that the worst was over; yet he could not, for he suspected the worst was still to come. The South was doomed to defeat, of that he was now certain. When the end came, when the last shot was fired, their troubles would just be beginning. Then, more than ever, Kitty would need an inner strength on which to rely, a strength derived from faith. Determined she should have such faith, he answered her with patience rather than reproach.

"You're not thinking straight, Kitty. God is always there when you need Him, though you may not realize it at the time. When you were a little girl, you used to run to me for everything, and most of the time, your wishes were granted. There were some occasions, however, when I had to refuse you. Now, why do you suppose that was?''

''Well, I—I imagine I asked for some things that wouldn't have been good for me or that I didn't actually need,'' Kitty answered slowly. With a small grin, she added, ''Besides, if you hadn't occasionally said 'no,' I would have been spoiled rotten.''

''Exactly. As a child, however, you didn't understand that. Instead, you felt disappointed and frustrated—perhaps even unloved.''

''No, I never doubted your love,'' she returned quickly.

''Then how can you doubt God's love? Don't you realize that, as much as I love you, God loves you even more? If He denies your request, then He does so for a reason and always for your own good. Your prayers may not be answered immediately, or even as you expected, but they will be answered.''

Resting her head on his shoulder, Kitty gave a small sigh. ''I guess you're right, Pa. It's just that I'm so tired of all this, and I can't understand why God burdens us with so many problems.''

''Perhaps to strengthen us in some way. Whatever the reason, He must feel we're capable of handling those problems, or He wouldn't give them to us. Of course, not all difficulties are heaven sent. Some are self-imposed, and others are caused by those around us. But placed in God's hands, none are insolvable. He will either show you a solution, or He will give you the ability to accept the situation. Once the situation is accepted, the problem no longer exists.''

His words were reassuring, and, no longer depressed, Kitty smiled up at him. ''You always seem to know just what to say to make me feel better.''

''Maybe that's because we share a very special closeness,'' he said affectionately.

''A very nice closeness,'' she agreed, glancing up at the bleak sky overhead. ''Hmmm—look at those dark clouds. Do you think we're in for a storm?''

''Possibly.'' Seeing her worried frown, he sought to allay her fear. ''You mustn't be frightened of storms, my dear. Whatever is in store for us, we'll weather it together.''

As they returned to the house, Kitty was filled with renewed hope and determination. By the time they sat down to the noon meal, her optimistic outlook on life had been restored. As she chatted cheerfully with her father over the dinner table, she felt confident in her ability to cope with the future. After all, their situation could be much worse, she decided, and there were some blessings for which to be thankful.

After his wife's death, Charlie had joined the home guards but, like Tad, had returned home after being paroled. The return of their overseer would facilitate spring planting, provided they could scrape up enough money to buy seed and hire labor. Exactly how they were going to acquire the money was not clear, but she was sure her father would find a way. Together, they would find some means of restoring the plantation to its former prosperity.

Kitty's sense of well-being increased when Mammy Lou removed their soup bowls and informed them that the first batch of lady peas had been picked that morning. These were served with cornbread and tender, green-stemmed onions. Despite the absence of meat, no meal had ever tasted better to Kitty, who savored each bite of the tiny peas that had always been her favorite vegetable. It was obvious that Dave shared her pleasure, and as he bit into a crisp onion, she remembered the many times when, as a child, she had begged him to eat onion after onion so she could listen to the funny, crunching sound. Pushing aside the bittersweet memory of happier days, Kitty eagerly filled her plate with a second helping of peas and silently tucked into the meal with wholesome relish.

They had just finished eating when Mammy Lou rushed into the dining room and informed Dave that one of the Moores' servants was out back and needed to speak to him. Kitty went upstairs to put Scotty down for his nap. It was not until she returned downstairs some minutes later that her tranquillity was suddenly shattered. Her father was waiting for her at the foot of the stairs, and when she saw the grim look on his face, her light-hearted mood evaporated.

"What is it, Pa?" she asked with dread.

"The Moores' plantation was raided by a small band of Union soldiers this morning."

"Oh, no," Kitty gasped. "What happened?"

"From what I can understand, an expedition party had been sent out to obtain oaths of allegiance from plantation owners in the vicinity. There were about a dozen men in all, half of them Negroes. Sam, of course, refused to take the oath." He paused, remembering the elder Moore's quick temper. "They hung him from one of the oak trees on the front lawn. Mary Belle and her mother were forced to watch, as were the house servants. Nathan somehow managed to slip out the back during the commotion, but he doesn't think any of the other servants got away. There was nothing he could do, other than watch from the edge of the woods until it was over."

"How horrible!" Kitty whispered. "We must go to them, Pa, bring Mary Belle and her mother back here, at least for the time being. They mustn't stay in that house alone."

"The house was burned to the ground, Kitty, and afterwards . . ." He stopped, not knowing how to continue.

Kitty sensed she still had not heard the worst. Feeling giddy, she asked, "What happened to Mary Belle? The Yankees didn't . . . they wouldn't harm defenseless women, would they?"

"I wish to God I could spare you the truth, but I can't. Mary Belle, her mother, and every female servant were brutally and repeatedly defiled by every man in the group. Afterwards they were slaughtered, along with every slave on the place. No one was left alive to identify them, or so they thought."

With an anguished cry, Kitty was in his arms, yet there were no words with which to comfort her. He held her to him for several moments until her quivering subsided, and then he slowly put her from him.

"The only thing we can do for them now, my dear, is give them a decent burial. I doubt those bastards will do anything else today, but I'm going to leave Charlie and Lemme here with you in the event they do pay us a visit. Keep everyone inside the house, and be sure all the doors and windows are bolted. When Tad gets back, tell him to meet me at the Moores'."

"But what are you going to do? You'll need help to bury so many."

"I'll take Gus and several of our field hands with me. You might send Moses over to the Waddells' place. They'll probably want to give us a hand. Whatever you do, stay inside. If any expedition party turns up, shoot first and ask questions later."

Kitty nodded, then hugged him fiercely before he turned to go. Watching him ride away she was assailed with a premonition of doom. The feeling intensified throughout the long, dreary afternoon, even after Tad and Dede returned. Tad immediately left for the Moores' plantation, and for once Kitty was grateful for her sister-in-law's company. Though nervous, Dede was trying desperately to bear up under the strain, and her considerate attempt to keep Scotty occupied and out of the way did not go unnoticed. The unfortunate episode regarding her cats was mentioned only once, when Kitty offered an apology, which Dede quickly accepted.

By nightfall there was still no sign of Tad and Dave, and as the hours dragged by, Kitty's anxiety increased. When the threatening storm finally broke with unleashed fury, she was almost relieved, believing the torrential rain would surely force her father and brother to return home.

Lightning zigzagged across the sky as Kitty kept watch by the front window. Finally she saw the weary handful of men coming up the driveway. With a relieved cry, she rushed to the front door, threw it open, and stepped out to the veranda, unmindful that Dede was right behind her.

Wordlessly Kitty ushered her father inside, with Dede and Tad only a footstep behind. The men were drenched to the skin and obviously exhausted, yet this was not Kitty's prime concern as she knelt to remove Dave's soaked boots and instructed Dede to do likewise with Tad.

Even in the hallway's dim light, she recognized the look of pain in her father's face, though he tried to assure her that he was merely being plagued with a bad headache. Far from being convinced, she insisted he change immediately into dry clothes and get into bed, where his supper would be served to him on a tray. He made no protest, and as she watched him unsteadily climb the curving stairway, her uneasiness grew.

Dede excused herself to ensure that water was being drawn and heated for the men's baths. Once she was out of earshot, Kitty turned to Tad.

"How bad was it?" she asked.

"Worse than I can begin to describe." In a somewhat dazed voice, he continued, "I've never seen anything like it, not even in battle. Blood was everywhere, all over the place. Some of them had been shot, and others had been bayonetted. A few were mutilated beyond recognition, especially the women. After the swine had tired of raping them, they hacked them to ribbons, except for Mrs. Moore. They had hanged Sam from that large oak tree in front of the house, and they pinned her to that same tree with a bayonet. God, I've never seen such senseless slaughter." He covered his pale face with shaking hands.

Wishing she had not pressed him to enlighten her, Kitty was at a loss for words. Bret had brought Dave a decanter of brandy on his last visit, and, hoping to restore her brother's nerves, she poured a liberal amount into a glass and handed it to him. She was thankful when Dede reappeared with Doshe, who was carrying a supper tray upstairs to Dave. Tad finished his drink in a gulp, then smiled faintly as Dede urged him to retire to their room and change out of his wet clothes. The three of them had just started toward the hall when a loud crash sounded overhead, followed by an ear-splitting scream from Doshe. Darting past Tad and Dede, Kitty raced up the stairs and automatically headed for Dave's bedroom at the far end of the hall.

She had just reached his room when Doshe rushed through the door, almost colliding with her. Seeing that the normally calm-mannered woman was practically hysterical, Kitty took hold of her shoulders, forcing her to a standstill.

"What happened, Doshe? What's wrong?" she rasped, dimly aware that Tad and Dede were standing on either side of her.

"Hit's Mist' Dave! When Ah brung him his supper tray, he wuz settin' on de bed, holdin' his head an' groanin', an' den—den he jes' keeled ober!"

"Oh, no!" Kitty whispered as Tad stepped past them into Dave's room.

She swayed slightly, then moved through her father's bedroom door. The sight that greet her caused her to clutch at the doorjamb for support. Dave was sprawled on the floor near the bed, and Tad was bending over him, apparently listening for a heartbeat. In the next instant she was kneeling beside them, taking hold of Dave's limp hand. Tears streamed down her face as she stared at his inert body.

"Is he alive?" she asked fearfully.

"Yes, just barely. Doshe, tell Lemme to saddle up Pa's horse and ride into town for the doctor. Tell him to fetch Doctor Johnson, and for God's sake, hurry! I think Pa's had a stroke!"

Chapter 30

The next two months were filled with tension and worry while Dave slowly recovered from the stroke that had almost claimed his life. For more than a week he remained unconscious, hovering on the brink of death. It was not until consciousness returned that the extent of damage to his aging body was fully realized. His right side was partially paralyzed, and his speech was also slightly affected, but the doctor assured them that, for the most part, these were only temporary handicaps.

During the weeks that followed, his prognosis proved to be correct. Dave slowly regained the use of his right arm, and his speech, though a little slurred, improved with each passing day. Only his walking remained impaired. The stroke had immobilized his right leg, the same one that had been broken three years ago and had never mended properly. Now, as he attempted to move from his bed to a chair near the window, he leaned heavily on his cane and dragged his foot behind him.

Kitty had remained by his side throughout the critical period, until it became apparent that his life was no longer in danger. Only then did she allow others to share her bedside vigil. Since then she had found little rest, dividing her time between tending to her father, helping Tad run the plantation, and spending whatever time that was left with her son. The strain was beginning to tell on her. Not only had she lost weight, but there was a drawn look to her heart-shaped face, and dark circles shadowed violet eyes that no longer appeared vibrant.

Throughout the ordeal, Bret rode out to Belle Glen several times each week to visit Dave, always spending the remainder of his visit with the family, in particular, Scotty. It seemed to Kitty that he had no desire to be alone with her, and his manner toward her, though friendly, was so casual that she sometimes wondered if she had imagined his offhand proposal on the day Grant had captured Vicksburg. This feeling of neglect rekindled her old resentment of him, and when he asked her to go horseback riding one morning, she was tempted to refuse. The opportunity to break free from her monotonous routine, however, proved difficult to resist, especially once Bret ushered her to the stables and presented her with a new mare.

Now, as she galloped beside him over the open fields and felt the wind in her face, she was glad she had not allowed pride to stand in the way of pleasure. She had almost forgotten how enjoyable life could be when one was free of worry and responsibility. By the time they paused to rest beneath a clump of pine trees and Bret helped her to dismount, she was feeling quite light-hearted.

"Well, how do you like your new filly?" Bret grinned.

"Oh, she's wonderful!" Kitty answered, stroking the mare's long neck. "I think I'll call her Rebel."

"Considering you own her, I would say that's an appropriate name." He chuckled and took her reins, securing them to a bush.

"Speaking of Rebels, what do you think of our victory at Chickamauga last month?" she asked smugly.

"Well, it was a tactical victory, but I doubt it will be a lasting one."

"How can you say that? Why, everyone knows our boys beat the Yankees so badly at Chickamauga Creek, they were forced to hightail it all the way back to Chattanooga. Now, we've got them pinned down there. With us holding Missionary Ridge and Lookout Mountain to the south of the city, and controlling the Tennessee River to the north, there's no way for them to escape. They're besieged just like we were, and it serves them right!"

"Yes, they're pinned down for the moment, but unless I miss my guess, Grant and Sherman will find some way to break through to them and get them out, probably in the near future." Seeing her frown, he smiled down at her. "But I didn't bring you all the way out here to argue about the war," he said meaningfully.

Not in the least mollified, Kitty lifted one eyebrow and gave him a withering look. "Then just why did you bring me out here?"

Tucking her hand through the crook of his arm, Bret promenaded her through the tall shade trees. "Because, my dear, I wanted to have you to myself for a while, especially since I'll be leaving for Memphis in the morning."

His casual reply took her by surprise. "How long will you be gone?"

"A couple of weeks or so, depending on how long it takes for the sale to go through on my brokerage."

"You're selling your brokerage in Memphis?"

"Yes, if the price is right, and I have every reason to believe it will be."

"Then I take it you plan to make a fairly nice profit," Kitty mused, an idea already forming in her mind.

Aware of her sudden interest, he grinned. "I plan to make a damned good profit, and when I do, I'll buy you a brand-new wardrobe."

Excited, yet not quite sure how to proceed, Kitty nibbled at her lower lip before casting a sidelong glance at him. "New clothes would be nice, of course," she agreed slowly, giving him an angelical smile. "But there's something else I'd like much more."

"I figured there would be," Bret answered with amusement as they paused in the shade. Turning her to face him, he lifted her chin with a forefinger so that she was forced to meet his eyes. "Well, let's have it, Kitten. What does your scheming little heart desire now?"

"A loan, Bret. I need a loan—so we can make Belle Glen like it used to be." Without giving him a chance to reply, she continued, excitement sparkling in her eyes. "If we had the money, we could repair and refurnish the house, build new barns, and replenish our livestock. Of course, that would mean replacing a lot of broken-down fencing, but I'm sure we could manage that by March. Then we could buy seed and hire additional hands to help with the spring planting, and—"

"Whoa, now." Bret chuckled. "Just hold your horses! What you're planning will cost a small fortune. Money doesn't grow on trees, you know!"

"But you're going to make a lot of money soon. You just said so. Besides, you'll get your money back just as soon as the crops are in and the first bales of cotton are sold," Kitty assured him.

"And what happens if the crops fail next summer? How will you repay me then? What are you prepared to offer as collateral?"

No longer smiling, Bret was deadly serious, or so it seemed to Kitty. Momentarily dumbfounded by his cold, businesslike manner, she hesitated before coming to a reluctant decision. "I don't think the crops will fail next summer, but to ease your mind, I'm prepared to offer one thousand acres of land as collateral."

"I'm afraid that's not good enough. You see, I already hold a mortgage on Belle Glen."

Kitty's eyes widened with surprise. "On all of it?" she whispered, suddenly feeling out of her depth.

He nodded. "The summer I returned to Vicksburg, Dave asked me for a loan. The crops had been bad for a couple of years, and having borrowed all he could from the bank, he was in a financial bind. I offered to let him have the money until he was on his feet again, but he insisted on giving me a mortgage on the place. The loan has never been repaid, so I'm afraid you'll have to come up with some—er . . . other kind of collateral."

"What other kind of collateral?" Kitty asked irritably. "I have nothing else to offer you."

"Ah, but you have." He smiled, placing his hands on her waist and drawing her close to the hard planes of his body. "Yourself. Marry me, Kitty. Let me give our son his rightful name, and I'll rebuild Belle Glen for you. You know how I feel about you."

The offer was tempting, but unacceptable to her. She wanted more than his name for their son, more than the love and security he was offering. She wanted the one thing he had withheld—his loyalty to the South.

"You know I'll never marry a traitor," came her bitter reply.

The last of his patience snapped, and with a muttered oath his hand fastened on her chin, ruthlessly tilting her head backward until she was forced to meet his angry gaze.

"Dammit, Kitty, when are you going to come to your senses? The siege is over."

"The siege, yes—but not the war. The fact remains that you're still a Yankee sympathizer. How can I marry a man I don't even respect!"

"To hell with the war! I'm fed up with you accusing me of matters you know nothing about. I want you, Kitty—with or without your precious respect—and I don't intend to wait much longer.'' Savagely he took possession of her lips.

For seconds Kitty struggled, futilely pushing against his chest with her clenched fists. But when his hand unexpectedly brushed one taut breast, her resistance slowly capitulated to desire. She had not the strength to fight him, nor could she contain her own arousal when his arm tightened around her, crushing her to him until her soft curves were molded against his hard virility.

A low moan rumbled deep in her throat as his fingers deftly unfastened the buttons on her blouse and slipped inside to caress one breast. Past differences faded from her mind, and instinctively she wound her arms around his neck, her lips parting of their own volition while he masterfully coaxed her into total submission. A familiar ache stirred deeply within her, filling her with impatience as unleashed desire consumed her like a flame. Had he tried to take her at that moment, she would not have resisted, but he did not. Instead, his hand slid tantalizingly to the nape of her arched neck.

"This is what I want from you, Kitty," he murmured against her lips. "This and much more. Stop fighting the inevitable. Marry me. Let me take care of you and the boy."

Trembling against him, she longed to say "Yes," yearned to belong to him for the rest of her life. But the words would not come. Nothing had changed, and remembering they were still on opposite sides, she deliberately steeled herself against him.

"No, Bret. I don't want you or your protection."

He released her, amusement tugging at the corners of his mouth as he watched her fumbling with the buttons of her blouse. "But you do want my money," he countered wryly.

"I want a loan," she snapped, "but not if I have to take you with it!"

Forcing back his anger, Bret walked over and unhitched the horses, leading them to where she stood. "Very well. As soon as I get back from Memphis, I'll see to it you have sufficient funds to restore the house, rebuild the barns, and replenish the livestock, with enough left over to enable you to put in a crop this spring."

Kitty was immediately suspicious. "And just how am I supposed to repay you if the crops do fail?"

"Oh, I'm sure I'll think of something," he answered enigmatically. "In the meantime, you can show your appreciation by helping me furnish my house."

"What house?"

"The one I'm building in town," he replied as he lifted her into the saddle.

"You're building a house!" Kitty exclaimed. "Where?"

"Near Cedar Grove, on a high bluff that overlooks the river. When I get back I'll show you, if you like," he said as he watched her adjust her riding skirt over the sidesaddle. Noticing the wine-colored material was patched in several places, he frowned as he vaulted into his own saddle.

"This afternoon I'll open an account for you at Collins's store. Buy whatever is necessary, and above all, get yourself some decent clothes. I'm tired of seeing you look like a field hand."

The excitement that had sparkled in Kitty's eyes was instantly dispelled by his blunt criticism. Field hand, indeed!

"That remark is going to cost you dearly, Mr. O'Rourke!"

Before he could reply, she was galloping away from him, pride stiffening her backbone when she realized he was not following her. So he's displeased with my appearance, is he? she thought. Well, just wait 'til he sees me when he gets back from Memphis! Vowing to extract vengeance for his unkind remark, she reflected that her only regret was that she would not be able to witness his dismayed expression when he received the bill for her new wardrobe!

Mammy Lou frowned with disapproval as she watched Kitty carelessly choose still another bolt of material and bring it over to the counter, which was already covered with her numerous other selections. It was obvious that her mistress was being willfully extravagant, for her purchases were not only in excess, but the most expensive to be found in each item, ranging from wallpaper and house paint to frivolous bonnets and dress fabrics. Her concern was not minimized by the knowledge that Mr. Bret would be footing the bill, and when Kitty appeared to be on the verge of returning for another bolt of material, her rebuke was automatic.

"Miz Kitty, hit ain' right you spendin' Mist' Bret's money lak dis. You dun already bought mos' haf de store as t'is!"

Kitty would have argued the point had she not remembered the necessity of returning to her house on Cherry Street. After all, the primary reason she had spent the last week in town was to repair the house, then sell it—hopefully at a good price. The town was still overcrowded, real estate was scarce and in great demand.

Her house was in a good location, and now that Lemme had replaced the shattered windows, repaired the holes in the roof, and whitewashed the exterior, all that remained to be done was wallpapering the interior.

"I suppose you're right," she agreed reluctantly. "Besides, I really should get that wallpaper back to Lemme so he can start on the parlor this afternoon." Tapping her finger on the counter, she glanced over to where Henry Collins was conversing with one of his Negro customers. When she got the gist of their disagreement, an amused smile lifted the corners of her mouth.

"Ah tell you, Mist' Henry, dat mule you sold me is plumb blind," the old man wailed.

"Aw, Tom, that mule's not blind."

"Yas, suh, he sho' is. Didn't Ah see 'im walk into a big oak tree an' almos' butt his brains out?"

Not doubting the man for a minute, Henry nevertheless gave him a disdainful look. "Hell, that mule ain't blind—he just don't give a damn!"

The discussion was terminated abruptly by the arrival of another customer, an attractive man whom Kitty was sure she had never seen. His impeccable attire and obvious assurance suggested affluence, which was soon confirmed by Henry's affability as he eagerly ushered him into the store.

He had apparently dropped by to purchase some cigars, and while he leaned over the counter to make his selection, Kitty stole another glance at him. He was of average height and build. His neatly trimmed mustache complemented aquiline features, as did the smattering of gray in his long, dark sideburns. Judging from his appearance, Kitty imagined him to be somewhere in his late thirties. It was not until he straightened and unexpectedly turned to face her that she noted the ruthlessness in his eyes, a coldness that caused her to shiver inwardly even though he was now smiling at her.

In the next instant Henry was introducing them. Garth Talbot, it turned out, had spent most of his boyhood in Vicksburg, though he now hailed from Missouri. Remembering Missouri was a border state, Kitty wondered if his sympathies lay with the North or South; at last she decided he must be neutral, since he was not wearing a uniform. As she conversed politely with the suave stranger, her curiosity increased.

"Tell me, Mr. Talbot, what do you think of the Yankees' occupy-ing our town?"

"I think they should all go back home, don't you?" he answered with a charming grin that caused Kitty to chuckle.

"Yes, indeed. Don't you agree, Mr. Collins?" Kitty asked imp-ishly, aware that Henry's business was booming and most of his paying customers were Yankees. No one else had any money. His answer, therefore, was not surprising.

"Well, yeah, I reckon I do. Of course, when they pull out, it's going to be mighty bad for business." He frowned, then added, "Though I doubt yours will be affected, Mr. Talbot."

"Oh, and just what is your line of business, Mr. Talbot?"

"I've recently opened a loan company down on Washington Street," he replied.

Kitty was immediately interested. "What kind of loans do you make?"

"Large and small ones, mostly on real estate."

"I imagine quite a few people need loans now, but what happens if they can't repay the money to you? Aren't you taking a big risk?"

Garth smiled at her naiveté. "Not at all. If the loan is paid back on time, I make a modest profit on the interest. If the loan is not repaid, however, I still have the collateral, which is usually real estate. Of course, I would prefer the former means of transaction," he said in a manner that did not quite ring true.

"Yes, I'm sure it must be unpleasant to evict people from their homes," Kitty answered, disturbed by the growing suspicion that Garth Talbot would not be inclined to leniency where money was concerned.

"Unpleasant, but occasionally necessary." Sensing his image had suddenly become somewhat tarnished, he added almost piously, "I assure you, it gives me no pleasure to profit from the misfortunes of others, but if I allowed people to renege on loans, I would soon be out of business and, therefore, unable to help others."

Still not completely convinced of his sincerity, Kitty was relieved when Henry informed her that the last of her purchases had been wrapped. He offered to help Mammy Lou transport them to their carriage.

"It's been a privilege to meet you, Mrs. Blake. I look forward to meeting your husband as well," Garth said after Henry and Mammy Lou had left.

"My husband died last spring, Mr. Talbot."

Garth did not bother with meaningless condolences but replied with unusual frankness. "Then I shall certainly look forward to seeing you again."

Confused by his forthrightness, as well as his obvious admiration, Kitty smiled uncertainly, then turned and walked quickly from the store. There was something about the man that made her feel uneasy. She was attracted to him, yet repelled at the same time. Still, it would not hurt to cultivate his friendship, she decided, especially since he owned a loan company. It never hurt to have friends in the right places, though she knew instinctively it would be unwise to be in Garth Talbot's debt. He simply did not strike her as being completely honest or trustworthy, and this thought was echoed by Mammy Lou while they rode back to the house.

By the time the carriage stopped, there was little doubt in Kitty's mind that, as far as Mammy Lou was concerned, Garth Talbot was "nuttin' but white trash." The fact that the bossy old woman was displeased with her for even conversing with the man was also evident, and, tired of being reprimanded, Kitty immediately put the grumbling servant to work once they were home.

Three hours later Kitty squirmed on the sofa in the back parlor and attempted to feign interest in the latest tidbits of gossip that Phoebe, Dolly, and Mattie had been exuberantly conveying to her for over an hour. Flora, unfortunately, was confined to bed with a nasty cold, and being free of her sister's censorship for a change, Dolly's tongue wagged endlessly. In minutes Kitty had been well informed on everything that had happened in Vicksburg over the past three months and had heard some incidents for the second or third time. Now they were back on the subject of the harsh treatment Negro soldiers were inflicting upon the white civilians, verbally and physically.

"Hmph, we're not safe in our homes, much less on the streets," Mattie said. "Last week, three black soldiers forced their way into the Jamisons' home and demanded—*demanded, mind you*—to be fed. When Mr. Jamison ordered them out, they actually pulled a gun on him. The incident was reported to the military authorities, but needless to say, no action was taken."

Wishing to change the subject, Kitty said, "Cora Crane dropped by yesterday and brought me a jar of her mint jelly. I suppose you've heard that Bess and Mark are planning to be married after Christmas.''

"Oh, yes." Dolly beamed. "And just yesterday, Flora said she wouldn't be a bit surprised if—''

She was interrupted by an unexpected pounding on the front door. Seconds later, Mammy Lou's raised voice sailed back to them, causing them to stiffen with alarm.

"Take one mo' step, niggah, an' hit'll be yo' last! Now, step aside whilst Ah gits de missus," she ordered, slamming the door shut.

Kitty bolted from the sofa and rushed out into the hall. "What's wrong, Mammy Lou? Who's at the door?"

"Hit's two ob dem niggah Yankees, Miz Kitty, an' dey say dey wanna see you 'bout dat "Fo Sale" sign out front. Dey say dat de sign'll haf tuh come down, less'n you kin prove you dun took de oath.''

"Give 'em an inch and they'll take a mile," Kitty muttered, and sailed back into the parlor, her expression one of outrage as she stalked over to the small secretary in the corner, jerked open the top drawer, and extracted a large revolver. Checking to see that it was loaded, she started toward the hall but was stopped when Phoebe frantically clutched at her arm.

"Oh, Kitty, you mustn't antagonize them! Just do as they ask, then perhaps they'll leave us in peace," she begged.

Her plea was quickly echoed by her distraught companions, but Kitty paid them no mind. Without bothering to answer, she strode determinedly from the room. Almost hysterical with fear, the elderly matrons immediately began twittering about what they should do, agreeing that the wisest course would be to leave. But how? None were feeling brave enough to venture through the hallway to the back door, which, aside from the front door, was their only exit.

"Oh, dear, I think I'm going to be sick," Dolly whimpered, mopping the perspiration from her plump face with a crumpled handkerchief.

"Don't you dare, Dolly Drummond," Mattie hissed. "We've got to find some way out of this house before that foolish girl gets us all killed.''

"But how, Mattie?" Phoebe whispered. "Our only means of escape is— Unless . . .'' Her voice trailed off as she glanced over her shoulder to the open window that overlooked the backyard.

As she followed Phoebe's gaze, Mattie's expression was one of shrewd reckoning, Dolly's of sheer dismay. The window was of average width, but there was no doubt that getting Dolly's corpulent figure through the opening was going going to be difficult, if not impossible.

Deciding she would rather deal with the Yankees than with the alternative, Dolly quickly shook her head. "Oh, no, I can't. I just can't! Besides, what if someone should see? Why, we'd be the laughingstock of town!"

"No one is going to see," Mattie answered sharply.

By now Dolly was on the verge of tears. "But—but what if I get stuck?"

"Perhaps we're jumping to conclusions," Phoebe said. "After all, we don't know that we're actually in any danger."

Motioning for the others to follow, she tiptoed across the room and cautiously cracked the sliding doors that opened to the hall. In stair-step fashion, the three women peeped through the narrow opening and spotted Kitty confronting two burly soldiers, who, even from a distance, looked quite menacing. The sound of deep, angry voices floated back to them, confirming their worst fears; yet it was Kitty's reaction that caused them to gasp aloud, for she suddenly brought forth the revolver she had been holding behind her skirts and pointed it at the soldiers.

"That sign stays where it is, and I'll shoot anyone who tries to pull it down. Now, get off my property!"

Apparently unconvinced, the taller soldier stepped forward, but he came to an abrupt halt when Kitty pulled the trigger and shot the dusty cap from his head with deadly accuracy. The loud report immediately produced squeals of terror from the matronly onlookers, who, in a state of panic, collided into each other as they scurried across the room and simultaneously tried to crawl over the windowsill. After a futile moment of pushing and shoving, Phoebe whispered, "You go first, Mattie, then you can pull Dolly from the front while I push her from behind."

It was in this unorthodox manner that the frantic ladies finally managed to escape, much to the amusement of Lemme, who, asleep on the back porch, awakened in time to witness their hasty departure. In the meantime, Kitty's dilemma had been solved by a Federal officer who happened to be passing by the house just as she fired the gun. Quickly sizing up the situation, he ordered the two soldiers to be on their way. After they had gone, the man turned to Kitty with a kind smile.

Giving a relieved sigh, she thanked the man and conversed politely for a few minutes. Having just arrived in town that morning, he was unable to enlighten her as to whether or not she would be allowed to sell her house without first swearing allegiance to the Union, but he strongly urged her, for her own well-being in the future, to take the oath.

It did not take her long to reach a decision. As soon as she had freshened up and changed into her one decent outfit, a black-and-white-striped taffeta skirt with a black velvet bolero worn over a full-sleeved white blouse, she headed straight for the headquarters of General McPherson, the officer in command of Vicksburg.

As Lemme guided the carriage down Cherry Street, then turned left onto Crawford Street and pulled to a halt, Kitty's nervousness was replaced by resentment. How dare the Yankees take over Balfour House and turn it into their headquarters! she fumed inwardly. Alighting from the carriage, she curtly instructed Lemme to wait for her, then marched up the steps and down the walk that led to the house. Without knocking, she opened the door and went inside, halting before a neatly uniformed soldier who was seated behind a makeshift desk in the hall.

Fear was far from her mind when she confronted the man with a disdainful look, haughtily demanding to see General McPherson. Clearly amused, the young orderly took her name and, with a wry grin, asked the nature of her business.

"When I meet the general, he will learn the nature of my business," she retorted.

"I see. Well, I'm afraid General McPherson is busy at the moment, but if you would like to wait," he suggested, gesturing to a long wooden bench against the opposite wall.

Kitty frowned with displeasure but nevertheless followed his suggestion and seated herself on the uncomfortable bench. The dining room doors had been left slightly ajar, and while she waited for the commander to see her, she watched an endless line of women filing past a long dining table that was ladened with all sorts of tinned, boxed, and bagged food supplies. Each of them sullenly accepted the ten-day rations that were being doled out in exchange for their oaths of allegiance. Many were strangers to her, probably refugees, but some of the ladies she recognized, despite the fact that they nodded quickly and then, ashamed, glanced away from her. Her heart went out to them, for they were all ladies of gentility and, she knew, staunchly patriotic to the South. Only starvation could have forced them into submitting to the enemy's demand and taking the despicable oath.

It seemed a meaningless gesture to Kitty. Did the Yankees really believe they could obtain loyalty by means of bribery? If so, they were a passel of fools.

It was rumored that General McPherson had formerly been a West Point cadet and that he was a well-mannered and fair-minded officer. Despite these flattering rumors, Kitty was totally unprepared for the chivalrous manner in which he greeted her. After being seated in a chair next to his desk, she steeled herself against his kindly gaze and came right to the point. Indignantly, she informed him that two of his Negro soldiers had trespassed on her property this morning and had actually attempted to take down her "For Sale" sign simply because she had not taken the oath.

"Tell me, General," she said, "is it customary for your men to threaten and bully defenseless women?"

A trace of a smile flitted across his face as he looked at the lovely woman who, though petite, appeared to be anything but defenseless. Somewhat dazzled by her spirit, he answered with controlled politeness, "Indeed not, madam, and certainly not with my approval. I sincerely regret this unfortunate incident, and I appreciate your bringing it to my attention. There is one fact, however, which I must make clear to you. You are living in a conquered land—and since we are still at war, property belonging to disloyal American citizens is subject to confiscation. In other words, those who refuse to take the oath of allegiance are placing themselves in a very vulnerable position."

"What you're saying is that you can't guarantee the safety of my property or myself unless I take the oath."

"In time of war, there are no guarantees. If, however, you do take the oath, I shall certainly be in a better position to offer you the protection of the Federal government."

"Very well, General, I'll take the oath and sign whatever is necessary," she informed him with a look of defiance.

The distasteful procedure took only a few minutes, though the painful experience could not end quickly enough for Kitty. After signing her name to the document that supposedly testified to her allegiance, she faced the general coldly.

"You realize, of course, that this changes nothing. My first loyalty will always be to the South."

"I had rather suspected as much," he answered wryly, then wrote something on a sheet of paper and handed it to her. "This verifies you have taken the oath and that you have my personal assurance of our government's protection. If anyone attempts to harass you in the future, show it to them. While I'm at it, I might as well sign a permit which will enable you to procure rations for you and your family," he added, filling in a short form and signing it at the bottom.

Glancing over the permit, Kitty frowned. "You've allotted me thirty days of rations rather than ten. Why?"

"Let's just say that I admire your spunk," he answered with a slight grin.

Arching one brow, Kitty studied the general for a moment. Deciding it would be advantageous to prevail upon his present good humor, she pressed her luck farther. After all, one did not stumble across opportunities like this every day!

"Well, since you feel that way, perhaps you'd be willing to grant me one other thing," she suggested with a fetching smile.

"And what might that be?"

"Last spring, your soldiers raided our plantation to the north of town. They ransacked our house, destroyed a barn, and took our livestock." Kitty paused, uncertain as how to proceed.

"You have my sympathy, madam," the general responded with obvious sincerity.

"I don't need your sympathy, sir, but I do need six shoats and a boar."

The commander chuckled. "So you want some pigs, do you?"

"Not pigs, shoats—young hogs about a year old and fat enough to be slaughtered as soon as the weather turns cold. Four would sufficiently supply us with pork this winter, but we need two more young sows and a boar to supply us with litters this spring."

"Hmmm." McPherson stroked his beard thoughtfully. "If I provided you with these animals, how would you transport them to your farm?"

"A friend of mine owns a warehouse in town. He has wagons, and I'm sure he'd be willing to help me."

"Very well, I'll grant your request. Tell your friend to have his wagon at our stockyard in the morning and instruct him to give the soldier in charge this permit," he said, filling out another form and handing it to her.

Kitty could hardly believe her good fortune as she read the narrow slip of paper. It clearly stated that she was to receive six *fattened* shoats and a boar. Her expression was one of surprised pleasure when she found the commander observing her reaction.

"Thank you, General. You've been most accommodating," she admitted reluctantly.

A devilish twinkle sparkled in his shrewd eyes, for he recognized her unwillingness to be indebted to him. "The pleasure is mine. In fact, it's quite refreshing to meet a Southerner who isn't too proud to accept a favor."

His subtle humor was not lost on Kitty, who returned his look with an impish smile. "I'd hardly call it a favor, General," she replied saucily. "After all, you Yankees have robbed us blind, so why shouldn't I take some of it back?" And with that pert reminder, she sailed from the room before he could think of an appropriate answer.

His amused laughter followed her, however, and her smile broadened. Again, she had met a Yankee she liked, and remembering the kind officer who had come to her aid earlier that morning, she decided that she might be judging the Federalists too harshly. Not all Yankees were monsters—just most of them!

Chapter 31

The winter of '64 gave way to spring, but since the Union's victory at Chattanooga in late November, no other major battle had occurred. Raids and guerrilla activities continued throughout the country, however, with frequent skirmishes erupting in Arkansas and Louisiana. There was a growing interest in the forthcoming presidential election in the North, particularly since Lincoln had been unsuccessful in finding a general who was capable of defeating Robert Lee's Army of Northern Virginia. Realizing the necessity of appointing a general on whom he could rely, Lincoln commissioned Grant to act as general-in-chief of the northern armies, thus giving him overall command.

In the South, confidence in President Davis and his administration was slowly deteriorating, as were dreams of ultimate victory. Tension mounted while everyone waited to discover when and where the next major confrontation would occur. By May two things had become evident: Grant's and Lee's armies were going to clash in Virginia, and Sherman, determined to cripple the Army of the Tennessee, was going for Joe Johnston in Georgia.

Like others, Kitty was beginning to feel that the war would never end, but in spite of grim rumors, she refused to consider the possibility of defeat. It was a blessing that her busy schedule kept her from dwelling on the matter.

The sale of her town house, plus financial assistance from Bret, had enabled her to begin restoring Belle Glen, but there was still much to be accomplished before the plantation could operate efficiently. Fortunately, many of their former field hands had returned throughout the winter and, though free, seemed content to pick up the threads of their previous lives. Happy to see their familiar faces, Kitty had nevertheless made it plain to one and all that, in lieu of money, they would receive food, clothing, and other necessities from the commissary, plus rent-free living quarters; in return, she expected an honest day's work from each of them. In other words, those who stayed would have to pull their own weight.

It often seemed to Kitty that she, alone, was shouldering all the problems, and there were times when she resented being responsible for everyone's welfare. Tad was a capable bookkeeper, but a dreamer when it came to managing people or money. He simply did not know how to say no to anyone and was easily touched by hard-luck stories. To his way of thinking, any field hand who did not feel up to working should not be required to do so. After all, hadn't they proved their loyalty by returning to Belle Glen? To add to her burdens, Dede had given birth to a little girl in the spring, and though Melissa was a good baby, she would be still another mouth to feed and an added responsibility.

There were times when Kitty longed to run to her father for advice, yet she never did. Dave had not fully recovered from his stroke, and she could not bring herself to tax what little strength he had left by burdening him with problems. Instead, she dealt with the worrisome situation on her own and tried to have faith in her decisions once they were made.

For a while Bret had been a frequent visitor and someone in whom she could occasionally confide, but his visits had become less and less frequent over the past two months. She realized that tending to his brokerage and supervising the construction of his house kept him busy. She also shrewdly suspected he was spending most of his spare time at Dixie's new establishment, a casino and theater that catered only to an affluent and respectable male clientele, including Federal officers. The question foremost in her mind was, were Bret and Dixie having an intimate relationship? It was galling to think Bret might prefer Dixie's company to her own, particularly when she was stuck on the plantation, raising his son and having no fun whatsoever.

To break the monotony, Kitty decided to spend a week in town with Aunt Phoebe. Though some of the land still lay fallow, the spring planting had been completed, so there was no reason for her not to indulge in a little pleasure. She chose the week of Beth and

Mark's wedding, knowing those days would be filled with numerous supper parties, teas, and dances honoring the young couple. She was not disappointed, and for one of the few times since her marriage to Miles, she felt totally carefree as she laughed and flirted with the bevy of admirers who flocked around her.

Shocked that a young widow should behave in such an unseemly manner, many a matron cast a disapproving frown in Kitty's direction, looks she pointedly ignored. To her surprise, it was Flora who put an end to the wagging tongues, Mattie's in particular, by staunchly defending Kitty and reminding the indignant ladies that, not only was she still young, but she had been widowed for well over a year.

During the week of social festivities, Kitty became better acquainted with Garth Talbot, who, to her surprise, was also a guest at several of the parties. It was obvious that though Garth was an unwelcome outsider, many of the old elite were heavily indebted to him and dared not exclude him from their guest lists.

She soon realized that Garth was not only aware of this hypocrisy, but amused by it as well. He held the upper hand, and he knew it. His manner and appearance were above reproach, but for all his savoir faire, Kitty suspected he was capable of cunning and ruthlessness.

Still, times were hard, and it never hurt to have friends in the right places, particularly affluent ones like Garth. Besides, he was always charmingly attentive and entertaining, so she did not discourage him from becoming a caller at Belle Glen in the weeks that followed. On several occasions she even allowed him to escort her to various social functions in town.

Though Dave was obviously not in favor of his daughter's association with Garth, he stopped short of actually forbidding her to see him. Kitty's main opposition came from Mammy Lou, whose low opinion of Garth had not changed in the least. In fact, she was downright belligerent upon learning that Garth was taking Kitty to the minstrel show one night. Her grumpiness failed to dampen Kitty's spirits, however, for she was determined to proceed with the outing.

The evening proved to be quite enjoyable, though Kitty's pleasure in the show was temporarily sidetracked when she spied Bret seated across the aisle from them. Determined not to allow him to spoil the evening for her, she politely returned his acknowledging nod, then turned her attention back to the black-faced performer who was doing a soft-shoe dance to "Swanee River." If she was more flirtatious than usual, it was quite unconscious.

The ride back to Belle Glen was pleasant enough at first, the conversation centering on the evening's performance. As Kitty listened to Garth, it occurred to her that she knew virtually nothing about him, other than that his family had been socially prominent in Vicksburg and had moved to St. Louis when he was a boy.

"You know, Garth, you never talk about yourself or your family."

Caught off guard, he tensed, though his reply was deliberately casual. "There's not much to tell. My father was president of the bank here until he resigned and we moved to St. Louis. I was twelve at the time, and being an only child—well, it was quite an adjustment to make." His voice became solemn when he added slowly: "I always swore I'd come back here someday."

Unaware that she had unwittingly caused him to recall bitter memories, Kitty smiled. "And so you have. After the war, perhaps your parents will visit you and I'll have the opportunity of meeting them."

"My parents died shortly after we moved to St. Louis. Having no other relatives, I spent the remainder of my youth in an orphanage—until I was old enough to go out and fend for myself."

There was no mistaking the tension in his voice now, and after expressing her sympathy, Kitty wisely remained silent for the rest of the ride.

As they rode along, Garth inwardly recalled the past. His father had not actually resigned from the bank; he had been quietly dismissed after having been accused of embezzlement.

Garth had realized long ago that his father had not been a dishonest man, merely a weak one, especially when it had come to pleasing his socially conscious wife, whose extravagance had far exceeded his income. Unable to satisfy his beautiful wife's frivolous demands and afraid of losing her if he didn't, Jonathan had unsuccessfully tried his hand at gambling, which had only worsened matters.

As a last resort, he had sought help from friends, begging for loans he had no way of repaying. But to no avail. One and all had rejected him, including Kitty's own father. With no other recourse, he had resorted to embezzlement.

Garth had inadvertently overheard the entire story when his parents' loud voices had awakened him one night. The argument had intensified, with Garth's mother accusing his father of being a failure and threatening to leave him. Within seconds two shots rang out, followed soon by a third. Berserk with anger, Jonathan Talbot had fired two bullets into his wife from close range, then, placing the revolver to his temple, had pulled the trigger again. By the time Garth reached them, it was too late. Both his parents were dead.

He had never forgotten that night, nor had he forgiven the men who had turned their backs on his father in his time of need—*especially* not Dave Devan, who had been the most affluent of them all. As a boy, he could not comprehend that the country was in the midst of a depression that even the affluent were struggling to survive. As a man, he would not try to comprehend the truth of the matter. As far as he was concerned, the men who had refused to help his father were solely responsible for his parents' deaths, just as surely as if they had pulled the trigger themselves. He had long ago vowed to make each and every one of them pay. He had worked, cheated, and connived to obtain money and power—not out of greed, but for vengeance. Now, the time was at hand.

It was ironic that he had become interested in Dave Devan's daughter—but even that could be worked to his own advantage.

It was not until the carriage pulled up in front of the house that Kitty sensed something had changed in their relationship. Instead of alighting as usual, Garth let his arm steal around her shoulders. In all the times they had been together, he had never attempted to kiss her, but she knew he was about to do so now. The thought was unappealing, and thinking to extricate herself from an embarrassing situation, she gave a pretentiously tired sigh and moved slightly away from him.

"It's been a lovely evening, Garth, but I really must be getting inside now. I'm rather tired, and I have a full day ahead of me tomorrow."

Instead of releasing her, however, Garth's arm tightened, and in the next instant, Kitty found herself trapped in his embrace.

"Kitty, when are you going to stop struggling to put this place back on its feet? Running a plantation is a man's job, not a woman's. Keep going the way you are and you'll be old before your time," he murmured, his eyes raking over her upturned face as his fingers traced the delicate curve of her chin.

His remark nettled her. "And just what do you suggest I do—let everything go to ruin until Pa's able to take charge again?"

"No, but I do suggest you let me help you," came the smooth reply as his fingers trailed down her neck.

Repelled by his touch, Kitty eyed him suspiciously. "How?"

"Let me stake you to whatever you need."

"I've already made a loan—"

"This wouldn't necessarily have to be a loan," he interrupted. "If you play your cards right, it could be, shall we say, a gift."

His hand stilled on her neck, and feeling suddenly out of her depths, Kitty shot him a perplexed look. "Are you asking me to marry you?"

"No. I'm asking you to be my mistress."

Her reaction was automatic, but even as her hand lashed out at his face, Garth's fingers captured her wrist, jerking her to him. The idea of being tied down to one woman had never appealed to him, nor did it now, despite the fact that Kitty was by far the most exciting female he had ever encountered. She had aroused him from the beginning, and he intended to have her, even if it meant using bribery or force. Her resistance merely excited him all the more, unleashing his savage lust as his mouth slanted down on hers, brutally forcing her lips apart while his free hand roughly fondled her heaving breasts.

Terrified, Kitty struggled against him as she felt his weight thrusting her down in the seat, but it was not until his mouth slid down to her half-exposed breasts that she was afforded the chance to effectively fight back. She sank her teeth into his earlobe, the salty taste of his blood almost causing her to gag as he cursed aloud and jerked away from her. In that instant, she scampered from the carriage and turned to vent her wrath on him.

"Don't ever touch me again," she ordered furiously. "I'd rather be dead than be your mistress! Now, get off our land and don't ever come back."

His menacing expression told her she had made a formidable enemy, but she was undaunted by the knowledge. Had she possessed a gun at that moment, she would have gladly shot him. Instead, she retreated to the house, relief flooding over her when she saw Lemme opening the front door for her. He wisely made no comment about her disheveled appearance, but a troubled frown marred his brow as he watched Garth's carriage disappear from view.

Not bothering with explanations, Kitty made her way upstairs and, after quickly undressing, collapsed into bed. It was some time, however, before she was able to put Garth from her mind and almost dawn before she finally fell asleep.

It seemed she had slept only a few minutes when Mammy Lou arrived with her breakfast tray the next morning, but, glancing at the mantel clock, she discovered it was almost ten o'clock.

"Come on, chile—wake up an' eat yo' breakfast. Mist' Bret's heah, an' he wants tuh see you in de pa'lor jes' as soon as he's finished visitin' wid Mist' Dave."

"Oh, Mammy Lou, I don't want to talk to him this morning," Kitty groaned. "Can't you get rid of him?"

"Naw'm, Ah don' think so. Ah don' know whut's de matter wid dat man, but he sho' seems tuh be in a tempuh dis mawnin'. Course, he don' let on to Mist' Dave, but dat don' fool me none. When he tole me tuh git you downstairs on the double, Ah knowed right den he wuz riled up. Whut you done now?"

"Nothing." Kitty frowned, throwing back the sheet and getting out of bed. "Now, stop asking questions and get my red gingham dress from the wardrobe."

After what she'd been through last night, she was in no mood to confront Bret, much less put up with a lecture. Unfortunately, there was no way to avoid him. If she did not come downstairs, there was no doubt in her mind he would barge into her room. When she finally descended the stairs, she saw that he was, indeed, in a disagreeable mood as he greeted her coolly, then sardonically remarked on her appearance.

"I must say you're looking quite rested this morning, considering you probably didn't get home until midnight. In fact, you look fresh as a daisy in that get-up you're wearing. New, isn't it?"

Realizing he was merely leading up to what he had really come to say, she sought to distract him. With feigned innocence, she dimpled into a smile. "Yes, as a matter of fact, it is. Do you like it?" she asked. "Of course, I wouldn't have a decent thing to wear if it weren't for you. I do hope I'm not spending too much, though," she added with elaborate concern.

"I haven't complained, have I?" he returned, amused by her obvious attempt to appease him, though not distracted by her tactics.

"No, you've been quite generous. I daresay I'm probably the best-dressed pauper in the county, thanks to you." When he did not reply, she turned nervously away from him and walked over to the window. "Naturally, I intend to repay you as soon as I can. Charlie says if the weather holds, we ought to have some good cotton this year, even if it is a small crop. If you can help us get a good price for it, maybe we can pay back most of the money you loaned us, and eventually . . .''

Her voice faltered as she felt Bret take hold of her shoulders and turn her around to face him. Refusing to meet his gaze, she stared at the buttons on his waistcoat until he lifted her chin with his forefinger and forced her to look up at him. "It won't work, Kitty. I'm sure you're aware I didn't come out here to discuss your clothes or your cotton. Let's stop fencing, shall we, and get to the point."

"Which is?" Defiance sparkled in her blue eyes as she haughtily met his gaze.

"Your association with Garth Talbot is causing a flurry of gossip in town. I want it stopped."

"Oh, do you indeed! Well, for your information, Mr. O'Rourke, I don't really care what you want. I shall see whom I please when I please, and there's not a blessed thing you can do about it."

"Aren't you forgetting something, Kitty? Not only do I hold the mortgage on this place, I also happen to be the source of your credit. It would be a pity to deprive the rest of your family simply because you refuse to be reasonable. Don't you agree?"

If looks could have killed, Bret would have been dead on the spot. Filled with rage, Kitty was almost incapable of speaking.

"You wouldn't!"

"You know I don't make idle threats. You also know I'll go to any lengths to ensure our son's happiness and protect his name—which means protecting yours as well. Your actions have a direct bearing on his future well-being, and it's high time you realized it. I won't stand for your reputation being tarnished in any way. Do I make myself clear?"

"Quite," she retorted. "But while you're worrying about my reputation, you might give some thought to your own. I understand you frequently visit Dixie's new gambling house."

"That's right." He grinned wickedly, amused by her childish barb. "But fortunately my social life can't harm Scott, since no one suspects him of being my son."

"What a hypocrite you are. It's fine for you to do as you please," she fumed, "but you object to my going to a few social functions with a perfectly respectable man."

"What makes you think Talbot is respectable?"

"Well, he's certainly influential," she replied, determined to defend Garth even though she no longer liked him.

"Influence and respect don't always go hand in hand, Kitty, especially not where Garth's concerned."

"Why do you say that?"

"You're aware that some citizens have formed a vigilance committee called the Rebel Scouts?" When she nodded affirmatively, he continued. "As you know, they've been operating on the outskirts of town, raiding the Yankees' supply lines and ambushing their expeditions, plus ridding some of the planters of troublesome Negroes."

"I know. Tad told me they wear Confederate uniforms and masks but that no one knows who they are or who their leader is. Whoever they are, they certainly have my admiration and respect," she declared, not realizing she was, in fact, addressing the very man who led the Scouts. "I fail to see what Garth has to do with any of this, though."

"Last week, the Baily plantation was raided by a dozen or so men who were dressed like the Scouts, but were actually a band of cutthroat guerrillas. One of them was killed, a man by the name of Thompson, who incidentally happened to be one of Garth's collection men. Unless I miss my guess, your friend Talbot is not only mixed up with these guerrillas, he's probably the head man."

"I don't believe you. Garth may be shrewd, even ruthless, but he's not a thief. You're being ridiculous."

"If I am, I'm not alone. A lot of people share my suspicion. Unfortunately, we have no proof—at least, not yet. There have been four guerrilla raids during the past month, and ironically, each time they occurred Garth was seen escorting you around town. In other words, my dear, you happen to be his alibi."

Flabbergasted, Kitty recognized the ring of truth in his accusation, though she was not ready to admit it. "How do I know you're telling me the truth, that you're not just saying this to make me stop seeing him?"

"You don't. As I said, I can't offer you proof just now, but if my hunch is correct, I don't want you mixed up in it."

"Oh, all right." Kitty sighed. "I'll do as you ask."

"I rather thought you might, especially since you didn't part with him on the best of terms last night." He grinned.

Kitty gave him a surprised look, then thrust her fists on her hips.

"Just wait 'til I see Lemme," she said through clenched teeth. "How dare he spy on me, then run taddlin' to you! And how dare you make me go through all this when you knew all along I wasn't going to see him again!"

"Let's just say I wanted to be sure."

"Well, now that you are, you can leave."

"Not so fast, Kitten. There's something I want to show you," he replied, leading her to the front door.

Though she was tempted to resist, curiosity prevailed. Sullenly, she followed him outside and around the side of the house, her anger fading completely when she saw Scotty sitting astride a new Shetland pony.

"Oh, Bret, what a darling pony!" she exclaimed.

"Mama, Mama—see what Unca Bwet gave me," Scotty chortled.

"I see, precious." Kitty smiled, brushing the damp curls from his forehead. "Did you thank Uncle Bret properly?"

"I gave him a big kiss, didn't I, Unca Bwet?"

"Yes, indeed." Bret chuckled. "Three, as a matter of fact."

"Pwease let me ride 'im now, pwease," Scotty pleaded, never taking his eyes from Bret's face.

"All right, young man, I guess you've been patient long enough. Your mother and I can watch from the porch while Terry leads you around the yard a few times." He motioned to a slender youth of about fifteen who was standing a few feet away.

As the boy drew abreast of them, Bret introduced him to Kitty. "This is Terry Dermott, my new right-hand man at the warehouse," he said, deliberately exaggerating to put the youngster at ease.

His ploy worked, and when Terry's face lit up in a pleased grin, Kitty was immediately drawn to his boyish charm. "I'm pleased to meet you, Terry. Are you new around here?"

"Yes'm. I've only been here about a year or so," he answered politely, the happy twinkle fading from his hazel eyes.

Curious to know more about him, Kitty asked where he was from, but before the boy could answer, Bret intervened. "Tell you what, Terry, how about leading Scotty around the driveway a few times so he can get the feel of a saddle under him," he suggested, addressing his next remark to Scott, who was now squirming with impatience. "Hold on tight to that saddlehorn, son. We can't have you falling off, now, can we?"

"No, sir, but I won't fall. I a big boy," Scott answered seriously,

curling both his chubby hands around the leather device and gripping
it for all he was worth.

Kitty and Bret chuckled as they watched their son's erect figure
being led away from them. With a feeling of contentment, Kitty
allowed Bret to guide her back to the front veranda. Once seated, he
told her that Terry had been recently orphaned—his entire family
wiped out by diphtheria in one of the refugee camps outside town.
Minutes later, Terry returned with Scotty, who was obviously elated
with his first riding session. With a disappointed look, he allowed
Bret to lift him from the saddle, but his expression soon brightened
when Terry cheerfully addressed his mother.

"I tell you, Miss Kitty, that boy of yours is going to be a good
rider in no time. Did you see the way he was sittin' in that saddle—
just like he was born to it. He hardly bounced around a'tall."

"Thank you, Terry. It's mighty good of you to take the time with
him," Kitty replied.

"Tell you what, Terry," Bret interceded. "How would you like
to ride out here a couple of times a week and help Scott with his
riding? That is, if Miss Kitty has no objections."

"Of course I have no objections. You're welcome to come anytime, Terry, anytime at all."

Scotty clapped his hands gleefully, for not only was he excited
about his riding lessons, but he had taken quite a fancy to his
youthful instructor. His happy expression evaporated, however, when
Bret stated that he needed to be getting back to the warehouse.

"Can I go wif you, Unca Bwet?" he asked in a pleading note.

Bret set the child on his feet and gave him an affectionate pat on
the head. "Not this time, son, but maybe next week I can drive you
and your mother into town to do some shopping. In fact, the three of
us will make a day of it. We'll get you some riding boots, maybe a
whole new riding outfit, then we'll stop by Mr. Collins's store and
see if he's got any of those licorice and peppermint sticks you like.
How about that?"

Scotty was delighted with this suggestion, but as soon as Bret and
Terry had ridden from view, he became suddenly pensive. Tugging
at his mother's skirt, he gave her a puzzled look.

"Why does Unca Bwet call me son? Am I really his son?" he
asked with innocent hopefulness.

Kneeling down beside him, Kitty gathered him to her breast. For
a moment tears misted her eyes while she tried to think of a suitable

answer. "He calls you that because it's a pet name, like when I call you 'precious' or 'sugar.' "

"But if he's not my real uncle, and he's not my daddy, what is he?" Scotty persisted, much to his mother's distress.

"He's your friend, Scotty. A friend who loves you very much," she told him with a barely discernible catch to her voice.

As Kitty rose to her feet, the child looked up at her, and there was no mistaking the disappointment in his innocent eyes. With a small sigh, he followed her into the house, but not before she heard the heartbreaking words he whispered.

"I wish he wuz my daddy. I wish I had a daddy like Unca Bwet."

His words echoed in her mind throughout the remainder of the morning, leaving her with a feeling of inadequacy and loneliness as she wandered about the house. For once, she would even have welcomed her sister-in-law's constant chattering, but Tad had taken his wife and child to visit Dede's aunt in Natchez. They would not be returning for at least several weeks.

As was customary in the summertime, Kitty retired to her room shortly after dinner. Attempting to escape the hottest part of the day, she tried to take a nap, but sleep would not come. As she lay on her moss-filled mattress and stared unseeingly at the overhead canopy, she was unmindful of the mockingbird that sang loudly just outside her shuttered window. Her thoughts were of Bret and the life they should have been sharing together. Yes, he had asked her to marry him, but pride had made her refuse.

Now Scotty was beginning to ask questions that were becoming more and more difficult to answer. She sighed, realizing that the older Scotty became, the more questions he would undoubtedly ask, especially if Bret were constantly present. The situation was getting out of hand, and something was going to have to be done about it. Unfortunately, no quick solution came to mind.

When she later visited with Dave in his bedroom, her thoughts were still on the problem. Nevertheless, she feigned interest in what he was saying about the Rebel Scouts and their efforts to end the guerrillas' skulduggery and keep troublesome Negroes in line. There saw no mistaking her father's admiration for the vigilantes. His voice even sounded stronger, and for the first time in months Kitty saw an unmistakable spark of vitality in her father that had been missing since his stroke. Finally Dave tired of the subject and asked how Scotty liked his new pony.

"Oh, he's tickled to death with it," she admitted, "but I wish Bret wouldn't spoil him so. In fact, I really think it would be best if Scotty saw less of Bret in the future. He's becoming too attached to him."

Dave's lips curved in a sad smile as he regarded his daughter. "Under the circumstances, is that so surprising? Isn't it only natural for the boy to be attached to his father?"

Kitty had long ago suspected Dave's perception of the truth, but now that he had openly confirmed her suspicion, she felt embarrassed and ashamed. Looking down at her clasped hands, she asked: "How long have you known?"

"Right from the beginning. Having known Bret as a child, there was no doubt in my mind that Scotty was his son. The two of them bear a striking resemblance, more so with each passing day. The older Scotty gets, the more he favors his father."

"Then that's all the more reason for Bret to stop seeing him. If you can see the resemblance between them, it's only a question of time before others will see it, too. I live in fear of that happening, but I don't know what to do about it."

Dave held out his hand to her. Sinking down beside his armchair, Kitty rested her cheek on his knee. She was somehow relieved that her father knew the truth, yet his knowledge did not solve her problem. Several seconds ticked by while Dave stroked his daughter's bent head and stared out the window. When the silence was broken, his voice was gentle and without reproach.

"I've never asked what happened between you and Bret, and I won't ask now. I've lived long enough to realize that everyone makes mistakes, but mistakes can often be rectified. There is one thing, however, that has always puzzled me. Was Bret aware of your condition when he left for Europe?"

"No, he had no idea I was carrying his child. I didn't want him on those terms then, nor do I now," she answered firmly.

"Then Bret has asked you to marry him?"

"Yes, some time ago, as a matter of fact." She sighed and looked up at him. "I refused."

"Why?"

"Because no matter how hard I try, I just can't forget how he betrayed us."

Dave frowned and shook his head. "So, you still think he was a Yankee spy?"

"I *know* he was, Pa. In fact, it wouldn't surprise me a bit if he still worked for them in some capacity."

"Believe me, sugar, you're wrong. As I've said before, things are not always what they seem. Just because you saw Bret talking to that Yankee down by the river prior to their attack doesn't give you the right to condemn him as a spy."

"But that was just one reason, Pa. You know there were others as well."

"Such as?"

"His friendship with General Sherman, for one thing, and for another, his willingness to help Sherman's troops bypass the swamps and reach the river that time. Remember?"

"Yes, I remember, and I also remember my relief when Bret led them away from the plantation. Had it not been for his shrewdness, Sherman's men might have been camping on our doorstep for days."

Considering her father's words and his inference that Bret had been trying to protect the family, Kitty was momentarily seized with doubt. Then she remembered Bret had never denied being a spy, and her prejudice returned, particularly when she recalled his occasional and unexplained disappearances during the siege.

"I wish I could see it that way, but I just don't," she said. "Bret has never believed we could win this war. He's never wanted us to win it. He's a traitor, and I can never forgive him for that."

"Then I pity you, my dear. Forgiveness is something we all need from time to time—but to receive it, we must first be willing to give it." Seeing her puzzled expression, he continued. "Has it ever occurred to you that you betrayed Bret when you married Miles? By doing so, you robbed Bret of a son."

"I did what I thought was best, Pa."

"But was it for the best?"

Kitty slowly shook her head, her blue eyes clouding with sadness upon remembering her unhappy marriage. "No, I don't suppose it was."

Dave smiled slightly, then rubbed his forehead. "You know, living one's life can be rather like climbing a mountain. There are many plateaus along the way, each one a little higher and a little more promising than the last. No matter how difficult the path, each of us instinctively struggles to reach that top plateau, for only then can we glimpse the future and understand the past. Lately, I've begun to feel I've almost reached the last plateau and that my usefulness here is almost ended. I'm not anxious for death, but neither do I fear it. Before I go, however, I'd like to know you and Bret have mended your fences."

"Don't talk like that, Pa. What would I do without you? How could I go on?" Her voice trembled.

"I'm not trying to frighten you, honey, but I want you to be prepared when the time comes. As I said, I'm not eager to die, but I certainly don't dread it. I'd just like to know that if something should happen to me, your happiness and well-being are ensured. Yours and Scott's. You've got to forget the past, Kitty, and look to the future. Marry Bret. Let him help you give Scott the home he deserves. You can't do it alone, you know. The boy needs his father."

Later that night as she sat on the veranda, she considered her father's advice. She knew he was right, of course, but how could she marry a man she did not trust? What kind of a marriage could they possibly have as long as their loyalties were divided?

Chapter 32

The Fourth of July arrived and was pointedly ignored by the citizens of Vicksburg. Bitterly remembering that Independence Day marked the anniversary of their town's surrender, Vicksburgers went about their business as though it were a day like any other. Only Yankees had cause to celebrate, and only disloyal Confederates, those who had "turned blue," participated in their captors' noisy festivities or viewed the colorful display of fireworks that night. Like most of her friends, Kitty deliberately kept busy on the Fourth and was greatly relieved when the dismal day ended.

Dede's aunt had suffered a mild heart attack, making it necessary for Tad and Dede to remain in Natchez longer than originally planned. The weeks sped by as Kitty took complete charge and efficiently managed the entire plantation. By August she began to realize the fruits of her labor.

Waiting for Charlie to call quittin' time, she was filled with pride as her eyes scanned the stretch of land that was thickly dotted with white, fluffy bolls. The first of the cotton had been picked that morning and was already at the gin. It was a prime crop, she decided, but as she watched the workers and listened to them hum while one of the older women sang a familiar spiritual, "Sometimes I Feel Like a Motherless Child," she was reminded of bygone days. No field had laid fallow then, whereas now only a small portion of land was planted. Dissatisfaction suddenly filled her, and she vowed silently to remedy this situation next year. No matter what it cost, every inch of Belle Glen's rich bottomland was going to be cultivated in the future.

Nudging her mount, she rode over to where Charlie was instructing the new Negro foreman, Amos, to call in the field hands. The big man did so in a deep, booming voice that was tinged with pride as he executed his newly acquired authority. His pleased expression was replaced by a dark scowl, however, when he spied one of the younger workers carrying a half-filled cotton sack.

"Whut's de matter wid you, Felix? Why ain' you totin' uh full sack lak de rest?" he growled.

"Ah's feelin' por'ly, Amos, moughty por'ly. Been down in de back all aft'noon," the young man whined.

"Huh, you jes' playin' possum tuh git outta wurk. If'n you duz hit t'morrow, Ah's gwine tuh tell Mist' Charlie. Den you's gwine tuh find yo'sef in uh peck ob truble fo' sho'. Don' forgit whut de missus dun tole us—if'n you don' wurk, you don' stay."

Kitty smiled and watched as Amos marched alongside Felix. "Looks like we've got a good foreman, Charlie," she commented.

"Yes'm, he'll do," Charlie agreed, mounting his own horse.

As they rode leisurely back to the house, Kitty asked, "By the way, do you think we can start ginning the cotton in a couple of days?"

"Reckon so." Charlie grinned. "If'n the good Lord's willin' and the creek don't rise!"

"I wish we could have planted more acres, but at least we've gotten a good yield out of this section. How many bales do you think we'll get?"

"Shucks, the way that cotton's growin', ain't no tellin'! Looks like we're gonna have a bumper crop, though."

"With the price of cotton going sky high, we oughta make a nice profit if we do get a good yield. Then I can start paying off our loan to Bret and still hold back enough to hire extra hands next spring. We'll need a lot of workers if we're going to plant all our fields next year."

"Don't you fret, Miss Kitty. Why, in no time a'tall, this plantation's gonna be jest like it wuz before the war," he assured her.

"I swear I don't know what I'd do without you, Charlie. With Pa sick and all, you're about the only one left around here I can count on. But you're been working too hard. Why don't you ride into town and have some fun?"

"Lord, I'd really like to, but Mr. Bret done tole me to stick 'round here, leastways 'til them guerrillas get caught."

"I'm running this plantation, not Bret. If I say you can go into town, then you can. Besides, there hasn't been a guerrilla raid in over a month. Far as we know, they've already hightailed it out of the county."

"Maybe so," he replied dubiously.

"Oh, quit being such an ol' worrywart, Charlie. For heaven's sake, I've got a house full of servants, so I'll hardly be left alone. It's high time you had a little fun, and now's as good a time as any."

Temptation battled caution, and the overseer thoughtfully scratched his head. "You sure you want me to go, Miss Kitty?"

"Quite sure," she reaffirmed as they reached the house. "Just be sure to get back before midnight. We've all got a full day ahead of us."

With a cheerful wave, she stood on the veranda steps and watched Charlie lead her horse around the side of the house toward the stable. It had been a good day, she felt—a very good day! Humming to herself, she turned and went inside the house. For the first time in years, she felt confident about the future.

Dixie paused at the wide double doors that opened from the foyer into the large, ornately decorated gambling casino, her eyes scanning the crowded room and coming to rest on a group of men playing poker in the far corner. Relieved when she discovered Bret was seated at the table, she quickly made her way over to him and tapped him on the shoulder.

"Bret, as soon as you finish this hand, could I see you in the foyer?" she asked.

"Sure, Dixie. I'll be with you in a minute," he answered, tossing another gold piece on the table. Three of the players folded, but the fourth called the bet. Bret spread his ace-high heart flush on the table, grinning when his opponent gave a low whistle.

"Sure beats the hell out of my full house," he admitted good-naturedly. Watching Bret rake in the pot, the man asked if he would be returning to the table.

"No, I think I'll call it a night. It's been a pleasure, gentlemen," he said. With a friendly nod, he left them and sauntered out to the foyer, where Dixie was waiting for him.

"Sorry to interrupt you like that, Bret, but one of your Rebel

Scouts is out back," she whispered. "Says he's got to see you right away. It's urgent."

"Who is it?" he asked, striding toward the back entrance.

"It's one of the Hartz boys, but I don't know which. They look a lot alike," she answered, turning the key in the back door and flinging it open. "He's over there, waiting for you by the stable."

"Thanks, Dixie." Bret smiled and strode over to where a young man was lingering in the shadows. "What's up, Steve?" he asked, immediately recognizing the oldest of the Hartz boys.

"We're in for another guerrilla raid, Bret," Steve replied soberly.

"Hell! Where do they plan to strike, now?"

"The Devan plantation. Scott's out right now roundin' up the other Scouts. They'll meet us about a mile outside of town, near the bend of the river. I figured those bastards would have a head start on us, so I told Scott to tell our boys to forget their uniforms tonight and just get out there."

"Right," Bret muttered, his nerves tensing as he imagined the brutality Kitty might suffer if he could not reach her in time. Swearing softly, he grabbed hold of Steve's arm. "Are you sure about this?"

"Positive. One of our boys has been seeing a lot of Ada, that tall chorus girl at Ed's Saloon. She stepped out in the alley to get a breath of air tonight, and that's when she overheard several men talking about the raid."

"Who were they?"

"I don't know. Ada said they were strangers—maybe hired guns from out of town."

"Probably hired by Talbot," Bret ventured.

"I had Terry saddle up your horse so I could bring him to you," Steve informed him, nodding to where he had tied their two horses to a hitching rail at the far end of the stable.

"Good. Let's get a move on. I just hope to God we're not too late!"

Kitty glanced up at the grandfather clock in the hall and saw that it was almost ten. Realizing the time had slipped up on her and that it was now way past Scotty's bedtime, she walked out to the back porch, which was where the house servants usually congregated on warm summer nights.

Spying his mother, Scotty scooted from Doshe's lap and ran over to her.

"Mommy, Mommy," he exclaimed, "Gus's teaching me a song, an' Lemme says when I's bigger, he'll teach me to play the banjo! Can Gus an' me sing our song? Can we, please?" he begged, shifting from one foot to the other with excitement.

"Not t'night, you ain', chile," Mammy Lou intervened, scooping the boy up in her arms and waddling toward the door. "Time you's in bed, an' dat's jes' whar you's a'gwine."

After promising Scotty that she would come up presently to kiss him good night, Kitty leaned on the porch railing. The sweet fragrance of night-blooming jasmine scented the night air, and glancing up at the star-filled sky, she felt reluctant to return inside.

"Want Moses tuh blow out de lamps on de porch?" Daisy asked.

"Yes, I guess we'd all better turn in." Kitty sighed. "We've got a busy day ahead of us."

She was on the verge of turning away from the banister when a faint whiff of smoke assailed her nostrils. Her gaze swung in the direction of the cotton fields, her eyes widening with horror when she saw an ominous pink glow in the distance.

"Lawd, Miz Kitty, de cotton field's on fire!" Lemme suddenly shouted.

Even as the others cried out in alarm, Kitty heard the distant sound of thundering hooves and saw the faint outline of riders silhouetted against the fiery background.

"Guerrillas!" she gasped, unmindful of the ripple of terror that was washing over the servants.

She was momentarily paralyzed by fear. Not long after the guerrilla raids had begun, Bret had provided them with a crate of rifles and ammunition, which were now stored in the cellar. He had also gone to great lengths to map out a feasible plan of defense, should Belle Glen ever be subjected to a raid. At his suggestion, Charlie had picked a handful of trustworthy field hands, plus Lemme and Gus, and had been giving them target practice on a regular basis. Thankful for Bret's wisdom and foresight, Kitty felt slightly reassured when she turned to the alarmed servants and quickly issued orders. Her assurance increased as she remembered that Charlie had returned from town an hour ago.

"Lemme, go down to the cellar and get the rifles and ammunition. Bring 'em out here on the back porch. Moses, run over and ring the plantation bell three times. Ring it hard, so it can be heard for miles. If the Waddells hear it, they'll know we're in trouble and try to help us.'' Pausing for breath, she was about to instruct Gus to get Charlie, but before she could issue the order she saw the overseer heading toward them, still in the process of hitching up his trousers as he ran. Had the situation not been so serious, Kitty would have been amused by his words.

"Damn polecats have caught us with our pants down!" he swore, then swung around to face Gus. "Where in the hell's them darkies I been teachin' to shoot? Go round 'em up and git 'em over here on the double, so's I kin pass out the rifles and show 'em where to take cover. Wait—never mind, Gus, here they come now," he muttered with relief.

Not waiting for the field hands to reach the porch, Kitty motioned for Doshe and Daisy to accompany her inside the house, then told them to lock all the windows and doors. As she entered the hall, she spotted Mammy Lou at the top of the stairs.

"Go tell Pa we're being raided by the guerrillas, but there's no need for him to come downstairs. Charlie's got everything under control, so he's not to worry. Tell him I'll join him as soon as I can," she rapped out quickly, fearful of Dave's becoming overly distraught and having another stroke. "Make sure Pa's all right, Mammy Lou, then get Scotty and go down to the cellar with Doshe and Daisy until all of this is over."

"Whut's you gwine tuh do?"

"Soon as I've double-checked the windows and doors, I'll put out the lights. No sense giving those varmints an easy target."

Daisy scurried down the winding staircase as Mammy Lou hurried off to get Scotty. "Did you check every window upstairs?" Kitty asked.

"Yas'm, dey's all locked," Daisy replied breathlessly, tensing with fear when a loud burst of rifle shots suddenly rent the air and intermingled with the deafening sounds of racing horses and blood-curdling yells.

Doshe came rushing into the hall just as Mammy Lou was coming downstairs with Scotty. "Get down to the cellar, all of you," Kitty ordered. Noticing Moses standing uncertainly in the back hall, she frowned with exasperation. "Don't stand there like a bump on a log, Moses. Go!"

"I wanna stay wif you, Mommy," Scotty protested tearfully.

"No, honey, you go 'long with Mammy Lou," Kitty answered
with as much patience as she could muster. Seeing his rebellious
look, she sought to appease him. "I want you to be my brave little
man, and do exactly as I say. Go on, now. Take care of Mammy
Lou and the others for me. Will you do that?" she asked, giving the
troubled boy a fierce hug after he had nodded reluctantly.

Heaven help them if the guerrillas set fire to the house, she
thought. Though the others could escape through the cellar door, she
would have to assist her father down the long flight of stairs,
supporting his weight as best she could. It would be a slow, pain-
staking process, and she seriously doubted they could reach safety
before the burning structure fell in on them. With luck, perhaps
Charlie and his men could prevent the riders from getting close
enough to toss their burning torches on top of the roof.

Trying to feel reassured by this slim chance, Kitty hurried to the
study and, standing on tiptoe, took down a rifle from a wall rack.
Checking to see that it was loaded, she returned to the hall and was
about to proceed to the front parlor to extinguish the lamps when she
heard a succession of shots being exchanged near the front veranda.

The raiders were circling the house now, and the ear-splitting
combination of thundering hoofbeats and gunfire made it impossible
for Kitty to determine what was happening. She knew Charlie had
stationed two of their men on the porch to protect the house's main
entrance, which explained the shots coming from that direction. Had
they succeeded in warding off the attackers, she wondered frantically, or had they been overpowered, perhaps killed?

Soon it became apparent that the guerrillas were trying to break
down the front door. The question was, how many would confront
her once the door was knocked off its hinges? Crouching beside the
curving staircase, Kitty slowly raised the rifle and braced it against
her shoulder, aiming the barrel directly at the center of the front
door. As it shuddered, then splintered, she cocked the hammer and
waited. Seconds later it flew open with a loud crash. Seeing two
rough-looking men come through the entrance, she aimed at the one
in front and pulled the trigger. Relief flooded through her when she
saw him clutch at his stomach, then fall face forward. Before she
could reload, the second guerrilla was upon her, swearing profanely
as he tried to wrench the rifle from her. For several seconds, Kitty
pitted her strength against his, hanging on to the rifle for all she was
worth while they scuffled around in a circle. Just when she felt she

could struggle no longer, a shot rang out, and the man stiffened, then thudded to the floor. Surprised, Kitty stared down at him for a moment, then glanced up at Dave just as he yelled out a warning.

"Behind you!"

Before Dave could get off a shot, a loud report sounded from the doorway. With a stunned look, he grabbed his chest. A scream was torn from Kitty's lips as she whirled to see a third guerrilla rushing her, but even as she lifted the barrel of the rifle, it was yanked from her hands, and she was knocked to the floor. With an evil grin, the scurvy man tossed the rifle aside, holstering his own gun and leering down at her. Kitty instinctively knew his intent. Rape!

Panting from exertion, she tried to roll away from him, but in a split second he had straddled her, imprisoning her beneath his considerable weight. A feeling of rage washed over her, lending her strength while she struggled against him and finally managed to rake her nails down the side of his face. With a muttered oath he backhanded her, the force of the blow snapping her head sideways and almost rendering her senseless.

Weak with dizziness, Kitty whimpered when he roughly fondled her breasts and slowly lowered his head. The foul smell of his breath fanned her face, causing nausea to well up in her throat as the room seemed to tilt and recede. Semiconscious, she dimly heard the roar of a gun and felt the man sagging against her, weighing her down, down . . . And then Bret was kneeling beside her, holding her in his arms. Her mind slowly cleared, as did her vision, and she saw the unmistakable concern in his searching eyes.

"Are you all right?" he asked hoarsely.

Kitty nodded but could not speak. With a choked sob, she buried her face against his chest and cried for several minutes, until finally he gently lifted her chin with his forefinger.

"Look at me, Kitty," he commanded softly. "You're sure you're not hurt? You . . . you weren't molested?"

"No, I'm not hurt, but thank heaven you arrived when you did." Suddenly remembering her father, she stiffened in his arms. "Pa! Pa's been shot!" she cried, pulling away from him.

Bret helped her to stand, and together they raced up the stairs. Dave was lying near the banister, and for a moment Kitty feared he was already dead. Kneeling beside Bret, she watched him cradle Dave in his arms, relief washing over her when she saw his eyelids flicker, then open.

"Oh, Pa, thank God you're alive!" she exclaimed, taking hold of his hand.

"You . . . you all right?" he whispered weakly.

Kitty nodded and quickly brushed a tear from her cheek. "Yes, I'm fine. Bret got here just in time," she informed him with a tremulous smile.

A peculiar noise sounded in Dave's chest, a rasping noise that Kitty had heard in the hospitals during the siege. She had often heard it referred to as a "death rattle," but she refused to associate the term with her father now. Pa isn't dying, she thought frantically, he can't be! Yet even as she tried to believe this, her mind told her differently. Realizing that his breathing was becoming more labored with each passing second, she glanced at Bret.

"I'll go downstairs and send someone for the doctor," she said, pausing when she felt Dave tug weakly at her hand.

"No, don't go," he gasped.

"But, Pa, you need a doctor."

"All I need is you now. You and Bret," he panted, pausing briefly to catch his breath. "Forget the past, Kitty . . . Promise me . . ."

"Yes, Pa, I promise," she answered in a choked voice, knowing he was referring to her past differences with Bret.

He smiled faintly and gave her hand an affectionate squeeze, then looked away, lifting his gaze to Bret's troubled face. "You've been like a son to me," he whispered.

"And you, like a father to me," came the husky reply.

"Kitty thinks you were a spy. Tell her the truth—before it's too late," he implored, struggling for breath. "Take care of her."

"I will, Dave. *Always,*" he promised solemnly.

Dave nodded and wearily closed his eyes. Seeing his pallor and sensing the end was near, Kitty clutched Bret's arm with her free hand, seeking reassurance that never came. With a sob, she rested her head against his shoulder, completely unaware that Mammy Lou had come to stand behind her, tears streaming down her face.

As the seconds ticked by and Dave's breathing became noticeably fainter, Kitty began fearing each breath would be his last. Suddenly his eyes opened wide and, staring beyond them, his face lit up in a smile of recognition. With surprising strength, he freed his hand from Kitty's and extended his arm, as if reaching for some intangible object.

"Jody!" he whispered. Then, with a shuddering sigh, he slumped lifelessly against Bret's chest, his eyes closing for the last time.

Stunned, Kitty watched as Bret slowly released Dave and lowered him to the floor. Even then she could not accept the fact that her father was dead. Tears rolled down her cheeks as she grabbed his limp arm, willing him to move, to show some sign of life.

"Oh, Pa, don't leave me," she cried. "Please, please don't leave me!"

The lack of response forced reality upon her, and she began to tremble. As if in a dream, she felt Bret lifting her to her feet, pulling her to him. Glancing up at him, she recognized the sorrow in his eyes and knew he shared her grief.

"He's gone," she whispered brokenly.

"Yes, he's gone."

Her pain increased while Mammy Lou knelt beside her father and, crying softly, folded his hands, then brushed a stray lock of hair from his wrinkled brow. She did not resist when Bret lifted her in his arms and carried her down the long corridor. But after he gently deposited her on the bed, she took hold of his hand.

"Don't go," she pleaded. "I . . . I need you."

Bret nodded and, seating himself beside her on the bed, extracted a handkerchief from his coat. Tenderly wiping the tears from her pale cheeks, he spoke to her, his voice husky.

"I'll always be near, Kitty—whenever you need me." Pale moonlight sifted through the half-closed shutters, faintly illuminating the room. Seeing the weariness in her drawn face, he stroked the damp tendrils of hair from her forehead. "You've been through a lot, little one. Try to rest now," he murmured.

The touch of his hand was somehow comforting, and within minutes Kitty gradually relaxed. As her eyelids grew heavy and finally closed, she was dimly aware of Lemme's sorrowful voice floating to her from the back porch, his words rising in song above the soft humming of other Negroes who, like himself, mourned the loss of a man they had loved and trusted.

Kitty stood at her bedroom window and watched while a handful of friends and neighbors solemnly made their way toward the family cemetery. Two nights had passed since her father's death, miserable hours for Kitty, who until now had refused to leave her room. She needed time to adjust to her loss, to learn to cope with it, but her efforts so far had failed miserably. Her every waking moment was filled with memories of her father. Bittersweet memories that merely increased her pain.

Now, the time was at hand that she had dreaded the most, for within the hour her father would be buried. Without troubling her with the details, Bret had made the necessary arrangements, setting the day and contacting their preacher. He had also telegraphed the tragic news to Tad and Dede, who had returned home that morning.

Both had been prostrate with grief when they had met with her in her room just before noon. Completely distraught, Dede had broken down in tears, looking almost faint as Tad had led her from the room. Kitty had not seen her brother since then, nor had she wanted to talk further with him; not yet. She was beyond giving or receiving comfort.

A light tap sounded at the door, followed by the familiar sound of Doshe's voice. "Miz Kitty, hit's almos' time tuh start fo' de cem'tery. De rest ob de fam'ly's waitin' fo' you on de porch. Lou's dun tole 'em not tuh close de coffin 'til you has uh chance to pay yo' las' respecks. Is you comin', now?"

"Yes, I'll be down directly."

Steeling herself for the ordeal, Kitty made her way slowly down the curving staircase and walked over to where Mammy Lou was waiting for her just outside the parlor door. As if sensing her mistress's reluctance to go further, she gently led Kitty into the room and guided her over to the casket.

"Come on, chile, dey ain' nuttin' fo' you tuh be 'fraid ob. Why, Mist' Dave luks so nat'ral lyin' dere, hit's jes' lak he wuz sleepin' almos'," Mammy Lou tried to assure her, sniffing and dabbing the tears from her eyes with the corner of her apron. Seeing Kitty's grief-stricken face, she shook her turbaned head and backed away, relieved to see Bret quietly entering the room. "Ah'll be in de hall, ef you needs me."

Kitty nodded and continued to stare down at the man in the coffin, bewilderment filling her eyes as she studied her father's immobile features. Mammy Lou had said he looked natural, but he didn't. Not to her. The traits she had always found so endearing in him, his warmth and gentleness, were missing, and now he seemed a stranger to her.

The unfamiliar feeling greatly disturbed and confused her, adding to her misery. How could she experience such estrangement when she had loved him so dearly? How could she not know him, when she had known him so well? Utterly bereft, she sank to her knees.

"Oh, Pa, why did you have to die? How can I possibly go on without you? I—I miss you so," she cried softly, her head bowed.

She did not resist when Bret gently lifted her to her feet, nor was she surprised by his presence, which seemed only natural. Wasn't he always at hand when she needed him? She allowed him to brush the tears from her cheeks with his handkerchief, a choked sob escaping her lips when his arms enfolded her a moment later.

"Mammy Lou said he looks the same, but he doesn't. Not to me," she said brokenly. "I recognize his face, yet he seems so different and . . . and I don't understand why. We were always so close, but now it's as though I don't even know him. I don't feel that closeness anymore, Bret. Why?"

"Kitty, tell me something. Since you moved out of your house on Cherry Street, does it still seem like home to you?"

"No, of course not."

"Why? It's still the same house, isn't it?"

"Of course, it is, but we don't live there anymore. No one does. It's just an empty shell, now."

"Exactly—which is my point. That's not Dave Devan in that casket, Kitty. It's only an empty shell. The man you loved, his spirit, hasn't ceased to exist. He's just in another place."

Hope flickered as she considered his words. "Do you really believe that?" she asked.

"I know it. Oh, I can't prove it. No one can. You either believe in God or you don't, but if you believe, you know death is not the end, but the beginning. You also know there *has* to be something beyond this life, something far greater than any human is capable of understanding."

His sincerity strengthened her, and her anguish lessened as she stared down at her father's remains. Heartache persisted, yet her despair diminished as she recalled Dave's last moments, when he had called her mother's name and stretched out his hand as though reaching for some invisible object. Then, she had thought he was delirious, but now she wasn't so sure. A strange serenity filled her as she touched Dave's withered hand for the last time.

Moments later she stood aside as Charlie and a few of her father's friends carried the casket outside. Taking hold of Bret's arm, she followed the procession to the family cemetery, where some of their people were softly singing in the background:

> *Swing low, sweet chariot,*
> *Coming for to carry me home . . .*

Her lips curved in a slight smile. If heaven existed, as surely it must, she would someday see her father again—in another time, another place.

Chapter 33

Summer green faded into an autumn glow as leaves turned amber and tall spikes of goldenrod dotted the countryside. Southerners still clung to dreams of victory, but as October rolled into November, their dreams began to disintegrate. Having taken Atlanta in September, Sherman waited until the week after Lincoln's reelection, then started his march to the sea. It was a campaign that heaped destruction on Southerners from Atlanta to Savannah and dealt a crippling blow to Confederate morale. By early December news of his horrendous actions in Georgia had spread throughout the South, causing even the most stout-hearted to begin having serious doubts about the Confederacy's ability to win the war. If Sherman could march his army through the South's very heartland, was any hope left?

Alarmed by the grim news, Kitty was equally distressed with the state of affairs at Belle Glen. The guerrillas had destroyed their cotton crop, and unless she asked Bret for another loan, they could not possibly plant again in the spring. Tad shared her concern but could offer no solution. Like Kitty, he was reluctant to turn to Bret for another loan, particularly since there was no guarantee that next year's crop would be a good one. After discussing the situation at length, they agreed their only alternative was to sell at least one-fourth of their land. Once the decision was made, Tad rode into town and made arrangements for the property to be listed in the weekly newspaper.

On the day the ad was to appear, Charlie made a trip into town for supplies and brought back a copy of the paper. Tad solemnly read their advertisement aloud, then handed the newspaper to Kitty, who retreated to the study to lick her wounds. For more than fifty years her family had owned this land. Her father had worked hard to purchase additional acreage to add to her grandfather Alan's original tract, eventually making Belle Glen one of the largest and finest plantations in Mississippi. Now, she and Tad were trying to sell a part of their heritage. It's wrong, she thought dismally, but what else can we do?

Her mind snapped back to the present when the study door unexpectedly flew open and Bret strode into the room, a rolled-up copy of the newspaper clenched in one hand. His expression was grim as he flopped the paper down in front of her. Resting his large fists on the desk, he glared down at her.

"Just what in heaven's name do you think you're doing?" he demanded.

Alarmed by his anger, Kitty was nevertheless determined not to be intimidated by him. With a defiant lift of her chin, she shot him a disparaging look that belied her misgivings.

"Since you've seen the listing, I should think the answer is obvious," she answered. "We're trying to sell some land."

"I can see that. What I want to know is why."

"Because we need the money, and there's no other way for us to get it. How else can we plant in the spring?"

"You know damn well I'm willing to back you."

With a tired sigh, Kitty got up and walked over to the window. "Yes, I know you are, but I can't keep asking you for handouts. I won't. Even Tad agrees that it's unfair to you and . . . and degrading for us. Don't you see—if we sell the land, not only will we have money for the spring planting, but we can return the money you loaned us this year and, eventually, pay off the mortgage you hold on Belle Glen."

"To hell with the mortgage!" he snapped, turning her to face him. "You know damn well I'm not going to foreclose."

"Then all the more reason for us to sell. Do you think I enjoy accepting your charity?"

His jaw tightened when he saw the stubborn determination in her upturned face. This time it was he who turned away and gazed out the window.

"I've never thought of it as charity. Belle Glen is the only home I've ever known. I know every field, every acre, like the back of my hand. Once, it was a prospering plantation, the finest in the county.

It can be again, but not if you start selling it off piece by piece. Since Tad was his stepson, Dave left all this to you. He worked hard to make it what it is. Don't ruin it, Kitty. Don't destroy his dream.''

Tears misted her vision as she stood beside him and, following his gaze, witnessed the acres of fallow land that stretched as far as the eye could see. The sight caused her to ache deep inside, and her voice quavered slightly when she answered him.

''Do you think I want to sell?'' she whispered. ''It breaks my heart to part with an inch of this land, but there's no other way.''

''There *is* another way, and you know it,'' he said, turning to face her.

''What? Let you go on footing the bills for me?''

''Why shouldn't I, if it means protecting our son's heritage? Someday Belle Glen will belong to him—if there's anything left.''

''Of course there'll be something left. You know I'd never sell all of it.''

''Maybe not willingly, but unless this place is run more efficiently, there may come a day when you have no choice.''

His was not a pessimistic viewpoint; it was, in fact, a possibility that had already occurred to Kitty. Fear flitted briefly across her face, then was replaced by a look of obstinacy.

''Belle Glen will not be sold. I'll do anything, anything at all, to prevent that from happening,'' she vowed.

Watching her, Bret knew he had every intention of using her precarious financial situation to his own advantage. He wanted her as he had never wanted another woman, and he was tired of waiting for her to come to her senses and agree to marry him. Remembering how she had flatly refused his last proposal, he decided to use a slightly different approach—one she would find difficult to refuse. He did not intend to be rejected again.

Cupping her chin in his hand, he forced her to meet his penetrating gaze. ''Do you mean that?'' he asked.

''Yes!''

''Then marry me. As your husband, I'd be in a better position to help you, to protect you and the boy. Give me my son, and I'll see to it that Belle Glen prospers again. You have my word on it.''

Kitty could hardly believe her ears. What callousness! It was as though she were some kind of an object he could buy!

Hurt that he had not even said he loved her, she was nevertheless forced to seriously consider his offer. There seemed to be no other alternative. Her expression was petulant when, after a slight hesitation, she said, "I see. What you're really suggesting is a business arrangement—a marriage of convenience." Even as she said it, she hoped he would deny it.

"Such marriages are not unusual, Kitty, nor are they totally without satisfaction. In our case, I think the advantages would outweigh the disadvantages, since we happen to have a mutual interest in our son's future." Seeing her uncertainty, he gave her a wry smile. "Who knows—you might actually enjoy being married to me."

"That, I seriously doubt," she retorted. "Most of the time, I don't even trust you."

Nettled by her answer, Bret nevertheless hid his irritation beneath a mocking façade. "Be that as it may, you can't deny there's a certain attraction between us. As I recall, we've had a few . . . er, intimate moments you quite enjoyed!"

"That's in the past. If I agree to marry you, it will be under one condition."

"Which is?"

Kitty hesitated, feeling unsure of what she actually did want. The condition she was about to demand was, in truth, totally unappealing to her, and she doubted Bret was going to agree to it. Still, she was hurt by the callous manner in which he had proposed, and the fact remained that she had never forgiven him for being a traitor.

With a defiant lift of her chin, she met his inquisitive look. "I want your promise that it will be a marriage in name only."

Surprise flitted across his face but was quickly masked as he studied her upturned face.

"You realize what you're suggesting?"

"Perfectly. I'll marry you, but only if you'll agree to respect my privacy."

Anger and frustration filled him, yet he gave no sign of it, other than a slight tensing of his jaw. "Very well. I'll forego my marital rights—provided you're willing to forego yours," he replied with only a trace of sarcasm.

"Mine?"

"Yes, yours. Celibacy has never appealed to me. my dear, so don't complain if I occasionally satisfy my needs elsewhere. You'll have only yourself to blame."

"I don't care where you satisfy your vile needs, as long as it's not with me!"

"Believe me, your virtue will be quite safe," he wryly assured her. "Unless, of course, you change your mind. And now that we've disposed of that matter, perhaps we can set the date. I rather like the idea of being married on the first of January. The beginning of a new year—and a new life."

"That's entirely too soon. In case you've forgotten, I'm still in mourning."

"You know Dave never cared for traditional mourning."

"Maybe he didn't, but others do. It's only a little more than three months since Pa died. Why, if we get married this soon, everyone in town will be talking about us. They'll all think we *had* to get married."

"And time will prove them wrong. We'll survive the gossip, Kitty. Our friends will stick by us. The rest won't matter."

"I suppose not," she admitted. "But I still think January is too soon. Why, we won't even have time for a proper courtship."

Her belated sense of propriety amused him, causing a devilish gleam to appear in his emerald eyes. "It's a little late for that, don't you think?" He chuckled. "Besides, courtship, my love, is merely a man pursuing a woman until she catches him. Having received my proposal, you can rest assured that I have, indeed, been caught."

Angered by his arrogant conceit, Kitty fumed inwardly, but before she could think of a scathing reply, she was hauled into his powerful arms and soundly kissed. Her resistance lasted only a moment before she began to respond, her pride and anger forgotten as his lips began moving sensuously against hers, rekindling embers of desire. Intense yearning was suddenly released, blotting all else from her mind as her lips parted beneath his and she pressed closer to him, her passion increasing as she felt the hard planes of his masculine body surging against her. It was, therefore, something of a shock when he unexpectedly released her seconds later. Bemused, she glanced up at him, wincing inwardly when she saw the sardonic expression on his face.

"Frankly, Kitten, I don't think you know what the hell you do want!" he remarked dryly, then turned to go.

Confused and embarrassed, Kitty said nothing as he strode from the room. Nor did she move until she heard the front door close behind him. Only then did she come to her senses and vent her frustration.

"Damn you, Bret O'Rourke! I won't marry you—I won't!" she whispered vehemently. Yet she knew the words were meaningless. She could fight him until the end of time, but she'd never stop loving him.

Their wedding was held at Belle Glen on the first day of January, but since the family was still officially in mourning, only a few friends were invited to attend the ceremony. The reception that followed was simple and brief. After a few toasts were made, Bret bundled Kitty into his carriage and started for Vicksburg, where they would spend their wedding night in his newly constructed home.

The ride was made mostly in silence, with neither of them feeling much inclined to talk. It was difficult for Kitty to realize they were actually married. She did not feel like a bride, and she was certain she did not look like one. Instead of wearing white, the symbol of virginity, she wore a velvet gown of deep blue, simply designed with a modest sweetheart neckline and long pointed sleeves.

The gown was undeniably becoming, and she was glad Bret had refused to let her continue wearing mourning clothes after they had become engaged. She would have detested being married in black. People might talk, but let them. At least she would have the pleasure of knowing she did not look like an ole crow, and were he alive, she knew her father would have approved.

By the time they reached town, it was near dusk. The streets were almost deserted, and for the first time that day, Kitty began to relax and look forward to reaching her new home. She had seen it just once, long before its completion, and she had not the faintest idea what to expect.

The location, however, had immediately appealed to her, since it was on the outskirts of town and near the Mississippi River, which could easily be seen from the upper balcony. For this reason she had suggested they name the house "Riverview," and Bret had readily agreed.

When the carriage halted in front of a white picket fence, Kitty's eyes danced with surprised pleasure. The three-storied house was even lovelier than she had anticipated. Twilight cast a rosy hue to the redbrick exterior and darkened the long, green shutters at each window. By contrast, the four round columns that supported both upper and lower verandas appeared stark white against the fading light.

"Oh, Bret, it's lovely," she cried as, arm in arm, they strolled up the long walk that was bordered with neatly trimmed box hedges. Taking note of the spacious front lawn, which was attractively dotted with trees and shrubbery, she asked if some were crepe myrtle.

"Yes, I had them transplanted here a couple of months ago, along with some dogwood and wisteria. The shrubs in front of the veranda are gardenias, camellias, and holly bushes," he said, pointing them out to her when they reached the wide porch steps. "Oh, and there's a rose garden in back."

"A rose garden!" she exclaimed, her eyes sparkling with undisguised delight. "It seems you've thought of everything. I can hardly wait until it all blooms this spring."

"Ah, but the best is yet to come. You've still to see what's inside." He grinned and opened the wide front door.

Without warning, Kitty was scooped up in his arms, carried over the threshold, and gently deposited on her feet just inside the wide foyer.

"Welcome home, Mrs. O'Rourke. Welcome to Riverview," Bret murmured as his arm encircled her waist.

The warmth of his deep voice stirred her, and she was too filled with emotion to speak for a moment. It was, therefore, something of a relief when she spied a middle-aged Negress standing in the dining room door. Slightly behind the smiling woman was a mulatto girl, whom Kitty judged to be in her middle teens.

"My dear, this is Liza and her daughter, Artie," Bret informed her. Directing his next remark at the servants, he said, "This is your new mistress, Miss Kitty."

"Lawsy me, Mist' Bret, you sho' dun yo'sef fine." Liza beamed. "We's moughty proud tuh be wurkin' fo' you, Miz Kitty. Ain' dat so, Artie?"

The younger girl nodded with a shy smile, which Kitty instantly returned. "Thank you, Liza. I'm very pleased Mister Bret hired you. I know both of you will be a big help to Mammy Lou, particularly when it comes to the housework and minding Scotty."

"Yas'm, we's sho' gwine tuh try, an' don' you fret none 'bout us gittin' 'long wid yo' mammy. We's gwine tuh git 'long jes' fine,"

Liza assured her enthusiastically. "Now, if'n y'all 'scuse us, we'll git on back tuh de kitchen an' finish fixin' supper."

After the pair departed, Kitty turned and smiled at Bret. "I like them, Bret, especially Liza. I think they'll get along with Mammy Lou, providing they can put up with her bossiness."

"I don't think that will be a problem. Both understand Mammy Lou will be in charge of the household, just as she was at Belle Glen. I've already warned them that her bark is worse than her bite."

"Well, I hope Mammy Lou won't be too high-handed with them. You know how she is. Do they know Gus is coming, too?"

"Yes, I explained he'll tend to the carriage, stable, and lawn. I've had separate quarters prepared for Gus and Terry Dermott over the carriage house. Terry has already moved in."

"I still don't see why you didn't let Mammy Lou, Gus, and Scotty come with us."

"I believe it's customary for newlyweds to enjoy a certain amount of privacy on their wedding night," he remarked wryly.

Her happiness suddenly faded, and frowning slightly, she shot him a wary look. "Under the circumstances, that seems unnecessary. We made a bargain, or have you forgotten?"

"No, I haven't forgotten, nor do I intend to go back on my word. I have no desire to bed an unwilling woman, not even my wife, so you can relax. And now that we've laid that problem to rest, perhaps you'd like to see the rest of the house before supper."

"Yes, I'd love to," Kitty murmured, somehow disappointed by his reassurance.

Moments later her spirits lifted as he guided her into a huge double parlor that had been tastefully furnished with rosewood furniture, French-crystal chandeliers, and exquisite fireplaces with mantels of Italian marble. White walls enhanced the beauty of peach brocade draperies, which, suspended from gilded cornices, matched the silk damask sofas and chairs and blended becomingly with the peach-and-gold floral carpet.

The dining room, library, and ballroom were equally elegant, and by the time Kitty reached the second floor, she was almost speechless with excitement. She had suspected the house would be attractive, but she had never expected to find such grandeur. Bret had spared no expense in building Riverview, she decided, realizing that this discovery should not have come as a surprise. Despite his shortcomings, which she had often enumerated, he was certainly no skinflint!

There were six bedrooms on the second floor and a large sleeping porch. Scotty's bedroom had been stocked with every conceivable toy a child could want, and behind the nursery was Mammy Lou's room. Liza and Artie were to sleep in the servants' quarters on the third floor, rather than over the stables. Kitty agreed that this arrangement would be more convenient for everybody, and she was particularly pleased that Mammy Lou would not have to climb a third flight of stairs to get to her room.

After Kitty had seen all the other rooms, Bret finally got around to showing her the bedroom that was to be hers, situated at the front of the house and a corridor's length from the nursery. The room was femininely decorated in white and blue, daintily flowered wallpaper perfectly matching the blue satin trim on the frilly canopy bed and dressing table. A large double wardrobe with mirrored doors was arranged against one wall, and a small rocker, upholstered in blue velvet, had been placed near the marble bedside table.

With feminine curiosity, Kitty walked slowly around the room, commenting first on one thing and then another before coming to a halt in front of the window. Parting the lace curtains, she looked toward the river.

"The view is lovely from here," she said as he came to stand beside her.

"I thought you'd like it. My room is just down the hall. Would you care to see it?"

"Yes, of course," Kitty replied, curious to know what kind of decor he had chosen for his own living quarters.

As soon as she stepped inside the room, she was favorably impressed with the wine-and-gold color scheme, which provided a perfect foil for the heavy oak furnishings. A large bed was centered on the far wall, its wine tester matching the brocaded draperies at the windows and blending well with the intricately designed rug. The decor was masculine, well suited to the owner's personality.

Again, Kitty complimented his taste, noting his unmistakable look of pleasure when she voiced her approval. It seemed he valued her opinion on such matters more than she had realized.

As Bret escorted her down the long flight of stairs, the tinkling of a bell sounded from the dining room, informing them that supper was ready. To her surprise Kitty realized she was hungry, but then

she remembered she'd been too nervous to eat earlier in the day.
After Bret had seated her next to his place at the head of the long
banquet table, Kitty appreciatively noticed the exquisite silverware
and Sèvres china. She was about to comment on them when Liza
and Artie began serving; then all else fled from her mind. The meal
was an epicurean delight: small quail browned to a golden crisp and
a varied assortment of vegetables seasoned to perfection. It occurred
to Kitty that Mammy Lou would have to put forth her best to outdo
Liza in the kitchen.

Conversation flowed congenially between them while they ate,
and after drinking several glasses of wine, Kitty was not only totally
relaxed, but also slightly giddy. Only when they adjourned to the
parlor did her apprehension return. As if sensing her renewed uneasiness, Bret offered her another glass of wine, but this time she
refused. She was not sure what was in store for her later, yet she felt
instinctively she had best regain her equilibrium before it was time
to retire.

To put her at ease, Bret casually mentioned the wedding ceremony and reception. "Everything went smoothly, don't you agree?"

"Yes, it did. Of course, Aunt Phoebe cried all the way through
the ceremony, but that was to be expected. Actually, I think she was
delighted over our marriage."

"I hope so," he replied, sipping brandy and studying her with an
appreciative eye. "Incidentally, I don't think I've mentioned how
lovely you look in that gown. You make a beautiful bride."

"Thank you," she murmured, discomfited by his scrutiny. "Everyone certainly seemed to enjoy the reception, especially the spiked
punch. I do believe Judge Crane was about three sheets to the
wind!"

"So I noticed," Bret answered, lighting a cheroot.

"I swear I don't know who was the most upset with him, his wife
or Miss Flora. If looks could have killed, he'd have been dead on
the spot!" Kitty giggled softly. "And to think I always believed the
judge was a teetotaler."

"Few men are strict teetotalers, my dear, at least not in this day
and time. Perhaps the judge was merely doing what a lot of Southerners are doing—trying to forget the war."

Kitty's amusement faded. "I suppose so," she agreed. "We've
all felt down this week, ever since we heard about Sherman's march
into Savannah three days before Christmas. Is it true what they're

saying, that his troops have cut a wide path of destruction all the way from Atlanta to Savannah?''

"Probably, but I daresay bummers did far more looting and burning than the Federals.''

"Bummers?''

"Yes, runaway slaves and deserters from both sides who are straggling behind Sherman's army and brutally reaping the rewards. Unless I miss my guess, these parasites are creating more havoc in Georgia than the Yankees.''

"But can't Sherman control them?'' she gasped. "Surely even he doesn't condone lawlessness.''

"I doubt Cump could control them even if he wanted to, which he probably doesn't. It's to his advantage to let them alone, seeing as how they're helping him to heap destruction on Georgia. What better way to lower morale and make Georgians howl?''

"What a terrible thing to say!'' Kitty exclaimed. "But, of course, I keep forgetting General Sherman is a friend of yours.''

"He may be a friend, but that doesn't mean I approve of his actions.''

"And don't you?''

Bret's mouth quirked into an enigmatic smile as he walked over to her. "Would you believe me if I said I didn't?''

Kitty also rose, hesitating only briefly before answering him. "No, I don't think I would,'' she replied.

"Then I won't waste my breath trying to convince you otherwise.'' Extracting a gold watch from his vest pocket, he glanced down at it. "It's getting late, and I imagine you're tired. I suggest we call it a day.''

Kitty accepted his proffered arm and allowed him to lead her from the parlor. Neither spoke as they mounted the long flight of stairs, and when they proceeded down the long corridor and the silence persisted, her previous anxieties returned.

Did Bret actually intend to keep his promise and leave her alone tonight? she wondered. If so, was this what she really wanted? Confused by conflicting emotions and, despite Bret's earlier assurance, uncertain of his intentions, she suddenly felt very vulnerable.

Her nerves were frayed by the time they reached her bedroom, and she almost jumped when Bret thrust open the door and unceremoniously ushered her over the threshold. Leaving her in the doorway, he walked over to the bedside table and turned up the wick on the lamp, then straightened to face her. The flickering light dimly illuminated his features, revealing the naked desire in his eyes for a split second before his expression became shuttered.

"I took the liberty of having Artie unpack your valise earlier. Your other clothes, of course, will arrive tomorrow," he informed her calmly.

Not knowing what to say, she merely looked at him while he continued. "If you need anything, just ring for the servants. The cord is by the bed. Perhaps you'd like Liza to help you undress?"

"No, that won't be necessary. I believe I can manage," Kitty replied in a small voice, not at all willing for the servants to discover the strange circumstances of their wedding night.

"Then if there's nothing else, I'll bid you good night," he said, raising her hand to his lips.

Their eyes locked as his mouth lightly brushed over her fingers, reminding her of other times when they had been on far more intimate terms. As if motivated by an unseen force, she reached up and shyly touched the strong line of his jaw, too befuddled by his nearness to consider the consequences. Excitement rippled through her when he pulled her roughly to him, crushing her against his muscular chest. With deliberate slowness, his head descended until his mouth hovered less than an inch above her own.

"I'll forgo my husbandly right," he muttered angrily, "but this is one thing, by God, I won't be denied!"

The savagery of his kiss took her by surprise, causing her to tense, then tremble with an intense desire that could no longer be suppressed. Instinctively aware of her submission, Bret relaxed his hold, and his mouth gradually gentled, moving sensuously over her parted lips and evoking an immediate response. The unexpected touch of his hand on her breasts caused her senses to reel, unleashing a dam of passion that made her whole being ache with longing while she hungrily returned his kiss. Her mounting need for him was sweet torment, and with an impatient moan she pressed closer to him, splaying her hands over his broad chest in a silent appeal for fulfillment as she waited for him to carry her to bed. Instead, his head slowly lifted, and he released her. Startled, her eyes flew open, and she stared at him with undisguised bewilderment.

"That, my sweet, was a mere sample," he remarked sardonically, "but when you're finished playing the virtuous madam, just let me know. Then we'll get down to the serious aspects of marriage!"

Filled with rage, Kitty clenched her fists to keep from hitting him. "You—you dirty, low-down skunk," she sputtered, "leading me on just so you could laugh at me and make me feel like some kind of a cheap harlot! Well, let me tell you one thing—every dog has its day, and I fully intend to have mine. No matter how long it takes, someday I'll personally see to it you get your just desserts!"

Arching one brow, he returned her hostile glare with a look of devilment. "That, dear wife, is precisely what I'd like—my *just* desserts," he answered mockingly, sauntering over to the door. "Incidentally, you can stop feeling like a harlot. You haven't the experience!" And on that stinging note, he exited, leaving her to her own fury.

Chapter 34

"Go 'way," Kitty groaned, pulling the eiderdown comforter half-over her face as Mammy Lou shook her for a second time.

"Come on, chile, wake up. Mist' Bret's waitin' on you downstairs, an' you knows how dat man hates to wait."

Kitty did indeed, for during the short month they had been married, he had impatiently hurried her to every function they had attended, even church. She often thought he derived perverse delight in seeing her scurrying around in a futile attempt to be ready on time, though there was no doubt that he really disliked being late.

"Then he shouldn't have married me," she muttered sleepily, still not budging. "What time is it?"

Mammy Lou glanced at the clock on the mantel and, seeing it was only eight o'clock, wisely sidestepped the question. "Time tuh rise an' shine," she said, adding shrewdly, "If'n you's gwine tuh git out in all dat snow."

Kitty's eyes flew open, then narrowed suspiciously. "You're just saying that to make me get up," she accused. "It's been years since we had a good snow."

"Hmph, you sho' gots one now, but don' take mah word fo' hit. Git up an' see fo' yo'sef."

Curious, though not at all convinced, Kitty threw back the covers and made her way over to the window. She parted the draperies and looked dubiously outside. Her scowl faded as soon as she saw that the entire countryside was blanketed in white.

"Good heavens—it did snow!" she exclaimed.

"Sho' did. Snowed all night. Now, you jes' git dressed an' hur'hy downstairs, so's Mist' Bret kin show you his su'prize."

"What surprise?"

"De one he gots fo' you an' de boy." Mammy Lou grinned. "He's been wurkin' on't wid Gus an' Mist' Terry eber since day-break, an' he wants you tuh cum on down an' see."

"Well, what on earth is it?" Kitty asked impatiently, shrugging out of her nightgown and stepping into the pantalets that, along with her other clothes, had just been laid on the bed.

"Ah knows, but Ah ain' tellin'. You jes' git on downstairs, an' den you'll find out," Mammy Lou replied as she laced up Kitty's corset.

Knowing it would be useless to question Mammy Lou further, Kitty fell silent as layers of petticoats were lowered over her head, followed by a slate-blue gown of soft cashmere. Next came the black boots, trimmed in silver-gray fur that matched her muff and the fur-rimmed hood of her dark blue cloak. It was difficult for her to keep still while Mammy Lou arranged her hair, for she was eager to see the surprise, romp in the fresh snow, and most of all—be with Bret.

Since their marriage, Bret had taken her demand for privacy literally, leaving her to her own devices and spending most of his free time with Scotty. It seemed they were never alone, except at mealtimes, and this was only because their son was still too young to join them in the dining room. Invariably Scotty was allowed to join them in the parlor afterward, but just as soon as the child's bedtime arrived, Bret always retreated to his study or rode off in the carriage. Whether he went back to the warehouse to work late or visited Dixie's establishment, Kitty never knew. She was too proud to ask.

At best, her relationship with Bret was strained. When others were present, they were forced to masquerade as a devoted couple for the sake of appearances. In private, however, there was little rapport between them, despite the fact that Bret was always thought-ful of her every need. He was courteous, yet impersonal, displaying an aloofness that baffled her. It was as though he were completely indifferent to her, a possibility that worried her to no little extent.

There were times when she regretted the restrictions she had placed on their marriage, but she was not about to back down from her position. She wanted more than his lust. She wanted his love, a feeling he had never expressed in words. Until he did, she had no intention of granting him *any* husbandly rights, for passion without love had become meaningless to her. Never once had it occurred to her that his past actions had spoken far louder than words, and as a result their relationship remained at an impasse.

Her one comfort was that Scotty was happy and had adjusted easily to his new home. Too young to understand that legal steps were already being taken to adopt him, the boy readily accepted the fact that Bret was his new daddy and his last name was now O'Rourke. There was no mistaking the mutual affection between father and son, and, witnessing their closeness, Kitty felt somewhat envious.

Now, a flickering of renewed hope welled up inside her as she descended the stairs and found Bret and Scotty waiting for her in the foyer. Catching the glimmer of admiration in Bret's eyes as he looked at her, she was thankful he had sought to include her in their outing. Today, at least, they would enjoy being a real family, sharing an infrequent camaraderie that most families simply took for granted. For Kitty, this rare companionship would be a welcome change, a real treat.

As she joined Bret in helping Scotty and Terry build a huge snowman, she was reminded of those few occasions in her youth when she, Bret, and Tad had romped for hours in the snow. As excited as a child, she listened with increased enjoyment to Scotty's squeals of delight while Bret and Terry took turns pulling him around the yard on the surprise Bret had brought—a new sled.

By the time they returned to the house for the noon meal, Kitty was frozen to the bone, but when Bret pulled her aside and offered to take her sledding after Scotty had been put down for a nap, she enthusiastically accepted. Looking forward to spending a whole afternoon alone with her husband, she eagerly rejoined Bret on the front lawn and was not surprised when he suggested taking the sled to a secluded bluff not far from the house.

Time flew as, forgetting past differences, they took turns sliding down the icy slope. The sled was long enough to accompany both of them if they sat upright, and after a while Bret suggested they ride double. Kitty welcomed his nearness when he seated himself behind her and reached for the steering rope. Excitement coursed through her as his arms circled her midriff, drawing her against his broad chest, and his strong legs molded against hers, pressing firmly into her thighs.

Filled with sensual pleasure, she dared not look at him for fear of exposing her arousal, and she was relieved when they shoved off and went zipping down the steep incline. As the sled picked up speed, her squeals of excitement intermingled with Bret's rumbling laughter, but it was not until they repeated the ride for a third time that she actually had cause for alarm. The sled had sped halfway down the hill when it suddenly veered to the right and struck a concealed hollow so forcefully that both riders catapulted into the snow. Over and over they rolled, finally landing in separate heaps at the foot of the precipitous embankment. Dazed and winded, Kitty was dimly aware that Bret was kneeling beside her and cradling her tenderly in his arms, but it was not until her vision cleared that she saw his haggard expression and heard the anxiety in his voice as he murmured her name.

"Are you hurt?" he asked, gently brushing the snow from her face with an unsteady hand.

"No, I'm all right," she whispered breathlessly, her eyes locking with his as his fingers stilled in her disheveled hair.

For seconds neither spoke, and then she felt his arm tightening around her, drawing her to him as he slowly lowered his head. His kiss was tender, filled with an expertise that immediately brought forth the desired response. Her pulse racing, Kitty clung to his broad shoulders while his lips moved languidly against hers, his tongue exploring the soft inner recess of her mouth.

Breathless moments passed, capturing them in a spell of sweet ecstasy, until, at last, Bret reluctantly put her from him and assisted her to her feet. No words were needed to express their feelings. It was as though their hearts and minds, their very souls, had been fused into one.

Kitty sensed that a turning point in their relationship had been reached, but knowing Bret as she did, she also realized she would have to make the first move toward a reconciliation. She had been the one to impose restrictions on their marriage, and she was going to have to remove them.

As they walked back to the house, arm in arm, she felt almost light-hearted. It was not until they reached the front door and Bret reminded her of Celia Collins's engagement party, which they were to attend tonight, that her happiness dissipated.

"I wish we didn't have to go. I've never cared for Celia, but even so, I thought she had better sense than to get engaged to a man who's old enough to be her father. I can't imagine why Mr. Collins has agreed to such a match.''

''I can,'' Bret replied wryly. ''Money. Sam Benson may not be young, but he is rich.''

''Celia has always gone hog wild spending money. Still, I should think Mr. Collins would be embarrassed to have a son-in-law who's older than he is.''

''In case you haven't noticed, there happens to be a shortage of eligible bachelors in town at the moment, discounting the Federals, of course. Ever since Lela Shelton ran off with that Yankee captain, I imagine many a doting papa has feared his daughter might do the same, including Henry.''

''I imagine so.'' Kitty sighed. ''But I still wish we didn't have to go. Maybe it will snow again and we can stay home.''

''Even if it does, we're still going to Celia's party. There is such a thing as etiquette, you know.''

''Etiquette, sir, is merely doing the little things you *have* to do that you don't really *want* to do!'' she replied saucily.

''Be that as it may, we're still going.'' He chuckled. ''Incidentally, the party begins at eight, so let's plan to leave here around seven.'' His mouth quirked into a wry smile. ''For once, try to be ready on time!''

Cocking her head, she shot him an impish look. ''Aren't I always?'' she quipped. Silently, however, she vowed to be prompt.

Yet as the appointed hour arrived, Kitty was running true to form, searching frantically for the long white gloves that had been laid out earlier but that now, apparently, were concealed beneath numerous fripperies scattered about the room. Hitching up her voluminous skirt, she went down on her hands and knees to look under the bed, where she immediately spied the lost items. Panting, she got to her feet and thrust her hands and forearms into the elegant gloves, extending them to Mammy Lou, who fastened the tiny pearl buttons at both wrists.

Ignoring the old woman's disapproving remarks about her tardiness, Kitty hastened to the floor-length mirror in the corner and surveyed her appearance, pleased with what she saw. The red velvet gown she wore was simply designed and most becoming, particularly in its off-the-shoulder décolletage, which Kitty had offset with a short strand of pearls. The only other adornment she wore was a dainty tiara of red velvet and seed pearls that held her long raven curls in place.

"Mis Kitty, hit ain' rat you pokin' along lak dis an' makin' Mist' Bret wait, jes' 'cause you laks tuh be late," Mammy Lou scolded.

"I don't like to be late," Kitty refuted, picking up her lace fan. "I just don't like to hurry."

"Hmph! You ain' neber tried hit. Hit ain' fittin', dat's whut. Mos' ladies lak tuh be early," she added, helping her mistress into a short fur cape.

"Well, I don't. Why should I be early? Then I'd just have to sit around and wait for everybody else to get there."

At that moment, Artie came scurrying into the room, a worried look on her face. "Mist' Bret dun sent me up heah tuh hur'hy you along, an' he sho' looks lak he's fit tuh be tied!"

Frowning, Mammy Lou shoved a fur muff into Kitty's hand. "You better git on downstairs befo' he cums up heah tuh git'cha. No sense rilin' him mo' den you already has."

"All right, I'm going, but this is the last time I intend to be rushed. If I've got to get in a nervous tizzy to go some place, I'd just as soon not go at all," Kitty muttered, sweeping past the two servants.

Bret was waiting for her at the foot of the stairs. When he glanced up and saw her gracefully descending, his displeased scowl was replaced with a look of unconcealed admiration. Relieved that her appearance pleased him, thus sparing her a lecture on promptness, she quickened her footsteps as she glided down to meet him. The breath caught in her throat when she noticed how extraordinarily handsome he looked in his black evening clothes. Many a wife would envy her tonight!

"Well, well," he murmured appreciatively, his tanned features appearing rakish as, stretching forth his hand, he assisted her down the last step. "You may not be the speediest woman in town, but you're definitely the most beautiful—and, I confess, well worth waiting for."

"I'm flattered you think so," she said, dimpling into a provocatively charming smile as she allowed him to usher her to the front door.

Excitement welled up inside her as she began to anticipate the evening ahead, particularly those precious moments when he would hold her in his arms while they danced. A subtle change had taken place in their relationship, and she fully intended to make the most of it. Tonight was going to be different, filled with a special kind of enchantment that would bind them closer together. She was sure of it, determined it should be so.

The next few hours were the happiest she had known since her marriage, despite the fact that she often found herself dancing with someone other than her husband. Courtesy demanded that she accept all invitations, but she felt Bret's eyes on her across the crowded ballroom floor and sensed his impatience to reclaim her—an impatience she shared.

As their eyes invariably met, however briefly, she knew Bret's mind was not on his partner, but on her. Only once did she experience an uncomfortable moment, when Garth Talbot asked her to dance and she saw Bret's dark look of displeasure. Her acceptance was automatic, for to have turned down his invitation would have seemed rude, especially since she had accepted all others.

Remembering how their brief courtship had ended unpleasantly, she hardly welcomed Garth's attention now, though it did boost her confidence to discover that, like herself, Bret was capable of jealousy. But did his obvious displeasure stem from jealousy, she wondered, or from the suspicion that Garth was the leader of the lawless guerrillas who had raided Belle Glen and killed her father? She tried to assure herself that his suspicion was totally unfounded, but she could not convince herself this was so. Involuntarily she tensed in Garth's arms while they waltzed around the room and politely conversed in a somewhat stilted manner.

Finally, to ease the awkwardness between them, Kitty casually mentioned she had heard he was acquiring quite a bit of real estate in town, along with several plantations that had recently been raided by bands of Yankee pillagers or lawless guerrillas.

His eyes narrowed momentarily before his expression became shuttered, his thin lips curving into an enigmatical smile. "Yes, I have," he admitted. "But, of course, so have the other two mortgage and loan companies in town."

"Both owned by Northerners, I notice."

"I'm no Northerner, Kitty, but neither am I squeamish about mixing with them to further my own business."

"As the saying goes, Garth, birds of a feather flock together. As far as I'm concerned, you're no better than the Yankees, profiting from other folks' miseries. All of you remind me of a bunch of vultures.''

Amused by her frankness, he replied in kind. ''I've always admired your grit, Kitty—particularly your straightforwardness. Unlike most of the fools around here, you see me for what I really am, an unscrupulous scoundrel who preys on the weak and gains from their misfortunes. Yes, I am a vulture, but better that than a helpless sparrow. I'm a survivor, and so are you. Most planters sold out and skedaddled when their plantations were raided, but not you. Instead, you used your head and married O'Rourke. I hear he's put a lot of money into Belle Glen's restoration.''

The music stopped, and, livid with rage, Kitty jerked free of his arms. ''If you're implying I married for money, you're wrong. I happen to love my husband and, what's more, I respect him. He, at least, is honest, which is more than I can say for some cowardly rascals I know.''

''Meaning me, I suppose,'' he countered in a dangerously low voice.

''Meaning you.'' She started to turn away from him but found her wrist caught in his steellike grip.

''Never call me a coward, and never underestimate me. It could be your undoing,'' he warned softly, his eyes glittering.

His words held an ominous threat, and as his lips twisted into a sinister smile, Kitty felt suddenly afraid. Determined not to be intimidated by him, she tugged free of his grasp and shot him a contemptuous look.

''The likes of you will never be my undoing, Garth Talbot,'' she retorted as, from the corner of her eye, she spied Bret striding toward them.

Seeing his grim look, she realized he had probably guessed that Garth was upsetting her. Quickly she forced her lips into a stiff smile, silently imploring Bret to rescue her without creating a scene. Her appeal did not go unnoticed, and though his expression was still less than friendly, his anger was carefully leashed when he nodded curtly to Garth and tucked her hand in the crook of his arm.

''It's getting late, so perhaps we'd better leave. Excuse us, Talbot,'' he said in a controlled voice.

''Of course. You're a lucky man, O'Rourke, to have such a beautiful and *entertaining* wife.'' Deliberately Garth made the compliment sound familiar and insulting.

Feeling Bret tense beside her, Kitty intervened. "On the contrary, Garth. *I* am the lucky one. Not every woman has such a kind and considerate husband," she countered spiritedly, much to Bret's surprise.

Her sapphire eyes danced with satisfaction when she saw Garth's slight scowl and Bret's wry expression. "Shall we go, dearest?" she said demurely.

"By all means," Bret answered, showing no surprise over the endearing way she had addressed him, though it was the first time she had done so since their marriage.

They excused themselves from Garth and walked out to the foyer, where they bade good night to their hosts. Not until they were in their enclosed carriage did the extent of Bret's amusement become apparent. Kitty heard him chuckling to himself.

"I see I've amused you," she stated good-humoredly.

"Let's just say you certainly surprised me," he admitted, grinning. "I had no idea you held me in such high esteem."

"Well, don't let it go to your head. Garth was being deliberately rude and insulting, so I merely put him in his place."

"And to think I dared hope you were in earnest," Bret remarked wryly. "A pity you weren't."

Detecting the hint of wistfulness in his voice, Kitty hesitated before answering. "But I was in earnest—at least, partly. I mean, you have been kind and considerate, and I suppose I am lucky to be married to you."

"Until now, you've hardly given me that impression," he said. "But pray do continue."

"Oh, you know very well I find you attractive."

"And honorable?"

Kitty glanced nervously at him, uncertain how to reply. "Sometimes," she admitted.

"But not always," he suggested with a trace of humor.

"No, not always. Not when you side with the enemy."

"Has it ever occurred to you that you might be wrong about that?"

"Am I?"

When he finally answered, his somber reply did nothing to reassure her. "Someday, when the time is right, I'll tell you, but not now. Believe me, I'm only thinking of your best interests."

Kitty was perplexed, but rather than risk an argument, she changed the subject. "It was a nice party. I'm glad we went."

"So am I." He smiled, casually putting an arm around her.

Shivering with cold, Kitty snuggled closer to him, welcoming the warmth of his body as his arm tightened around her, pinning her to him. Her contentment was such that she hated to have the ride end, but all too soon they reached the house.

Once inside, the two of them checked on Scott, already asleep in the nursery; then Bret escorted her down the dimly lit corridor to her bedroom. He was on the verge of opening the door for her when a faint tapping sound caught Kitty's attention. Glancing toward the end of the hall, where double doors led onto a balcony, she spied a profusion of large snowflakes through the frosted panes.

"Oh, look—it's snowing again!" she exclaimed, moving past him to the wide doors.

Flinging them open, she stepped outside and, heedless of the cold, walked over to the railing, delighted with the icy crystals that swirled around her. Laughter bubbled deep in her throat as she felt the moist flakes nipping at her face. As Bret sauntered over to stand beside her, draping an arm around her shoulders, she smiled happily up at him, then returned her attention to the spectacle before her.

"Listen," she whispered. "Do you hear it?"

"What?"

"The silence. How quietly the snow is falling, hardly making a sound." Enraptured, she paused before continuing. "I love to watch it snow at night. It's so beautiful and peaceful—almost magical. Right now, I feel as though we're cut off from everyone and everything. As though—" She hesitated, seeking the words to describe what she meant.

"As though we're in a world of our own?" Bret suggested softly.

"Yes. As though we're in a world of our own," she murmured, touched by his understanding.

His arm tightened around her shoulders, pulling her even closer, and for several minutes neither of them spoke. It was not until he felt her shiver against him that he suggested they return inside. Chilled to the bone, Kitty offered no objection, though she was reluctant to break the spell.

As he escorted her back to her room, she wondered if he intended to stay with her tonight. When he paused at her door, uncertainty was mirrored in her eyes as she smiled up at him.

"It's been an enjoyable evening," he said, taking her hand in his, "and a rather full day in all. I'm sure you're tired, so I'll say good night." Lightly kissing her forehead, he turned and walked to his room.

Disappointed, Kitty slowly closed her door, a feeling of desolation washing over her as she began to undress. She was tired of the whole charade—tired of sleeping alone, yet always longing to be in his arms.

Not bothering to don a nightgown, she slipped into a dressing gown of teal-blue velvet and impatiently fastened the three buttons just below the plunging neckline.

Studying her appearance from every angle, she realized she looked quite provocative—exactly what she intended.

A feeling of reckless daring washed over her as she walked to the dressing table and sat down. Removing the hairpins and shell combs from her hair, she picked up a hairbrush and briskly brushed out her long curls, not stopping until her thick ebony hair gleamed halfway down her back. Pulling back the long tresses that fell from a center part and framed her heart-shaped face, she secured the unruly locks with the shell combs she had worn earlier. Carefully turning the doorknob so as not to make a sound, she stepped into the darkened corridor.

She paused for a moment until her eyes became accustomed to the darkness, but her determination did not waver. She was tired of being married to Bret yet living apart from him, and she was confident that what she was about to do was right. She had placed the restrictions on their relationship, restrictions Bret had naturally resented, but now she intended to remove them. If he would not come to her tonight, she would go to him, even if it meant abandoning her pride.

Her courage faltered, however, as she halted in front of his closed door, uncertain how to proceed. What would she say to him? How could she tactfully convey to him that she wanted to be his wife in the truest sense of the word? Would he be receptive or scornful? Perhaps it was already too late to mend her fences. Maybe he no longer desired her at all. The last remnants of her courage almost crumbled. Nevertheless, she was determined to proceed as planned.

Taking a deep breath, she raised a trembling hand and rapped softly on his door, halfway hoping he would be asleep and unable to hear her timid knock. But only an instant later the door swung open and she found herself face to face with him.

It was obvious he had been undressing for bed, since only a white towel draped loosely around his middle concealed his nakedness. Embarrassed and at a sudden loss for words, Kitty averted her eyes, fastening her gaze on the mat of dark hair that partially covered his muscular torso and tapered to a V below his narrow waist. Memories of the more intimate parts of his virile body caused her heart to lurch in her breast, and she lifted her eyes in confusion. His expression had become enigmatic, and it was impossible for her to guess his thoughts. Yet, when he did speak, his words were tinged with irony.

"Well, madam, to what do I owe this unexpected pleasure?" he asked, stepping aside so she could enter.

On trembling legs, she crossed the threshold, moving slightly past him before turning to meet his inquisitive look. Remembering he often had a nightcap before retiring, she said the first thing that came to mind.

"I . . . I've caught a slight chill, and I thought a touch of brandy might help—that is, if you have any," she replied hesitantly.

His white teeth contrasted sharply with his dark complexion as he shot her a sardonic grin, a look that clearly told her she was not fooling him in the least. His answer was casual.

"Of course. I usually have a nightcap before retiring," he drawled, "but then, I'm sure you're well aware of my habits by now. At least, most of them."

Not knowing how to reply, Kitty silently accepted the drink he handed her and allowed him to usher her to one of the two wing-back chairs situated on either side of the fireplace. His unfathomable mood was anything but encouraging, and as she watched him toss a few pieces of kindling onto the smoldering embers in the fireplace, she heartily wished she were back in her own room. Her nerves were on edge by the time he seated himself in the chair opposite her, but she somehow managed to retain her composure.

"I see you finally decided to wear the dressing gown I gave you," he said. "It's very becoming."

"Thank you," she murmured, then added without thinking, "I was saving it for a special occasion."

"Oh? And is tonight a special occasion?"

Vexed that she had inadvertently admitted more than she had intended, Kitty attempted a casual reply. "Yes, in a way. We've had a wonderful day, and I'm looking forward to tomorrow."

"So am I."

The conversation was more relaxed now, and unwilling for it to change, she continued brightly. "And tonight was special, too, particularly when we were standing on the balcony. Everything looked so white and beautiful, so clean. Wouldn't it be nice if it snowed for days on end?"

"For us, maybe, but I doubt many soldiers would agree, especially those lying in trenches."

Kitty's smile faded, and a look of distress flitted across her face as his words painted a grim picture in her mind. "No, I don't suppose they would," she agreed. "Folks say a lot of our boys are going barefoot and that many who do have boots have taken them off dead Yankees. Do you think that's true?"

"Probably. The North has money and factories. We don't."

"Oh, how I wish we could whip the tar out of them and end this mess," she said vehemently, then sighed. "We've held our own for so long, but now the only war news we get is bad. Sometimes, I think the South is snakebit, that our dreams are just dying on the vine."

"It's been a nice evening, Kitty. Let's not spoil it by talking about the war. I suggest we finish our brandy and turn in."

Again she sighed, this time from personal disappointment. She had come willingly to him, hoping he would make love to her, but somehow her plans had gone awry. Now, he was practically inviting her to leave, and she could think of no way to detain her visit, unless . . .

Taking another sip of the distasteful brandy, she rose gracefully and handed him the half-filled glass, her mind racing as she watched him set both glasses on the mantel. She had no intention of leaving his room tonight unless he physically forced her from it. There was a distinct look of awareness in his eyes when he walked over and took hold of her shoulders, caressing them with a slight movement of his thumbs.

"Feeling warmer?" he asked softly.

"Much." She smiled, then feigned a grimace. "Now, if only my head would stop hurting, I believe I could sleep."

The corner of his mouth quirked, and as he lazily arched one dark brow, Kitty had the uneasy feeling he was not taken in by her lie. Belatedly, she remembered that she had seldom been successful in fooling him. He knew her much too well.

"Hmmm, a headache, too. Well now, we can't have you suffering with that. Where does it hurt?'' he asked in a vaguely mocking voice.

''Back here,'' she answered meekly, rubbing the base of her skull.

''Ah, then perhaps I can help. Headaches in that area are usually caused by tiredness or tension,'' he told her, taking her by the arm and leading her to the bed. ''In either case, a good massage usually does the trick. Sit down, and I'll see what I can do.''

Kitty obeyed, turning her back to him when he sat down beside her. Without being told, she reached back and swept her long hair over one shoulder, then lowered her head slightly so he could reach her neck. Inwardly quivering with anticipation, she waited for him to begin, and when he did, she all but sighed with contentment. His hands were strong yet gentle, and as his fingers manipulated the taut muscles in her neck, a soft moan stirred deep in her throat. Within minutes she felt totally relaxed, and when he leisurely began unfastening the front buttons of her robe to have better access to her shoulders, she made no attempt to stop him. It was what she wanted—his nearness, the touch of his hands on her flesh, the ultimate fulfillment that he alone could give her.

Her eyes closed while he gently removed the combs from her hair and slipped the robe from her shoulders. Her arms slipped out of the loose sleeves, allowing the garment to fall to her waist, though she ineffectually attempted to cover her nakedness by clutching a fold of the soft material to her breasts.

Bret did not speak, nor did he need to express his feelings. She sensed his hungering gaze on her back, and it came as no surprise when his arm encircled her midriff and his hand splayed possessively over her flat stomach. Tense with longing, she caught her breath when she felt the tantalizing touch of his lips on her neck, then the sensual exploration of his tongue trailing provocatively to her bare shoulder.

A burning desire filled her, consuming her like a flame while his free hand caressed her breasts and his mouth slowly descended to the curve of her spine. His lips lingered on the sensitive area for a brief moment, arousing her to fever pitch. When his head unexpectedly lifted moments later, and he slowly turned her to face him, a low moan of protest rumbled deep in her throat.

''Look at me, Kitty,'' he said, lifting her chin with his forefinger. ''You came to me tonight. Why?''

Long, sooty lashes shadowed her pale cheeks as she stared blindly at his muscled chest for a brief instant, then slowly raised her eyes to meet his.

"You know why I came."

"Yes, I know—but it's not enough. I want you to tell me. God knows I've waited long enough. Say it, Kitty," he commanded, forcefully dragging her to him so that their lips were mere inches apart. "Say you love me."

His answer was mirrored in the blue gaze that flicked hungrily over his rugged features. "I love you!" she murmured passionately, winding her arms about his neck.

An unmistakable look of triumph flitted across his face, and then his mouth masterfully claimed her parted lips as he forced her down on the bed, pinning her beneath him. The feel of her bare skin against his chest, the soft curves of her body pressing wantonly against him, increased his urgent need for her. But as always, he had no intention of hurrying. He had taken her before, but he felt he had never completely possessed her. Now, he was determined to do so, body and soul.

Feverish with desire, Kitty slowly ran her fingers through the crisp hair at the back of his neck, her flesh tingling with awareness when his hands began exploring her body. Moaning with impatience, she silently begged him to fulfill her longing, to end the sweet torment that was becoming almost more than she could bear.

"Do you want me, sweetheart?" he asked huskily as his mouth moved to her throat.

"Yes," she whispered. "Yes, I want you!"

His breathing was ragged when he raised his head, but in spite of his consuming desire, the full extent of his passion was deliberately held in check. Releasing one of her hands from behind his neck, he dragged it down to his waist.

"Show me," he demanded huskily, tensing when her fingers brushed his abdomen as she released the towel at his waist and shoved it impatiently aside.

"Love me, Bret. Please love me," she implored, her voice barely audible as her lips caressed his neck.

Her response was everything he wanted, everything he had dreamed of for years, but still he was not totally satisfied.

"Be sure, my darling. Be very sure," he warned softly. "If I take you now, there'll be no turning back for either of us. We'll have a

real marriage or none at all. I want more than just your body. I want
your trust, your respect, and most of all, your love. Not just tonight,
but always."

"Oh, Bret, that's what I want, too," she answered. "It's what
I've always wanted, only—"

"Only what?"

"You've never said you loved me, not even once," she answered
with a trace of reproach.

"Haven't I? Don't you know by now that actions speak louder
than words? Why do you think I lived in that godforsaken hole
during the siege? Why do you think I've hung around all these
years, when I could've stayed in Memphis and been a helluva lot
better off? God in heaven, what do I have to do to make you realize
how I feel?"

Her mouth curved in a slight smile as she reached up and placed a
small hand on either side of his face. *He loved her.* She knew that
now, though she was still determined to hear it from his own lips.

"You might try telling me. It only takes three words."

His arms tightened around her as his mouth slowly, seductively,
found hers. "I love you," he breathed against her parted lips.
"You'll never know how much—"

A soft moan of pleasure stirred in her throat when his hands
moved to her hips and she felt his strength possessing her. She was
dimly aware of his impassioned words of love as they became one,
spiraling closer and closer to the brink of rapture until, finally, they
reached the ultimate peak and experienced an exquisite release that
was more perfect, by far, than either had dreamed possible.

Much later, Kitty snuggled contentedly in Bret's arms and listened
to his even breathing while he slept beside her. Peeping up at his
face, she studied his strong, rugged features in the pale shaft of
moonlight. Relaxed by sleep, he no longer appeared mocking or
overbearing, but curiously boyish and even vulnerable. She had
loved him for as long as she could remember, but never more than at
this moment. He had been the perfect lover tonight, satisfying her as
never before while repeatedly demonstrating his love, both verbally
and physically.

The past no longer mattered to her, only the future. A wonderful
future wrapped around Bret, Scotty, and, perhaps, an unborn child
who had been conceived this very night. She desperately hoped so,
and with this happy possibility in mind, she drifted to sleep.

Chapter 35

Winter slipped into spring, and Southerners gradually resigned themselves to the inevitable outcome of the war. Though fierce battles were still occurring in Virginia, North Carolina, and Alabama, it was now obvious that the spirited Rebels could not hold out much longer. Only determination remained, but even that waned during the first week of April, when Union troops took over Richmond, the evacuated capital of the Confederacy. The Confederacy was doomed, and the realization of defeat was a bitter pill for Southerners to swallow. The fact that Lincoln had been reelected for another term did not help.

Kitty found it hard to relinquish hope, no matter how grim the situation appeared. For the first time since the war began, she was enjoying life to the fullest, and she refused to let anything mar her newfound happiness.

The past two months had proved one thing to her. Marriage was not an abomination, not if one were married to the right man—and she was! Being married to Bret was not only satisfying, but fun. The happy weeks following their reconciliation had been filled with exciting activities, all planned by Bret. It was as though he were trying to make up for lost time, particularly where his son was concerned. Family outings had been numerous, much to Scotty's delight, and if Bret bordered on spoiling the child, Kitty was not unduly worried about it. She, too, was being spoiled—and loving every minute of it.

There had been picnics, church socials, a minstrel show, and a circus, each enjoyable event binding the three of them closer together. Last month Bret had bought a larger pony for Scotty, and since then Sunday afternoons had been reserved for short riding excursions along the bluff.

All outings did not include their child, however, for though Bret was bent on getting to know the boy better, he was also determined to enjoy some activities alone with his wife. Whenever a showboat docked, they would dine on board and enjoy the musical performance that followed the delectable meal. Twice, a troupe of traveling actors had arrived by railway and paid a brief visit to Vicksburg, thus enabling them to see several good plays. In addition, there had been numerous shopping sprees, and each time Bret had extravagantly encouraged Kitty to buy far more than she could ever wear, much less fit into her limited wardrobe space. She soon learned that her husband had impeccable taste when it came to women's wearing apparel, and where she was concerned, price was no object with him. He was intent on providing her with whatever her heart desired, whether she needed it or not.

There seemed no end to his generosity. His thoughtfulness always pleased her, but his unusual display of tenderness, particularly during their more intimate moments, touched her as nothing else could. There was no doubting the sincerity of his devotion, which made her realize how foolish she had been to believe he had married her merely to gain his son. He loved her, and though there were still occasional flare-ups between them, she was finally beginning to understand the complex man she had married. He might be proud, stubborn, and arrogantly domineering at times, but he was also capable of displaying far more warmth and affection than she had realized.

She was learning to respect his integrity more with each passing day, though she still could not overlook the fact that he had previously been a Yankee spy. She would never understand why he had turned against his own kind and sided with the enemy, nor was she sure even now where his sympathies lay. It was a subject she preferred not to dwell upon and a topic both of them avoided discussing.

As far as she was concerned, the past was dead and buried, and she had no intention of dragging it up again. She was happy and secure for the first time in years, and as her love for Bret intensified, so did her desire to please him in every way possible. He had given her so much, and she desperately wanted to give him something special in return.

Now, at last, she could. The past week had confirmed that she was carrying his child, for not only had she missed her menses for the second time, she was also beginning to have bouts of morning sickness. She had suspected she was pregnant for several weeks but had decided not to mention it to Bret until she was positive. As yet, she had not had the chance, since he had been out of town on business all week. Fortunately, he would be returning on the *Natchez* early that evening.

Such business trips were not unusual, and as a rule Lemme was the one who met the riverboat and drove Bret home in the carriage. But since it was a lovely Palm Sunday, Kitty decided to drive down to the wharf and meet Bret when his boat docked at half-past six.

She knew he would be surprised to see her, though she doubted he would be pleased that she had come by herself. The town was still teeming with Yankee soldiers, many of them Negroes, and their disrespect and rudeness toward the townspeople made it unfeasible for ladies to venture out unaccompanied. Normally she would not have done so, but today was different. She had missed her husband and was anxious to have him all to herself. If he had missed her even half as much, perhaps he would not scold her for coming to meet him alone.

As she drove down to the docks, it dawned on her that Bret, having been away a week, might need to stop and check on the warehouse. Occasionally it had even been necessary for him to stay overnight at his office, working on ledgers or tending to other business matters. She hoped such would not be the case this evening. Her frown faded and was replaced with a smile when she realized that, having been separated from her, Bret would hardly be inclined to think about business tonight. After all, he was an extremely virile man—and it *had* been a whole week!

The wharf was crowded and noisy. Looking toward the riverboat *Natchez*, Kitty saw that the passengers were just disembarking. The steep embankment that led down to the docks was paved with rough cobblestones that were treacherously slick, and for several seconds she debated whether to risk the tricky descent or remain where she was and wait for Bret to find her. Hoping to catch a glimpse of him, she scanned the people milling around the gangplank, but to no avail. It occurred to her that it was going to be difficult to spot him

in the bustling throng below, but the thought of trying to descend the
risky slope without assistance was unappealing. Her two-piece outfit
was new, and glancing down at the billowing skirt of bone moiré
taffeta trimmed with black braided scrollwork, she decided to stay
put. After all, she was hardly dressed to go traipsing up and down
bluffs.

With a resigned sigh, she turned her attention from the gangplank
to the Negro dockhands who were dexterously carrying valises and
trunks ashore. Her lips curved in a smile as one of the blacks began
to sing:

> *Gwine to lay down my burden, down by the river side,*
> *Down by the river side, down by the river side;*
> *Gwine to lay down my burden, down by the river side,*
> *To study war no more.*
> *I ain't gwine study war no more . . .*

As the catchy tune continued, folks stopped to listen, some even
clapping their hands to the music's rhythm. Kitty began tapping her
foot to the time, her eyes sparkling with delight until, minutes later,
her gaze swung back to the empty gangplank, then traveled over the
docks, the smile fading from her lips when she finally spied Bret at
the crowd's edge—conversing with a woman she immediately recognized. Dixie!

For seconds she was too stunned to move. Then she saw Dixie
brazenly take hold of Bret's arm as they began moving through the
crowd, and she was immediately consumed with fury. The trust she
had begun to place in him over the past weeks vanished as though it
had never been. She had been duped.

Bret had probably been seeing Dixie all along. In fact, he had
probably been having an affair with her, which certainly explained
those evenings when he had *supposedly* worked all night at the
warehouse. What a goose she had been to believe he could ever be
faithful to one woman! Her naiveté must have seemed amusing to
the low-down varmint.

Getting back into the carriage, Kitty jerked up the reins and
whipped the startled bay into a fast trot, her eyes glittering with
anger as she headed for home. She would never forgive him for this.
Never! Nor did she have any intention of living with him after today.

Tomorrow morning she would take Scotty and her servants back to Belle Glen, where they belonged.

There would be nothing Bret could do or say to stop her, not when he learned that she had caught him in the act. She was half tempted to leave this very night, but that would mean denying herself the pleasure of telling him exactly what she thought of him—and that was one satisfaction she fully intended to have.

It came as no surprise when a young colored boy appeared at the house soon after her own arrival, nor was the message he delivered anything other than what she had expected. In a hastily scribbled note, Bret informed her he had arrived safely, adding that the business he had transacted during the past week needed to be recorded in the ledgers and it would be a couple of hours before he would be able to come home.

"Business indeed!" Kitty snorted, angrily crushing the note in her hand and tossing it aside. "Just wait 'til he gets home and I give him a piece of my mind!"

The evening hours passed slowly while she paced back and forth in the front parlor, mentally rehearsing exactly how she would handle the situation. First, she would allow him to make his excuses for being so late, let him sink irretrievably into the lie he would undoubtedly offer. Then she would coldly inform him that she knew exactly where he had been since his return—and with whom. Let him get out of that one, she thought with perverse satisfaction.

She had promised Scotty earlier that he could stay up at least until Bret returned home, but since it was so late and the boy was yawning sleepily, she realized she would have to renege on her word this time. As was customary, she tucked him into bed and heard his prayers, but seeing the disappointment in her child's eyes as she leaned over to kiss him, her heart constricted with pain.

Thinking to make amends and hoping to pave the way for tomorrow, she said, "You know, it's been quite a spell since we've seen Uncle Tad and Aunt Dede, so I was thinking we might go to Belle Glen tomorrow. Would you like that?" She forced cheerfulness into her voice just as Mammy Lou shuffled into the room to bid them good night.

"Yes'm," the youngster replied with a happy smile. "Will Daddy come, too?"

"No, not this time," Kitty replied a trifle unsteadily, blowing out the lamp on the bedside table to conceal her expression.

"Then it'll be his time to miss us, won't it?" Scotty remarked with a tired yawn.

"Yes, I suppose it will," Kitty agreed huskily. "Now close your eyes and Mammy Lou will sing you a bedtime song." She motioned for the woman to take her place beside the drowsy boy.

Kissing him again, she hurried from the room and made her way downstairs. The song Mammy Lou was singing was one she had heard many times as a child, and sinking down on the bottom step, she listened to the familiar lyrics:

> Go to sleep little baby,
> When you wake, you'll have some cake,
> And all the pretty little horses . . .

How often her father had sung those same words to her, and how simple life had been in those days. But nothing was simple now, least of all the prospect of having to tear Scotty away from Bret. With a dispirited sigh, she rose slowly to her feet, her hand tightening on the banister when she detected heavy footsteps on the front porch.

Rooted to the spot, she strove to appear calm as Bret walked through the doorway, dropped his valise on the floor, and pulled her into his arms.

"God, I've missed you," he groaned, drinking in the loveliness of her upturned face.

"Have you?" Kitty asked, turning her face aside so that his descending lips merely grazed her cheek.

Sensing something was amiss, Bret frowned slightly, yet he said nothing when she eased out of his embrace and stepped down on the landing. Her unusual remoteness warned him of her displeasure, which he attributed at first to his belated arrival. But as he watched her move toward the parlor, another thought occurred to him that seemed more plausible.

"I sent a note by messenger saying I would be detained at the office. Did you get it?"

Kitty turned to face him. "Yes, I received it. How very thoughtful of you to inform me of your whereabouts," she replied scathingly.

His broad mouth quirked in a smile, and he sauntered over to her. Lifting her determined chin with his thumb and forefinger, he said,

"Look, I'm sorry I was so late getting home, but there was some business I had to tend to."

His lame excuse riled her all the more. Slapping his hand away from her chin, Kitty glared at him. "Oh, I'm sure there was. In fact, I'm surprised you found time to come home at all."

"All right, Kitten," he interrupted, "if you've got a burr under your saddle, let's have it. What's wrong?"

Kitty's voice was laced with sarcasm. "Wrong? What could possibly be wrong?" Suddenly her blue eyes narrowed, blazing with unmistakable indignation as her control snapped. "*I* went down to the dock to get you, and what did I find? You and that . . . that harlot strolling around and having a cozy little chat in front of half the town. How could you? How could you humiliate me like that?"

"You've no cause to feel humiliated, and you've certainly no axe to grind with Dixie. She's a friend—nothing more."

"Fiddlesticks! Don't deny she's been your mistress, because I happen to know better."

"No, I won't deny we had an intimate relationship at one time, but that's in the past. Since our marriage, there's been no one but you. I can't prove it, of course, so I'm afraid you're just going to have to trust me."

"Trust you! Why should I? You still haven't explained what Dixie was doing down at the wharf, and don't expect me to believe she just happened to be passing by."

Bret hesitated, considering whether or not to tell her the truth. Finally he said in a noncommittal voice: "What would you say if I told you I'm one of the Rebel Scouts—and that Dixie supplies us with vital information from time to time?"

"I'd say I didn't believe you. Besides, how could Dixie supply you with information, vital or otherwise?"

"Being the owner of a casino, she comes in contact with all sorts of men, including Union officers. Whiskey has loosened many a man's tongue, particularly when he's gambling or enjoying himself in other . . . er, unmentionable ways upstairs."

"That may be, but I still don't believe you. Why would a former Yankee spy throw in his lot with the Scouts? It wouldn't make sense."

"No, it wouldn't, would it?" Bret agreed wryly.

Doubt briefly clouded her thoughts. What if he were telling her the truth? Was it possible that he *was* a Scout, and Dixie was merely a source of information? If so, it was highly unlikely that he had ever acted as a spy for the Union, yet he had never denied doing so. No, it would be totally out of character for Bret, a Yankee sympathizer, to join the Rebel Scouts, and arriving at this conclusion, she strengthened her resolve.

"In any case, I don't intend to live with you under these circumstances. Tomorrow morning I'm moving back to Belle Glen, and I'm taking Scotty with me."

"Like hell!" Bret muttered. Jerking her to him, he was strongly tempted to shake her, but he refused to give in to anger. "Now, you listen to me, and listen well. You knew what I was when you married me, and nothing's changed since then. This is your home—yours and the boy's—and this, by God, is where you're going to stay! You can forget running back to Belle Glen, my dear, because it won't do you a damn bit of good. I'd just come after you."

"Then you're going to have to make a lot of trips, because I don't intend to live here, and I certainly don't intend to share your bed."

His mouth curved into a humorless smile as he released her. "That remains to be seen, though you can do as you please for now. It's been a long day, and frankly, I'm too damned tired to care where you sleep tonight."

Enraged all the more by his apparent indifference, Kitty pushed angrily away from him and, with a haughty lift of her chin, marched past him to the stairs. Somewhat surprised he did not immediately follow her, she was disappointed some minutes later when she heard him entering his bedroom.

Feeling forlorn, she looked around the room that was hers—a room she had not slept in for months, not since their reconciliation. The prospect of doing so tonight was depressing, for she had grown accustomed to sleeping beside him and having his arms wrapped securely around her. The thought of never doing so again brought sudden tears to her eyes, and it took every ounce of determination she possessed not to back down from her earlier avowal and go to him. Only pride held her back, pride and the unpleasant remembrance of his questionable association with Dixie.

Not wishing to disturb the servants at such a late hour, Kitty undressed herself, muttering soft curses while she struggled to remove the tightly laced corset, then slipped into a new batiste nightgown. Jerking back the frilly coverlet, she crawled into bed.

Sleep would not come easily tonight, she realized, for no matter how hard she tried to blot Bret from her mind, she failed. His words kept ringing in her mind, especially his insinuation that he and Dixie were working for the Rebel Scouts. No one knew the Scouts' identity or where they got their information, but since they always seemed to know exactly when and where to attack, it was obvious the group was well supplied with knowledgeable informants. A menace to both Federals and lawless guerrillas, the Scouts had become a legend in their own time, heroes to every loyal Southerner in the county. Could Bret have actually joined this fearless group of Confederate patriots? Then she again rejected the possibility. For him to do such a thing simply would not make sense.

By two-thirty, Kitty still had not found a plausible answer, and sleep was out of the question. Perhaps a glass of wine would relax her taut nerves and enable her to get at least a couple hours of sleep. It was worth a try, she decided.

Throwing back the sheet, she got out of bed and shrugged into her wrapper, wishing she did not have to go all the way downstairs to fetch the wine decanter from the dining room. But as she reached for the latch on the door, an unexpected noise halted her. The realization that Bret was quietly closing his bedroom door held her motionless, and expecting to hear him come to her room, she felt her spirits momentarily lift, then plummet as she listened to his footsteps going down the hallway. Now, where was he going?

Her curiosity increased as she paced back and forth, until minutes later she heard the faint sound of a horse being walked from the stables to the front of the house. Rushing over to the window, she saw Bret mount his black stallion, pick up the reins, and head down the circular driveway. She watched until he disappeared into the night.

"Oh, just wait 'til I see him in the morning," she fumed aloud. "Sneaking out of here in the middle of the night, just so he can run to that painted hussy!"

Quickly lighting a candle, she made a beeline for the dining room. Knowing it was quite improper for a lady to drink anything stronger than wine, particularly when drinking alone, she felt not even a twinge of guilt when she jerked a bottle of Bret's best bourbon from beneath the sideboard. She poured a generous amount of the amber liquid into a glass and seated herself at the dining room table.

The grandfather clock in the hall ticked loudly but did not disrupt her vengeful thoughts as she took a sizable drink, wincing when she swallowed the distasteful mouthful. She was about to take another sip when a knock sounded loudly at the front door. Surprised that anyone should come calling at three o'clock in the morning, she picked up the candle and went to the hall. A knock sounded again.

"Who is it?" she called.

"It's Dixie. Let me in," came the urgent response.

Baffled, Kitty shot back the bolt and opened the door, her puzzlement increasing when Dixie whisked into the hall and anxiously turned to face her.

"Kitty, where's Bret?"

"I rather assumed he was with you."

"What on earth gave you that idea?"

"Because I happened to see the two of you down at the dock yesterday."

"*And* jumped to the wrong conclusion. But that's something we'll have to sort out later. When did Bret leave?"

"About twenty minutes ago," Kitty answered, puzzled.

"Damn! If only I could have gotten here sooner." Dixie frowned and clenched her hands together.

"What's wrong, Dixie? Is he in some kind of trouble?"

"Unless he's warned, he'll be riding into a trap just after daybreak. Garth's guerrillas are waiting for him."

"Garth's guerrillas!" Kitty gasped with astonishment.

"Yes. The same bunch of cutthroats who raided Belle Glen and killed your father. Bret has suspected for some time that Garth was the head man, but he hasn't been able to prove it. So far, the scoundrel has managed to escape every time the Scouts have busted up one of his raids."

"I—I don't understand. Why would Garth's men be after Bret, and what does Bret have to do with the Scouts?"

"He's their leader."

"I don't believe you," Kitty scoffed. "Bret spied for the Yankees during the siege, so why would he risk his neck for a bunch of Rebels now?"

"What a blind little fool you are," Dixie said cuttingly. "Bret was a spy during the siege all right—but not for the Yankees. That was merely a front, a disguise he used to obtain invaluable information for Van Dorn, then Pemberton. Good Lord, you're his wife! Don't you know him at all?"

For a brief moment Kitty was too stunned to answer, but her

surprise quickly gave way to resentment. "Apparently not as well as you do. But then, of course, you *are* his mistress!"

"Don't be an idiot. Yes, I had an affair with him, a relationship that ended long before he married you. Oh, I'd take him back in a minute if he'd have me, but unfortunately he happens to be in love with you. God only knows why! You've always been more of a hindrance than a help to him, but you're the one he wants, the one he's *always* wanted."

It was obvious Dixie was telling her the truth. Recalling all the unjust accusations she had hurled at Bret, Kitty was suddenly swamped with remorse and shame. Tears misted her eyes when she finally raised her head and met Dixie's stern gaze.

"You're right," she murmured. "I have been a fool, but I swear I'll make it up to him." Remembering the initial reason behind Dixie's visit, she forced all thoughts of her own foolishness to the back of her mind and squared her shoulders resolutely. "You said Garth's men are planning an ambush. Are you sure?"

"Yes. Lyle Redman worked for Garth up until yesterday, but they must have had some kind of a row. Anyway, Lyle's bearing a grudge now, or so Annie says."

"Annie?"

"One of my, er . . . employees," Dixie explained wryly. "She occasionally entertains upstairs, if you get my meaning, and tonight Lyle Redman happened to be her caller. From what Annie says, he was drunk as a skunk and talking his fool head off. It seems that Garth ordered a couple of his men to visit the casino last week, just so they could subtly drop a hint or two about this so-called raid. They looked like they'd had too much to drink, so it didn't occur to me they were deliberately leading me on, baiting the trap for an ambush. Dammit, I should have known better, but I swallowed their whole pack of lies—hook, line, and sinker!"

Kitty wanted to console her, but there simply was not time. "Where will the ambush be?"

"The raid was to be at the Taylor plantation, so it'll be somewhere in that vicinity."

"I know the place. It's just east of the Big Black and near a stretch of piney woods. Where will the Scouts meet?"

Dixie shook her head. "That, I can't say. All I know is that they usually rendezvous in a deserted cabin somewhere in the swamp just above the old island ferry landing."

The cabin was unknown to Kitty, though she was familiar with the area surrounding the landing. The ferry had been destroyed, but there was a rocky ford just north of it that made an excellent crossing whenever the Big Black River was not flooded. Only a couple of weeks ago she and Bret had ridden out to the Big Black on a Sunday afternoon. Then they had taken a shortcut through a cane thicket just off the main road, and when they had reached the woods, Bret had shown her a narrow trail that had once been used by the Indians. He had laughingly referred to it as his "secret byway," and at the time she had believed him to be joking. She knew differently now. Few were aware of the trail's existence, and she had no doubt that this was the route Bret had taken tonight. She did not know where the cabin was located, yet she was almost certain Bret and his men would ford the river at an old Indian crossing, the Gravel Branch Ford.

Kitty came to a quick decision. "We've got to get word to them, warn them before it's too late."

"Yes, but how? Every able-bodied man who can be trusted is riding with the Scouts, which leaves only a few of those old codgers who were in the Home Guard."

"That's it, the home guard!" Kitty exclaimed, taking hold of Dixie's shoulders. "Now, listen to me. Go to Judge Crane and tell him what you've told me. Tell him to round up as many in the home guard as he can and ride out to the Taylor plantation. If Bret rides into an ambush, he's going to need help. I only hope I can reach him in time."

"What do you mean, 'reach him in time'?"

"I mean that I'm going to try to intercept him at the Gravel Branch Ford. The river isn't high yet, so I'm sure that's where they'll try to cross. Bret left about thirty minutes ago, but he's still got to rendezvous with the other Scouts. That delay just might enable me to get to the ford before he does."

"You can't, Kitty!" Dixie gasped with astonishment. "It's far too dangerous. You could be killed."

"I *must*. There's no other way. Besides, Bret showed me a shortcut to the river when we were out riding a couple of weeks ago, and I'm almost sure I can reach the ford in time. Don't you see, I have to try!"

"But there are pickets on every road leading out of town. What if you run into them?"

"I won't. I'll bypass the main road, cut through the cane thicket at the edge of town, then take the byway Bret showed me. Few know about it, so it's unlikely I'll run into anybody. Don't worry about me. I'll take a gun, and if I have to, I'll use it."

Dixie's expression was one of dismay and indecision. "I don't know, Kitty. What you're suggesting makes sense, but it's just too risky. If anything happened to you . . ."

"Nothing's going to happen to me," Kitty interrupted. "Now please just do as I ask. There's not a moment to spare!"

Realizing the younger woman was determined, Dixie gave a defeated sigh and turned to go. As she reached the door, however, she stopped and glanced over her shoulder.

"You know, I guess I've been wrong about you. You may be pigheaded and proud, but you've got a lot of spunk. Be careful, Kitty—and good luck."

Kitty smiled but made no reply. Even before the front door closed behind Dixie, she was racing upstairs to change into some riding clothes. With luck, she could be on her way in fifteen minutes. No, not luck, she corrected herself. This was one time she was definitely going to have to hurry!

Chapter 36

The overhead sky had slowly turned to a murky gray by the time Kitty reached the Big Black, yet visibility was still poor and offered only a dim view of the opposite bank. Both rider and horse were winded, for as the narrow trail had widened, Kitty had urged Rebel into a full gallop. Pausing at the water's edge, her gaze swung northward to where the river curved. If memory served her correctly, Gravel Branch Ford was just beyond the bend. Praying she had made it in time, she resolutely guided her lathered mount in that direction.

Minutes later, her lips curved slightly with satisfaction as she saw that her estimation had been accurate. The shallow ford was just ahead. Nerves tensing, she gently nudged the tired mare across the gravel riverbed to the middle of the ford, then halted. A whippoorwill called out in the distance, briefly dispelling the eerie silence that enveloped her. It was quiet, almost too quiet, she thought uneasily as she surveyed her surroundings.

A slight sound came unexpectedly from the east bank, the unmistakable rustling of leaves, and her hands tightened on the reins as she scanned the area for some sign of life. Seeing none, and taking a deep breath, she forced herself to relax and turned her attention back to the west bank, since it was from this direction that Bret and his men would be riding.

The darkness of night had all but faded, and though the sun had not risen yet, the gray sky was becoming lighter with each passing second. Had she been right in assuming the Rebel Scouts would come this route? she wondered. And if so, had she arrived in time?

Her spirits were quickly revived when she heard the sound of hoofbeats coming through the dense woods. A flock of mallards noisily took flight from the east bank, causing her to glance in that direction. Her eyes widened with fear as she spotted a tall, scurvy-looking man duck behind a large walnut tree. One of Garth's guerrillas! The ambush would not take place at the Taylors' plantation, but *here!* Even as she jerked up the reins and turned Rebel toward the west bank, Bret and his men rode into view.

"Go back, Bret!" she yelled frantically. "It's an ambush—"

From the east bank, a volley of gunshots rang out, causing her startled mount to rear and almost unseat her. Tightening the reins, she dug her heels into the flanks of the skittish mare and tried to head for Bret, who was already riding out to rescue her from the line of fire. There was no mistaking his fury when his arm encircled her waist and she was yanked from the saddle and carried like a sack of potatoes as they galloped at breakneck speed back to the safety of the woods.

Dumping her unceremoniously on the ground, he vaulted from the saddle and prodded her toward the huge trunk of an uprooted tree that was lying horizontal to the river near the bank. Rebel shouts intermingled with the sound of thundering hoofbeats as the Scouts rode past them, heading for a direct confrontation with the guerrillas, who were now galloping out into the ford.

A quick glance revealed that the Scouts were evenly matched in number. There were a dozen or so masked guerrillas being led by a man whom Kitty instantly recognized, in spite of the kerchief that concealed the lower part of his face. Garth Talbot!

Before she could utter a word, Bret shoved her roughly into a lower position behind the fallen tree, thus putting an end to her view.

"Keep down," he ordered. "What in the hell are you doing here anyway?"

Miffed by his apparent ingratitude, Kitty shot him a mutinous look. "Trying to save *your* neck. Dixie came by to tell you about the ambush, but you'd already gone. Somebody had to warn you, and there wasn't time to find anybody else."

Bret fired a shot, knocking one of the guerrillas from his horse, then glanced down at her with a vexed expression. "So you came charging out here by yourself. Dammit, didn't it occur to you that you could have been killed?"

"Well, I wasn't," Kitty snapped.

After firing several more shots, he looked at her again, but this time there was no anger in his face. "I ought to throttle you, but I won't," he told her. "For once, you happened to be in the right place at the right time! Now stay put, and for God's sake, keep down."

As he started to move away from her, Kitty clutched fearfully at his arm. "You're not going to leave me, are you?" She gasped with alarm.

"You'll be all right."

Before she could argue, he was remounting. "Just stay put until I come back for you," he ordered, and then he was gone.

Horrified, Kitty watched him ride out to the middle of the ford, where the battle was taking place. Her fear for her own safety was forgotten as she witnessed the fierce struggle taking place before her very eyes.

Some men wielded sabers while others fired point-blank at charging riders. As the battle intensified, Kitty began to fear that none of them would escape alive. The Scouts, at least, seemed to be holding their own, for though some of them had been wounded, only one had fallen from his horse.

Several times she caught a glimpse of Garth but lost sight of him when other riders galloped by and obscured her view. Her main concern, however, was Bret. Jerking a small revolver from the holster at her waist, she fired at a guerrilla who was charging him from behind. Her aim was true—the man fell into the ford, and as the confrontation accelerated, she had to repeat the action on one other occasion.

It was becoming apparent that the outlaws were losing ground and could not hope to win. Several of them were lying facedown in the shallow water, but as far as Kitty could determine, only one Scout had been killed. Wounds were numerous on both sides, however, and as the fighting dragged on and on, her fear for Bret's safety increased tenfold.

It seemed a lifetime before the struggle finally ended and the few remaining guerrillas made a break for the east bank and disappeared through the woods. Bret stayed behind when several of his men pursued them, and with a sigh of relief, Kitty lowered her gun and rose wearily to her feet.

"Drop the gun, Kitty, and turn around," an ominous voice said.

She instantly recognized it as belonging to Garth, the vicious killer who had raided Belle Glen and attempted to burn it to the ground. The man who was responsible for her father's death. Rage filled her as she whirled around to confront him, the revolver still clenched in her hand.

"You despicable swine!" she exclaimed furiously.

His thin lips twisted into an evil smile as he met her hostile glare. "I've always admired your beauty and your spirit, but never more than now. A pity you had to interfere and upset my plans. Since you have, though, I might as well make the most of it."

"What do you mean?"

"Just this. You're going to be my ticket out of here, but first I have an old score to settle with your husband. Now, drop the gun and come over here," he ordered, his own gun pointed directly at her.

His expression was sinister, and not doubting he would cold-bloodedly shoot her if she disobeyed, Kitty did as she was told. Bret would be coming for her at any moment, unaware that Garth was waiting to kill him. Realizing this, she was determined to protect him.

"I'd forget old scores if I were you, Garth. Shoot Bret and you'll never get out of here alive. His men will gun you down on the spot. So if you plan to use me as hostage, I suggest we leave now," she said in a calm manner that belied her fear.

Seeing no sign of Garth's horse, she decided he must now be on foot, a fact that might enable her to find some means of escape when she accompanied him through the woods. Hope flickered briefly in her but was quickly extinguished when he jerked both of her arms forward with his free hand and deftly bound her wrists with his kerchief.

"I think not, Kitty. At least, not yet. First, I'm going to kill your husband, then we'll leave. With you as my shield, I seriously doubt anyone will take a shot at me. My only regret is not being able to watch him writhing in torment while he dies. I understand stomach wounds are quite agonizing—so that, of course, is where I'll aim. Being an excellent shot, it's unlikely I'll miss," he boasted. "What a shame I'll have to forgo the pleasure of seeing him suffer, but we'll probably hear him screaming for miles. That, at least, will be some satisfaction."

It was no idle threat, and Kitty knew it. He was going to kill her husband unless she could stop him. She *must* stop him, even if it meant sacrificing her own life.

His gun was aimed directly at her, but the element of surprise might catch him off guard for a split second, giving her the edge she needed. Deliberately shifting her gaze past him, she feigned a look of sudden recognition.

"Oh, thank God you're here!" she exclaimed, pretending to see a rescuer who did not exist.

Her ploy worked, diverting Garth's attention for a moment as he glanced over his shoulder. Heedless of the consequences, she made a frantic grab for her gun, but Garth was too quick for her. Even as her tied hands fumbled for the weapon, he closed the gap between them, kicking the gun out of her reach while his free arm encircled her neck. She tried to scream, but the sound was choked off when his stranglehold tightened painfully and he maneuvered to get behind her, pinning her rigid back firmly against his chest.

They were facing the ford, yet completely hidden from view by the dense foliage. Rendered helpless, Kitty strained to see Bret, who was now standing on the opposite bank talking to the other men. Seconds later her terror intensified as, one by one, the Scouts remounted, and she heard Bret's raised voice instructing them to split up and take different routes into town to avoid arousing suspicion. Two Scouts, Steve and Scott Hartz, stayed long enough to dispose of the dead bodies, dragging them from the shallow ford to where the river deepened, then dumping them in the swirling water that would inevitably carry the floating corpses downstream. Only the dead Scout remained, and as she watched the older Hartz brother pick up the lifeless body and carry it to his horse, she wondered if the man would be buried in the woods or taken to his family. Did it really matter? Unless a miracle occurred, her own husband would be killed before her very eyes.

A wave of dizziness swept over her when she heard the Hartz boys galloping off into the woods, then saw Bret crossing the ford toward them. Unable to scream, she squirmed weakly against Garth, but his arm merely tightened around her bruised throat, cutting off her air supply. As Bret reached the bank, she saw his gun was holstered, and with a sinking heart, she realized it was unlikely he would be able to draw fast enough to defend himself in time. He was only a few feet away when Garth stepped from behind the clump of bushes that had completely concealed them, his arm still firmly around her neck while he propelled her forward.

"That's far enough, O'Rourke," he announced.

Caught off guard, Bret halted abruptly, a look of surprise on his face as he turned to face them. Seeing Garth's vicious hold on Kitty, his expression changed to one of fury.

"Let her go, Talbot," he said, his voice ominously quiet. "I'm the one you want."

"How very noble of you," Garth remarked, "though I'm sure you know I have no intention of letting Kitty go—at least, not for a while. Ah, the times I've dreamed of taking her, of possessing her totally and completely. You stood in my way, but no more. As soon as I've killed you, we'll head for Natchez, then board the first riverboat for New Orleans. From there, we'll catch a steamer to Nassau, where I happen to own a small sugar plantation. In other words, O'Rourke, your wife will simply disappear. I tell you this merely so you'll have something to think about when you're squirming around on the ground, waiting to die. If my aim is true, that should take several excruciating hours. Pity I can't stay to enjoy your agony."

Kitty saw Bret's hands clench and unclench by his sides, and she knew he was going to charge Garth, which was exactly what Garth wanted. The closer Bret was, the more accurate Garth's aim would be.

Bret's only chance depended on her, and realizing this, she reacted instinctively. Though her tied hands were not much use, she was not immobile. Clenching her fingers together in a fist, she made a quick thrust at Garth's gun when Bret charged, hitting Garth's wrist just as he squeezed the trigger. The shot went awry, and taken by surprise, he loosened his stranglehold on her throat for a split second. It was all Kitty needed. Sinking her teeth into the forearm that still imprisoned her neck, she clamped down on it with all her might.

Cursing angrily, Garth slung her roughly from him and fired again. Her scream intermingled with the loud explosion as she collided into a large pine tree. As the side of her head struck the sturdy trunk, she was only dimly aware of another shot being fired. Then she lost consciousness and sank to the ground.

She had no way of knowing that Garth's second bullet had also gone astray and that the last shot had been accurately fired from Bret's gun, striking the guerrilla in the head and killing him instantly. She was also unaware of Bret's anxiety when he rushed over and knelt beside her, fearfully cradling her in his arms until, minutes later, she slowly regained consciousness. She only knew that, as the blackness gradually receded, there was a painful throbbing in her head, and a familiar voice was hoarsely speaking her name.

It was Bret, and, recognizing the unmistakable sound of alarm in his deep voice, she struggled to open her eyes.

"Are you all right?" he asked, relieved when she nodded affirmatively. Feeling her shudder against him, he said, "You're safe, dearest. Garth's dead."

"And you?" she whispered with concern. "Are you all right?"

"Now I am—as long as I have you," he murmured, his arms tightening around her while his eyes devoured the loveliness of her upturned face.

"I mean so much to you?"

"You mean *everything* to me," he affirmed, nuzzling her cheek. "For God's sake, don't ever scare me like that again. You could have been killed."

She gave him a slightly reproachful look. "When Dixie told me what was going on, I had to come. I had to warn you—"

Her words were terminated as Bret's mouth slanted down on hers, capturing her lips in a passionate kiss that momentarily made her forget everything while she responded with equal fervor. When he eventually lifted his head, however, her thoughts returned to the present.

"Bret," she began hesitantly, "Dixie told me you were just posing as a Yankee spy so you could get information for Van Dorn and Pemberton. Is that true?"

"Yes, it's true."

Her heart constricted with pain upon recalling the many times she had unjustly accused him of being a traitor; yet never once had he denied it or made any effort to defend his actions. The realization that he had revealed the truth to Dixie but not to her added to her pain, and her expression was one of hurt bewilderment as she pulled away from him and rose to her feet. Turning to face him, she saw his perplexed look when he stood and closed the gap between them.

"Why?" she whispered. "Why did you let me believe the worst of you all these years? Did you trust me so little?"

"Trust had nothing to do with it," he replied, spanning her waist with his hands. "Spying is dangerous business, and I didn't want you mixed up in it. I figured the less you knew, the safer you'd be in the event I was caught."

Remorse coursed through her, and with a choked sob, she melted against him. "Oh, Bret, I've been such a blind fool. I should have trusted you, at least given you the benefit of the doubt. But I didn't. Can you ever forgive me?"

Her penitent expression reminded him of the numerous times when, as a child, she had been caught in mischievous acts, acts for which she had always been grievously sorry. Remembering those occasions, he found it impossible to remain solemn, and his mouth quirked into a grin.

"It seems I'll have to," he drawled, amused. "Living with you may be difficult at times, but living without you is sheer hell!" His voice deepened with emotion as he added seriously, "You see, Kitten, I happen to love you very much. More than life itself. I have for years."

"Oh, Bret—*never* let me go!"

"Don't you know, my darling, I could never let you go, even if I wanted to. There *is* no life for me without you. You're my heart, my soul—my reason for living. You and Scott are all that matter to me." His lips confirmed the vow in a brief, passionate kiss. "Let's go home," he said at last.

Home! Never had the word sounded so good to her.

Wrapped in contentment, she remained silent as they rode through the budding forest, which was dotted with flowering dogwood. When they emerged from the pine-scented forest that bordered the edge of town, a familiar rumble sounded in the distance, immediately capturing her attention. Cannonfire!

As Bret reined in, she realized he had also heard the alarming explosions, which were apparently coming from town.

"Bret, why are the cannons being fired?"

"I don't know, but as soon as we reach the top of that ridge, maybe we'll find out," he said, nudging his stallion into a canter.

Just as they reached the foot of the high ridge that overlooked the town and river, a small band of men galloped over the crest and headed directly for them. It was the judge, accompanied by five other elderly men who had once belonged to the home guard. When they drew abreast, Kitty winced inwardly, remembering how she had urged Dixie to recruit their help to thwart the guerrillas' ambush. Considering they were all well past their prime, they probably would have been more of a hindrance than a help. Seeing their haggard expressions, she regretted having worried them unnecessarily. Dismounting, she and Bret walked over to them.

"You two all right?" the judge asked breathlessly.

Before Bret could answer, Kitty said, "We're fine, Judge. The ambush failed. I'm sorry I had Dixie trouble you unnecessarily."

"No trouble a'tall. We'd have come sooner, but all hell's broken out in town."

"Sounds like it," Bret remarked. "What's happening?"

Tears sprang to the old man's eyes. "We've lost, Bret. Lee surrendered to Grant yesterday at a place called Appomattox."

"I don't believe it!" Kitty gasped. "General Lee would never surrender to the Yankees—especially not on Palm Sunday. It's probably just another rumor."

The judge shook his shaggy head and regarded her sadly. "No, my dear, it's no rumor. The news arrived by telegraph this morning."

"The war is over, Kitty," Bret told her gently, placing a hand on her shoulder.

Refusing to believe the worst, she clung fiercely to the last shred of hope. "It isn't over!" she cried. "Even if Lee's army in Virginia did surrender, that doesn't mean the rest of the Confederacy has done the same. What about our soldiers in Arkansas, Tennessee, and Alabama, not to mention the other southern states? And what about General Johnston? Do you honestly believe he's going to surrender North Carolina just because Lee's given up?" she challenged.

Bret shook his head. "He'll have no choice, nor will our other commanders. Our men have done their best, Kitty, but the odds were against them from the beginning. The South's military equipment and manpower have never equaled the North's. No army, however brave, can continue fighting with inadequate supplies and on empty stomachs, not even ours. It's a wonder they've held out this long."

"Damn right about that," the judge asserted. "The Yankees may have licked us, but by heaven, we gave 'em a run for their money!"

"We did at that," Bret agreed, his eyes never leaving Kitty's. "We've lost, Kitty—but we're not dishonored."

His words finally got through to her, forcing her to face reality. Deprived of hope, she turned and slowly made her way up the steep ridge that overlooked the town. The men's voices followed her, and she heard one of them saying Lee's men had been paroled and given permission to return home. Even that was small comfort to her. She understood only one thing: the South had been defeated.

She had almost reached the top of the hill when she heard the judge and his cronies bid farewell to Bret. Pausing to catch her breath, she glanced over her shoulder and saw they were leaving, heading back toward Vicksburg. Her eyes burned with unshed tears.

"I won't cry," she swore fiercely to herself, "and I won't be beaten—not by the Yankees or anyone else!"

By the time Bret reached her side, she had regained her composure, though she was still filled with bitterness. Sensing her mood, he offered no words of comfort but merely put his arm around her waist as they made their way to the top of the ridge.

A faint din drifted to them from the other side, gradually intensifying and becoming more distinct as they reached the crest that overlooked the town and river. Shouts of joy intermingled with cries of distress, reminding Kitty of the day Vicksburg had been forced to surrender. Now, Union soldiers were again flocking to the courthouse hill, fervently singing "The Battle Hymn of the Republic." A short distance away another familiar song erupted. Not to be outdone, die-hard Southerners were proudly launching into "Dixie." Ironically, as the two melodies crescendoed, they seemed to blend into one.

Feeling Bret's arms tightening around her waist, she leaned against him. "Somehow, I can't believe it's really over," she murmured in a dazed voice. When he did not answer, she glanced up at him questioningly.

"Oh, Bret, will anything ever be the same again?"

"No, my love, it won't," he answered. "The South we knew and loved is gone. But we'll rebuild it in time."

"How? Now that the Yankees have won, they'll never leave us alone. How can Southerners possibly survive?"

"Southerners will survive because that's what we know how to do best. We can't go back to the past, but we can look to the future."

"The future," she repeated softly, her lips slowly curving into a smile as she considered his words. A flicker of hope stirred within her, gradually strengthening as her gaze swept over the town again. This time she felt no sorrow, only determination.

"Yes, we *do* have the future," she said at last, "and this time we'll build it together!"

Author's Note

The people of Vicksburg who experienced the siege did not forget that their town had been forced to surrender to Grant on July 4, 1863—nor did their descendants. The holiday was not officially celebrated again in Vicksburg until 1945.

KAREN JOHNS

Having lived in Arkansas, Florida, and Tennessee for most of her life, Karen Johns considers herself a true southerner. She has been happily married to Terry for 30 years and has three sons—Steve, Mark, and Scott. Teaching singing and piano in her home parttime allows her to pursue writing, and in her free time she enjoys playing cards—especially canasta and bridge—and caring for the family dog, Baby, and cat, Lady. PROUD SURRENDER is a sequel to Karen's first novel, BELLE GLEN, which was published several years ago.